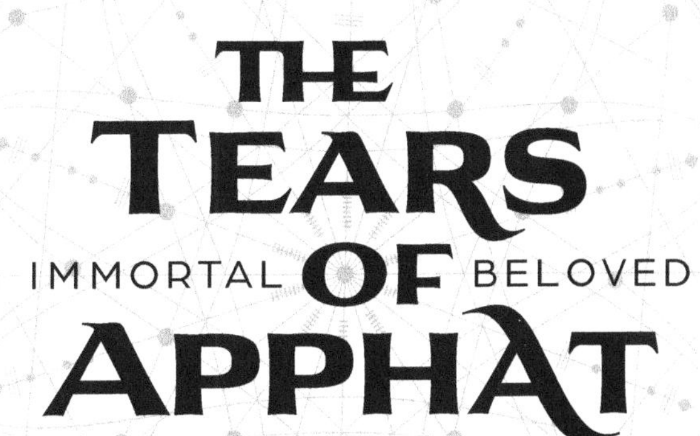

THE TEARS OF APPHAT

IMMORTAL BELOVED

ALAIN LOUIS CAMUS

Copyright © 2023 by Alain Jean Francois
(Alain Louis Camus – nom de plume)

Copy-editing by Gillian Rodgerson
Cover design and layout by Arjan van Woensel
Map design by Alain Jean Francois

Library of Congress Cataloguing-in-Publication Data

ISBN paperback 978-0-6457676-0-5
ISBN ebook 978-0-6457676-2-9

Contact: Alain Francois.
alainlouiscamus@gmail.com

DEDICATION AND ACKNOWLEDGEMENT

To

Dimitri

My mother, Blanche Francois for her enduring support and encouragement.

My Great Grandmother Alice Camus for always being by my side, encouraging me and guiding me throughout this journey.

David Phillips, my friend and night listener, whom I would call late at night from Melbourne, and who patiently with eager anticipation listened on the phone in Adelaide to each new instalment and begged for the next chapter.

Asfaine Mountains
The Kingdom of Gleskerell
Cave of Gibrar
Naassée
Ishmus of Mina
The Giants Steps
Dessert of Keira
The Great Marshlands
Oasis of Shahreza
The Huda Pass
Walled Desert City
Ocean of Malkizar
Schiraz
Ocean of Elwah

In a land that is not on any of your maps,
a culture based on ancient Lore beyond
your understanding, in a language that is barely
able to be translated into yours, I exist.
My name is Azizi; it means 'beloved' in the ancient
tongue of the desert people.
I will be known as the Immortal Beloved.

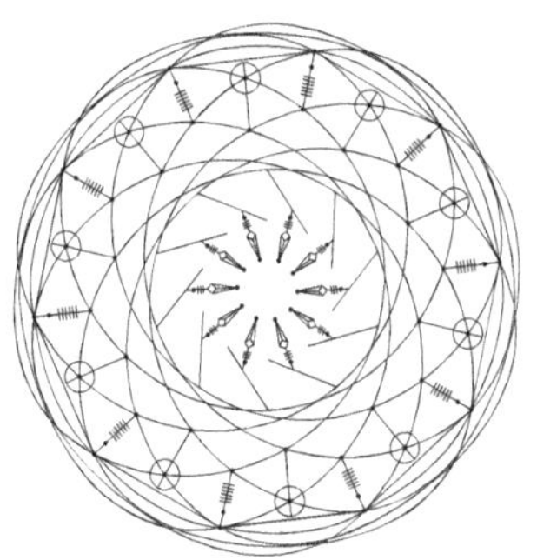

CHAPTER ONE

"Hummel! Hummel!"

The shouts pursue me. Too late, I realize I have taken the usual way home. Out of the corner of my eye, I catch a movement from behind one of the buildings. A shout goes up; Knut and his friends are in pursuit. I break into a run. My heart starts pounding. Perhaps I can outrun them. Planning my escape, I head for the forest; there at least I can lose them. I know the secret paths of the Hills people.

"Hummel! Hummel!" The insults stab at my back.

My face flushes with shame. Anger boils within me. They are calling me a stag that cannot grow horns. A stag that prefers the company of other stags. Running past houses and shopfronts, like unspoken accusations, feeling the eyes of villagers on my back. My lungs are hurting. I take big gulps of air. My legs are burning with the effort, urging me to stop and rest. Gritting my teeth and ignoring the pain I run faster.

I glance back; Knut is catching up, a vicious smile of victory on his lips.

"Get him!" he yells.

One of his friends has circled around and is coming at me from my right. He goes to intercept. At the last moment, I dodge left down a laneway. The sound behind me dies down; I want to slow and ease the pain. My breath comes in short bursts, rasping in my throat. Pushing the pain away, I force myself to run harder. This laneway will take me into the main square and past the fountain. A track then leads out of the village to the forest.

The fountain is just around the corner.

Knut casually turns the corner, both hands by his sides in tight fists.

I look back; the other two boys are behind me coming up at a jog.

I'm trapped. I've stopped running. A tight knot re-forms in my stomach. My whole body is shaking. Struggling to catch my breath, I stand as straight as I can, bravado prevents me from showing how desperate I am to breathe normally. My head is spinning from the effort. The world seems to recede. One of the boys is laughing and starts to walk towards me. He comes close. Anger boils up inside me like nothing I have ever known, a rage that threatens to explode from inside my chest. My vision blurs. Without a thought I throw a punch and hit him in the face.

He yells, and his eyes wide open in shock. His hand flies to his nose: blood is oozing out all over his fingers. He looks at his bloody hand and continues to yell. I think I've broken his nose. I start to laugh; a sense of satisfaction and triumph fills me at his pain. My body continues to shake. I want to hit someone else.

Knut grabs me from behind, his arm around my neck. I stumble. My head hits the pavement. He sits astride me, pinning my arms against my body and holding me down by the shoulders.

Suddenly, something black appears. A pain erupts in my left eye. A flash, colours explode; he's punched me in the eye.

"What visions are you having now witch's brat?" He spits his words at me. His breath stinks of stale cabbage. He bends his head close to my ears. I try to turn away, but my head is jammed. "Don't ever go near my girlfriend again!"

I'm confused. Is he mad? There is a girl who sat next to me in class once. She's very plain looking, the type who just giggles at anything behind her hand. She chews her own hair!

"Why would I? She's ugly!" I blurt out.

His body shifts with his upraised fist. This time I manage to move my head quickly and he slams his fist into the pavement. He lets out a curse.

Twisting my body, I throw him off. Scrambling to get up before he can pin me again, I stumble, the pain in my left eye making me dizzy.

I'm on my feet. Knut is nursing his right hand, cursing and yelling. His two friends are standing by, unsure.

"Hey! You lads stop that noise and go home!" It's the grocer from the town square.

I don't wait; I make a dash for the fountain. I am on to the path that leads to the forest when I hear my pursuers' footfalls shortly followed by a loud curse from the grocer.

The anger in my blood eases the pain in my legs. I run, breathing in the ecstasy of flight. Finally, I reach the first line of trees and head for the thickest part of the forest. Everything becomes a blur of colours and movement.

Finding a thick bush, I squeeze myself through the brambles. The darkness of the surrounding leaves and branches is a relief to my aching eyes. Trying not to move, I huddle, cramming my head between my knees to muffle my breathing, and wait. The smell of bruised leaves surrounds me like a faint barrier. It's not long before I hear the careless stomping of Knut and his friends. Anger rages inside me at their disregard for my forest. I squeeze myself into a tighter ball.

"This forest gives me the creeps. Come on, we can get him tomorrow."

"I'm going to get you, brat!" Knut yells out.

The noise of breaking twigs underfoot gets closer and closer to my hideout.

Suddenly a low, distant howl echoes in the forest.

Stillness.

"Shit! It's a wolf!"

"Don't be a baby. There are no wolves this far down."

"I dunno. My dad said they seen one last season."

Silence.

Another howl this time closer, and then another but from a different direction.

"I ain't staying here to find out! I'm going."

The sound of trudging feet, uncaringly kicking leaves as they go, begins to move away.

Another howl and a short bark; the stomping feet break out into a run.

Silence. The forest is unusually quiet.

My heart is pounding. I dare to peer through some of the branches.

Soft, irregular footsteps approach. They pass by. Stop and then continue through the forest. Another howl and a short bark. This time it's followed by a soft snigger, quickly muffled.

I lower one of the branches and see a shape. A shadow is moving stealthily through the trees. It's on two legs. I can't see anymore, and it disappears.

Wrapping my arms around my knees, I let go of my breath, and the pain in my eye overwhelms me. The unfairness of the bullying overcomes me, and I sob, my tears wetting my arms and knees. I scream in pain at the wrongness of it all. Everything inside me hurts.

"Mother," I whisper in between sobs.

Weak and exhausted, I slowly make my way out of my hiding place. I wipe my eyes hurriedly, my left eye bursts with pain, and I let out a curse. The forest is dark. It's past sunset. The air is cooling quickly, and shivers course through my body. The smell of damp leaves rises from the forest floor. The darkness and pain confuse me. I look around trying to get my bearings.

"Aldrik." A soft voice speaks my name.

A beautiful woman stands a few paces before me. Her garments flow, creating a strange, pale aura that surrounds her. She smiles gently and her face glows with a soft light.

"Who—" I swallow hard, my voice is no more than a whisper. "Who are you?"

Her smile is gentle. Her hair moves with the slightest breath of air.

"Are you a spirit of the forest?"

She smiles again and my fear melts away. "I am always here when you search for your herbs."

I dare not move. I try to remember if I have ever seen her before. Her eyes and smile remind me of someone. Shaking my head, trying to focus my mind, I ask her, "But I have never seen you. How can you be near me without me seeing you?" And then it dawns on me: the wood sprites and small elves occasionally appear. They never speak but always point me towards the clearings where the best herbs grow. A sense of awe fills me, a shiver runs up my spine, and my body is suddenly covered with goosebumps.

In a low whisper I ask, "Are you the Lady of the Forest? My godmother told me of the Lady of the Forest, the one who protects and guides all other spirits. Is it you who guides the sprites to find my herbs?"

She smiles gently at me but just looks me in the eyes. "Come, Aldrik, I have something wonderful to show you."

We walk quietly side by side. She leads me into a thick part of the forest I have never seen.

All at once, we come to a place where the trees seem fewer but taller. They stand majestic and more ancient. A strange soft light glows filling the immediate surrounds, but there is no visible source. She turns to face me and points to the base of the largest tree.

"There. Go there and look."

Following her direction, I step to the tree, and at its base behold a carpet of the most beautiful, delicate flowers. Each one a fragile star shape of pure white and at its centre a small bulb of the purest blue I have ever seen. Kneeling on the ground, I stare at this wonder. They are out of season, normally blooming at the end of the season of Malkizar.

Wonderful warmth fills my chest, all the hurt of the day dissolves, and, mesmerized, my eyes begin to brim with tears of joy. I look up. "How? How is it possible?"

She smiles. "They could not help it. I pleaded, telling them that it was for you, my sweet."

My heart is filled with gratitude. "Thank you. They are so beautiful."

Even before my eyes, the petals begin to close; the flowers are returning to their sleep.

Reaching out to me, she brushes the left side of my face. "Now you must go home and let Aïschah take care of that." Her hand feels like the touch of a feather, sending shivers up my spine. "Aldrik, do not be afraid. Tell her everything. All will be fine."

Her form becomes translucent and melts into the forest. Like a whisper of the wind amongst the trees, I hear her voice, "Follow the line of ferns on your left: that will take you directly to your godmother's cottage."

She is gone, and a feeling of being alone again almost overwhelms me. The carpet of flowers has blended back into the undergrowth.

The moon of Camlac is peeking over the mountaintops. A faint light edges a row of large ferns. Heading towards them, I can see that they follow a line of trees forming a border.

An icy breeze blows from the north, and my swollen eye hurts. I hurry towards the familiar slope at the edge of the forest where the cottage of my godmother, Aïschah, stands. I stomp my feet and clap my hands in the vain hope that feeling will return to my freezing extremities. The warm light of oil lamps and the fireplace glows through the closed window, a sharp contrast to the surrounding cool, shadowy landscape. I pause a moment, building my resolve. My godmother is my confidante; I can tell her anything and not fear any prejudice. She teaches me about the animals of the forest, and the whims of the weather and sometimes about her herbs and medicines.

I open the back door quietly and enter the kitchen. My godmother is standing at the stove, her back turned to me. She is leaning over a pot, her head clouded by steam.

"Godmother?" I call out, on the brink of tears. I want to tell her everything.

She gestures, raising a hand. "Hush, dear one!"

She murmurs a few words over the steaming pot, but I cannot identify what she is saying. I have learned to respect my godmother; her healing magic is renowned throughout the region. To interrupt her could mean that the potion sours.

She turns and smiles at me. She has long, light-coloured hair, which she sometimes ties back with a ribbon, but tonight it is loose and frames her face. It resembles the steam rising from the pot behind her. Her smile drops as she sees my face and my tattered clothes.

"Aldrik, what has happened?"

The anger, the humiliation, the pain I feel, and the hurt in my eye, bubble from deep down and suddenly burst out into tears. She comes over and folds me into a hug. The smell of fresh herbs on her apron comforts me. She lets me cry and then gently leads me to sit on a chair. She goes to her shelves and picks a small pot of ointment.

"Here, let me put something on that."

I look at my godmother, drawing comfort from her. The salve stings a little, but she is gentle.

Her face is very serene. Her eyes are clear blue, typical of the people of the Northern Region, and sometimes they sparkle with mischief. To me she looks kind, but I have seen her eyes grow cold like the midwinter ice when she is displeased with something or someone; I would not wish ever to be on the receiving end of that look. Her face is calm, with very few lines upon it, and her age to me is a mystery, though in my mind she appears to be ancient and wise.

"Now tell me, was it a mountain that you ran into?"

I can't help but smile. "Knut is what I ran into."

Her face goes severe. "That boy needs to be taught some manners! So, how did this start?"

Heat rises into my cheeks. I look down at the ground. I don't want her to think less of me. My body hurts with sadness. A cold river runs through my insides, and breathing is hard. Every time I take a breath to speak, a flood of tears threatens to burst out.

"Aldrik," she speaks my name softly, "You have nothing to fear."

Her words echo those of the lady of the forest. Reassurance creeps in. The knot in my stomach slowly unwinds. I clench my fists. Determination to speak my feelings finds form and the words come out.

"Knut and his friends push me around, calling me all sorts of names." Breathing becomes easier, relief at being able to finally tell someone. "I feel different. I know I'm different. It doesn't matter how much I try; my teacher always finds fault. I know the *Book of Parvus* off by heart and yet..."

Anger and sadness threaten to engulf me again. I pause distancing myself from the memory.

"My teacher says I show no promise. The other kids make fun of me, and some of them avoid me; they look scared. I don't belong there."

Ashamed to repeat the word that Knut and his friends called me, I speak of another instance.

"A different teacher once took our class while Delenna Tobba-ha was ill. I was able to give the correct definition of a sacred Parvus to the teacher. She praised me and pointed out to the others that they should apply themselves a little more to their study. During a break in the lessons, Knut and his friends cornered me and beat me up until I could not breathe. I didn't go back to class that day." I stop, considering all that I have just told her.

She looks at me with sadness in her eyes. "I am distressed to hear this. Why have you not spoken of this before, Aldrik?"

My eyes drop to the ground.

"Your gifts are what sets you apart, Aldrik. In terms of promise, it is useful to remember that Knut and his friends are repeating the year of school. If anyone shows little promise, it should be they."

"My teacher says that I do not have any gifts."

"I have my own opinion of that claim." Her eyes focus and a stillness fills the space between us. "Aldrik, describe what happens when you know the answer to a complex Parvus."

Only the trust I hold for my godmother makes me speak.

"I am not sure. It is as if someone whispers the words into my head. I am certain of the answer, and I say it before I can think about it."

"Do you remember last Spring, when you told me you could see a blue shimmer in the waters of the river? Tell me what you were feeling just before that."

I think back to that day. The memory of the clear sky, the gurgle of the river as it meanders among the rocks, are as clear to me as if I had gone back there.

"Everything becomes still. Even the sounds around me fade away. Then the surroundings become sharp; I can see every detail in the rocks and sometimes even the air shimmers as if it were solid. Sometimes it feels like I'm losing my mind. I see things that other people cannot see. That makes me feel different, weird, like a strange being."

"How does it start?"

"It always starts with a feeling of wanting to be somewhere else. My teacher says that I daydream. I guess it feels just like that. A dream, but while I am awake."

My godmother smiles gently.

"That is exactly what it is—a daydream or as you put it—a waking dream. Some would call it a vision."

"I don't want to have visions. People think I am mad. This is exactly what Knut says I am. Last year I saw what would happen to one of the girls in our class a whole day before it happened. I told her, hoping she would stay away and not get hurt. Now students are avoiding me and some of the teachers look at me strangely."

"Some of your teachers do not fully understand. Others are afraid. I would hope that at least one teacher, when she looks at you, is waiting with interest to see what other skills you have before making judgement. But all of them should be encouraging your skills. Your school is regarded by the Council of Elders as particularly fine in the search for magicians. I find it perplexing and sad that none of them have done anything at all."

My godmother grows silent and serious. She looks at me, and her eyes seem to focus beyond me. I start to fidget, I twist my fingers around, an awkward silence fills the room, and yet I know I have done no wrong.

The silence grows uneasy.

"Godmother?"

Aïschah blinks once, and her eyes focus back on me.

"Aldrik, next time you feel yourself slipping into a daydream, don't resist it. Allow yourself to see it fully. Your waking dreams, Dear One, are nothing to fear." She pauses a moment and sighs deeply. "However, I must go and see your father and speak with him. As for Knut and your teacher, don't worry; everything will be fine. I have to think carefully about your apprenticeship. Stay here in your usual room tonight."

Aïschah will not say anything else. I relax a little, but a sense of relief mixed with apprehension gnaws at my stomach. My father will undoubtedly hear of my poor schoolwork.

We eat our dinner in silence. I go to bed uncertain of the future but comforted that a burden that has weighed upon me for a long time has lifted.

CHAPTER TWO

High up on the side of the mountain, the small temple school of Asfaine is bathed in the late afternoon sunlight. The dim light filters through the high windows of the main classroom. The smell of ancient books fills the room, and specks of dust dance in the still air, defining the beams of sunlight. The elder leading the class is Delenna Tobba-ha, one of the few female high teachers. Her voice drones, repeating a Parvus from sacred scripture; the class echoes each word in a monotone, trying to emphasize every inflection taught. A short whistle of air cuts through the chanting as a narrow piece of cane finds a faltering student.

"Again!"

Bored of the senseless repetition, my attention drifts to the low-set northern windows. The mountaintops have turned a pure white. The snow line stops a little way down. It is early in the season of Malkizar, but it won't be long before the mountains are covered and the village of Asfaine will then be shut off from the plains below. The scent of pine trees wafts in through an open window, briefly clearing the atmosphere. I wonder if I can again find the place where the star flowers grow.

A beam of light from the setting sun bounces off one of the tower windows, throwing a shaft of faint blue light into the room. I remember my godmother's advice, not to resist and allow myself to see it fully. The air around me blurs.

A waft of warm air catches me by surprise; the smell of drying linen in the midday sun drifts across the air like woodsmoke. A crescent silver moon shines amidst a sky of a thousand stars. The curved blade of my scimitar reflects the moon; its razor-sharp edge turns from a white silver to pink and then to deep red. I hear the rustle of a light breeze in a palm grove, its leaves rustling in a strange language. I see low-lying, whitewashed buildings amongst beloved sand dunes. A sense of deep longing fills me. The scene grows dark. Bodies of young men lie on cold black stone. Blood pours from their severed limbs. I stare in horror but cannot turn away. My body is frozen. A presence stands near me. I try to move or turn but cannot. I open my mouth to scream, forcing air but no sound comes out of my mouth. Someone is whispering in my ear.

"You cannot defeat me. These are mine to have and do with as I please." Smoke stings my eyes.

Someone is screaming.

"Aldrik! Aldrik, stop daydreaming and answer the question!"

A small, dark, round woman with very mean dark eyes, her face flushed red with anger, is shouting at me. Delenna Tobba-ha's face is leaning into mine. Suddenly conscious of where I am,

I straighten, embarrassed. The other children are sniggering. A familiar mocking voice calls out, "The witch's brat is having a vision."

Another sharp whistle of the cane. "That's enough, Knut." It smacks loudly as it lands on the desk, narrowly missing his hands.

Knut looks at me fiercely, his free hand on the desk making a slow fist until his knuckles turn white. My stomach twists. In my mind I plan my way home to avoid Knut and his friends. My eye from yesterday is still swollen from yesterday.

"Well, Aldrik...answer. Please." The final word dripping with acid.

Placing my right fist into my open left hand, I bow. "I'm sorry, mistress. What is the question?"

She sighs as a bell tolls, announcing the end of lessons. "Never mind, Aldrik. Come and see me before you go home."

The class turns into a riot of chatter and scraping chairs.

I stand at my desk waiting for the classroom to clear, a heaviness weighing inside me. As Knut passes by, he purposely bumps into my desk, sending my things clattering onto the floor. I watch as pencils roll out of sight. Names and pictures have been carved into my ink-stained desk with sharpened pencils and even a small knife. I trace some of the pictures with my finger, lingering on the name Aldrik and a rude image. The image has since been scraped away, the raw wood still showing. I did not carve my name or the picture. I only scraped off the drawing that accompanied it. And yet, I was the one who got into trouble for it.

The voices of the other students fade into the background, their footsteps receding. The mocking laughter of Knut echoes last. The smells of dried apples and wood shavings rise from the empty desks. Another day ending in frustration, yet again calculating in my head how best to avoid Knut and his friends. The weight of it all, of this year, the relentless criticism and punishment from my teachers, the meals eaten alone in my father's house, all of it settles in my stomach threatening to make me sick.

A small wheezing sound intrudes on my thoughts. Delena Tobba-Ha is looking at me, with a mixture of anger and pity. I know what will follow. Endless and meaningless questions about my future, listing of my faults and weaknesses, and demands that I respond with answers on how to address these.

Resentment rises within me. Clenching my jaw shut, I decide not to speak.

She points to the front of her table. "Aldrik, come and stand here."

Slowly and deliberately, placing one foot in front of the other, I prepare to endure.

Apprehensive of the sting of the cane for her disapproval, I stop short of reaching her table, eyes downcast in mock submission. Her desk is in disarray, littered with papers and books. She is not very tidy for a teacher who expects it of us.

"Aldrik, I don't understand."

It begins. It seems that *she*, does not understand. The dialogue in my head sways between outright laughter and a scream of frustration. I don't understand why I'm here! I don't know why I must learn these meaningless verses and repeat them day after day.

The mountains outside the window beckon me.

"Look at me, Aldrik!" Her face is flushed, some of her hair no longer tucked neatly under her bonnet. Although she is looking at me, her eyes seem unfocused. Casually a thought occurs to me. I can hear my godmother saying that she probably eats too many spices. I bite off a smile.

"Aldrik, you are twelve years old. Very soon and before your thirteenth birthday, you will need to begin an apprenticeship. Do you have any idea what you will do?" She waits.

Shuffling my feet, I shrug my shoulders.

"Aldrik, your father is the village chief. It is through his efforts that this school still functions. Think how disappointing it will be for him to hear of your poor schoolwork."

I was wondering how long that was going to take. I am so bored of being reminded of that.

"If your mother were alive..."

My head whips up. Clenching my teeth, I openly stare at her. How dare she mention my mother!

Sensing my resentment, she quickly changes mid-sentence. "I will need to speak to your godmother, Aïschah. Tell her to come and see me tomorrow."

My heart sinks. I don't want my godmother involved in this.

"Do you understand, Aldrik? I need to know what to do with you."

Hoping to be released soon, I nod. A battle rages in my head. Resentment builds within me at being coerced, and anger at having to reveal my poor schoolwork. I am desperately trying to figure a way out.

The teacher sighs heavily. "Go Aldrik." She waves her hand wearily at me.

I turn to leave, and she adds, "Pick up your things off the floor first."

Quickly, before she adds anything else, I gather my pencils and shove them in my desk.

"Aldrik..."

Too late. Something else. Her tone of voice is suddenly sweet. "Can you ask your godmother for some more herbs? I have run out. And uh, tell her I will pay her when I see her. Here... " She hands me a note. "I have written the name of the herb on this."

Reluctantly, I take it, and this time I almost break into a run for the front door.

Filled with a sense of release, I scamper down the wooden stairs, skipping them two by two and jump off the last three.

I open the paper. Curcuma, written in a rushed handwriting, a small dark blot on the bottom corner where the ink has dripped. The paper smells slightly of cooking oil. I knew it, curcuma for inflammation. Ha! Too many spices! Disgusted that she thought I could not remember such a simple word, I pass a rubbish bin, crumple it, and angrily throw the piece of paper away. I'm not her errand boy!

My mind is preoccupied. How will I tell my godmother? Perhaps I ought to speak to Father first. He will look at me severely and at worst give me a lecture about my future.

The sight of the front door brings me to a sudden stop. My godmother, Aïshah, is standing in the doorway to the temple school. Confusion and fear mix, wondering why she is here.

"Hello, Aldrik."

"Why are you here?" Hearing the reproach in my voice I regret it immediately.

A thought occurs to me that she wants to make sure that yesterday's incident is not repeated. She has come to protect me from Knut and his friends. Shame and anger rise within me. I am not a baby. Aïshah looks at me with her cool gaze. She doesn't seem angry.

"I need to speak to your teacher. Where is Delenna?"

Only someone of importance would dare to call my teacher by her first name. I point back to the classroom. She nods and smiles at me.

"And I also came to speak with you about the vision you have just experienced."

I stand dumbfounded. How did she know? And then I remember, my godmother is one of the Council Elders. She is revered as a powerful healer and magician.

"First a word with your teacher. You have nothing to fear Aldrik. Wait for me here."

Curiosity and nervousness gnaw at me. On the one hand, I want to know what my godmother is saying to my teacher. On the other, I am nervous about my poor schoolwork. Hesitating, tempted to go and stand below the open window and listen in, but fearful of the shame of being discovered, I resolve to wait for my godmother.

The meeting did not last very long. Aïshah is back before I can summon the courage to change my mind. She walks briskly out of the long corridor that leads from the main rooms. The sun has set and in the remaining twilight, shadows fill the corners and vaulted ceilings.

Aïshah's eyes hold an air of seriousness. The kind I want to avoid. My stomach churns at the thought of what Delena Tobba-Ha has said to her about me.

Aïshah pauses a moment in front of me and smiles. "Come

Aldrik, let us leave this place. It tends to make me sad."

I take a breath of relief. I don't feel like hiding anymore.

We walk in silence for a while heading into the village. She makes straight for the village bakery. The town square is deserted. We sit at a small table that the baker has placed outside his shop to encourage people to purchase his wares and eat at their leisure. Aïschah goes inside. I am surprised, surely the bakery is shut by now and preparations for the next morning's baking underway.

She steps out looking triumphant, holding two small pastries. "These were left from this morning's baking. Here, eat this one."

It's a small barley cake filled with a soft, creamy centre. My mouth waters. It's one of my favourite sweets. My mind, on the other hand, reels in confusion. This is normally a reward for good work and for celebrating important occasions.

I look up inquiringly, suspicious of her motives.

"Godmother? What are we celebrating?"

She laughs openly.

"We are celebrating you. But first, let us discuss your vision."

"How did you know?"

She pauses a moment. "When a vision comes to you, it draws energy towards you. The more significant the vision, the more power flows. Because we are related, and because I am sensitive to power, I felt a surge and an image of you came to mind. That is how I knew. I do not know what you saw, only that it was a powerful vision."

Savouring the last morsel of barley cake to make it last, I let the soft centre melt slowly in my mouth.

The images of young men being tortured float into my mind. A sense of revulsion and embarrassment fills me. Not sure of what the images mean, I opt for the less threatening one.

"Is there such a place as I saw?"

"I do not know what you saw. Why don't you start from the beginning?"

Hesitating, not knowing how to start, and feeling a need to ask many questions, I shrug my shoulders. "I don't know where to start."

"Where were you? What were you doing? And what drew your attention that allowed you to slip into a trance?"

I almost laugh. "That's almost as many questions as I have."

Aïshah smiles. "All right. Where were you?"

"I was in the main room with the others. We were repeating the Parvus set for the day."

"What else were you doing?"

My face flushes with embarrassment. "Godmother, I was really bored. We kept repeating the same lines over and over again. Some of the students could not speak with the right inflection."

"Do you remember which of the sacred verses were being spoken?"

My face feels hot. "It was one of the Parvus that King Apphat wrote on the beauty of love. I cannot remember the specific one."

Aïshah's eyes are on me. "What happened next?"

"One of the windows was open and I could see the mountaintop. I remember thinking that I wanted to go to the forest, and I noticed that the light changed."

"How did it change?" Aïshah's tone is urgent.

I reflect a moment. "The sun was setting, and a beam of light struck one of the high windows, sending a ray of blue light across the room."

Aïshah's attention grows even more tense. Goosebumps suddenly cover my arms.

"A light breeze blew through the open window. I could smell the pine trees. I was thinking of how the village would soon be cut off by the snows. And then the breeze turned warm. I became confused. I found myself standing in a place full of sand. I could feel heat all around me as if on a bright summer day. I could smell the smoke from a campfire. Although I knew that where my body stood, it was still daylight, and yet I could see a night sky full of stars."

My stomach sinks at the memory of what came next. "And then everything went dark. I saw young men being tortured. A voice spoke to me. It was a horrible voice..." Tears well up in my eyes.

Aïshah places a hand on my cheek. "Go on, Aldrik."

"The voice said that I could not help them. She was torturing them, Godmother!"

Swallowing the memory down, I go on. "And then I saw a weapon by my side. Its blade was very sharp. I've never seen such a weapon and yet I knew its name. It is called a scimitar. I looked up into the sky and saw a crescent moon. Its light shone on my blade making the edge look sharper. But then the silver light turned, and the blade looked like it was dripping with blood." Pausing to take a breath and release my pent-up anger, I look at Aïshah. "I felt angry and wanted to use it to protect these young men. Smoke from the campfire blew across my face, stinging my eyes. I heard someone scream. Next, I saw Delena Tobba-Ha yelling at me to answer the question."

Aïschah sits deep in thought. Her eyes, unfocused, seem to be looking at something far away.

The silence grows uneasy.

"Godmother?"

She smiles. "Aldrik, your visions are of things that may yet happen. They are nothing to be afraid of."

Standing, she holds her hand out to me. "Come, Aldrik, stay with me again tonight. Tomorrow, we will see your father."

Although no longer a child, I derive a great sense of comfort holding her hand all the way back to her cottage.

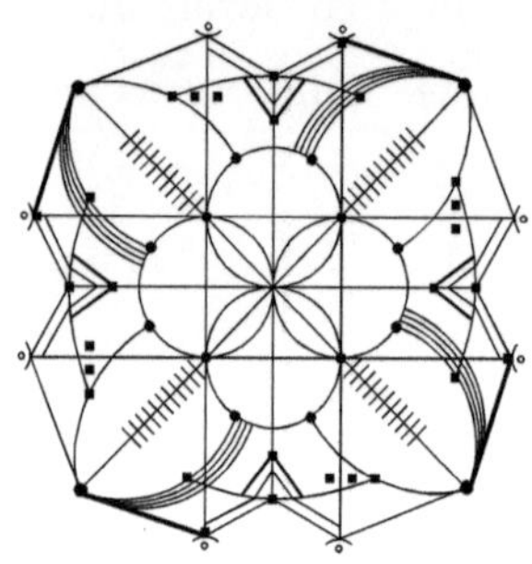

CHAPTER THREE

I wake from a dreamless sleep. The room is still dark. Although the sky outside my window is lighter, the sun has not yet risen. The feather-filled eiderdown looms large like a mountain on top of me. Testing the air, I stick my arm out. The fire must have gone out during the night; the air is cool on my skin. With a shiver, I quickly draw my arm back under the covers.

I struggle with an internal battle—the urge to get up and relieve myself or to stay warm under the covers for a little while longer. In the end, the feeling of fullness becomes uncomfortable and wins; I cannot hold on anymore.

Slowly and tentatively, I stick my feet out from under the covers. I slide my body sideways trying to keep as much of my body warm as I can. Struggling not to lose the eiderdown, I blindly feel with my feet until I sense the inevitable cold floor. I find my slippers quickly and, bracing myself, I deliberately plunge out from under the cover into the cold morning air. I shiver and race to the toilet.

I hear my godmother in the kitchen. The comforting smell of baking wafts past.

"Hurry Dear One; I have made warm cakes for breakfast."

Part of me wonders at the occasion but the thought of the cakes fills my stomach with longing.

Breakfast over, I help my godmother clear the table. She stands before me smiling warmly, yet I can sense a tension in her. She casually brushes my hair back with her hand.

"Now Dear One, go wash yourself and dress. We will go and speak with your father. He is expecting us."

I look at her in wonder: how could Father know already that we are on our way? My awe of my godmother only increases, a sense of importance fills me to be her godson.

We take the most direct path to the village. Meandering at first through the edge of the forest, the pine trees giving off their sharp, sweet scent in the cold morning air. Each breath I exhale turns into a cloud of mist before my face. I breathe out slowly and shape each breath, trying to make rings the way my father does with the smoke of his tobacco pipe.

The sky has just started to turn a pale blue; the tips of the mountains covered in snow begin to glow a faint pink with the early touch of the sun's first rays. I hug my jacket tighter around my neck.

My godmother walks briskly, showing little effort, while I occasionally hurry my steps to keep pace with her. We reach the outskirts of the village. Except for the silversmith and the baker, everyone else seems to still be in bed.

We reach the square; long icicles are hanging from the fountain spouts in a frozen dance both graceful and violent. Each spout is shaped differently according to its position relative to the sun. There is one I like best; its mouth is that of an eagle. There is also a fish, its cheeks puffed as with an effort to spit the water. The other two spouts are creatures that belong in stories told to children. One looks like a wolf with large fangs and the other a little like a bear but with wings and the beak of a bird. I heard my godmother once call it the fire beast. The metal of the fountain is dark with patches of slimy green. The water in the fountain is not yet frozen as this is just the beginning of Malkizar. The icicles will melt away with the midday sun. The smell of wet stone rises from the street. A waft of freshly baked bread drifts across our path from the bakery. Despite a full breakfast, my mouth waters.

We enter a wide street that rises heading to the top of the village. As we pass by, a boy about my age, and carrying a bucket, is making his sleepy way to the square's fountain to collect some water. His eyes meet mine and the sleep dissolves into hostility. He's a friend of Knut's. I straighten, confident, almost daring him. I make a brief sign with my left hand, knowing it to be a childish sign of witchcraft. His eyes widen, and his skin suddenly pales even in the cold air. He looks up at my godmother and as quickly looks away. His free hand turns into a fist.

"Come Dear One, let us hurry, your father is waiting." My godmother smiles at me, I'm sure she has not noticed the exchange.

We reach my father's house.

Aïschah doesn't bother to knock. She opens the door, and the warm air surrounds us. There is a sense of comfort mixed with authority. Dark wood panels line the walls. Some images hang on the walls, depicting the various clans in their traditional colours. Tall shelves hold books on various topics, ranging from law to histories of the four lands. To one side, a broad set of stairs climbs to the upper floor. The familiar smell of my father's pipe tobacco, rich and sweet, reminds me of a dark, spicy, fragrant spread the baker uses on some of the pastries he makes. The warm sweetness of spices mixed with old leather-bound books, envelops me like a warm blanket.

My father is in his study. He raises his eyes, a serious look on his face. "Aïschah, welcome." He sees me and his face softens. "Aldrik." He motions me forward. "Come let me look at you."

My father looks up briefly at my face and then my godmother. I see her smile and shake her head. Confidently I go to him. Even sitting down, he towers over me. He raises an arm to my shoulder, holding me gently.

"Does it still hurt?"

I shake my head.

"Tell me what you have been up to."

I know not to talk about my waking dreams with him. Nevertheless, I sense my godmother tense slightly. Hesitating, thinking he is referring to the recent fight, I change the subject.

Looking into his grave face, self-importantly I announce, "I know where the star flowers grow."

For a moment he looks astonished and then raises an eye to Aïschah who despite herself struggles to hold back a grin.

"He seems to know more of the forest than I do. I am just as astonished with the ease he takes to nature. Or..." she adds, "Perhaps it is nature that is taking to him."

My father frowns, then looks at me thoughtfully. A sigh escapes him. I can smell the bittersweet fragrance of his pipe tobacco. "Star flowers, eh?"

"I can take you there to see them."

He casually lets his arm drop away from my shoulder. "They were her favourites."

I understand he refers to my mother. A small painting of her, mounted in a gilded frame, sits on his desk. She has long dark hair, kind blue eyes and a lovely, unforced, gentle smile. I want to tell him about the Lady of the Forest, but something holds me back.

"Haakon, we need to speak."

My father shakes his head as if awakening from a dream. "Yes. Yes, of course. Aldrik, go upstairs and wait in your room."

My godmother smiles at me, and I walk out and up the narrow wooden stairs. The second last step creaks. It has always creaked.

I sense that my father and godmother are to talk about something important. I leave the door ajar and lie on the floorboards with my ear to the ground; my father's office is below.

"He has inherited her gifts." My godmother speaks gently.

"Her gifts?! He has inherited her looks. It breaks my heart each time I see him." Reproach and anger tinge his tone.

"Haakon, you knew she had the sight."

"Much good did the sight do her." I can hear my father's anger.

"Yes. She feared the gift of sight. There are some things that not even the sight will prevent from happening."

There is a long pause.

"What would you have me do Aïschah? Her gifts were her curse. His gifts, as you call them, will isolate him. He is already different from all the others. There are those who will ridicule him, and worse, they will make his life a misery. I know about the fight. The grocer came and saw me yesterday. Although I am told that he gave back as good as he got. Knut's father is a brute with his children and so his eldest takes it out on the weaker children. It becomes a cycle of violence. Look at him: is this what you want for him?"

Gently, my godmother continues, "You are right. He is different. He needs to stand up for himself at some point. But keeping him from his gifts and denying what he is will not save him either."

"Then what? The old ways are not what they were. There are many folks who are suspicious of the gifts you speak of."

Aïschah's voice changes, a subtle change but evident to me. "Haakon that is why I come to you. The teachers at his school are not qualified or experienced to handle a child with such gifts. As far as his other schoolwork is concerned, he could do with a more understanding hand. I'm offering to take up his education, to nurture his gifts and see that they are used properly. He is of age to begin an apprenticeship. He already knows most of the herbal medications I prepare, and he often collects the herbs from the forest with accuracy that is beyond his age. Let him begin his apprenticeship into healing and eventually magic with me and see where it leads."

I hear the chair scrape the floor as my father stands. He begins to pace in the study. "What makes you think that he is ready for that? Other than the herbs—and I am not saying that a healer is not a worthy profession, but what other abilities could he possibly have shown at his age?"

There is another pause.

"You know the importance of the three."

"Yes. So, what of it?"

"He has had a third vision and this one disturbs me, Haakon. It speaks of bigger events than those of this village."

The floorboards creak as my father shifts his weight. "What visions has he had?"

"The first came to him many months ago, although I dismissed it at first as an ordinary gift of sight. He saw what he calls the Lady of the Forest. It is she who led him to discover the place where the star flowers grow."

My breath against the floor almost sounds too loud. There is a slight wind outside, which whistles softly as it passes under the front door. A windowpane rattles. My stomach twists: my godmother is speaking about my visions to my father.

"You know who the Lady of the Forest is, Haakon. You only have to see how he looks at her image on your table."

My father begins to talk and then stifles a word.

"You should take comfort that she is looking after him."

The windowpane rattles again. I will my body to perfect stillness.

"His second vision is concerned with water. He sees a blue stone in the river that leads to Malkizar. He is the only one who can see this. He even pointed to it once when I walked with him. Even using the sight, I could not see it. But I did see the colour of the water change to a deep blue. Haakon, there is no mistaking the symbol of the water and a blue stone. According to legend, that would be one of the Sacred Tears."

"Aïschah, be careful. There are many who already call you a heretic and a witch!"

My godmother makes a small laughing sound. I picture her

dismissing the comment with a wave of her hand. "Let them call me what they will. Whom do they turn to when they are sick?"

"You said he had a third vision?"

"Yes, this one only yesterday. He was in class at the time. His previous visions required an external focus element, such as water or fire. This vision came to him suddenly, there was no point of focus—no water, no fire, nothing. It just came to him."

"Why is that important?"

"It means that his powers are developing beyond his ability to control them... " My godmother pauses. "If he does not understand what he is seeing, he could very well dismiss them out of hand or worse still, they could drive him to insanity—no longer make sense of the world around him."

A gust of wind whistles under the front door. The windowpane rattles once more.

"What..." My father's voice falters. "What did he see?"

"He saw a land far away, specifically the land of the desert people. He saw a weapon of power, a silver moon, a sky filled with a thousand stars, fire, and smoke. He also saw death and heard a voice warning him off. Of course, as with these things, they were embellished into a story; those, however, are the essential symbols of importance."

"Aïschah, you are the seeress in these matters. What do these mean?" My father's tone has changed from anger to resignation.

"The faraway land is where his destiny lies. The weapon of power is one that is waiting for him, though the latter is unclear, as the weapon did not reveal its purpose. The silver moon is a symbol of my name in the ancient tongue, and its light shining upon the blade signifies my guidance; the sky full of stars signifies those that he will save. The sight of death and the sound of warning are the consequence if he does nothing. Fire, as an elemental, calls him to action, and finally, darkness and smoke, which blew across the scene before he could see any more, is a symbol of deceit—that which is trying to prevent him from fulfilling his destiny." My godmother spoke with a voice that I knew would not be challenged.

The sound of my heartbeat in my chest is loud. The wind is silent, and the house suddenly seems still. A long moment passes before I hear my father once more pace in his study. His steps are measured; his weight makes the floorboards creak.

"Does he know the meaning of these? Have you spoken to him about it?" My father's voice sounds grave.

"No. I wait on your decision, Haakon. But it would be wise not to delay this."

"Call him downstairs."

I hear my godmother move to the bottom of the stairs. "Aldrik. Come, Dear One. Join us."

I get up slowly, trying not to give my listening position away. I am very careful coming down the stairs, looking where I place my feet, avoiding looking at my godmother. My cheeks burn. I look up and see my godmother smiling at me. She reaches out and gently brushes my hair away from my eyes.

"You heard everything?" Her question is gentle.

I nod guiltily.

"Good, I am glad." She is still smiling at me. "Come, your father wishes to speak with you and me."

My father is standing looking out of the window. He is holding the picture of my mother, and carefully, he places it back on his desk. Sitting down in his chair, he beckons me over to him. "Aldrik..." He pauses. "How old are you now?"

"Twelve, Father. Nearly thirteen."

He smiles at me. "Nearly thirteen, eh? Well, that means you are on your way to manhood." He looks at my mother's picture and sighs. "Your godmother and I have spoken about your future. You have skills that require tuition of a specialised kind." He looks at my godmother, "You are to stay and study with your godmother. You will not need to come home. Aïschah is a very powerful magician and healer. She will teach you the ways of healing and, in time, those of magic."

I swallow hard. I can hardly believe what I am hearing.

"Do you understand Aldrik?"

"Yes, Father."

"Do you have any questions for me, Aldrik?"

A little knot sits in my stomach. I look briefly at the picture of my mother. She is smiling. I look up at my father and see the courage in his eyes.

"Father?"

"Yes, Aldrik."

"Will I be able to come and visit you?"

For the first time in a long time, my father wraps his arms around me and draws me into a hug. His strong arms around me feel comforting. "Anytime you want, my son. You are always loved." He releases me and adds, "I am very proud of you. Do you remember what your name, 'Aldrik,' means in our tongue?"

"Yes Father. It means noble and kind as well as mighty."

"That is correct. It also means that you have a bright and wonderful future."

My godmother coughs. "Haakon, I have one more request."

My father looks up at her.

"Haakon, as you know he will have to take on a name of power. All who deal with him will know him by this name. It is a name that will resonate with his skills and protect him. Only you and those close to him will remember him as Aldrik..." My godmother pauses, as if thinking. "I have often referred to him as 'my Dear One.' In the language of the Tassili, the desert people, this would be Azizi. It means 'beloved.' This is to be his new name."

My father nods his agreement.

"Very well then. Azizi..." The sound of my new name resonates in my being. A thrill rises along my spine and ends in a shudder. "Go, my son, with your godmother and learn your lessons well."

I hug my father and releasing him, I place one hand on his cheek, feeling the stubble of his beard.

"Don't be sad Father. I will come and visit often."

My father smiles at me.

My godmother and I walk out into the cold early winter morning. The sky looks bright and full of sunlight. A weight has lifted off my shoulders. I stand tall and proud. I am to be an apprentice in healing and magic. Looking up, the sky seems within my reach. "Godmother?"

"Yes, Dear One?"

"Will I have to go back to school?"

"No Aldrik, that will not be necessary. I will take care of your studies. I have already spoken to your teacher."

A sense of relief fills me. "Godmother, Father said I would learn magic."

"Yes. And you will"

"Can I learn to fly?"

"That would depend, Dear One."

"On what?"

"On whether you could change yourself into a bird."

I look up to find my godmother smiling at my confusion. "However, there are other ways to fly."

"Will you teach me?"

"You already know how to."

I look up at her to see if she is making fun of me.

"How?"

"In your dreams, some nights ago, you told me you flew over the cottage and into the valley below."

"Yes, but that was a dream. I mean now! Could I fly now?"

I look up at my godmother. She shakes her head slightly with an expression of amusement and mild disbelief. My godmother sighs. "There is much to teach you, Dear One."

We reach the cottage and eagerly I go to the room I sleep in whenever I stayed with my godmother. This is my room now. I stand at the doorway, savouring the moment. I step inside. My chest expands, my body lengthens: this is my room. I look at it now as if for the first time. The walls are made of wooden logs, which make the room look and feel warm. A window looks out over the valley towards the south. The Asfaine Mountains rise in the distance, curving towards the west. A gentle slope of grass and pine trees falls away from my godmother's cottage. From the window, I have a clear view of the path that leads to the valley and the village. If I crane my head around to the left, I can see the line of pine trees that are the edge of the forest. In the season of Malkizar, the sun fills my room in the early morning, but late in the evening the sunlight disappears behind the cottage.

A small table sits underneath the window. Pencils and paper are neatly arranged on the table. This is where I will study and write my notes on healing and magic. I touch the desk, feeling the smoothness of the wood. No carvings or insulting images on this desk. Briefly, I touch the pencils, rearranging them. Filling my lungs with the cool dry air, I know I'm at home and a thrill of gratitude fills my heart. Some of the warm air flows through the open door from the main fireplace downstairs. There is a rug in the middle of the floor, which now I am thinking of moving closer to my bed to keep my feet warm when I get up in the mornings. A small shelf sits near the bed to hold some books that I will need to read and study. There is a small oil lamp on the table, lending the room a sense of comfort and serious scholarship.

"Come and have some food, Dear One."

With one last proud look at my room, I turn to go and eat with her.

The table is set for two, and now, knowing that I will be eating all my meals here, it looks different. The smell of freshly baked bread fills the room. A pot of steaming vegetable soup sits on the table.

My godmother looks up.

"How is your room?"

"Beautiful. Just fine, thank you."

"How do you feel?"

"I am so excited. I have my own room in your cottage. When will you begin to teach me?"

"I think tomorrow morning will be soon enough. But first, I will tell you what I will teach you and begin to tell you about the legends you will study."

I sit at the table opposite my godmother.

"First, tell me. What do people say I am?" she asks.

I have a mouthful of bread, which I am suddenly finding hard to chew and swallow.

"It's all right, Dear One, I am not easily offended."

"Some people call you a witch. I have heard others call you a magician and seeress, though I don't know what seeress means."

My godmother nods her head.

"A seer or seeress is one who is able interpret signs and sometimes is able to see the future. Those who call me a witch do not understand what they say. They use the term in a negative way, implying that I am responsible for making bad things happen. In the olden days, a witch was a woman who was versed in the Lore of healing herbs and potions. She would offer her knowledge to heal people of their sickness. A magician, although flattering, implies that I do tricks or at least do things that ordinary people are unable to explain."

"Dear One, have you heard the word 'Mahjir' or 'Mahjira'?"

"No." I realise I whispered the word. "No Godmother, I haven't," I say more decisively.

"The title of Mahjir for a man or Mahjira for a woman, is given to one who has mastered the arts of magic and seership."

"The first thing you must know, Dear One, is that the knowledge I give you has been given from one such a person to another. It is considered sacred knowledge and therefore must not be spoken of lightly. It is also forbidden to share that knowledge unless it is with one who is undertaking the role of apprentice. By agreeing to study with me, you are undertaking the role of apprenticeship into magic and seership."

My godmother's voice is quiet but full of authority. She is looking at me with that serious gaze that makes me feel very little.

"Do you understand Azizi?"

She used my name of power, and the result is to send a shudder up my spine. I swallow the lump of bread.

My heart is thumping in my chest. "Yes, Godmother I understand."

"Good." She begins to eat and continues her instructions. "Your apprenticeship will take four years unless you complete it earlier. Once you successfully complete your apprenticeship, you will be initiated first into the First Order of Apphat as a healer and then as a magician in training. To mark that occasion, a sign will be permanently tattooed into your right forearm. Like this one."

She draws her sleeve back and lets me see the sign painted on her arm. The sign is faded; it must have been made a long time ago. It looks like a double-headed axe with one line cutting across it. Above the line is a simple circle, and below the line a similar circle but this one had been painted in. I swallow hard. I dare not ask if it will be painful.

"To anyone who knows what this sign means, it will grant you respect as a powerful healer. This sign, however, is not to be paraded before just anyone. After initiation, it is wise to keep it covered."

"Beyond the first order of initiation, there are two more orders before you are able to be accepted as Master or Mahjir. Eventually another tattoo will be placed on your chest, to mark your initiation into the first order of magic."

My heart sinks a little. I realise now how difficult this will be.

In four years, I will be seventeen, practically a grown man. The smith's apprentice looks so much older than me, and he is fifteen. Although my godmother is a kind and loving person, I know that she will not settle for anything but complete dedication.

"Right now, Dear One, a small lesson in geography and history."

I look at her puzzled. I thought I would be learning magic, not ordinary schoolwork.

My godmother looks at me with a playful smile.

"Don't worry; this is not school. Azizi, do you know the names of the two great oceans?"

I think back for a while to my lessons at school.

"Yes, Godmother. The one where the sun rises, is called Elwah. Its name means 'joy' and the other where the sun sets is called Malkizar, meaning 'sorrow'. It is also the name of the winter season because the waters of Malkizar are cold and stormy... " I pause a moment. "I was born in the season of Malkizar, the time of sorrow. Is that why my mother died and made my father sad?"

"No, Dear One. Your mother died because she was not well, and she knew it. Your father is sad because he loved her very much and misses her." Aïshah looks at me with a kind smile. "You also need to know that you were born in the second hour of the second day of the second month of Malkizar. The astrological significance is important, Azizi. In esoteric terms, it makes you a child of stardust, holder of magic. This is the reason so few of your classmates understand you. To them, you appear to be aloof and disconnected from their world."

A long silence weighs over the room. I can still see my father's face as he looked at my mother's picture. A deep desire still dwells within me to tell my father that she now protects the forest and sometimes leads me to find wonders there.

"Dear One, you did not cause your mother's illness. It was not your fault."

I look at my godmother. "I know. She told me."

She takes a quick breath, releasing it slowly. "I am glad she did. You named the oceans well. Do you know the legend of the oceans, how they were created?"

I shake my head.

"What I am about to tell you should be spoken with great reverence. These things are not spoken of lightly, even by great sages.

"According to legend, at the beginning of creation, the two great oceans were whole and as one. But when mankind was created, and confusion and disharmony arose among men, a great cataclysm occurred upon the land and the ocean split into two. It was then that the Spirit Guardians of the land drew the energy from the waters and created a pair of magical stones, each representing the energy of the split. They are said to be sapphires, each a different hue of blue. The one representing Elwah shines the pure sky blue of a clear spring day, while the other representing Malkizar, glows with the gloom of the winter ocean, often streaked with bolts of pure white, resembling a fierce storm at sea that still rages within it. And hence the duality of joy and sorrow was born into the world.

"It is recorded that the Spirit Guardians initially gave the stones to the people of Elwah with a command to guard them and use the stones to re-establish the Great Harmony of the land. No instruction was given on how to use them, but a warning was issued that the power of the stones could not be used for evil: the result would be total annihilation.

"In stories told of ancient times and of King Apphat the Compassionate, legend also states that he who holds the sapphires in his hands knows himself truly, and nothing will stand in the way to achieving his heart's desire.

"King Apphat was given the sapphires in his youth by a seeress whose identity has remained secret. While King Apphat ruled with compassion and wisdom, even he could not bring about the Great Harmony written in the Sacred Parvus. It took him a lifetime to understand the warning given of the danger of using the stones. All that is left of the warning is a cryptic verse in an ancient book, that best translated states: 'The power of the Gateway is one or won, or both'. It is unclear whether the ancient script for the word 'One' means a singular entity or 'Won' as in victory. On his deathbed, Apphat surrounded by mystics and disciples, said that he had finally understood the warning. Urged by those around him to reveal the secret, in his wisdom, to ensure that the secret would be shared by all, he smiled and said he would inscribe it on a paper for all to see, but only those who were wise enough would understand.

"The following morning, his followers found him dead with a beatific smile upon his face, holding a parchment to his chest. His followers unfolded the document and found the Seer had drawn a line across the page, with a circle above it and a circle below it.

"Many arguments developed. Most agreed that he had begun to write the answer but had died before completing his message. Some said that he had tried to warn of the stone of sorrow. Others said that the warning was for the stone of joy and taught against all excesses. In the old script either could have been right or wrong since the symbol for joy is a line with a circle above it and the symbol for sorrow is a line with a circle below it."

It occurs to me that the same symbol appears on my godmother's tatoo on her right arm.

"Godmother, does anyone know where the Sacred Stones are?"

"No Azizi, no one knows. There are as many legends about their location as there are about the Stones themselves. Some say that for safe keeping the Stones were separated and each sent to a secret guardian."

"What I saw in the river last summer; was that one of the Stones?"

"You're very quick, Dear One. I do not think it was, but I think your last vision signifies something about your destiny."

"Am I meant to discover the Stones, Godmother?"

"That I do not know."

She pauses a moment and then adds, "Teaching you the ways of magic will eventually release your true destiny. I think that is enough stories for now. You need some rest before your lessons begin tomorrow. Take your time to arrange your room the way you want. Ask me if you need anything. Tomorrow, after breakfast come and meet me in the Herbarium."

"Thank you, Godmother."

My godmother smiles at me.

"Rest well Azizi."

I reposition the rug, made sure my pencils are sharpened. Caressed the clean unmarked surface of my desk. I open some of the books already on the shelf and flip through them without really reading anything. Hours passed quickly. The sky darkens early during the cold season.

When the time comes to slip into bed, I thought I would be too excited to sleep, but as soon as I lay in bed, I slip into a dreamless slumber.

43

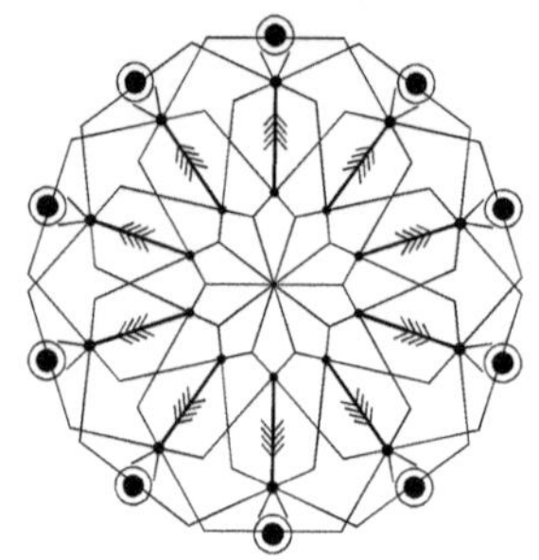

C H A P T E R F O U R

Lessons in Magic —Lesson 1—The dreamer awakens. Those are the words my godmother has written on a dark green slate with some chalk, and which I now stare at. The words, elegantly written, seem to take on an importance of their own. The early morning light fills the herbarium with a pale glow. The wood stove is already alight and fragrant apple woodsmoke fills the room. My godmother stands by the window and waits until I have seated myself at the large table, my pen and parchment ready.

"Magic is real. Reality as you perceive it, is a dream." Those words seem finite. There doesn't seem to be room for discussion. I sit motionless not knowing what to say or do. There follows a long pause I dare not break. I want to learn but this really confuses me. I wait for an explanation, but my godmother fixes me with a long, searching look.

"Ask any question you want."

"I don't understand Godmother. How can this be a dream?" I wave my arm to take in the room around us.

"Last night when you slept, did you dream?"

I think for a moment and remember. I was in a favourite part of the forest where the trees grow tall and dense.

"I did, yes..."

"And as you remember the dream, did you feel that at the time it was real? You could see the trees, the forest, the sky. Could you see the ground you walked on and feel the cold air around you?"

I fidget uncomfortably. I don't know how, but she knows my dream to the finest detail.

"Yes, Godmother...but—"

"Ask yourself, Dear One, with what eyes were you seeing your dream forest?"

I think for a moment and realise that asleep my eyes would be closed.

I must look confused. My godmother smiles.

"So, you see, it is not with your physical eyes that you look upon your dream landscapes."

"With what? How do I see?"

"With your mind, Dear One. And in that dream, as in all others, it is your mind that wanders in the woods and 'sees.'"

"But then, when I wake up and open my eyes, I see all of this."

"Your physical eyes merely register something and sends these signals to your brain. But in fact, it is your mind that interprets what has already been projected."

I could feel myself looking dumbfounded. This was going to be harder than I thought.

"Azizi, Dear One." My godmother has begun to call me by my

name of power. "Look at one point in this room. Look carefully. Now close your eyes and picture what you were looking at. Out loud, describe what you see in your mind."

"I can see the room, the window that looks out on the Asfaine Mountains."

"Be more precise; describe the things in the room as you perceived them a moment ago."

"I can see the shelves with jars of dried herbs. The jars are dark brown with labels on them that tell what is in them. The writing is too small for me to read. There is one jar on the table over there by the window." I raise my arm and point in the direction I knew would be the window.

"Describe it."

"It is one of the blue jars. It has a cork stopper. There are dried flowers in it. I know because only the blue jars have dried flowers."

"Keep your eyes closed. Tell me what is written on the label— the type of flower it is."

"I can't. It is too far away."

"Azizi, listen carefully. Relax and take a deep breath. Now in your mind move towards it; allow yourself to see the label as if you held it close."

I take a deep breath, but my body feels tense, frustrated. I let my breath out slowly as my godmother instructs me. Gradually, I feel very peaceful, as if I were floating on water on a warm summer's day. As though my mind fills the room, I expand. I hear myself gasp. The blue jar is right in front of me, its label as large as my hand. Clearly it reads: *Delphinium Dora*. Involuntarily I gasp.

"Stay focussed, Dear One. What does it say?"

I whisper, "Delphinium Dora."

"Let us go further." I sense my godmother smile. She then speaks in a very strong voice I have never heard her use. "Put that jar back where it belongs with the others!"

Without thinking, I see the empty spot on the shelf, where the jar belongs and see the jar slide back into place.

I hear a scraping sound and cannot help it. My eyes snap open. I quickly look and to my amazement, the blue jar is no longer on the table where it was, but back on the shelf with the others.

My godmother is still seated in front of me, a good ten paces from the shelves. No matter how quickly she moved, she could not have placed it back.

Aïschah smiles, reading the astonished question on my face. "Close your mouth, dear. You never know what could fly into it."

I close my mouth quickly. "But how?"

"You did it, Dear One, with your mind."

"But how?"

"If this 'reality' is a dream created by your mind, then you can control the elements in your dream with your mind. However," she pauses, "it requires will, which in this case you used unconsciously, merely responding to *my* will, when I ordered you to replace the jar. And of course," —this she adds with a mischievous smile— "you cannot go around re-ordering the world around you without affecting the sanity of the dreamers of this world. So, I urge you, be careful how you use your mind."

I sit there amazed, contemplating the possibilities.

"You did well, Azizi. There will be other lessons. Just think about this one, and what you have learned."

I sit motionless, fascinated by what has just happened.

Aïschah looks at me, smiling.

"It would do your mind good to walk through the forest. Go, enjoy yourself, there will be time enough to think this through."

I get up and walk outside. I am different, somewhat lighter. The air around me seems to shimmer. I head for my beloved forest. The forest looks unusual, almost as if I can see through it; the trees seem to shine with light. It is as if I can see them draw their power from the earth and send it to the very top leaves. I also catch movements throughout the forest; I assume these to be the birds, the squirrels. It is as though I can look into the forest and, in an instant, I am deeper into it than I have ever been.

Something catches my attention. I begin to perceive something dark moving amongst the trees; the odd shape begins to form and reform as if attempting to hide amongst the trees. A fog fills the forest and then suddenly, the feeling is gone. It is the old forest again, dense, and dark, moving with the wind. My heart sinks, and a heaviness fills my body in a way I have never noticed before. Energy seeps out of me. I decide that am tired and return to my godmother's cottage and rest a while.

My godmother's herbarium is where I spend most of my time. The room is large and airy; there are several windows that face the Asfaine Mountains to the north, and one that faces the mountains where the sun rises. The room is filled with jars, books, and old parchment rolls. The jars contain herbs, dried flowers, roots ground into fine powders, and ointments made from distilled fresh herbs. In the far corner, there is a woodstove, where the fire almost continuously burns. Above the stove hang a few different sized cauldrons, made of shiny copper, in which my godmother prepares her medicines. The air is warm, and the heavy scents of dried herbs mixed with those of dried flowers fills the room. Depending on which potions are being prepared, the air can become overly sweet or acrid. There are several tables, the largest of which is in the centre of the room. This is the table at which I sit and watch and learn how to prepare the healing potions from the herbs. Some potions require only certain parts of the plant, such as the root or the flower and sometimes the leaves. Others require the entire plant but prepared in different stages. Aïschah teaches me the difference between a salve, a tincture, and an infusion. She watches closely as I record the instructions in my books, taking great care that these are written in the accurate symbols of runes. She first introduced me to the language of runes some days after my first lesson in magic. I love the runes—they are a secret language of magic. She had explained that this was to ensure secrecy for the more advanced magic. Used improperly, certain recipes or incantations would cause more harm than good. It is vital to protect the secret knowledge.

Aïschah also continues with my ordinary studies: number skills, the study of the stars and their great movements that will allow the interpretation of future events. Within a very short time however, I know most of the herbs she uses, and I know exactly where to find them deep in the forest. Aïschah marvels at my thirst for this knowledge.

I lay down my pencil and pause waiting for the next instruction. Looking up I see my godmother smiling at me, satisfied with my work.

"You have done well Azizi. There is not much more for me to teach you with the herbs. This means that I can now begin to train you in other things."

She pauses for a moment with a look of mischief in her eyes.

"But first—have you forgotten what day it is?"

I frown thinking perhaps I have forgotten something important.

Aïschah carefully produces a small package wrapped in a leather pouch and hands it to me.

"Happy Naming Day, Aldrik."

Today is the day of my birth when I was given my first name. I am turning thirteen.

My heart leaps, and a smile spreads across my face. I had forgotten.

Carefully, I take the gift from her and unwrap it. My skin is covered in goosebumps. In front of me lies a beautiful silver knife with runes engraved on the blade. Its handle has been carefully carved from pear wood; it fits perfectly in my hand.

I look at my godmother in deep gratitude. I had seen her little knife, some time ago and so desperately wanted one of my own.

"Take good care of this Azizi; it is meant only for collecting and cutting your herbs and flowers. Do not spoil the blade by cutting anything else with it. The runes on the blade are to sanctify the flowers you will cut with it."

"Thank you, Godmother. This is so beautiful. It's... it's perfect!"

"You are thirteen now. This is a powerful and magical number. I want you to be especially alert to things that happen around you: they may give you a hint of important things that come into your life. You have worked hard today. Now, go and explore your forest."

With a sense of pride and importance, my pocketknife carefully wrapped in its leather pouch and in my pocket, I walk out of the cottage and head to my beloved hills. I take with me my small satchel with pieces of paper carefully folded into small pockets, where I can store any herbs, seeds, or flowers. Every now and again I reach into my pocket and hold the knife; it is such a wonderful gift. I try to decide which herb or flower I will collect with it first; it must be special.

The sharp scent of the pine trees and other flowering forest trees, mixed with the decaying leaves and moss, rises to my senses. The late afternoon sunlight filters through the thick canopy, sending rays of light that catch outcrops of rocks and moss; occasionally the light falls upon the damp bark of a tree making it glow.

I catch a flash of brown fur along one of the branches. It confirms what I have been looking for. There is a squirrel, and it has built its home in one of the highest trees. I reach in my other pocket where I have stored some food scraps. The forest seems to have become so accustomed to me that most of its inhabitants will pay me no heed. Others, a little hungrier and braver, will on occasion come to me for scraps of food.

I leave my bread crumbs on an outcrop and walk casually away. I look briefly over my shoulder, wondering if the squirrel has seen the crumbs where I have left them. I stop suddenly; from the corner of my eye I see a shadow slip through the trees and disappear. I turn but cannot see anything. The forest has gone very quiet. Perhaps the squirrel has come down and waits for me to leave. Something is not right. I look around; the forest is too quiet.

I shiver.

The early winter snows cover some of the forest, and random

white patches remain in the cooler parts of the undergrowth. The forest is silent and still, and everything seems muffled. The air is motionless; my breath comes out in small puffs of steam.

I turn around to survey the stark black trees against the failing sunlight. I sense that I am being watched. I have sensed this before. My godmother warned me about wolves and bears, but this is too low on the mountain slopes for either of these to be hunting.

I can only hear the soft crunch of my steps through the decaying leaves. The chirp of a bird breaks the silence. Over my right shoulder, I see a small bird. I am certain I have seen this one before, its peculiar brown and white colouring, and one wing that appears to droop a little. If it is the same, it usually comes to me for breadcrumbs. I stop in a small clearing and taking out a handful of crumbs from my pocket, I scatter some close at hand, keeping a portion in my hand. I want to see if it will come to me and eat from my hand.

The small bird flies down almost immediately, pecking at the crumbs on the ground, then eyes me once and flies onto my hand for richer and easier pickings. In one instant, the bird looks up and flies away and, in that moment, I sense a shadow behind me.

"The forest likes you, master."

I turn, startled, annoyed that the bird may not come down again. I stare. A boy about my age and slightly taller, dressed in sheep's skins stands there, grinning. His accent is thick and slightly raucous. His skin is darker than mine, and his hair is dishevelled as if he has been sleeping rough outdoors; a slight angular jaw frames a soft expression in his dark brown eyes, so dark that they appear almost black. His smile quickly fades at my angry stare.

"I'm sorry sir. I did not mean harm. I've been watching you for some time now."

In a flash I understand the furtive movements, always at the limit of my field of vision. The lack of tracks—this is a Hills boy who probably knows the ways of the forest as well as I, if not better.

"You've been watching me?"

I cannot hide the anger in my voice as he backs away a step. In truth I am more disappointed at having been caught like this, unawares.

"I'm sorry master. I wanted to make sure you weren't one of the town brats: they only destroy things. But you—the forest likes you."

As if to prove the point, the small bird at that moment flies down and begins pecking at the crumbs, which I had dropped in my surprise.

"You're Mistress Aïschah's apprentice. My folks said to make sure no harm comes to you. My ma says the mistress is teaching you the ways of magic."

The boy speaks this with some awe in his voice. I understand. Aïschah has often spoken of the Hills people. She regularly takes medicines to them and tends to their needs. These are poor people but in exchange, they give her milk, cheeses, and animal skins. She must have told them that I wandered the forest and to keep an eye on me and make sure I would be safe.

As much as I appreciate her concerns, I am a little hurt that she thinks I might not look after myself. Something else dawns on me; I wonder whether this is the 'friendly wolf' that chased

Knut and his friends away. I re-appraise this youth. He has the physical appearance of someone who spends most of the time outdoors. His shoulders are broad, and the loose shirt made of some rough material reveals a strong chest. There is a strength in his body that belies the gentleness of his face.

The boy still stands there, unsure. I want to apologise for my outburst and do not know how.

"What is your name?"

"Halim, Master."

I think for a moment. "There is no need to call me Master. Halim? In the ancient tongue that means 'gentle.' Did you know that?"

Halim smiles and shakes his head. I'm not sure whether he shakes his head because he doesn't know or whether he is too shy to acknowledge the meaning of his name.

I notice that a handmade wooden pipe is tucked through his leather belt. The belt itself is old and looped through a couple of metal rings.

"What do you do, Halim?"

He looks confused for a moment and realises the meaning of the question. "I tend the sheep, Master."

"Are you not very far from your sheep Halim?"

"Oh no, Master, the sheep are safe in the barns for the early winter nights."

There is a gentleness about him that does his name justice. I look at him and realise that I have been staring at his eyes. He meets my gaze without flinching. His dark eyes have the look of a friendly dog; I have the sense of falling into them as into a well. There is also a sadness about him that I cannot quite place. I find myself for the first time wanting company.

"Halim do you know where the red berries grow?"

Like the sun appearing from behind a cloud, his smile lights his face.

My heart skips a beat.

"Yes Master. I will show you."

"Please, Halim, do not call me Master. My name is Aldrik."

He smiles shyly and looks away.

I let him lead me, knowing full well that I know where the berries grow.

He steps carefully. I am amazed at how little sound his footsteps make and the way he moves. He seems to disguise his trail, making it look as if something small yet difficult to identify has moved through the forest. His shoulders are broader than mine, and I think about the strength that is required to carry a lamb that needs nurturing. Amazed, I realise that his footwear is also made of animal skin. His calves are bare, and I can see the muscles working, flexing with every step. I wonder how he can withstand the cold.

We arrive at a familiar clearing. I pretend that I have never seen it before. He holds a branch aside to let me through into the clearing.

"Thank you, Halim."

It's the same sunny smile again. I brush past him; the comforting warm smell of straw hangs about him.

"The berries grow just over there."

I recognise the small but robust bush; it is laden with berries fully ripened in the early winter; its name is Rosaceae, and it produces fruit twice a year. The leaves and the stem, when boiled in water, make a bitter but powerful medicine that will ease inflammation, as well as ease a sore throat.

Halim is at the bush, a mouthful of berries and another in his hand, the dark juices trickling from one corner of his mouth. His face twists at the bitter sweetness of the fruit. He laughs wiping his chin with the back of his hand, and offers me a handful of berries. I cannot help myself and laugh with him. I am at ease knowing that he has not judged me the way the village children do. I recognise what I miss from the company of boys my own age.

I taste some of the berries; they are ripe and not as bitter as others, still I make a funny face at the sourness and we both laugh.

Sitting next to the bush, I take out a large piece of paper from my satchel. I reach for the leather pouch in my pocket and unwrap the knife. Halim has grown serious and looks at my every move warily. Carefully, I cut several stems and leaves with my knife and place them on the sheet of paper. Cautiously, I fold the paper back over the stems. Replacing the package in my satchel, I am conscious of the awe Halim holds me in; he is openly staring at my knife.

"Master...Master Aldrik, is that a magic knife?"

I give up correcting his address. I show him the knife and he visibly recoils.

"No, Halim. It is not magic. The blade has runes inscribed on it. They are to bless the plant when I cut it to protect its healing powers."

I point out the runes to him. I can tell that even if I were to offer him a chance to hold the knife, he would not. He nods his head in understanding.

"It is a beautiful knife, Master."

"It is a gift from my godmother on my naming day, which is today."

He looks up with a half smile, looking somewhat ill at ease. I understand the conflict—he has no gift for me. Tradition requires him to acknowledge my naming with a gift no matter how small. He wasn't to know. I feel a little embarrassed that I have placed him in this position of obligation. I have an idea. Looking at his wooden flute, I ask him, "Halim, for my naming day, would you play me a tune on your pipe?"

He looks surprised at the request, then appreciation dawns on him. A song is a gift and traditionally, musicians are highly regarded. He now sees it as an honourable and valuable gift. He takes out his pipe from his belt and thoughtfully caresses it. The instrument is handmade and well looked after, oiled and polished.

He tilts his head for a moment and raising the pipe to his lips, places his fingers above some of the holes, then he takes a breath and gently blows. A high tender sound resonates throughout the forest; it seems a long, plaintive call. Halim closes his eyes, focussed on the music. The forest stands still, and I hold my breath. The note goes on and on, and then like a leaf in a capricious wind, it flutters and weaves. The tune first moves slowly and then as if in a chase, runs and turns, rises, and falls. I think of leaves blowing in the wind in the early autumn, birds chasing insects in mid air, ground creatures scampering and foraging for food. Then all goes quiet. It is music celebrating the forest. Tears have welled up in my eyes.

It is a most wondrous tune and too soon comes to an end in a soft whisper. Halim slowly and reverently lowers his pipe and looks at me. He sees my emotional response and breaks into a broad smile, revealing a perfect set of white teeth.

All is quiet. I cannot bring myself to break the echoes that still seem to resonate throughout the clearing. With reverence for the gift, I take a breath, and quietly I say to him, "Halim, thank you. That is the most wonderful song I have ever heard. Thank you for your gift. I will treasure it always."

He looks proud. With a rush of fervour, I also realise that custom requires me to share my naming feast.

"Halim, my godmother has baked fresh barley cakes for my naming feast. I would be honoured if you would come with me and share them with us."

Now he looks embarrassed.

"Oh Master, no, I could not. That would be... it would not be right to... the mistress will not know and..."

I cut him short. "Do not be concerned Halim. I will let my godmother know that you are with me. Besides, you have given me such a wonderful gift, it is only right that you share the feast with us."

He pauses for a moment, and his brow furrows into a worry line. "But how will you tell Mistress Aïschah?"

"That's easy. I will tell her now."

Now he really looks confused.

"Just be very still while I concentrate."

This is probably one of the easiest things my godmother has taught me—the art of mental speech. I relax to send a message.

I ease down next to the bush and allow myself to slip as if in a warm bath. Closing my eyes, I focus on the image of my godmother in her cottage. Mentally I think 'Godmother'. Almost instantly, I hear her voice in my head.

"Yes, Azizi. Are you well?"

"I wish to bring a guest tonight; his name is Halim."

There is a pause. The voice in my head responds, and her tone has warmth to it. "Bring him Azizi."

I open my eyes to see Halim staring in awe. "There, it is done. She is expecting us both. Come, I am hungry for barley cakes."

I start to laugh. I feel so wonderful. I have a friend.

Halim smiles shyly and then resolutely, "But Master... how did you?"

"I just spoke with her with my thoughts, and she replied with hers. That is all."

I can see that although I think it's simple, Halim thinks it would be easier to fight a bear with a stick.

"Come, Halim, I know the quickest way to my godmother's cottage."

We break into a run, laughing out loud and making whooping noises that frankly have probably scared all the forest creatures in the area.

~

WE ARRIVE AT MY godmother's cottage, out of breath and sweating. There are cuts across my hands and face from running through brambles and bushes, and dark streaks of green stain my shirt. I turn laughing to look at my friend Halim. He steps out of the bush behind me, not a mark on him. I frown puzzled as to how he could have managed that and just burst out laughing. It feels good to have a friend. A light film of perspiration is all that shows for his efforts in keeping up with me.

I motion him forward.

"Come, Halim, come and meet my godmother."

Suddenly he looks shy and reluctantly comes forward.

"Don't worry, she won't change you into a fire beast." I regret saying that the moment I see the fear and awe in his face. "Halim—seriously, she really is very nice. You have known her bringing medicines to your people for a long time. Come, let's have barley cakes for my naming day."

He stands there a moment, hesitating. I take his hand and gently lead him to the back door that opens into the kitchen. A wonderful smell of freshly baked barley and honey cakes greets us, mixed with the sweet and pungent fragrance of hot spiced drinks. Aïschah is nowhere to be seen. We walk in quietly; Halim timidly follows in my footsteps. We look at the rows of cakes still steaming on the kitchen table, and I wonder if she would notice if two went missing, when I hear a rustle behind me.

My godmother is standing at the kitchen door smiling warmly at us. She is dressed simply in long blue blouse and dark trousers and wears a long overcoat of pure white linen. I look at her in awe; she seems to radiate energy. Her eyes wander to Halim. I can feel he is frozen into a kind of subdued terror.

"Hello Halim, and welcome to our house. I am glad that you came to share Aldrik's naming feast."

Halim manages a whisper, "Hello Mistress."

I look at him; his head is bowed in a gesture of both shyness and deference. My heart goes out to him. I step close to him and placing a hand on his shoulder; I look at my godmother who gives a little nod. "Godmother, could we stay here in the kitchen and have the feast?"

She smiles, winking her understanding at putting Halim at ease. "Of course. That's an excellent idea."

"Come, Halim, sit next to me." I lead him gently to the kitchen table and sit next to him.

The cakes are delicious, the hot spiced drink sweet and warming. My godmother will not reveal to me the secret ingredient that she puts in it to make it so delicious, but I suspect I can guess.

"I know… it's cinnamon, I'm sure of it." And I gulp the last of my drink, wanting to bury my face in it to reach the last dregs.

She touches her nose knowingly, which surprisingly makes Halim laugh out loud. I realise he is laughing at the dark froth on the tip of my nose, and I laugh with him, trying in the process to place a stain of the dark spice on his face, which he avoids agilely.

The end of the feast comes too soon. It is late and the night is black as ink. I realise with a small sadness that Halim is far from home. An idea emerges in my head.

"Godmother, it is very late and dark. Could Halim stay with us tonight?"

She looks at me enquiringly.

"He can stay with me in my room."

Her eyes are warm, nevertheless she holds my gaze for a moment. "Yes. Yes, of course he can. Halim, you are most welcome to stay. It would be too dangerous for you to travel in the woods at this time of night on your own."

Halim looks at me then at Aïschah. He swallows hard and nods his head.

I give a whoop of joy. "Thank you, Godmother! Come Halim, I will show you my room and you can stay with me."

I lead Halim to my room and show him in. "Wait there a moment, Halim, I have to ask my godmother something."

Aïschah is still in the kitchen putting things away. I go to her and wrap my arms around her. "Thank you, Godmother, this has been the best naming day ever."

She hugs me warmly and tilting my chin towards her she adds, "I am glad you brought Halim with you. I haven't seen you this happy in a long time."

"Godmother, I will help you clean up."

"Thank you Aldrik, but you have a guest. Look after him and have a good night."

I turn to leave.

"Aldrik, remember Halim is a shepherd; he will have to leave very early in the morning to tend to his sheep."

"I understand. Good night, Godmother."

"Good night, Aldrik."

I return to my room to find Halim sitting on the edge of the bed. As soon as I enter, he stands, looking unsure.

"Godmother says good night and reminds me that you might have to leave early in the morning to tend to your sheep."

Halim nods, "Yes, Master, though if I am not there, my cousin will take them to the low pasture and wait for me."

I poke my finger in his chest in jest, "Please Halim, don't call me Master! It makes me feel like I'm an old man!"

At this he laughs, again that incredible laugh so full of joy and light.

"Do you want to sleep?"

"Yes, I am tired."

He goes to lie on the rug next to the bed. I pull him up. "Halim, look at this bed, it's huge. You could fit a whole village in here."

He laughs again. "Surely not Mast..," He gives a little cough. "Aldrik."

It sounds so strange and yet so wonderful when he says my name.

"Share my bed, Halim. I promise not to snore like an old man."

Again, that easy laugh. With absolute unconscious abandon, he undresses and lets his clothes drop to the floor. For a brief moment, I stare at his perfect naked form. My heart is pounding so hard in my chest that it's hurting my ears. I look away and shyly I take my day clothes off. He is already lying under the covers, and I slip in next to him. I lie there a while, my mind racing in a thousand directions, like a leaf caught on wild summer wind.

"Good night, Halim, and thank you."

Sleepily he answers, "Good night, Master Aldrik."

I feel the warmth of his body next to mine; a gentle fragrance of hay lingers about him.

He turns in his sleep and unwittingly, his leg lies on top of mine. I dare not move. The day catches up with me and I drift into a restless sleep.

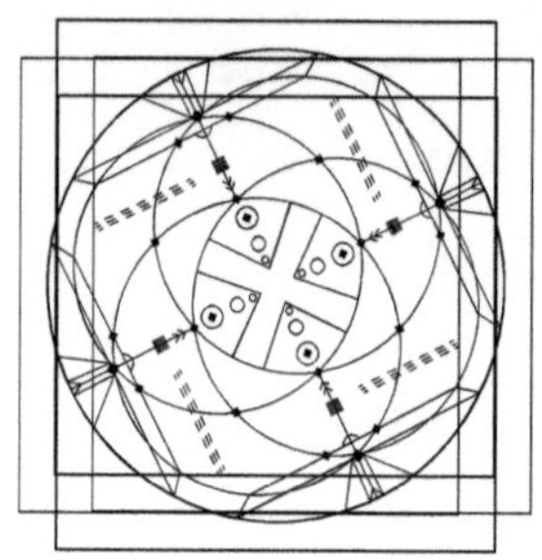

C H A P T E R   F I V E

I open my eyes, and cool grey early morning light filters through the half-drawn curtain. I lay in bed treasuring those moments of warmth under the covers. Looking up through the window, I see a large heavy cloud drift by slowly; woolly thoughts crowd in my mind, not making sense. Lazily, I wonder how late it is. I turn my body away from the window, intent on sleeping in. With a slight skip of my heart, I realise that Halim is not there. The sheets where his body had been the night before are cold to the touch. With a little sadness, I understand that he must have gone early to tend to his sheep. I bury my face in the pillow, inhaling the faintest fragrance of straw. He must have moved quietly not to wake me up.

Reluctantly, I decide to get up. Holding on to the covers, I stretch my legs out, feeling for my slippers and then make the decision to throw the covers back. The cold air wraps itself around me sending shivers along my arms and back. I quickly put on my day clothes and make my way to the kitchen. I see to the fire, stoking it and feeding two more logs, which slowly catch on.

I look around for evidence of yesterday's feast. My godmother has cleaned everything and put all the plates back. I stand daydreaming at the window that looks out over the valley. The light is cheerless, and a faint mist hangs in the air. Down in the village, small plumes of smoke struggle to flow upwards, bending instead under the weight of the cold air; a shiver runs up my spine. I look at the ground outside my godmother's cottage for any sign of footprints, hoping to see whether Halim took to the forest path or the lower slopes of the mountain. The ground is hard with early frost but there are no signs outside.

His laughter echoes in my mind; I see us running through the forest again, his smile making me feel warm.

"Azizi?" My godmother's voice startles me. She stands at the kitchen door, already dressed and holding a basket full of herbs and plants. She must have gone out early to collect those. Her cheeks are flushed with the bite of the cold winter morning. "Are you well Azizi? What were you thinking about?"

Heat rises into my cheeks. Aware that I am blushing and not knowing why, I quickly answer, "It is so quiet this morning. How early did you go to collect those?"

She looks at me briefly and places the basket on the kitchen table. "Before sunrise."

"Why did you not wake me? I would have come." I'm not sure that is entirely true. I don't like cold mornings.

"You were asleep, Dear One. I did not want to wake you."

"But Halim—" I chew my sentence off, aware of the real reason

I wanted to get up early.

My godmother smiles warmly at me. "He was already up and leaving. I walked with him to the forest edge and from there he went down to the lower pastures."

The fire crackles as a log settles in the wood oven.

"He is a gentle soul, Azizi. You're very fond of him."

It isn't a question. I hesitate before answering, "He's a good friend. I wanted so much to spend more time with him. But I don't know if he... if he..." The words sit in my heart and will not make it out of my mouth.

My godmother places her hand on my shoulder and gently looks at me. "Azizi, love is a gift. It is freely given. Do not put a price on it."

"I just want a friend." A small hurt has settled on my chest. "He sees me as your apprentice and calls me 'Master.'" Hesitantly, I add, "Will it always be like that Godmother? Those who don't understand make fun of me, and those who do, look upon me with awe and fear?"

"Do you love him as a friend?"

"Yes, I do."

"Then, that is your gift, priceless and without condition, his to accept or reject. You truly cannot make him do either. As for how he looks upon you, I am certain that he does not fear you, otherwise he would not trust you. As to the awe he holds for you, these folks are gentle and their respect for magic is profound."

A strange emptiness has crept within me. I realise that I want to see him again.

"Azizi, take your time with your heart. It is worth cultivating much like a precious flower. You will see Halim again and your friendship will grow if you nourish it. Much like some plants, though do not crowd it or overfeed it. Let it find its roots into a fertile soil that is your friendship."

I nod, not fully understanding what my godmother is telling me. At least I am reassured that I will see him again.

"Come, let us have breakfast and then we will resume your lessons." Then she adds with a slight mischievous smile, "Today I am teaching you how to unlock closed things."

⌒

THE FIRE IN THE herbarium has taken the chill out of the room. The sky outside still looks grey and heavy with early rains. Oil lamps set around the room give it a sense of warmth and comfort. I look at the table where I write my notes. It is clean and bare. In the centre of it is a small brown box made of oak. It is decorated with delicate white flowers made of some fine metal embedded into the wood. I have seen this box before on the shelves and wondered at it, as it appeared not to have a lid or other opening. It seemed a solid block of wood, yet when moved a small object inside makes a slight rattling sound.

"You will need to open this."

"Is there a key?"

"The key is inside."

I look at her puzzled, turning the box over and over, the object inside making a faint rattling sound.

"How can that be? There is no keyhole."

She smiles at me. "Not all keyholes are visible. And not all keys are the same."

This is a test. Another one of those seemingly impossible tasks that my godmother sets. Again, I turn the box over and over, looking for a clue. There must be something about it that will allow me to open it.

"See the box as no one else sees it. Remember your first lesson in magic, how you were able to place a jar back on the shelf without touching it physically. Use your mind."

I stare at the box not knowing how to perceive it. Then I realise the box may not open from the outside. But surely there would be a mechanism on the inside that would trigger it to open.

"Remember this is a dream. You have made the box."

I stare at it, not comprehending. "How can that be Godmother? The box was here before me."

"Are you sure of this?" She smiles mischievously, then adds, "How old is your mind, Azizi?"

"Godmother, I don't understand."

"Think of the dreams you dream at night. Which came first? The dream or your mind that dreams it?"

"My mind of course."

"Then, if this world and everything in it is a projection of your mind, then the box must have been created by your mind."

"But I didn't make the box. Someone else did."

"Hmm. Think of it this way, Azizi. You created the concept of the box. Sure, someone physically made it. But your mind created it, in other words you 'dreamed it' before it came into physical form. Since your mind is a part of the whole of creation, then you conceived it, and you are now responsible for it."

I think at this point my mind begins to spin, and yet there is something in what she says that resonates with me deep inside.

"Are you saying that this box existed long before it was made?"

"While your mind is unique, it is a part of a whole. Think of the Ocean of Elwah. Imagine that the rain is falling upon this ocean. Many raindrops mingle with the water that is already there. One raindrop is no less important than the others, for without that one drop, the ocean could not be said to be complete."

She pauses and looks to see if I am following her thoughts. "So yes. The mind of which you are a part conceived the box long before someone brought it into being. It was his task alone to bring it into form."

"So now, what I have to do is to look with my mind and see it as it was first conceived?"

Aïschah smiles at me and nodds.

I relax the way my godmother taught me when I first replaced the jar on the shelf. Closing my physical eyes, I hold the box and look upon it with my mind. I can see it there behind my closed eyelids. It shimmers as if it is made of light. Slowly, I will it to move around to look at it from all sides. Then, gently, I imagine that I can look inside the box. The sides of the box flicker and dissolve as my mind enters the confines of the box. In it I see an object, oddly shaped, but I cannot focus upon it. It is round at one end and stretches into a thin handle.

"I cannot see how this object is the key." I sense my godmother smile.

"The object you perceive is not the key; it is the prize."

Then I see it. On the inside, the box seems to be made of long rectangular pieces of wood that lie on top of each other like a wall. Each piece fits tightly against the others except for one small opening. My heart quickens, and what happens next is nothing short of extraordinary. The focus of my mind upon the interior of the box somehow activates it. One piece of wood slides into the small gap, which in turn creates a gap at the other end, allowing another to fall into it. This process continues more and more quickly until there is an audible click and the box splits in half. I open my eyes and the two halves of the box lie in my hands, the object inside now clearly visible. It is made of some metal and looks like the stamps that the leatherworker and silversmith use to make impressions upon their work. The large bulb at the end is carved. I draw a quick breath suddenly realising that the carving is a replica of the symbol of the first initiation: a double axe with a line in between and a circle above and below it.

I look up at my godmother who stands smiling broadly at me.

"Well done, Azizi. You have shown yourself worthy of the prize. The stamp you hold will be used to mark your right arm with the symbol of your first initiation."

A sense of pride wells up inside me.

"Godmother, why is this stamp kept in such a box?"

She takes a breath that I interpret as a sign of patience for my slow wits.

"This is a sacred symbol, only used to mark someone who has shown their readiness to be initiated into the first order of Apphat the Healer. It must be kept, therefore, away from anyone who cannot open the box."

There is a long silence while I think about the implication for me.

"But how does this test of mind demonstrate readiness for healing?"

Again, she smiles patiently. "That is a good question. You know

now how to open a box from the inside. How would you open someone's mind and read it to heal the body that holds it? The mind being one thing, how would you open someone's heart—and delve into its closely guarded secrets?"

My mind reels. I must look awed. "How... How would that be possible?"

"Just think, Azizi. What part of your being is the most vulnerable? Where do you experience your deepest feelings?

I did not have to think long. "My heart."

"Yes. Now imagine that someone's heart has been poisoned."

"How could that happen?"

"Through words, deeds, or even a physical poison."

"How could words or deeds poison someone's heart?"

"Imagine that someone wishes you ill, and that person knows of your friendship with Halim. They tell you that he does not actually care for you. How would you feel?"

"I would not believe them."

"Good. But let us say that circumstances arose that made you doubt. Where would you feel that doubt?"

"I'm... I'm not sure."

Halim, not caring for me? My stomach tightens at this thought as if someone has punched me in the stomach.

"Be conscious of your body. How does your skin feel and how is your heartbeat?"

I become aware of my pounding heart and my skin feels clammy. I swallow before answering, "My heart is beating faster."

"So, you see, by this mere suggestion, your body and your mind are now in conflict. Your heart, which knows this person, is rebelling against your mind; that voice that always argues with you, wants control, and always desires supremacy over you."

She pauses, looking at me carefully. "Your heart, on the other hand, knows only one truth and that is love. So now there is conflict, and your mind begins by creating a series of lies to convince your heart that your feelings are misplaced. Your heart now begins to yield piece by piece to this continuous onslaught until you perceive a lie disguised as truth. A poison has now entered your heart."

There is a long silence. Carefully she takes the box and the stamp from me. She places the stamp into one half of the box and holding the two halves together they meld almost instantly.

"Poison can take many forms. It is not always a physical one. The mind can be powerful; it can manipulate your perception of reality. There lies its strength and also its weakness, because it is aware that your perception is merely a projection of a dream.

"The heart, however, knows only one truth—Love. Love will ultimately conquer, but for a time, at least if not protected, it can be made a prisoner of the mind."

I sit motionless, aware of my feelings. I speak to my heart and tell it that I will always listen to it. A small voice, which I immediately recognise, tells me that this will not always be possible. In my head I tell it to be quiet, that it is a lie.

"So Azizi, this brings me back to my question. How would you enter someone's heart and heal it of the poison that has entered there?"

"I don't know, Godmother."

She smiles at me. "I hope you will not have need of this technique. However, there is a way, which is usually reserved for lovers; for who else would know your heart better than yourself than someone who loves you unconditionally?"

My cheeks burn. I look away. I am not sure what Aïschah is implying.

"Rest easy, Azizi. I will not require you to perform this task now. Suffice for me to tell you the principle of it."

I go to the writing desk and pick up my pencil and paper. Aïschah interrupts me and motions me to sit again. "This you should not write down but commit it to memory."

She instructs me in this healing technique, which requires for the healer to lie next to the one to be healed, holding his right hand with my right hand. Before proceeding, I would need to ensure that my mind is clear to guide my will into my own heart, focussing all my feelings of love. And then directing it to the other's heart, avoiding at all costs any resistance from the other's mind. Once there, identify the poison and direct my source of healing power to it. She explains that in such a heart and mind meld, the danger lies in one succumbing to the poison itself and beginning to doubt one's healing. The other danger is the fact that the person's heart will be laid bare, all secrets revealed. This could overwhelm an individual if he is not ready for the impact of pure love.

Aïschah then looks at me. Her eyes seem to soften, but with a serious note and strength of will in her voice, she adds, "Before you could ever attempt such a healing Azizi, you would need to come to know your own heart, for not until then will you receive the power to fulfil your destiny."

She shakes her head slightly as if clearing her mind. "I am not sure what was just said Azizi, and I do not need to know. But heed well the words you have just heard."

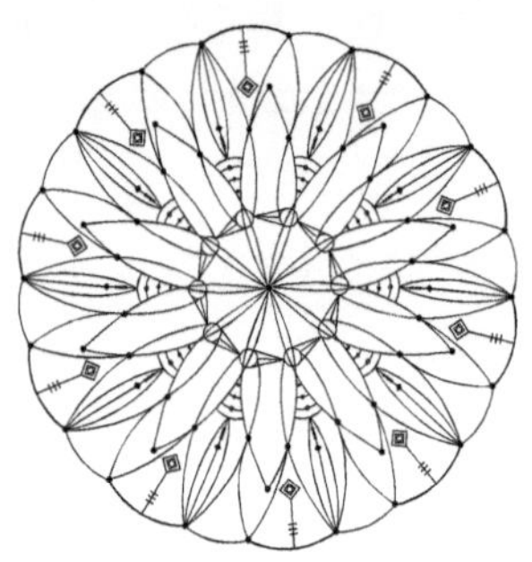

C H A P T E R   S I X

A balmy breeze blows through the open window, bringing with it the smell of warm grass and the fragrance of late blooming flowers; the air is filled with nostalgia. The snows have melted except for the top of the mountains, which remain covered in large patches of white, broken with green and grey. The seasons have come and gone; time seems to have slipped by. I have celebrated several naming days. It is the fourth year as my godmother's apprentice. My next naming day, I will be sixteen.

It is midway through the season of Elwah, and I wonder whether I will be able to find the row of ferns that leads to the star flowers. The Lady of the Forest, as I call her, my mother, or at least her spirit, has not appeared all year. My godmother tells me that I am making excellent progress and she is willing to initiate me into the first order of Apphat, but I must first pass a test of healing.

"Aldrik." A soft voice interrupts my reverie.

My godmother is looking at me, not so sternly but all the same slightly annoyed that I have allowed myself to wander off.

"I am sorry, Godmother."

"It's all right. It is the season of joy after all." She sighs and looks out of the window. "It will serve no purpose your being here, and your mind somewhere else. Go and find your star flowers, Aldrik."

A little embarrassed at being so transparent, I smile guiltily. "Yes, Godmother."

I am suddenly excited, and before I can thank her, she adds, "You may as well make your outing useful for me, though. I would like you to take some medicines to the Hills people. One of the women has come down with a fever."

She picks up a package from the table and hands it to me; she gives me instructions on how to prepare the herbs. I am hardly listening, I know what to do, and my mind is already wandering the forest, thinking of the path I should take.

"...twice a day. Do you understand Aldrik?"

"Yes, Godmother." And with that, I practically run out of the room.

I reach the forest and take great gulps of air. The air, laden with the scents of spring, is intoxicating. I run, laughing out loud, the sound of my voice echoing through the woods. Finally, out of breath, I slow down and listen to the noises around me. It's not long before I realise that I have no idea where I am or where I'm going. The paths look unfamiliar, and I walk aimlessly bathing in the pure joy of the forest, a thrill in my chest, and then it hits me. The forest thins out and opens onto a low valley. My purpose was to find Halim, and here, like soft moving clouds, white sheep roam on slopes of new green grass. The scene is so calm, the air so pure, and the sunlight so warm on the valley, that I pause there a moment, drinking in the peace. Halim is sitting on a rocky outcrop on the other side. A faint tune echoes through the hillside; he is playing his wooden flute.

I step out of the trees and stand in the light. I don't call out for fear of scaring and scattering the sheep. Instead, thinking that he has seen me I wave my arm at him. He looks up, I think he smiles, but then a moment later he places his flute on the rock beside him, stands, and starts towards me at a run. He reaches for something in his pocket. I stand there puzzled and delighted that he has seen me. Within a few moments he is near enough that I can see the features on his face. He looks tense. I see now that he is holding a slingshot, fully drawn with a small pebble at its centre. He lets go and I hear something whistle past me. I stand there in shock wondering what could possibly possess him to try to hurt me. I hear a small yelp behind me and turn, suddenly aware of a tingling on the back of my neck. Just paces behind me a young grey wolf bolts back into the cover of the trees and nearby bushes. Halim is by my side looking serious.

"Master, did you not hear it following you?" Halim looks at me incredulously.

I am abashed. "I'm sorry; my mind was somewhere else."

He shakes his head in disbelief, then smiles. "It was a young pup. The bigger wolf would not dare come this close into the open field." He looks thoughtful and adds, "Though the mother cannot be far off. Come, I must make sure my sheep are safe."

I follow him, feeling foolish.

Halim calls his sheep with a mixture of whistles and gurgling noises and astonishingly, they come to him. The flock gathers around him, and he leads them far from the line of trees.

He sits looking out over the flock. No words are spoken; my lack of judgement weighs heavily on my mind. I want some reassurance that he does not think too poorly of me.

"Halim?" He turns and looks at me. "Halim, I am sorry."

He looks perplexed. "Sorry, Master? I don't understand."

"For not keeping alert and letting a wolf get so close to me and your sheep."

"That was not your fault, Master. Wolves hunt: that is what they do." There is no judgement in his voice.

"Then, thank you."

"Thanks... for...?"

"For protecting me from the wolf."

His face lights up with a smile, "That, is what I do."

I sigh filled with relief, and smile back at him.

Suddenly, I remember the task my godmother has given me.

"Halim, I have to take some medicines to one of the women in your village. What is the quickest way to your village from here?"

He looks at the sky for a moment. It is still early morning; the sun is above the Asfaine Mountains.

"Follow the sun until it is above you. You should see the village in the next valley."

I stand, still feeling a little awkward.

"Master, if a wolf follows you—do not run. Stand very still." He picks up a large stick from the nearby trees handing it to me. "If it comes towards you wait and hit it hard, here or here." He motions to his chest and then his nose.

I take the stick, feeling unsure of myself. I knew there were wolves in the forest, but I had never seen one so close. I hesitate a moment and decide to go.

"Thank you, Halim." I turn and walk away in the direction of the rising sun. I look back once and wave at him, he waves back, and this fills me with courage.

I walk, keeping an eye on the sun above the canopy of trees. I estimate it will be another hour before I reach the next valley to the Hills people's village. I have never felt so uncertain of the forest as I do now. The forest seems unusually quiet, and I look behind me often, imagining grey shadows are stalking me.

It seems an eternity before I see the sun hovering above me, its heat warms in the cool air of the forest. I can smell woodsmoke before I see it. The forest thins out and I look over a small valley where the village is nestled. These are not grand houses but simple stone buildings with thatched roofs. Small wooden pens protect their vegetable gardens from marauding animals. Unsure and nervous, I realise that I do not know my way around the village, nor do I know the woman who suffers from the fever.

As I approach the village, a few children's faces peer up at me. The womenfolk are probably inside preparing the midday meal. An old man is walking slowly towards me, his cane assisting his every step. As I near him, he pauses, looking at me.

"Good day to you, young Master Aldrik."

I am taken aback that he should know who I am.

"Good day to you Father." I address him as Father in acknowledgement of his status as an elder. He seems pleased with that.

There is a long pause and not knowing the correct protocol, I take a chance to ask,

"Father, I bring medicine from Aïschah for the woman who has the fever. Where can I find her?"

He nods once and pointing his walking stick in the direction I have come from, indicates the first house I walked past.

"That would be Halim's mother."

I realise now that I did not listen to everything my godmother was telling me when she was giving me the instructions. I am also surprised that Halim did not say anything to me about his ill mother.

I make my way to the house, the old man in tow. I hesitate at the door. The old man bangs his stick on the wooden post beam and calls out, "Ulfa, Master Aldrik is here with the herbs for your fever."

A rough sound, interrupted by a cough that could have been 'come in' is all I hear. The old man motions me forward.

The room is dark; a single wax candle is lit. Stale smoke from the wood fire stove permeates the air. I will have to re-kindle the fire to make the tea. A woman rises from a cot bed looking at me. Even by this light I recognise the eyes—they are Halim's eyes only a little older.

Her face is pale; she looks drained of her strength. Her composure, though, is fierce; she would have been a woman of great beauty in her youth. There is an air of determination about her. If my memory of names serves me, Ulfa would mean 'she-wolf' in the ancient tongue. I can see that one would not easily stand between her and her offspring.

She looks at me silently and gives me a small smile. She coughs and I can hear that it sits on her chest. The herbs will alleviate her fever, but the chest cough must also be dealt with. My mind races through the herbs that would alleviate this, and I realise that it will take me several hours to collect them. I gesture to the cot bed.

"Please lie down, and I will prepare the tea infusion."

Reluctantly she goes and lies down; the cough shakes her several times. She watches my every move as I rekindle the fire and prepare the infusion. The room is simply furnished; there is a table and stools for meals. A set of shelves roughly hewn out of hard wood is set against a wall, with wooden cups, saucers, and plates for everyday use. There are some other personal items; a delicate porcelain cup painted with summer flowers appears to be in pride of place. There are also some small wooden carvings of animals, and these I assume to be Halim's creations. A little window at the far end of the room allows a little light in; it is simply covered with a piece of material for a curtain. The small stove where I am preparing the tea is the only source of heat for the room.

Finally, the infusion is ready, and I pour the steaming liquid into a wooden cup. She takes the cup graciously. I can see that she is not a woman used to being looked after. The old man is still here, sitting by the fire, and he watches her, occasionally shaking his head.

"How long have you had this cough?"

She looks at me and an awkward moment fills the space between us. I realise that I am asking questions Aïschah would be asking. Nevertheless, I stand my ground even as a fifteen-year-old, confident in the knowledge of healing my godmother has taught me.

Finally, she answers, "At the start of the lambing season."

That would mean only two lahé. Before I realise what is happening, my focus softens and my muscles relax. Looking at her with the sight, I can now see the dark patch that sits on her chest. It looks ugly, almost like a living thing with roots already spreading. If not treated, it will grow and possibly kill her.

"Mistress Ulfa, the herbs will bring down your fever somewhat, but they will not heal the cough that sits on your chest."

I call it a cough so as not to alarm her, but she pales visibly at that and slumps in her cot. I can see that she knows how ill she is. The silence becomes heavy, the occasional child's laughter the only audible sound.

The old man shuffles on his stool and clears his throat. "What is to be done then, young Master?"

"I need to ask Aïschah for her counsel."

I can see that a delay will only cause further stress and so I add, "I will attempt to speak with her now."

Ulfa looks up at me and makes an involuntary sign. I recognise the sign; it is one that acknowledges strong magic and seeks protection from harm. I smile inwardly, for all their superstition, at least the Hills people know about magic and recognise its power.

I sit cross-legged in front of the wood stove, seeking the flame as a point of focus, and make a sending to Aïscha. It isn't long before the familiar sound of her voice responds inside my head.

"What is it, Azizi? I cannot spend much time; I am making a complex potion."

"It is Ulfa, Halim's mother. She is not well. There is a darkness on her chest that makes her cough. The herbs will ease her fever, but I fear this is more serious."

There is a pause and I sense a mixture of thoughts, tension mixed with resolve.

"Your time has come, Azizi. Seek permission first, but I say, this is your time to apply the healing I have taught you."

A sudden fear grips my stomach. I am not sure I can do this without her guidance.

Very firmly she addresses me, "Put your fear aside, Azizi! Your fear is simply a doubt in the power that flows through you. Do not doubt! As I have so often explained, the power is not yours, it merely flows through you. Let it!"

I take a deep breath and releasing it slowly, I allow myself to relax. Aïscha breaks the link between us but not before I recognize her sending me love.

I open my eyes. The old man is looking at me, nodding his head. Ulfa openly stares at me, sitting as still as her condition will allow.

"Ulfa, I have spoken with my godmother. I seek your permission to heal this condition. Will you let me?"

She stares in disbelief, and then nodding her head she coughs a "Yes."

This is Halim's mother whom I have never met until now. Unsure of my own ability, my brave assertion that I can heal her condition sits uncomfortably in me. I remember my godmother's teachings: this is someone in need, so I put my awkwardness aside and take on the role of healer, giving instructions that inspire confidence. I take a deep breath and speak in the tone of power Aïscha has taught me.

"Ulfa, please lie down and relax."

Ulfa, without a second thought, lies on the cot with her arms by her sides. The old man sits still and looks on intently.

I take a moment to focus on allowing the power to flow through me. It begins with a prickling sensation at the base of my spine, and travels quickly upwards, leaving me with an intense sense of warmth. I take another breath and the power flows, this time from the top of my head. I extend my right arm and move it in an upward motion from her feet to her head. This, Aïscha explained to me is the preamble of an Apphat healer; it serves to balance the patient's energies and enables the healing to flow more effectively. My hand feels warm and tingles: this is the sign that her energies are balanced. I soften my gaze and once more behold the dark shape upon her chest. I let the power flow down my arm intent on sending it directly to her chest. Something is not right. It is as if my head will burst. Slowly, the power gathers down my arm and surges forth: it looks as if the dark shape is suddenly ignited in white fire. Sweat pours down my face; I can taste salt on my lips. Darkness invades my senses; I fall as if down a deep, black hole.

I open my eyes. The old man is looking down at me, concern in his eyes. I realise I am lying on the floor.

"Mistress, he is awake."

Aïscha's face comes into focus. I am puzzled and wonder how long I have been lying there.

"Godmother!"

My head feels as though Knut and his friends have pounded me with wooden clubs. I fall back.

"Hush, Dear One. Take your time."

With a shock, I realise that the light is different. It is already dusk. I must have been unconscious for a while. Suddenly I realise where I am.

"Ulfa? How is she?"

My godmother smiles at me.

"She is well." Then enigmatically she adds, "The amount of healing power you delivered to her, I will not be surprised if you have added a score of years to her life."

I cannot remember anything of the healing.

"Azizi, whose permission did you seek for the healing?"

"Ulfa's, of course," I answer, confused.

"Azizi, though the patient is important, permission should be sought from your Source." She smiles again, shaking her head. "No wonder the power flowed with such intensity. You had not specified the intent of it." She sighs, then adds, "We will speak of this later, but for now rest easy. She is well."

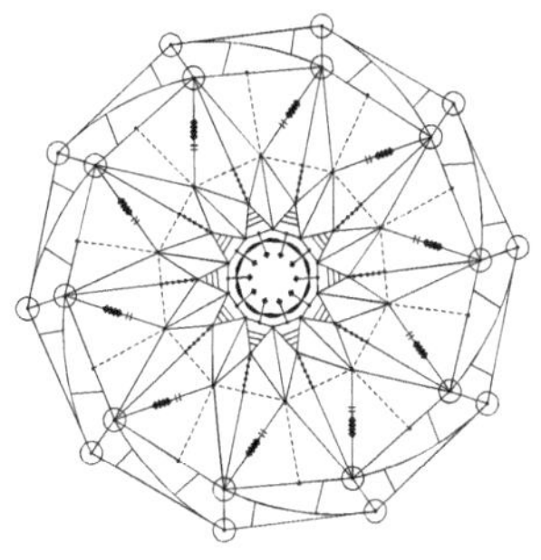

Rumours amongst the Hills people that Aïschah's apprentice is becoming a great healer have finally subsided. The leaves of the forest have changed colour. Snow has gathered at the top of the Asfaine Mountains, covering them like nightcaps and readying them for a long sleep. Grey clouds roll in from the north. Icy gusts of wind catch the remaining leaves from the trees taking them into a wild dance. Strands of cold mist meander through the valley and make their way through the streets of the village. The air smells of wet moss mixed with damp earth. The season of Malkizar is looming and my sixteenth naming day is approaching. I can see my body is changing, and this brings on more questions than answers. Conversations with my father in past years are making me apprehensive. I feel awkward. I love my father very much, but there are things I feel I cannot speak to him about.

"Are there any girls that you like?" he had asked me during one of our chats.

That question inexplicably made me angry. Why should he ask that? Girls are silly: they spend their time preening themselves and are always giggling at the most idiotic things.

"I don't like girls!" was my abrupt answer.

My father looked at me for a long time. Then nodding his head, he had said, "According to the great philosophers, and especially Apphat the Wise, in every man and woman lies their opposite. It is possible for a man or woman to love only their kind."

I was lost. I had no idea what he was talking about, but if the 'chat' came to an early end I would be happy.

"Aldrik, there are rituals for the passage into manhood. In our culture, it suffices for you to take your place within the community and make a contribution." He paused thoughtfully for a moment and then added, "There are probably types of initiations required as a healer."

I nodded, thinking of the days spent at school, and the boys' whispered conversations, who often talked about the rituals of initiation into manhood. Some more gory than others, and there was always a notion that whoever could conjure up the worst ritual was in the know. I decided to speak to my godmother and ask her what rituals were required.

Aïschah sat down, contemplating my question. "Azizi, there are many types of initiation into adulthood. For boys, some cultures will have them experiencing excruciating pain. This may involve burning marks into their body, being bitten by insects, or even bodily mutilation. I find these barbaric and unnecessary; they are designed to test resilience to physical pain. I don't understand how that proves that you are a man, as it implies that men must suffer, and they must suffer silently."

I breathe a sigh of relief; at least my godmother is on my side.

"You have to remember, pain is not in your body, it is of the mind. Think for a moment of the following pain: the breaking of a heart when one says goodbye to a lover, the doubt that someone does not care for you, or the pain in your heart when you see an animal suffer uselessly; the longing one feels to be in the arms of a loved one. Those are painful, yet the body does not bleed." She pauses for a moment. "I can teach you a mindset that will allow you to never feel physical pain. So, what is the point of initiation by inflicting pain? Even the tattoos you will bear as a healer of Apphat may be momentarily painful, but this will pass quickly. The pain itself is not the purpose of the initiation: the tattoo marks you as one who has studied and been found worthy." Her eyes focus on something distant before she goes on, "No, for my part, initiation into adulthood is the proof that your mind is no longer concerned with childish toys and games and yet has not lost its childlike quality of awe, love, and imagination."

She looks at me a while with her piercing blue eyes. "Do you feel you are ready to be a man, Azizi?"

Looking at her, her eyes full of wisdom and kindness, she who expresses joy at the first fall of snow and knows the right combination of herbs to heal the sick; under that gaze I still feel like a boy.

"I'm not sure, Godmother. I don't think I will ever be completely a man."

She smiles at me. "That is a wise thing to say, Azizi. I think you are truly on your way to being a great man."

My sixteenth naming day is celebrated quietly with my

godmother; my father is away negotiating trading terms with the Northern Regions, and Halim is tending to his sheep a long way off.

I am eating my third cake. Aïscha smiles at me and mischievously, silently points out that there are three more. "Azizi, you have worked well. You are ready for your initiation into the First Order of Apphat the Healer."

A piece of honey barley cake suddenly feels very large in my mouth. I am not sure I should have started this third one. My stomach, for some reason, is now rebelling at the thought of anything else.

"Chew your food carefully, Azizi." Aïschah almost laughs at my composure. "The instrument that you have released from the box will be used to mark your right arm with its symbol."

I remember the symbol of a double-headed axe with one line cutting across it. Aïschah rolls up her sleeve to reveal the tatoo I will be marked with.

"Since I have trained you in your skills, the rules and tradition require that an Elder other than me will perform the ceremony of initiation. This is to ensure that you are ready according to the laws and not according to my personal desire for you to be initiated."

I stop chewing midway through my honey and barley cake. I no longer want to swallow but make an effort to do so and focus on what my godmother is saying. A wave of cold seems to fill me; my body feels heavy. This day seems to have arrived so quickly and so quietly.

Aïschah pauses a moment. "Some days ago, I contacted the Council of Elders, and one has been selected to carry out this task. He will arrive in the morning. Tonight, you will need to go to bed early. In the morning, you should abstain from having breakfast. The ceremony is conducted on an empty stomach to ensure that you focus your energies on the initiation process."

I am conscious of the smell of the wood fire mixed with the fragrance of the honey barley cakes. A stillness fills the air. I can hear the whisper of a slight breeze blowing through the pine trees behind the cottage. A bird occasionally calls out. I look at my hands, pale objects against the wood of the table. I wonder if these are the hands of a healer. I tentatively stretch my fingers out and turn my hands face up.

My godmother is looking at me with some concern.

"Azizi, you have nothing to fear. You are ready for this step; it is one that should be celebrated in your heart."

So many thoughts crowd my mind. A swell of pride fills my heart knowing that I have reached this step. A tinge of fear bubbles up like boiling porridge in the pit of my stomach. I want to make her proud, but a part of my mind is trying to convince me that I could delay this process and avoid any pain. I look up at my godmother and smile with all the courage I can muster. "I will be ready. Thank you, good mother."

Aïschah smiles broadly. "You have not called me that, since you were six years old." She continues, "Today you should rest and do what pleases you the most."

~

I OPEN MY EYES and dreamily turn to look out of the window. The sky is clear of the storm clouds from the day before. A sense of anticipation fills me and for a moment I cannot recall why. Sitting bolt upright, I remember; this is the day of my initiation. I leap out of bed, not caring about the cold. My heart is racing, my stomach complains, and I remember that I must not eat. Hurriedly, I run my way to the bathroom to wash myself and dress.

I make my way to the herbarium. A sweet yet acrid smell fills the air. Aïschah is there, and so is a wizened, elderly man who must have arrived very early. Dressed in ceremonial robes I have only seen in ancient texts, he moves slowly and with precision, as if his every gesture has a singular purpose. Despite the age showing in the lines of his face, his full head of hair is still dark with only a single white strand.

I pause to take a deep breath and then enter the room cautiously. Both have been busy over a smoking concoction that emits the acrid smell. I recognise some of the herbs used. My godmother turns first.

"Good morning, Azizi. Let me present you to Mahjir Suffrah, one of the Elders who sits on the Great Council of Master Magicians. He is to initiate you today."

I bow my head in deference to the Master and whisper, "Mahjir."

Dark brown eyes, almost so dark that they appear almost black, peer at me with an expression of great interest. I had heard of the dark-skinned Mages of the Southern Lands. His skin black as ebony, is a sharp contrast to his light-coloured ceremonial robes. I am suddenly gripped with apprehension. When he speaks, his voice is just above a murmur, yet resonant enough to send chills up my spine.

"Greetings, Azizi, and welcome." His eyes wander in the space above and around me. He turns to Aïschah. "I can see what prompts you to celebrate his powers, Silver One. His Hala is filled with golden strands of light."

I understand that using the second sight, he is examining my energy field. He turns back to look at me and pauses for moment, the gaze becoming more intent. "Perhaps however, this initiation will fulfil the flow of energy to his heart."

A flutter of panic rises from my stomach. Aïscha has explained the process but now that the moment has arrived, so many uncertainties surface in my mind. Will I be worthy; am I ready; will it hurt? And what of my heart, what does he mean?

"Come Azizi and stand before me. It is customary to ask questions of the initiate. Answer them truthfully and know that I will know if your answers are not sincere."

The seriousness of the moment suddenly weighs upon my shoulders. I stand before him trying not to tremble.

"Azizi, do you know the nature of your heart?"

I hesitate, the stern look of his eyes demanding no less that absolute genuineness.

"Truly, not entirely."

He smiles and nodds approvingly.

"Do you promise to use your skills for the highest good only, and not desire to gain earthly benefits from them?"

A swell of emotion begins to pound in my chest. It has begun.

"I do."

"Do you promise to use the healing power that flows through you from the Great Spirit for all those who are in need?"

"Yes."

"Do you, Azizi, accept the Mores of Apphat the Great, the Healer and the Wise, and know that all are created equal in the eyes of the Source of All?"

"Yes."

"Will you, Azizi, allow the Power of the Source to flow freely through your heart and accept whatever it is that is revealed to you?"

A mixture of excitement and dread fills me. Aïscha has told me that all questions were different for each initiate. Realising I cannot be hurt, I answer,

"Yes."

"Then, Azizi, young master in training, accept the mark that hails you as a healer of Apphat and revered magician, able to call upon your Source for the greater good of your fellow beings."

He motions me to the chair that faces the mountains.

"Sit in this chair and face the rising sun."

As I sit, I look up to see my godmother beaming with pride. She whispers, "To better prepare yourself for the mark, Azizi, focus your attention, all of it, on the source of your power."

I close my eyes and focus on my mind. Aïscha interrupts me with a gentle voice sounding slightly amused. "Azizi, the source of your power is not in your head, it is in your heart. Focus there."

I focus once more; the centre of my chest begins to feel warm and fills me with a sense of peace.

The stamp I have delivered out of its box has been heated to sterilise it. Mahjir Suffrah is now dipping it in the concoction of distilled herbs. The liquid is almost black. The process of heating and dipping is repeated several times. Each time it is accompanied by Mahjir Suffrah's incantation, spoken so softly that I cannot understand the sense of them but can feel the power flowing from the words.

The old man holds my arm steady and surprisingly with great strength for such an aged person.

The shock of the initial contact of the stamp with my skin takes me by surprise and I draw my breath in quickly; the pain is intense. I will my focus back to my heart and the pain subsides almost immediately.

My vision swirls, and scents around me arise from thin air. I recognise the warmth of cinnamon mixed with more ancient ceremonial fragrances. Smoke churns, rising and bewildering my senses. A calm voice pierces the haze, chanting old verses in an ageless tongue, words I recognise but cannot understand. The verses weave a tapestry of sensations. The unmistakable feeling of floating, the sudden thrill singing through my body, and the sound of a deep, resonant voice I know but cannot identify. I know I have fallen into a trance.

The voice of Mahjir Suffrah seems far away. "This is not uncommon Aïshah, do not be concerned."

The air around me cools and heats alternately. It is as if I am caught in a whirlwind.

"Although, he seems to have gone much deeper than the average apprentice."

My godmother's presence is palpable; I can sense her concern. All at once, the air is still, and a light surrounds me.

"Oh, this is unusual." Again, the voice of the Mahjir. "What do you see Azizi? Take your time."

For some strange reason, his question appears so simple that I want to laugh. My body takes a deep breath as a profound peace seems to wrap me in its arms. I hear myself answer, slowly and clearly, and yet my voice is not my voice. "What I see is meaningless; it is how I see." I sense tension in the room. Mahjir Suffrah takes a sudden quick breath. "It is with the Tears of Sorrow that I see. My name is Azizi. It means beloved in the ancient tongue. I will be known as the Immortal Beloved."

As if with a brief gust of wind, the light that surrounds me suddenly dissipates. Sadness fills my being like a heavy weight and removes me from the world. Daylight slowly filters through my consciousness. The acrid smell of the tatoo potion fills my nostrils, and it overwhelms me. The room around me begins to dance and sway. I open my eyes. Mahjir Suffrah is gaping at me, his mouth open, as if in mid sentence. My godmother's face appears in front of me. She holds me up by the shoulders as my body slumps forward and everything goes black.

I hear a whisper in my head. With great compassion, it says, "Your last test will be to heal yourself."

~

I DON'T REMEMBER RUNNING into Knut, and yet my head is pounding. Struggling, I open my eyes; the room is spinning, making me want to throw up. I close my eyes quickly and desperately focus on ignoring the rising nausea.

The door to my room opens with a creak.

"Azizi, are you awake?"

I can't help but groan in response. My godmother quietly makes her way to my side, standing in front of the window. I am grateful that at least when I open my eyes, I won't be blinded by the early afternoon light that is beaming in. I am disoriented; I vaguely remember speaking to Mahjir Suffrah not long ago, this morning.

Aïschah draws a chair next to my bed and sits down. I can smell a concoction of strong herbs. "Your head must be aching. That is normal. I have made you a tea that will restore you. Let me help you sit up and have a sip at least."

She gently places her hands behind my head and helps me sit up. The liquid in the cup is steaming. Carefully, I take a sip. The tea is slightly bitter with a not-too-unpleasant, deep, earthy aftertaste. Taking another sip, my head begins to clear. The room has stopped spinning. My stomach makes a loud growl, and my godmother laughs. "It sounds like a hungry bear. I had better make you some breakfast. Finish the tea first and then come downstairs."

The door to my room closes softly behind her. I turn my head towards the window and almost let out a cry. A sudden searing pain pulls my attention to my right hand. I stare at the dark mark above my wrist, still fresh where the skin has not quite recovered from the tattoo. Aïschah must have put a clear salve on it. The skin around the tattoo is still red and glistening from the salve. Strangely, the pain almost at once eases, and I stare at the mark that identifies me as an initiated healer of Apphat. My back straightens. I sit up in bed, and I can hear my heart beating. My mind is still as I contemplate the importance of that mark.

The kitchen is filled with the comforting fragrance of freshly baked bread. Aïschah lays out the table. A loaf of bread fresh out of the oven is cooling on a board. Two jars of different jam and a block of rich golden butter adorn the centre of the table. She has laid out white plates, rimmed with gold and adorned with one single blue star flower. I stare at them, knowing that these plates are only ever meant for important occasions.

Aïschah looks up and smiles broadly at me. Something in my heart softens, and I walk quickly around the table and throw my arms around her. I hold her for a moment while she gently strokes the back of my head.

"Congratulations Azizi. Come, eat, and celebrate this important occasion."

I look up at her and briefly look around, taking a place at the table. "Has Mahjir Suffrah left already?"

Aïschah smiles briefly. "He left immediately after your initiation. You slept the rest of that day and the next, only waking up this morning."

Puzzled and disoriented, I look around. A moment of panic seizes me to think that somehow, I have lost an entire day and two nights.

I pull the chair back and sit down and as I reach for the bread, I realise that it is with my right hand, exposing the tattoo. My hand hovers in mid air as I stare once more at the mark. Aïschah looks at it, smiles, and pulls up her sleeve to reveal her mark. A moment of silent understanding passes between us.

"It will heal quickly. Remember though to make sure you keep this hidden unless necessary. So, from now on, you should wear shirts with long sleeves, or you could just wear light gloves."

"Godmother, what happened after the mark was applied? I remember being overwhelmed by the smell of burning herbs. I could hear Mahjir Suffrah chanting an incantation, and I sensed what appeared as bright light surrounding me. Beyond that, I don't remember anything."

Aïschah briefly looks away. When she returns my gaze, a strange emotion fills her eyes.

"You fell into a trance, which is not unusual. Most initiates will experience that." Aïschah pauses and takes a deep breath. "But then you spoke in a strange tone. Although it was your voice, there was a deep resonance within it that commanded attention. I can vouch that Mahjir Suffrah was visibly shaken."

My heart is beating loudly in my chest. A palpable stillness fills my body.

"I am not sure that I can repeat the words you spoke, for they are not mine to speak." I must have looked disappointed, as she adds, "But I think you will come to know what words they were. They are a prediction of what you are to become." She raises a hand to stop me from asking. "It is something I have not clearly foreseen. It is a mystery that hints at great events, in the distant future. Mahjir Suffrah will consult the Council of Elders before I or anyone is allowed to reveal those words. The Elders will review the Sacred Books of Records, especially those that contain prophesies made long ago." She pauses and the air fills with a silence that is heavy with questions.

"Once you made those pronoucements, you lost consciousness. Mahjir Suffrah has instructed me to focus my teaching on making sure that you remain conscious while in a trance. To this end, I will give you exercises in maintaining a link with your physical body while allowing your mind to perceive what you are shown." She hands me my favourite jam, made with the small wild strawberries that grow in shade of the tallest trees of my beloved forest.

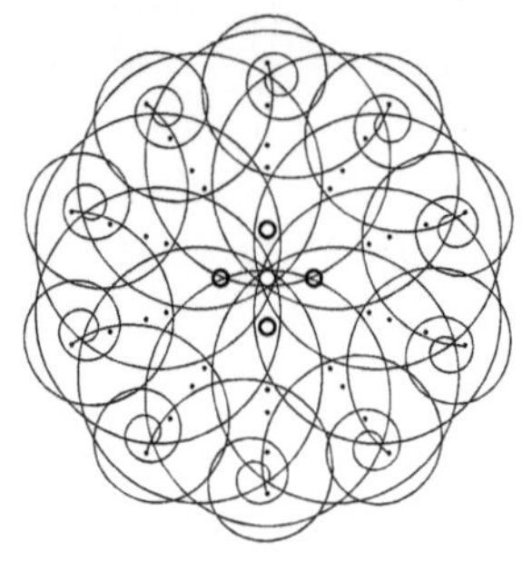

CHAPTER EIGHT

My first initiation into mastering healing is complete. According to Aïschah, I completed this stage well ahead of time. She is pleased with my progress. It is now the final year of my apprenticeship. I am now seventeen, and this is the final step to complete the First Order of Apphat, that of magicians; but I am still on the long road to mastering magic. A fire is lit in the herbarium for it is a cold winter's day outside; the snow has raged all night. The light that comes through the window is grey and cheerless, emphasising the warm orange heart of the fire.

"Come, Azizi," my god mother addresses me. "I will guide you to master your sight and train you not to lose consciousness during your trance."

She asks me to sit comfortably in front of her and offers me two stones, one clear as a winter sky when the winds have blown all clouds from its path; the other a dark stone that is as black as the deepest cavern. The stones feel cool in my hands.

"Hold the clear stone in your right hand and the other in your left. Now relax your body and still your mind. These stones will help ground you and guide your sight to the truth. One day you will do without them.

"Allow yourself to slip into a kind of dream state. Simply observe what you experience," she adds. "Let your mind see this room, then slowly move your attention outside this room." She pauses waiting to make sure that I am following her directions. "I want you to imagine that you are walking away from here. See the path you will take to your father's house. You will go through the town square... "

I am aware of the heat in the room. I think I must be sitting too close to the fire yet dare not move for fear of breaking my godmother's instructions. The room is getting hotter. I can feel perspiration beading on my forehead. My eyes begin to sting.

"... good boy, just relax. Now tell me what you see in the square..."

I hear my godmother's voice fading and echoing. I can feel tears rolling from my eyes; I hear my voice speak as if a long way away. "... Salty... I can taste salt... "

A blinding flash cuts across my sight and everything recedes; I float in an immensity of blue and feel both joy and grief in the one instant. For a long time, I hear a distant voice droning. The ethereal words have a sense of warning of some dangers, and elaborate instructions that make no sense to my mind. I cannot tell whose voice it is.

All at once, everything goes black, and the room is spinning. I am disoriented; my head hurts. I hear myself moan.

"Where am I... ?"

"Hush, Dear One, I am here. You are with me in my house."
I recognize my godmother's voice and feel her touch on my
shoulder. I shiver.

"I'm cold... It's cold in here."

"Hush, Dear One," she says again as she wraps a blanket
around me.

My eyes begin to clear, and I recognise my godmother's
herbarium, but everything is different. It takes me a few
moments to realise that it is dark. My mind staggers; only a few
moments ago it had been morning. The flames of the fire have
died to embers.

"What happened?" I ask drowsily.

My godmother guides me to my bedroom.

"You went further than the town square. I'll explain in the
morning, Dear One. You need to rest now."

⌇

I AWAKE WITH THE first pale strains of morning and arise, feeling
a little confused with vague memories of the previous day. My
head still hurts. On my bedside table is a cup. I reach for it and
examine it. I can smell the remnants of a powerful herbal drink.
My godmother must have made this for me last night, but I
don't remember.

I go to the kitchen where my godmother is preparing breakfast.
As I sit eating, silently absorbed in my own thoughts, I become
aware that she is staring at me. I have not experienced this gaze
and discomfort since the age of twelve when I told her of my
third waking dream.

I shudder and put my spoon down. Unsure of myself, not knowing what has happened, as calmly as I can, wanting to try at least to break this gaze, I look into her eyes,

"Godmother, I am scared. What happened last night?"

"Finish your breakfast, Azizi. I will explain as much as I can after that." With that she leaves the room.

I find her in the herbarium. There are no potions brewing, the air smells clean, tinged with a slight fragrance of the apple wood burning in the stove. I sit on a chair near the table where she writes her notes on herbal remedies. She is looking out of the window across at the mountains. It is a bright winter's day; the snow clouds have cleared. The sky is a crisp sapphire blue, and the white peaks of the mountains are fast turning golden with the sun's first rays.

After a long pause, she turns from the window. There is an air of sadness about her. She sits in a chair at the table near me.

"Dear Child, I will teach you all I know. That, I have promised to your father. But the day will soon come when even my knowledge will not be sufficient to guide you."

I make to protest, and she quiets me with her raised hand.

She then explains the vision that I had. "The exercise I had planned for you last night was meant to train your sight by guiding you on a mental journey around the village. I had intended for you to remain conscious while using the sight and report on your surroundings. I was following your mind to check your accuracy. You fell into a trance, and all was going well when, without warning, you spoke of the sacred symbol of Salt. My mind link was suddenly blocked, and I could only listen to you. You were in ecstasy as you described the blue light of the Tears of Apphat."

Aïschah pauses visibly shaken. She looks at me deeply, her expression troubled as if she is hesitating to tell me something. I begin to sense the import of her words and must have looked worried; the Tears of Apphat are legendary. Objects of sacredness, spoken of with great reverence by initiated Master Magicians and philosophers.

She sees the impact her words have on me, and taking a deep breath she relaxes her brow and explains. "The Sacred Stones have not been seen in over two hundred years. The import of your vision is that they must be found and made manifest. They will be needed soon to prevent the world from falling into chaos. You spoke of other things, mostly in brief phrases so that I could not make sense of what was to come. Your words echo the waking dream that you had when you were twelve. You are to play an important role in what is to come. You spoke of the dunes of the Great Desert of Keyab and far away cultures. Every now and again, with great sadness in your voice, you would say, 'he is so beautiful, I must find him, for the sake of the love that they bear.' You would repeat 'He is so beautiful.'"

Heat rises in my cheeks, confused but not knowing why I blush. I stare at the neat rows of flowers and herbs on the table. I begin classifying them in my head: *Mentha spicata for indigestion, fevers, nausea. Salvia Officinalis, for sores.*

"Dear One," my godmother interrupts my mental classification, "you have nothing to be ashamed about. I love you as you are, and before long you will fully understand your feelings."

I am confused. I am not sure what she is talking about, so I change the subject.

"Godmother, this dream."

"Vision, Dear One, it was a vision."

"Ah... Well, this vision then, Godmother, in this, I speak again of the hills of sand as in my waking dream when I was twelve. You call them by another name."

"Dunes. You used that word in your vision. This is how we know a vision is a true one. You are using a true word that you have not heard before. The word 'dunes' is to describe the hills of sand as you call them."

"But where is this land? It seems so different from this..." I gesture to the window to encompass the frozen scene outside our house.

"Child, there are some things you should listen to more closely. I have already shown you a map of our world, but that day, as I remember, you were too interested in the star flowers that were just beginning to grow through the last snows."

She says all this taking down a map and once more showing me the various parts of our world; she points to a vast area of land all coloured a dull, dusty yellow, well south of our mountains. She explains that this is the Great Desert of Keyab. It is apparently all made of sand. The thought baffles me; I cannot comprehend such a vastness of nothingness.

"Oh, it is not nothingness, by far." My godmother explains that the desert is dotted with oases, small pockets of water that the people there use as stopovers on their journeys. She also talks about the sudden bursts of colour that the desert explodes into overnight after a rare shower of rain.

"I should like to visit there some day." I say this in wonder.

My godmother looks into my eyes and smiles saying, "You will, Dear One, you will."

She rolls the map and puts it out of sight. "I told your father once that I would teach you all that I know about healing and magic. You have learned well. I also gave you a new name, Azizi. It is a name I have chosen for you after studying your stars. It is a name of power as well as one that binds you to my heart. More than ever now, this name is to shield you against evil; it is both protection and a way of preventing strangers to use your real name as a means of power over you."

I remember the first time my father called me by that name, how it had sent a shudder up my spine. Again, the feeling is the same except this time, there is an energy about it that surrounds me.

Aïschah continues, "I must accelerate your Lore. There is a lot to learn; first and foremost, you will train yourself to keep conscious throughout your vision state and be able to remember all that you see."

I sigh, thinking of the long days ahead.

"But not before you have taken a walk in the forest and made snowballs. Go and seek out Halim."

I look up to see my godmother smile warmly. As great a teacher and magician as she is she nevertheless understands the heart of a seventeen-year-old boy.

And so, my final year of apprenticeship ends as it began, with a walk in my beloved forest.

~~~

I WAKE WITH A start, the words of a male voice still ringing in my ears.

"I saw him who dances like the fire. Deep embers are his eyes,
~~~

and one smile of his lips could set a thousand hearts aflame."

I hear this voice in my dream and I have had this dream for several nights now. The dream is always the same. I am walking along one of my favourite paths in the forest when suddenly the surroundings change. I look up and there are no trees, only a midnight blue sky dotted with brilliant stars. The barren ground undulates and seems to spread all the way to meet the sky. The colour of it is pale under a full moon and almost looks like snow in winter. It is soft and warm underfoot. My feet sink slightly into it, and the texture is unlike anything I have known. Disoriented, I realise that I am no longer in my beloved mountains. Instead of feeling the cold of winter, I feel as if I am standing in the full blaze of the sun in the middle of summer. Yet it is night. This dream is full of contradictions. I walk over a hill and come across a fire in the open—there is no fireplace. Here, my eyes sting as the smoke blows across my face. Near the fire someone is dancing, but I cannot see who it is. Someone steps in front, blocking my vision, but his back is turned to me. I hear his voice; it is a young man's voice, full and resonant but with a strange tune to it. It is melodious but the words come out as a strange mixture of sounds like the gurgling brook and the whispering wind. Each time he repeats, "I saw him who dances like the fire. Deep embers are his eyes, and one smile of his lips could set a thousand hearts aflame."

Then the speaker of these words turns and faces me. His head and face are covered with a dark blue cloth that seem to blend into the night sky. He then removes the cloth covering his face and looking directly at me, he smiles such a beautiful smile that my heart aches in my sleep. I struggle to see what is behind him but all I see are flames dancing high against the night sky.

The stranger facing me adds pleadingly, "He is so beautiful; he is so beautiful".

I noticed that around his neck he is wearing a golden pendant with a figurine that looks like two snakes intertwined. I awake with a start and with such an ache in my heart that leaves me with an indescribable feeling of longing.

For many weeks, I say nothing to my godmother about this dream. Of late she is adamant that I develop my own interpretations of my dreams and visions, insisting that it is for my own good and that I must develop my own sense of seership.

I meditate on this dream daily and still no answer comes. I do not know the stranger in the dream nor the place. I do however find out the significance of the pendant. Looking in a book of talismans, leafing through the pages casually, a page falls out, loosened from the binding, and in front of me lies the Lore of the intertwined snakes, known by the great sages as 'Jörmungandr'.

The snakes signify primal power. Two snakes stand for both energies of the universe. If they are intertwined this signifies that they are in perfect harmony. In addition, the Lore of the talisman goes on to say that the representation of two snakes in the form of a circle stands for a love that reaches out beyond the stars and into the beginnings of time itself.

I understand almost all the Lore, but the last part seems somehow to elude me. No matter how many times I read it, it makes no sense at all.

There are further references to the legendary King Apphat and the mores of the culture he founded. I read with fascination, not understanding everything I read, yet knowing that somehow it speaks of something intimate, something my heart knows, and yet in some way something I find both elusive and secretive.

Many thousands of years ago, the god-king Apphat had founded a culture upon which the current laws are based. His greatest legacy is a culture based on the spirituality of androgyny. To be an initiate of the sacred sect of Apphat means to join an exclusive and secret order that is revered as holy. Love, as well as the initiation into love, is held as sacred. The act of love is regarded as sublime and not merely sexual. In this culture, love between men and men, women and women, men and women, is all regarded as equally holy. The priests of this order are seers and are held in high regard. Yet it is the initiated soldiers of Apphat who are revered as the sacred guardians of the sect. I search all the parchments on culture and history for such a civilization, and many reference the Naasséenes. They are a strange people ruled by High Priests, according to historical facts, and they are also feared as their highly trained soldiers have never been defeated in written history. The other passages on family life and art I skip, interested only in the passages that deal with Apphat and the healing arts, and yet very little is written on that subject.

As I try to understand this Lore, I become more and more obsessed with the figurine. So much so, that I copy it on parchment until it is drawn to my satisfaction. I then decide to take it to the town smith to have a talisman made of it in gold and silver. It feels like such an extravagance, but I am convinced that I must do this. Secretly, I want the talisman for myself, hoping that it will reveal its secrets to me once made and worn.

The town smith has his workshop on the edge of the village. It is an older house, with windows that face the rising sun. A large sign hangs above his door: a dark circle enclosing a small white hammer behind the head of a white reindeer that names his trade. I open the door; a soft bell announces my entry. The large front room is where the smith makes his more delicate works. It is warm, but the light is cold, almost blue. The heavier works, such as shoes for horses, is done in a large barn at the back. A slightly acrid smell hangs in the air; it's a mixture of charcoal burning and a slight sulphuric smell, not altogether unpleasant. My eyes are still adjusting to the dark shadows, and dust dances slowly in shafts of light that cross the room. At the far end is a large window with a bright light pouring in. It seems somewhat unnatural and I realise that the window acts like a loupe, amplifying the light that falls on his desk.

A dark shape is outlined, bent over some work. I stand there a moment and give a little cough to announce my presence. The smith turns and rising, walks towards me, and stands two paces from me. He is smaller than I remember, barely taller than me, but his muscular body is a testament to the heavier work he did for years; his apprentice now mostly does the shoeing of the horses. He has unruly white hair. His light blue eyes have the ability to focus sharply over his rimmed glasses, and I am sure that under his scrutiny he will find fault with my drawing. He looks at me rather severely when I present him with my request. I pray silently that he will not ask me to explain the talisman. He handles the parchment several times before speaking.

"This is mighty detailed work you require. How will you pay for it?"

I show him the coins that I have saved over the years from the allowance that my father gives me.

He looks up briefly and seems to sniff at them before looking back at the parchment, almost uninterested in the coins. In an almost offhanded way he dismisses me, saying it will be ready in a week. I tell him that I will call during the week to see how the work is progressing.

I thought his eyes would pop, and before he can speak, I add, "The drawing is based on sacred Lore; it must be exact." With that I leave hurriedly.

Early in the week, I come to look at the work in progress, and the smith seems pleased at my approval. A week later, I take possession of the finished talisman. It is a pleasing piece of work to look at. The two snakes are intertwined around an ornate circle of symbols of stars and leaves. The talisman combines both silver and gold, better setting the work into relief. The new metals shine brightly. Once in my hands though, a sense of foolishness fills me at what I now consider an extravagance. I hold onto the talisman for a while and then decide to put it away. It is clear that the meaning of the Lore is not going to reveal itself to me. If anything, the dreams come on even more urgently and the images become almost life like.

One detail changes. As the young man who is wearing the talisman pleads to me, I now catch a glimpse of a person dancing behind him. I still cannot see his face, but only parts of his body. It is another young man and now I begin to doubt that there has ever been a fire, for the body of this young man moves like firelight and even his limbs glow like the gold of flames. Now as I hear the voice pleading, I catch glimpses of the talisman alight with fire—the dancer wears it.

Finally, I decide to speak to my godmother about it.

I relate to her my dream and tell her of my discovery of the

Lore and its meaning. I do not tell her my foolishness with the making of the talisman.

There is a long silence, and then she looks up from her books and, looking deeply at me, smiles with a hint of mischief saying, "So, it seems that there are two of you who think 'He is so beautiful.'"

For a moment I am left bewildered and then with a flash of memory, I understand her reference to my words in a vision I had when I was seventeen. Heat rises in my cheeks and yet again feeling annoyed that I do not know why I blush, I ask, "Godmother, what is the significance of this dream?"

She asks me again to tell her the dream and asks how recently I have had this dream.

"It has been two nights ago since the last dream."

She asks me if there has been any difference the last time, or whether the dream remained the same.

I begin to say that it is always the same when I suddenly remember, "No. Though I have never been able to see him clearly, I see the dancer now wears the talisman. In addition, the last time, just as the dream ends, I hear a clap of thunder. I wake up and think that there is a storm outside, and when I get up to look out of the window, the sky is always clear."

"And what have I told you of such symbols in dreams?"

I think for a moment and remember, "That something is to be made manifest on the third night."

My godmother looks at me approvingly. She looks back at her books. There is another long pause that leaves me uncertain. Then she looks up again.

"What do you think will manifest itself from your dream?"

I answer without thinking, "The prince will... "

I have no knowledge that the young man in my dream is a prince. My godmother looks at me with slightly raised eyebrows, waiting for me to finish my sentence.

"You should learn to believe in your intuition, for it has always proved to be correct in the past."

I look at her bewildered. "But... "

"We had better prepare for a royal visitor. It appears that you have forecast his arrival for tomorrow night."

There is a pause in which I am slowly absorbing all of this, and she adds, "Your destiny is reaching out to you. Trust in yourself, Azizi, trust."

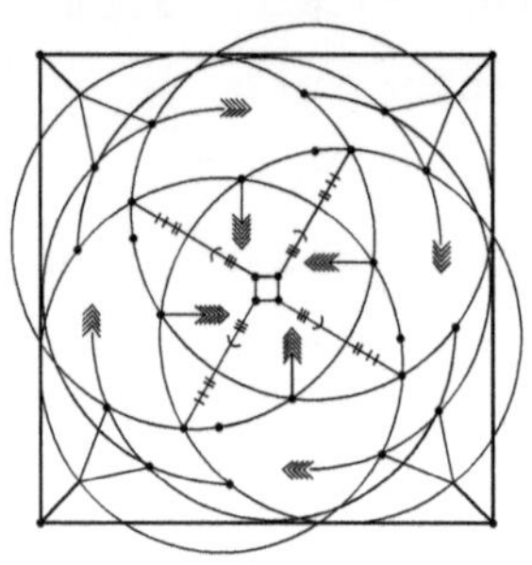

C H A P T E R   N I N E

The fire has settled down to a gentle heat. I sit with my godmother in the herbarium ready for another story, which according to her will give me a deeper understanding of the Mores of Apphat. And so she begins, as always with a preamble that is meant to warn me about the dangers of misusing magic.

"The greatest king of our times was King Apphat, the mystic. Also known as the wise, because he formed a spiritual belief system based on the balance of duality. He had ordered his priests and wise counsellors to search the world for all the known religions, mystical Lore, and ancient customs and beliefs. He concluded that though the world appeared to be split into binary opposites, such as day and night, male and female, fire and water, and so on, the true purpose of one's destiny was to find balance. So, he formed an order based on Oneness—he actively encouraged androgyny, the balance between male and female.

Many mystics, who knew the secrets to Oneness, came from a mysterious land of healers and magicians. These individuals, therefore, have always been held in high regard, because of their ability—they are the keepers of the sacred knowledge. As a result, our homeland is known for its magic Lore and Magicians; the secret Lore is kept to the initiated, and the deeper truths are not paraded before the crowds of awe seekers. Clever tricks and illusionary magic are still popular, regarded by the simple folks as true magic. You can still see them in the marketplaces, their practitioners earning a few coins. There is a saying amongst the seekers of the deeper knowledge: 'Do not cast water upon the sand.' Do you understand what this means Azizi?"

I thought for a while. "I think so. Pouring water on sand serves no purpose as nothing would grow from it."

"Yes. And like water amongst the desert tribes of the Tassili, our precious knowledge is fiercely guarded and kept in tight secrecy. Though most have witnessed the more common magic, the tricks of the marketplace, few have witnessed True Power, and so legends and stories abound, and any that have witnessed an act of True Magic are well paid for the tale. The tales grow but few have witnessed it.

"Of all the Greatest Magic, Azizi, the supreme one is said to be that of True Love. It is said that the power wielded by two who share a common bond is immeasurable. Not in a hundred years has there been any account of the Great Love Magic.

"There are certainly everyday accounts of Love, such as mysterious warnings from distant loved ones, or sudden perfumes pervading the air at the thought of a loved one. But none are so great as the Love of Star Souls.

"According to legend," my godmother continues, "the Princess Baltazar of the far-off land of Moeurs became enamoured of a young foreign prince against her father's wishes. The pair could not be separated. The Sultan engineered the young prince's disappearance, but not before the lovers had exchanged their vows of love, and had fashioned, each for the other, a talisman of love. Using this talisman as a voyager would use a compass, through long and arduous search, the princess found her lover at the door of death, in a dank cavern guarded by bandits in the hire of her father.

"She managed by ruse to get into the cavern and threw herself at her lover's side. She was at once discovered but when the bandits came to take her, awe and terror struck them. The lovely princess transformed before their eyes into a beast of fire and metal claws. Many men who braved the beast died there and then, and those who lived to tell the tale would be haunted by nightmares for the rest of their days.

"According to the legend, the princess stood guard over her prince for thirty days and nights and any who dared approach were confronted by the awesome transformation, until one day both prince and princess disappeared without a trace. The cavern to this day is said to still bear the marks of the Fire Beast and its deep chambers still echo with the moans of the lovers' despair. For though she could protect her prince, she could not escape. Every night, she again took her earthly form of womanhood and collapsed with exhaustion at her lover's side.

"It is believed that they were spirited away from the cave by a great magician who took pity upon their plight. They were hidden amongst the stars. That is why the last constellation to be seen in the night sky as the dawn breaks, is the brilliant fire beast. The princess is still making ready to confront her enemies, and beside the fire beast, paling fast in the oncoming daylight, is a group of stars in the form of a man lying unconscious."

My godmother paused, concluding, "There are other tales of great love, and so many customs and rituals have developed amongst our people, for the proclamation of Love of two who seek eternal companionship. Gifts are exchanged, vows are taken, and talismans made to protect and unify their love especially when apart and in the face of adversity."

I am annoyed at the story, not really knowing why, and I blurt out, "Such a pretty story, but what is its purpose?"

My godmother pauses and looks at me with a slight air of annoyance, the same look she often gives me when I make such remarks.

"Perhaps young cynic, it is to be appreciated for its prettiness."

I begin to laugh, and she cannot help but smile.

"Aïschah, you know what I mean. There must be more than the story itself."

"That is part of its wonder—for you and any other who seeks the truth, to delve at its mystery."

This is not the first time that my godmother had spoken of the Great Love Transformation. This was an act of pure magic not witnessed in a hundred years. I have always treasured our deep conversations in the past about the meaning of the transformation and the reasons why certain animals are made manifest.

My godmother, an assiduous scholar, often spends days researching old mystical Lore. She holds the view that this is based in ancient times when mighty spirits guarded the land.

Certain forests and mountains are sacred to the gods of the land itself, and then there are smaller spirits that work in forests and streams together with the greater gods of the air, whose power breathes through cloud and frost and the whispering wind.

Some of the original spirits often take on the form of the animal they were created to protect. People of the land, who associate with one of the Powers whether consciously or not, will be drawn to a particular animal spirit and worship it.

I want to engage in this kind of conversation, a scholarly argument as she calls it. Tonight though, Aïscha looks tired. She rises abruptly saying, "Dear One, there are some things I cannot do for you. This story is meant for you. It is you who must find the deeper secrets hidden within, for the time is fast approaching when you will need them." She hesitates a moment and then adds, "Azizi, listen carefully. You will not come truly into your power unless you open your heart and allow the power of Love to flow through."

She turns slowly and leaves the room. I am suddenly alone, and a sense of isolation from the world surrounds me and fills my inner being. I wonder at my godmother's mood and remarks.

This is a story of Love. What does love have to do with me? I am seventeen and barely a man. Boys do not call themselves men until they reach the age of eighteen. I pause and breathe deeply wanting to examine my thoughts with sincerity, as my godmother has always urged me to do. I focus upon my heart, and there in its depth I find something, large yet fragile, almost like the bud of a fruit waiting for sunlight. I open my eyes quickly; this feeling seems too intense.

The fire is slowly dying to embers in the fireplace. The cold of the winter's night is again creeping into the herbarium. I watch silently as the embers play cat and mouse with the gusts of hot air, whispering around the ashes. My heart is aching. I am longing for something, and I do not even know what it is.

Little eruptions of colour now and again burst forth from the embers, I watch as pretty displays of fire entrance me. A corner of the fireplace draws my attention. There, in the middle of some remnants of logs, little puffs of flames erupt every now and again and produce brilliant pockets of colour. I wrap myself more tightly in the blanket and allow my feelings to sink. A small shot of blue flame comes and goes, taking all my attention. I watch, wanting to see again such an attractive colour. Again, it comes unexpectedly. This time, though, it grows. I can see the flames engulfing the remains of the log it has burst from. The flame takes shape, now a dancing figurine, and now a gently rolling wave.

All at once, a pair of eyes float above the flame and stare at me. The colour is as blue as the early spring star flowers that burst forth deep in the forest, too shy for the open fields. All the warmth of the fire enters my heart. I melt; I float. Oh, these eyes are so blue, so deep and so gentle. I see justice and compassion, joy and sorrow.

I hear a whisper as if from a great distance, "This is my gift to you, Azizi."

I hear myself answer to the fire. "Joy and sorrow... Thank you, Godmother... "

"What did you say?"

My godmother is standing at the door, looking at me intently but in a manner that suggests that she does not want to startle me.

Absent-mindedly I answer, "Joy and sorrow, cannot without

the other be... "

The fire dies. Sorrow fills my heart at the end of the dream. My godmother comes in. She sits beside me.

"That is not an interpretation that an apprentice would give to that 'pretty' story. I am proud of you, Dear One. Did you find this in the fire?"

Dreamily, still affected by the vision, I answer, "No, Godmother. I found it in his blue eyes, that came from the fire."

My godmother stares at me for a long time. She strokes my hair her fingers smelling of fresh herbs. Finally, she says, "Child, sometimes your visions frighten me."

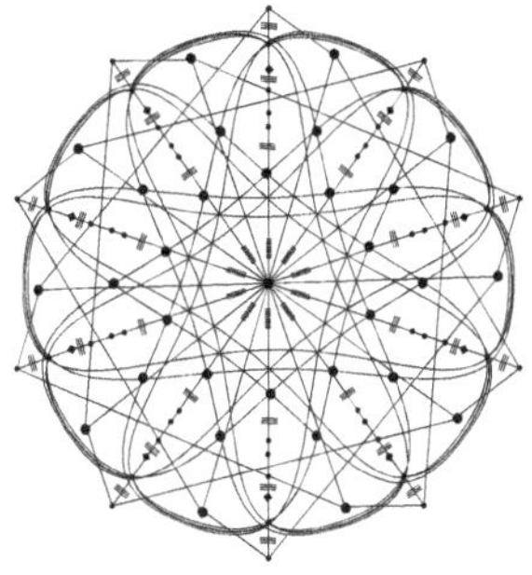

C H A P T E R   T E N

It is the third day since my last dream. The nights come quickly in winter. I help my godmother in the house with preparations for our guests. A part of me is scared. What if my dream interpretation is false, and the visitors do not come? Aïschah's quiet confidence in me makes me nervous.

At times she senses my uncertainty and asks me to prepare something else; this has the effect of my believing at least in Aïschah's confidence.

It is dark well before supper. Warm aromas of freshly baked herb bread waft throughout the house, teasing my senses and gnawing at my stomach.

I stand at the doorway to the kitchen staring at the hearth. Aïschah opens the wood stove; the fire burns a brilliant orange. I shiver. Like cold icicles, beads of perspiration trickle down my spine. I stand paralyzed. At the sudden and palpable change in energy, Aïschah whips her head around and looks directly at me. "Stay focused, Azizi. What do you see?"

The kitchen dissolves. I can see my beloved forest, and it is dark, yet all the details are etched out as clear as day. The forest races at me.

My mouth is dry. I whisper, "Danger. The Shadows walk the forest. There is danger all around."

"Where are you now?"

The forest opens up, and the road to the village appears white under a blanket of snow.

Just around the first bend, the bridge stands clearly over the dark, raging torrent that has not yet frozen over.

"I am by the first bridge to the south of the town."

"Do you see anyone there?"

I look along the road, which meanders like a white ribbon into the grey night. It is deserted.

"No one."

"Look carefully."

I sharpen my gaze and intensify the power of the sight. The first hill that obstructs my view melts away and there on the road, wearily making their way on foot leading their horses, two figures are walking towards the bridge.

My sight zooms in. I gasp.

"Stay focused, Azizi. Are these our guests?

"I cannot say. They are strangers."

"How far are they from the bridge?"

"About half an hour's travel."

"Listen to me closely, Azizi. I sense the danger you perceive. I will seek help now. I implore you: stay by the bridge. Do not attempt anything. I will join you shortly. The light is with us."

This will be a real test of my staying powers; I have never intentionally stayed in one 'mental' spot before. The landscape appears strange and calm, yet I know, Shadows move with evil intent amongst the forest trees.

I sense my godmother's physical presence nearby in my physical consciousness but nothing else. I gather she must be travelling on the mental plane elsewhere. I am not sure what she can achieve.

An eternity seems to pass. All is quiet. The travellers appear around the first bend, and they seem so lightly dressed for our winter. I mentally jump. Just a short distance to my left, a rock suddenly stands and takes the shape of a man. It quickly melts amongst the trees. I catch a flash of deep scarlet in the flow of the fabric. I sense great danger for the travellers. They are close to the bridge and at once the leader stops and looks up. His companion catches up and asks something in a foreign tongue, which is answered with a short harsh word. A part of me struggles at the recognition of that sound. They resume their walking.

I pray for my godmother to hurry.

Just behind me and slightly to my left, a sphere of light appears. In a halo of iridescent blue flames, my godmother is walking towards me. She is in her astral form. Beauty and power flow from her. It is only the second time I have seen her in this form.

I hear her thoughts. "These are our guests; they are in danger. We must either delay them on their journey until help arrives or help them. However, we must not use magic, for I sense that one of the Scarlet ones is here, and we must not give away the source of protective power. You may use your thoughts and some telekinetic power, but not the Greater Magic. Do you understand?"

"Yes Godmother." I reply, really not knowing what I can do.

With this Aïschah steps to the horses. The first horse at once jerks his head up; ears sharply pointed, it neighs and refuses to go further.

The leader stops and looks around worriedly. He holds tightly onto the horse's reins lest the beast bolts. A quick exchange is made between the two men, in that deep, whispering, gurgling sound I heard before. The leader peers into the night beyond the road and into the forest.

Slowly and cautiously, the leader looks around, calming his mount. They have just crossed the bridge, when suddenly three Shadows erupt from the forest and leap towards the travellers.

The leader at once reaches to his side; a flash of silver appears in the shape of a crescent moon.

"A scimitar." I hear the name in my head. I have only ever seen one in my dreams.

With one fluid movement of his arm, belying his apparent age, the leader dispatches one of the Shadows and the body rolls over the side into the torrent below. The other two Shadows use the distraction to attack the second traveller. Caught by surprise, he falls, stumbling and is wrestling with them.

His companion turns to his aid but before he can raise his hand, three more Shadows appear behind him.

I am unable to assist, filling me with a sense of helplessness. The horses neigh, the leader grunts under the attack, and yet the Shadows have not uttered a sound—not even in death do they make a sound.

"Godmother, how do we help them?"

At that very moment a veritable rain of stones showers the Shadows with uncanny accuracy, and there follows a tide of smaller shadows from the woods.

"The Hills people! Godmother, that's who you went to get?"

"Yes, Dear One. Take care of the horses; they are about to bolt."

This would be easy; the teachings of my godmother on animals will pay off. I impress upon the minds of the two horses thoughts of peace and safety and approach gently. Animals have second sight and will readily understand what we can impress upon them. Sensing the source of my thoughts, they easily follow me out of harm's way. I lead them into the forest amongst the safety of the trees, and out of sight.

I turn to look down the road to see the attackers run away from the village. I also see my godmother using her power to throw wave after wave of fear energy after the Shadows. The energy is grey and takes the form of darts with hooks. When they reach their victims, they envelop them with a grey cloud of doubt and diffuse strands of ugly yellow. The darts then gnaw at the attackers, eroding their resolve in the most irrational ways. The Hills people disappear as quickly as they have come.

A wave of blackness darted with red flashes erupts close by. I stare at this mental manifestation as once more an apparent boulder takes the shape of a man. I can now see him clearly. He is staring at the road; his eyes are pure black and drip with hatred. He mutters in a foreign tongue and quickly and silently seems to melt away into the forest and in that movement, I catch once more a flash of scarlet.

I am left standing in my mental body feeling dirty and drained at the experience of such evil.

My godmother appears beside me.

"The travellers are safe. A little bewildered but safe. Come let us go home and prepare to greet them."

"What of the horses?"

"Let Halim take them to the travellers."

Just as she is vanishing from sight she adds, "Speak to his mind, do not materialise."

At that, my friend Halim the shepherd boy is walking through the forest, carrying his leather sling. These slings, the Hills people normally use to chase off wolves, but tonight they have used them to great effect against soundless Shadows.

He has just seen the horses and is walking gently towards them. Almost as if sensing something, he pauses. I take my opportunity.

"Halim, Halim, peace. Halim, listen."

I hear his thought back to me,

"Master?"

I have tried over the years to get him out of the habit of calling me that. As Aïschah's apprentice, he regards me as a mystical being and it is no use.

"Halim, it is I. Take the horses to the travellers."

"I understand," he replies. "It is an honour to serve you and the Mistress."

"Thank you, Halim. Bring the travellers to Aïschah."

Halim as equally gifted at taming an apprentice magician's heart as animals of the forest, gently takes the reins of the horses which, docile and at peace, happily follow their small human friend.

I stay long enough to watch the amazement of the travellers

as this poor shepherd boy brings them their mounts, intact and calm.

"Please sirs, follow. I will take you to the house of Aïschah."

The older man in a thick accent asks, "Was it Aïschah, then, who helped back there?"

"Yes, sir, and her Dear One, who is a magician."

The man looks puzzled. Narrowing his eyes, he looks briefly around, then shrugs and helps his companion to his horse before mounting his own. They follow Halim through a dark winter's night to the warm hearth of my godmother's house.

This night my life is changing.

I come back to my body; the house seems dull compared to the light of the mental plane. I am exhausted, my clothes drenched with perspiration.

My godmother is there, smiling.

"Well done Dear One. Go and change; you have time, and I will fix you an herbal restorer."

"Godmother, why did I have this warning vision and... " I hesitate, not wanting to injure her feelings and unsure of my own ego.

"And why did I not see anything?"

"Yes."

My godmother smiles at me. "Azizi, I have told you before, you do not choose the Power. It chooses you. Now ready yourself for our guests, they are not far away."

I step out of the bath to dry myself and find in my room an herbal drink. These, my godmother prescribes from time to time after long visions or long periods of astral travel, to calm and restore a balance of energy. I have often come out of visions with headaches or slight giddiness, as my energies are not grounded. I drink the bittersweet liquid and find that I am calmer, more assured, and ready to face the world.

I hear grave muffled voices coming from the welcoming room. My godmother's measured and calm voice over the sharp staccato of a deeper man's voice whose tongue finds the words of our language difficult. I walk into the room. An older man with a white beard is facing the door through which I come. My godmother has her back to me and even so, as I come in, she turns around and greets me with a smile. Further down the room and standing near the fireplace facing away from me is another figure. I cannot tell from looking at the clothes whether it is a man or woman. Long, flowing clothes adorn both strangers and part of the material even covers their heads.

"Ah!" the older one exclaims, as I enter the room. He gives a quick look at my godmother and then a long, appraising one for me. I look on indifferently and bow slightly towards the guests.

My godmother begins to speak but before she can utter a word the older man interrupts her.

"So, this is your 'Dear One.' I was beginning to think that he was either a figment of a shepherd's imagination, or a powerful spirit at your command, Aïschah. It is good to see he is flesh and blood."

At this the person at the rear of the room turns. His face is uncovered. I gasp as our eyes meet.

There is a long pause, and then my godmother pointedly clears her throat and says, "Come, Azizi, you can see that such a stare is causing our guests some discomfort. Will you not come in and meet them?"

"I have seen those eyes in my dreams."

I cannot break my gaze. Here are the eyes that have haunted me night after night before the arrival of our guests. Here then are those mournful dark eyes, mysterious like deep caverns. My heart leaps in my throat. I cannot speak.

"I understand what you are saying, Azizi, but now it would be polite to greet our guests and we will discuss your dreams later."

This she says with enough strength that I understand I must obey her. I break my gaze. It is now the young man's turn to stare at me. He looks at me more with curiosity than anything else. He certainly is beautiful. His face is like a chiselled piece of dark wood, polished and deep honey brown in colour, even more emphasised by the white cloth he wears around his face. His features are even and well proportioned, and slight and pleasant angularities to his face lend him an air of authority.

I bow my head and stare at the ground as I can feel myself blush.

"This is my god son. He has been with me now for almost five years. Azizi, this is the Grand Vizier His Highness Giafar. General and advisor to the Sultan of Schiraz, and his..." At this she pauses, looking directly at the older man's face. He nods slightly in her direction "... and his nephew Ijlal, the crown prince of the land and son of the great Sultan Rashãd."

"I hope you will tell me of your dream soon. I am intrigued that I should be in one of your dreams."

My knees nearly give way at the sound of his voice; this is also the voice in my dreams.

I notice that both adults in the room wait upon this young man's words. Neither make to speak, as if there is a silent agreement between them all, that when he speaks, all others should listen.

This is the prince in my dreams.

Still, my head is bowed as my ears burn.

"I am sorry, I did not intend to make you feel embarrassment. I also bring a dream that I hope your godmother will interpret for me. But more of this later, I have interrupted your conversation, Uncle."

The older man whom he addresses as 'Uncle,' nods briefly in the young man's direction and resumes his conversation with Aïschah.

"So, then you are of the opinion that the Scarlet Robes were responsible for the attack. Did you see any of them? It would be unusual for them to give up so easily."

"I did not see them as much as sense their presence. These are trained to disguise themselves well, even on the psychic planes."

"Godmother... "

"Yes, Azizi."

The Grand Vizier looks annoyed at the interruption.

"Are they also able to take on the shape of a rock?"

"I have heard it said that they are able to make themselves look like anything they choose. Why do you ask?"

"In that case there was but one."

"You saw one?" This she asks with a note of incredulity.

Feeling that at last I can contribute something to this conversation in the presence of the prince, I continue, "Yes. There was one who was by the bridge just before the attack. I had mistaken it for a rock, but as he moved, I caught a flash of the red robe he wore beneath his black one. He then took to the woods. Later, after the Hills people attacked the Shadows, there was an explosion of anger and hatred near to where I was sheltering the horses. Again, it was a rock that took the shape of a man. I saw him then clearly in the light. His eyes were very dark, and hatred poured from them."

A silence follows in which the Grand Vizier re-appraises me.

"This is most unusual." My godmother looks on with concern. "Are you sure that he did not see you?"

"He never once looked at me. I am certain that he was not aware of my presence."

"The Robes are trained in second sight. Standing that close to one of them, you should have been visible to his sight. It appears that the evil one sent a Robe whose training was incomplete after you, Giafar."

"For what reason?" Giafar asks impatiently. "I thought these were trained killers."

"It begins to look to me that this one was sent to follow you and report. Greedy for power as they are, he instigated an attack to see how far he could get and perhaps gain kudos for himself. Once the attack failed, he retired knowing that he had exposed himself unnecessarily."

"This begins to fit into the whole scheme of events that have developed."

He explains that for some time now, the kingdom of Schiraz has suffered many attacks along its borders. This seemed to be the work of the Over Lord, but the disturbing factor was that there were obvious signs of the Scarlet Robes, which are the servants of the Sorceress. This Sorceress is an evil woman with twisted desires and an unquenchable thirst for power. It is said that she manipulates the Over Lord who has become weak and a mere puppet in her political intrigue. Many kings are now afraid of open confrontation with the Over Lord for fear that their kingdom will be annihilated. Over the last years, those who have dared to voice such opposition have disappeared without trace only to be found many months later, dead and in a state, which spoke of horrendous torture. The Sultan Rashãd has consulted his magician and seer, who have advised him to seek help from Aïschah in the Asfaine Mountains.

Still later, it appears that the crown prince had a dream that no one could interpret but which foretold both magical and political intrigue. In a three-fold mission they decided to seek help from the great Seeress Aïschah. The voyage would also serve as a test of skill for the prince, who had just turned seventeen, as well as 'spiriting' him away from potential harm. For his protection, his maternal uncle, Giafar, would accompany the prince. A trained soldier, Giafar is also the most senior and trusted general of the Sultan.

It appears now that their plans have become known to the Sorceress and to the Scarlet Robes.

In a quiet voice, Aïschah responds, "For some time now, I have been watching the signs in the heavens. I could sense that something was afoot. What you tell me now confirms this." I look at her with some wonder; she has never spoken to me about this, and yet now I understand her night vigils and her withdrawn moods.

"But now, Prince Ijlal, you spoke of a dream you wish to have interpreted."

The prince clears his throat. He sits down near the fire on a cushion and he takes a moment to collect his thoughts.

"The dream came to me on the day after the Feast of the

Double Axe of the Sacred Order of the Naasséenes. In my dream, it was night and as I looked over the sand dunes, I saw the moon of Camlac full and round in the sky. The moon appeared yellow and sickly, and as I wondered about this, there appeared upon the sand two golden snakes, which although they came from opposite directions, met upon the sand, and raising their heads to each other, began to dance in a harmonious rhythm. At this, could be heard many cries of joy and cheer. This noise attracted the attention of the sickly moon and seeing the snakes, the moon dropped a shadow upon the sand, which quickly engulfed one of the snakes. At once a great bird flew over the sands of the desert. It cried reproachfully at the moon, for of itself it could not fly so high.

"Next, I saw the snake inside the moon, as if suspended in a bubble; it was pale and sickly as well, and the sight of it made me ill to my heart. Very soon after this happened, the moon began to bleed, and the serpent within it grew smaller as the moon grew larger. A drop of blood fell to the sand and spread, staining the land. Cries of despair could be heard everywhere. Here in my dream, I turned and looked behind me.

"On the other side of the land there lay a great ocean. A drop of water rose from this ocean into the night sky, and as it trailed across the sky, it left a path of silver dust. Beneath it, another moon in the shape of a crescent appeared; this one was silver and bright. As the drop of water fell it was caught by the half moon. It rested there for a while. As the moon sank towards the sea, its reflection formed a double axe head. The great bird that had reproached the sickly moon, flew towards the silver moon and circled above. At once, the drop of water within the moon spun and became transparent, taking on two shades of blue, one light and one dark. The drop of water was now surrounded by seven stars and accompanied by the great bird, moved forward to the bleeding moon. Suddenly, the drop of water showered the moon of Camlac with its water, and the snake within it was released and joined its mate upon the sand. The sickly moon shrivelled and where it was, black nothingness remained."

The prince stops. Everyone is silent.

"This is where the dream ended," adds the prince.

My godmother takes a breath. "I will interpret the first part of your dream; its significance has been written in the stars for many nights now. The second part of your dream is not mine to speak of."

She pauses a moment and begins in a voice that holds authority.

"There is a woman who, greedy for power and at the peak of her fertility, seeks to capture a male child of royal blood, and one who follows the Mores of Apphat. This one will fall in love with another of royal blood, their love, an object of political power. She will manipulate the capture of the lover and exploit the rivalry of the kingdoms to gain supremacy. With his capture, she intends to use this youth's primal energies to enhance her own. She intends to sacrifice him at the full moon at the height of the season of Malkizar when the power of Nature is at ebb. His death will plunge the nations into war and chaos. Disturbed, an Ancient Spirit, guardian of the land will waken from slumber. This I have spoken, for this is at hand, so sayeth I."

There is a long pause.

"Is there no hope then?" asks Giafar.

"The second part of the dream needs interpretation, for therein lies the hope of the world."

"Will you not give it to us Aïschah?"

"I have told you that it is not mine to speak of."

"Aïschah, we run short of time. Where will we seek another seer to give us the second interpretation?"

"My godson will give it to you."

This is said with such authority that there is a silence that even I who love and know Aïschah well, dare not challenge.

All eyes are on me now. I am scared. Never has my godmother asked me to interpret another's dreams, and certainly not royalty at that.

My godmother looks at me sternly. There is a command in her eyes that demands I set my fears aside.

I look briefly at the flames in the fireplace, and let my feelings subside. A slow settling feeling comes over me, and I can feel my attention withdraw from my physical consciousness. From far away I hear my voice speak slowly and clearly.

"Behold, from the salt of sorrow and the water of joy, will spring forth a beloved of the light. The venerable Silver Moon has prepared him for his sacred Lore. The Silver Moon of her own power cannot in this matter intervene, for it is the power of a seer of Apphat that is needed to conquer the sickness of the land. He, accompanied by seven followers and led by the Spirit of Hadid will seek the Evil One. Through the sorrow of his heart, he will bring about the destruction of this evil one and save the beloved of the land's crown. This is at hand, it is to begin, so sayeth I."

I can feel the eyes of the prince gazing fiercely upon my face. A strange feeling fills me; I seem unable to wrench myself from the deep meditative state I am in. A part of me is wrestling to be let go of a giant hand that holds me in its grasp.

I hear from a distance the Vizier speak animatedly to my godmother.

"Aïschah, your name means 'silver moon' in the ancient tongue. Surely the boy speaks of you. Who is then this apprentice that you have versed in your Lore?"

"None other than my godson, Giafar. This child is a child of the light and speaks truly of himself. I glimpsed his destiny a long time ago."

"But he is still a child, only just past his first initiation."

A flood of sorrow fills my heart, tears roll down my cheeks, and salt touches my lips. I am helpless to move. Shafts of blue light pierce the darkness of the room; I sense myself floating; my heart is ready to burst. Like the softness of snow falling, a light penetrates the very core of my body, and I open my mouth,

"Vizier... " I hear my godmother begin but then is suddenly silenced.

The sound that comes from my mouth is not mine. The voice is deep and resonant and fills every part of me and the room all around me.

"O Great Ones, behold my beloved, born of my tears. The heart of this child speaks truly, for only he can seek the Great Harmony. My sacred sorrow is already bound and begs to be released. Joy must be vouchsafed or great and long will the darkness be that will descend upon this land."

Like a great wind the light departs, the darkness of the room engulfs my sight, my throat is dry, and yet I can taste sweetness. But with every gulp I take, the bitterness of salt invades my senses.

I gasp for breath and stumble forward. The prince catches me in his arms. He feels strong. I look at him dimly and see tears in his eyes. I turn to my godmother and call out to her.

"Godmother... salt, sorrow... " is all I can manage to say.

She gently takes me in her arms as the prince stands aside. I sob on her shoulder for a time. She helps me to my room and without undressing me puts me to bed. I cry still, for it seems all the sorrow of the world has invaded my heart. Then, exhausted I drift off to sleep.

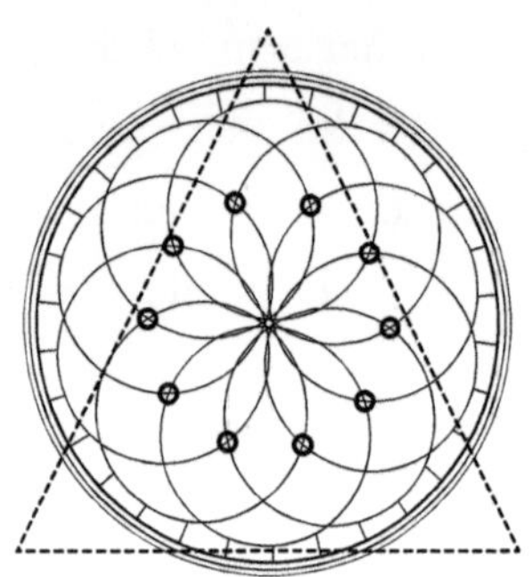

C H A P T E R   E L E V E N

Giant waves of water toss me about like a plaything. In my dream I am alone, yet whenever I call out in fear, a giant beast rises to the surface and holds me afloat. Then suddenly, as if bored or it has remembered something, it abandons me. This is repeated time and time again.

Exhausted and ready to give up, I see a log in the distance, also tossed about by the fury of the waves. All at once it is near me and clutching it desperately is the figure of a semi-conscious man. I cling to the log.

The man then raises his head and, opening his eyes, looks at me. His eyes are blue as the summer sky and softly he speaks to me, "My love will keep you afloat."

I wake with a start. Shafts of sunlight blind me and I am momentarily disoriented. An odd ache fills my heart.

I remember where I am. This is my bedroom. I rub my eyes. I

sense that I am in my nightclothes and not remembering how I got there, I try to recollect the previous night's events.

"Greetings."

Startled I look in the direction of the voice. The prince is there.

"I am glad to see you rested. Your godmother asked me to bring you this."

He offers me a cup of hot liquid.

I can smell the sweet aroma of my favourite drink. Sitting up, I take one sip and immediately feel the warmth fill my body. A heady taste of honey from the hills fills my senses and as if sunshine fills my being, my mood lifts.

I am awkwardly conscious of the prince, standing next to me.

He is openly staring at me. I hear him softly say something in his native tongue,

"Eaynak zarqa' lilghayat, tudhkiruni bisama' alsahra'I."

Puzzled, I look at him. Realising he has spoken in a language I do not understand, he apologises, "Forgive me. I meant no disrespect. I simply said that your eyes remind me of the desert sky, they are so blue."

Heat rises in my cheeks. I look away and not knowing what else to do, I look up at his dark brown eyes that seem to be bottomless wells. I smile shyly and look down again. My fingers fidget with the bed covers.

There is a tension about him as if he is waiting for something and either does not know what to say or does not know how to ask. Finally, he blurts out, "Does it hurt much when the Great Guardian Spirit speaks through you?"

The prince looks as though he regrets his question the moment he utters it.

"Please, forgive me. I did not mean to intrude."

He looks kind, and there is something about this young man I like. Although he could only be one year older than I am, he commands respect.

"Thank you for catching me. It is the first time I remained conscious." I pause, thinking about the experience. "My consciousness is pushed aside as the Presence fills me completely, and though it does not hurt in the physical sense, it leaves me with an unbearable longing for the next time and yet it frightens me at the same time."

"Ah, like a young lover."

This is said more as a statement than a question. For some reason it makes sense, yet I can feel myself blushing.

He smiles briefly and adds, "You fairly froze my uncle's blood. Nothing else could have convinced him of your worthiness."

He laughs briefly to himself for a moment. I want to ask him if I am worthy in his eyes.

"You have not been initiated?"

The question seems ambiguous.

"Yes. I have received the first Order."

The prince looks awkwardly at me. "I meant the initiation into the Mores of Apphat."

Comprehension dawns on me. My ears burn. I feel a strange stirring in my stomach.

"No... I ... no."

"Are you not certain of your heart?" he asks, a little incredulously.

I look down at the bed, conscious of the form of my body beneath the coverings.

"Truly, Azizi, only a prophet of Apphat could speak of such

things as you have and with such authority."

Ijlal senses my discomfort and does not press further.

Slowly he edges his way to the bed, again looking unsure of himself. Then all at once, making up his mind, he sits on the edge. My heart races to have this handsome prince sitting so close to me, in such intimate circumstances as my bed. He takes my hand in his; his palm is cool, his skin is soft, and yet the hold is firm; I can easily feel the strength of it. I look down. The dark honey of his skin stands in sharp contrast to my pale skin and the white cotton sheet.

He looks directly into my eyes. His eyes are so dark that I cannot distinguish the pupils. There is an intensity of purpose, a passion, yet gentleness. He feels fragile.

"To you only Azizi, can I speak these words, for only you, prophet of Apphat, will understand my heart. I ask your counsel, favourite of the Guardian Spirit. I have given my heart, yet I know not if the love I feel is true."

"Tell me of the one who so inflames your heart."

His gaze becomes distant. A smile flutters across his lips and like a brief spot of sunlight appearing on a cloudy day, his face lights up.

A shudder runs through my spine, warmth fills my inner being, and I can smell the heat of the sun on dry linen.

He begins, "I once saw him... "

Like an echo to his words, I hear my voice intone, "... him, who dances like the fire. Deep embers are his eyes, and one smile of his lips could set a thousand hearts aflame." An old ache fills my heart. I look at him. His mouth is gaping still in mid sentence. By way of explanation, I add, "That is the dream in which you spoke these words to me, which has filled my sleep for many nights."

His hand grips mine tighter until it begins to hurt.

I smile at him and pat his hand with my free one.

His eyes fill with tears, he lets go of my hand and, throwing his arms around me, he embraces me.

A mixture of feelings floods me. Initial embarrassment gives way to a desire to be held like this forever. His skin smells vaguely of cinnamon. I am safe.

He breaks away, tears freely streaming down his face. He looks like a little boy.

"Then truly you say my beloved is my intended, the Star Soul I yearn to be with?"

"Yes."

The answer is so simple it does not need embellishment.

A thought nagging at the back of my head suddenly jumps clearly into my mind.

"Please wait." I get up, feeling conscious of my nightwear. I go to my set of drawers and there, I take out a small, forgotten package wrapped in white silk. I come back to the prince and standing in front of him, I hand the package to him saying, "My dream has come full circle."

With great care he unwraps the silk and there, glistening in the sunlight seemingly come alive for the first time, is the pendant of the two entwined snakes.

The prince stares at the gift and then back to me.

"You must give your beloved this charm as a token of your eternal love. It will bind you to each other in the eyes of God and men. In my dream, he already wears this. It is a gift of my making to become a gift of your heart. It is a charm of Sacred Lore."

"Truly you are a prophet and a seer."

A small hurt enters my heart at the thought that the awe he now feels for me will place this distance between the two of us. A knot forms in my stomach. I see myself atop of a mountain; an insurmountable distance separates us. A sad turmoil fills me like a wind that could break me to pieces.

Almost as if reading my thoughts, he takes me in his arms, and wrapping me with his strength he kisses me on both cheeks.

"This is our custom between brothers Azizi. Will you be like a brother to me?"

CHAPTER TWELVE

For their safety, Giafar agreed with Aïschah that they should stay until the end of Malkizar and wait for the melting snows to make the roads passable. Even so, there are many preparations to be made.

My godmother explains, as far as she can, the meaning of the words I had spoken in my trance the previous night. Their practical application is that for some deep spiritual reason I am chosen for a sacred mission. This mission Aïschah foresaw in part when I was twelve. It is also decided that I will accompany the prince back to his kingdom. The Sacred Tears must be found, and the kingdoms healed and united. How this is to be achieved, no one seems to know, least of all my godmother. With her usual trust in the stars, she urges me to let go of my doubts and go to the desert as foreseen in my previous vision.

Following the interpretation of Ijlal's dream, my godmother

foresaw that the prince was in danger. Ijlal and his uncle take up residence at my godmother's guest cottage, adjacent to the main house, awaiting the thawing of the snows. This gives me ample time with Ijlal, delighting in his discovery of my beloved forest. This is also the season of my next naming day. I turn eighteen in just a few lahae. I speak to my godmother and request, so as not to embarrass our guests, to celebrate my naming day some other time.

I truly feel that Ijlal is like a brother I never had. He lends me strength like no other. His friendship as well as his ease of manner is a comfort, and his laughter fills me with warmth and light. He teaches me some of the language of his people. I sense that the days spent in laughter are preparing me for a long and dark journey.

~

TODAY THOUGH, IJLAL SEEMS a little distant. At first, I thought I had done something to offend but quickly understood how he must be longing for his land and people; but most of all he's eager to behold his beloved of beloveds once more. He now wears the talisman next to his heart to imbue it with his love energy for the man he is to make a gift of it.

Malkizar is quickly coming to an end and the roads will soon again be safe to travel. I am in search of the blue star flowers, delighting in the knowledge that Ijlal will not have seen such beauties. Delicate blooms of bright blue, tiny, pointed petals, these flowers appear through the melting snow announcing the onset of Elwah. Since I was a young child, their appearance heralding the rebirth of the forest has fascinated me. Every year I go in search of them, locating them amongst ferns and in secret locations deep in the forest.

We are walking among the moss and soft earth, careful not to take a tumble on the wet and slippery ground. I delight in showing him all the secrets and wonders of the things I have grown accustomed to over the years. Eventually, the talk between us becomes sparse and then turns to the tales and politics of his land.

He tells me of his kingdom and of the legend of the Schiraz tree. "This tree only bears fruit once every twenty-two years. The fruit is sweet and has great healing powers. The most amazing thing though is that left to mature, the stone of the fruit transmutes into a highly coveted red gemstone."

Curiosity has the better of me, and I ask, "How can a tree that bears gemstones then possibly reproduce itself? Or does it die once it has produced its fruits?"

"There is another plant, which always grows near this tree. It will, if its roots encounter one of the fallen red gems, draw from it a special substance. This plant in its natural state is quite plain, yet once it has drawn the energy from the gemstone it will blossom, into the Schiraz tree and in turn produce the coveted fruits."

"Your land is full of magic, Ijlal. I long to see the Schiraz tree one day."

He tells me also of his Companions, a band of young lords, sons of desert noble men, with whom he roams the sandy kingdom, guarding its borders and generally looking for adventure. The band of Companions are loved and respected. Many a time they have come to assist the common people in their hour of need. Tales of their prowess have grown almost to legend status. They once rescued a baby and its mother who had become separated from their caravan. Mother and child had found themselves alone without food or water in the middle of the most ferocious of all desert lands—the marsh near the cave of Gibrar.

"The colours of our brotherhood are that of the Tassili people—deep blue. They also bear a crest on their outfit—a double axe of gold with a serpent entwined around its stem."

Ijlal gives me a sidelong glance before adding: "All the Companions who are of age are initiates of the order of the Naasséenes."

This I knew to be a secret sect whose customs and rituals are practiced by the tribe of Apphat.

As he speaks of his Companions, Ijlal's eyes light up and the pride he bears for his band is clear. "Ah Azizi, you must come to my land soon and meet my brothers. We will welcome you with open arms."

As he speaks, a rarely seen tekbyek bird takes off from a tree, screeching once in that eerie cry so typical of its kind. I shudder. The disturbance of the tekbyek is not a good sign in the forest. The common folk associate it with the dark spirits.

I break the silence, wanting to release the tension left by such a sinister cry. I ask him about the politics of the land as we walk on. He explains to me the complex structure of kings and noblemen and how each pay tribute to one higher until all give tribute to the Over Lord.

His father's is the second largest kingdom and as such gives tribute directly to the Over Lord.

There has been growing discontent amongst the smaller kings over the years. The Over Lord is seen as greedy for both power and riches. He exacts so much from the people that slowly the land is being destroyed. All hate his chief adviser—a Sorceress whom few have seen but whose reputation for cruelty and thirst for power is well known. She has created a personal guard of evil men known as the Scarlet Robes. They are known to train in the dark arts.

Ijlal suddenly seems weary and slows down his pace, walking towards an outcrop of rock. The forest feels heavy and at once darkens as if the sun has passed behind a cloud. My skin prickles and a sickening feeling of abhorrence overwhelms me.

Quickly I turn to Ijlal and using the voice of power my godmother taught me, I command with all my will, "Brother, come to me."

Ijlal stops, a furrow creasing his brow he hesitates.

"Come to me now!"

Almost dreamlike, Ijlal obeys yet I can sense his mind questioning my command. His will is very strong.

He takes three steps when, out of the woods behind him, a Shadow detaches itself and comes straight for him. My immediate reaction is to raise my arm and call the power; my skin tingles as if I am standing too close to a fire. A strong foreboding stops me from using the power. At that same moment, the Shadow, which is now within striking distance stops, appearing to savour the moment. The air around it reeks of the foulest smell. Ijlal stands his ground caught in my command. The creature's features cannot be discerned; it is cloaked from head to foot in a dark robe. Its momentary hesitation saves the prince. A flash of brown pelts out from behind me and makes straight for the Shadow. My heart sinks as in that instant I recognise Halim with nothing but his shepherd's staff for protection. The courage that his heart possesses to confront a bear or wolf attacking his sheep is the same courage that now drives him to attack a creature possibly ten times as dangerous in defence of his friends.

There is a sound like a sharp intake of breath followed by a heart-rending grind. Halim falls to the ground as the Shadow takes flight. In my recognition of Halim, I released Ijlal from my will. The prince at once draws his scimitar. Ijlal lets out a cry of rage at the disappearing Shadow. I rush to Halim's side. There is wildness in his eyes; he lies motionless, and I fear for the worst. Carefully I examine his body. Fortunately, it appears that the shepherd's staff has taken the brunt of the Shadow's deadly knife and it has only made a cut to Halim's side.

Nevertheless, the cut is deep enough to bleed profusely, and the surrounding skin begins to swell and discolour to a deep purple, a sure sign of poison on the blade.

Ijlal standing above me looks at me with concern and confusion.

"Ijlal, I will need your help to carry him back to Aïschah for healing. I am not familiar with the poison. We must hurry."

Ijlal kneels to take hold of Halim, then looks at me straight in the eyes.

"Why did you command me so and held my will?"

His question will not find rest until he has an answer. I will have to do it quickly and convincingly, for Halim's sake.

"Ijlal, as you were talking to me, what was in your mind? Think, what is it that you wanted to do?"

"What..?"

"Think carefully: what was uppermost in your mind?"

"I was weary. I wanted to sit down to finish my story."

"Where were you going to sit down?"

"On that outcrop of rock..."

He turns to point at it and stops mid sentence, staring. Where the outcrop had been, now it is occupied by a small shrub surrounded by moss.

Ijlal stares at me, visibly pale.

"It was a Scarlet Robe in disguise. I sensed his presence too late. I am sorry I had to take hold of your will like that, but your safety was uppermost in my mind."

To an unspoken question in his eyes, I add, "I sensed that I must not use the Power as to have done so would have made us vulnerable to the dark arts."

His eyes at once soften and gently he picks up Halim. I go to help but the ease and determination with which Ijlal carries this poor shepherd boy is enough to warn me that amid magicians, this at least is Ijlal's way of feeling useful.

As we walk, I must focus on several things all at once. I must find the quickest way to my godmother's house and perceive any further danger. I also need to keep a sense on Halim's body energy, which is rapidly weakening. I contact my godmother mentally and warn her to prepare for the injured boy we are bringing.

She was speaking with Giafar, when all at once she stops and gives him clear directions of the path he is to take on which he will find us. Giafar too stunned simply stands and obeys.

Shortly, Giafar comes at a jog around the bend in the path ahead of us and breaks into a run when he sees the burden the prince is carrying.

"Nephew, let me help you."

Without stopping, Ijlal looking straight ahead, answers, "This shepherd boy saved my life; I will carry him."

"Grand Vizier, show Ijlal the way back to Aïschah's house. I must go into the forest for a plant to heal Halim's wound. I think you should be safe; I have not sensed any other danger. Nevertheless, keep a watchful eye."

Giafar at once draws his scimitar and placing himself to the right of the prince, they walk off along the path.

CHAPTER THIRTEEN

I will have to hurry if my search for the plant is going to be of assistance to Aïschah in her healing.

When I finally reach the house, perspiration has drenched my clothes; my hands are dirty and cut from the rummage through the undergrowth. I had to go deeper into the forest than I thought to find the plant I required. Just as I was exasperated in my search, a wood spirit materialized and guided me to the exact spot of the forest where I found the plant. It is an extremely rare plant and is the strongest antidote to a variety of poisons, especially unknown ones.

Aïschah placed Halim in my bed. He looks pale and fragile; his skin is covered in perspiration and his head tosses from side to side in delirium. He is muttering in his native dialect, and nothing he says makes any sense. My godmother has taken his shirt off and the wound has been washed. The surrounding skin is heavily swollen and has gone a dark brown fading to a deep purple at the outer edge. I offer the plant to Aïschah. She immediately takes it and macerates it in a bowl of hot water on the edge of the bed. Prying off the roots of the plant she carefully applies the wet plant directly to the wound and dresses it with a small linen bandage. She hands the roots to me.

"Go and make an infusion of this."

She hardly looks at me. I gather the wound is a serious one.

All the while, the prince stands in a corner of the room looking on. I come back a little while later with the infusion. The steam rising from the bowl smells strongly of wet earth and moss.

Aïschah tests the temperature of the liquid on the back of her hand,

"Prince Ijlal, please help raise him; we need to make sure he takes in at least a cup of this tea."

The prince steps forward and gently holds Halim's body into a half-sitting position, while my godmother with one hand keeping Halim's head still, pours as much of the liquid as will go into his mouth without spilling. At first, the potion dribbles out of the corner of his mouth. Ijlal then strokes Halim's throat in a downward motion as my godmother pours more of the liquid. This time mercifully the liquid goes down.

Aïschah quietly looks at the prince and thanks him, handing me back the cup. I think at first her silence towards me is reproach at having been caught unaware.

She turns to me with concern. Slowly she says, weighing every word, "Azizi, these creatures are dangerous beyond measure. Their disguise has fooled many a trained magician. You are fortunate to have sensed his presence in time."

Yet I am helpless and scared, that a poor shepherd boy should die to protect me or worse still, die to do what I had been supposed to do: protect the prince.

She sighs and brushes my cheek with her hand, "You cannot alter the past. Let it be."

Long hours crawl into the night; Halim lies delirious, his body burning with an insatiable fever that has gripped him. His breathing becomes more laboured, and his limbs have gone completely limp. Gone are the previous spasms that contorted his body.

My godmother looks on concerned for some time and then leaves the room, asking me to call her if there is any change. Her manner implies that she expects none other than a change for the worst. My heart sinks and I find myself on the brink of tears, willing with all my might for a solution.

I sit by Halim, holding his hand; I am aware of Ijlal's gaze and looking up find the prince looking on with a mixture of deep sadness and confusion.

I hear my godmother speak with Giafar in the other room, and I catch snatches of the conversation.

"The poison is a powerful one used only by practitioners of the dark arts. There are no known effective antidotes. The poison is designed to torture the body and mind alike, while keeping its victim alive for a while. With this latest attack, Giafar, the prince is in danger. There must not be any further delay in your departure."

Other things are said, but they all blur in my concern for Halim. Suddenly Halim starts to make small plaintive noises with every breath. I call Aïschah. She comes into the room quickly. She takes one look at Halim and sighs, whispering more to herself than anyone in the room, "The power of the poison holds his heart."

With a hoarse whisper, Ijlal speaks, "Can you not heal him?"

Tears brimming in my eyes, I look briefly to my godmother. "Aïschah is doing everything she can."

Ijlal looks at me puzzled. "Do you not love him?"

I look at Ijlal. "Of course I love Halim. He is very dear to me." Suddenly I understand the meaning of his words. My face burns with embarrassment. My godmother is looking at me deeply and calmly.

"Prince Ijlal is right. You may be able to reach Halim with your heart where my skill cannot."

It takes a moment for the full import of her words to sink in. There is a method of healing, where all else has failed, that involves the heart. It is particularly suited to lovers. It involves calling the heart energy and with it entering the other's mind and heart, taking over the poison and with one's own energy conquering the illness. No secrets would be barred from such a heart-to-mind meld. The greatest danger would be to allow myself to succumb to the poison of my own ego, under the heavy burden of the naked truth of his heart.

Many doubts race across my mind. I am scared, torn between the knowing of my duty and the realisation of all that it implies.

Softly, the prince speaks directly to my fears: "Truly Azizi, if you are a healer of Apphat, initiated or not, you can heal a brother of your heart."

Yet again I can feel my face burn, I look at Halim, white and weak, still as a sparrow in the claws of a tekbyek bird. My heart goes out to him. If he can show such courage, surely, I can do the same for him.

I look briefly at my godmother. "Godmother, I have not done this before."

"Neither had he."

I look down.

"Let your heart be your guide. It is true." She adds, "I will help you if and where I can."

I take a deep breath. "Tell me what I must do."

"First put your pride aside. You did all you could in the forest; you could not have done other than what you did."

Aïschah can be very direct when the moment is called upon. Those words from her are all I need to set aside my confusion and feelings of guilt. My godmother continues revising the detailed instructions she had once given me some years ago, on how to achieve a mind and heart meld. It is not unlike travelling upon the ether but with a different goal—the destination is not a place but rather a concept—another person's heart and mind. I lie on the bed next to Halim, my head to his feet, and holding his right hand in my right hand, I relax, calling to his heart.

<center>~~~</center>

COLOURS RACE PAST ME; I experience a sensation of both falling and rushing headlong; my greatest fear is the perceived inevitable hard landing.

Like a rush of wind, I find myself standing in a dark place. Standing is probably not the right word. I do not know which is centre, up, or down. Everything around is a palpable darkness. The darkness does not last long: flashes of light echo and race past me. I look around. I am in the middle of a garden; weeds are visibly twisting out of the ground, encroaching, and matting the surrounding landscape. They are stifling the flowers, which quickly fade and drop their blooms. The light is dim, almost like night. The details of the garden are etched against an eerie pale sky. The beautiful limbs of small trees are slowly changing into grotesque shapes. The grass is taking on the texture of fine bleached bones. Here and there in pools of shadows stand gnarled trunks covered with holes that resemble festering tumours more than knots. Instead of foliage, webs spread from branch to branch and trapped in the webs, already cocooned, I see shapes that resemble small animals.

My heart sinks and my stomach churns at such a sight. I hear whispers, questioning and threatening. I cannot make out what the words are. I turn; one enormous yellow cat's eye is staring at me from above. All at once the eye becomes so large that it fills the space around me. Yellow and cold and totally impassive it stares. There is no where to hide from this all-seeing eye. The eye blinks once and then vanishes.

Quick movements of shadows catch my awareness. There are strange creatures lurking amongst the trees. I cannot say that I see these as much as I am aware of them, as I am aware of everything that is all around me, behind, in front, and in all other directions. This feeling of complete omni-awareness is difficult to become accustomed to.

I see a river of fire pouring from a far point that seems to spread in all directions. Dark clouds hover above me and below me. A foreboding presence fills the air. I see in the distance a flickering light like the light of a candle guttering in a strong breeze. Beside the light I see a small boy, frightened and looking around him with wide eyes, terror pouring out of his being like waves of grey smoke. Every now and then he whimpers and every time he lets out a whimper, a shadow appears next to him and reaches out with a cold, clammy finger. The boy then freezes once more into terror. All my compassion goes out to this boy. I step forward in my mind and find myself instantly before him.

I address him directly, "Do not be afraid. I am here to help."

He looks upon me with awe, fear in his eyes not quite sure whether I am friend or foe. I step towards the shadows and with an almighty roar command them to be gone. Momentarily as if taken by surprise, the air clears, and the shadows recede but then hang like hungry wolves on the outer limits of my consciousness. I turn to the little boy who in one instant has bolted into my arms and is clinging on desperately. He is crying uncontrollably.

"Do not let me die. Please, I don't want to die."

I hold him tightly, letting him sob on my shoulder. He is soft and vulnerable; I am sure that in one instant he will slip from me into an abyss.

"Take me to your heart," I whisper to the little boy.

"I have lost the way; I do not remember which way to go."

"Tell me where you would feel safe. That is the way to go."

He clings to me suddenly crying again. "Please do not let me die. I don't want to die."

"I promise to protect you. Take me to the garden where you feel safe."

"It is overgrown with weeds and bad things are there that have killed my flowers."

"Then let us find it together and pull out the weeds and chase the bad things out of your garden.”

“I do not remember the way. I became frightened and ran off.”

For a while we walk together side by side. He still clings to my hand and walks as close to me as our movements will allow. The shadows are following us and are again creeping in closer. Insidious despair begins to edge in all around me. It takes all my will not to let it affect me. Panic begins to insinuate itself. I need to find his heart quickly. I hear rather than feel a soft breeze stir in what I take to be the sky in this forsaken land. Behind a veil of mist, a very pale distant moon appears.

“Call to his heart.” The voice seems to come from the moon. In a moment of confusion, I do not understand what it says. Again, it repeats, “Call to his heart.”

All at once, angry dark clouds gather and cover the moon and I lose sight of it. I am confused. Heaviness creeps into my being; I want to lie down and sleep. *How*, I think, *can I call to his heart?* Something on the edge of my subconscious is calling out to be heard. Then I remember. His heart would have a secret word that is the sacred name of his inner being.

I ask him for the name of his heart.

He looks at me long and seriously, then deciding that he trusts me, he leans close to my ear and whispers. He gives me a word like the sound of a bell. This is the key to his heart; its resonance will open the doors.

When I call the sacred name of his heart, the shadows fall away momentarily. Then, as if a signal has been given, they creep together in one movement towards us. A soft echo resounds somewhere near me. I look down; the little boy glows with an inward light and his young face is at once old and baby-like. The light shifts and with it he appears different. There in his eyes I know the truth of Halim's heart. It overwhelms me; my inner mind begins to crumble under the weight of the knowledge. The little boy looks at me with Halim's eyes and with all the power of innocence says, "I love you."

At once the shadows erupt in a hoarse whisper of mocking laughter. My mind, forever the arguer and the doubter, gives me all the reasons why I should not believe him. A shadow creeps closer to me and touches me. A searing pain explodes in my body at once cold and hot. I begin to cry.

The little boy shudders and holding onto me once more cries out, "Please do not let me die."

And then in an old man's voice, "You promised not to let me die."

I fall to my knees the weight of an unbearable sadness filling me.

The shadows creep closer.

All at once a warlike cry in a foreign tongue pierces the darkness. A cry filled with determination and wrath; a beam of light plunges through the darkness from above and becomes a shield around me. It is vibrant this shield.

The child looks at me, beaming.

"The Protector is protected."

The boy's face now resembles my godmother and softly almost haltingly he adds, "You are the magician."

All my Lore comes to me then. Everything is clear.

I speak all the words of power that I know, words to dispel darkness, words to conquer and command, and then sacred words to heal.

A flash of bright white light pierces the shadows and with a great moan they recede and melt before the light.

The last thing I remember is the little boy kissing me full on my lips and whispering, "You hold my heart."

I awake choking on my tears.

"He is healed. You have done well, Dear One. Let your sorrow be over; he is well again."

Halim lies there breathing easily now, though still pale.

My godmother is sitting on the edge of my bed, smiling at me, and caressing my face with one hand and drying my eyes with the other. The prince sits on the opposite side of the bed and is holding my hand firmly in his; his eyes hold pride and a fierceness that tells me what his words cannot express. I notice around his neck, the talisman I have given him; it seems unusually bright, as if it has just been polished.

I cannot say for certain how I resisted the shadows' poison that had invaded Halim's heart. The shadows know me now almost as well as if they had invaded my being. I still feel icy cold where one of them touched me.

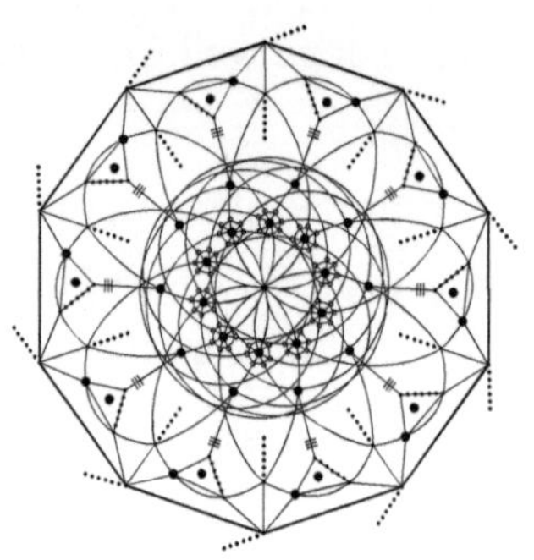

CHAPTER FOURTEEN

The next day Halim is still lying in bed weak from his ordeal, but his beaming smile tells me he's well and glad he is to be awake. Gently I question him, but he cannot tell me anything of our mind meld. Some things are best left a mystery. Ijlal enters the room, almost timidly. Halim looks up at him. Not a word is spoken as Ijlal gently takes Halim in his arms and embraces him. I hear him whisper, "Thank you."

That evening, Halim joins us as we sit around the table for our supper. He hardly speaks a word but often his eyes meet mine with a look of devotion that touches my heart.

"Aïschah, I heed well your advice to leave. Many things however have not been sorted. When will your apprentice be ready to accompany us?"

It was Giafar in his grave voice who had spoken.

"Surely the danger is as great on the road as it is here."

"I do not see everything, Giafar. My instincts tell me it is time. However, I sense it would be safer for now if you left separately and Azizi can join you later. It is better not to attract undue attention."

There is a pause. Clearly Giafar disagrees with Aïschah. He is a soldier and for a soldier, it is safety in numbers that count.

"But who will show him the way? He has never been out of his village. This is a great journey he will undertake."

I want to say something but cannot think of what. My godmother gives a sigh.

"I will show him the way." Halim's soft voice could have been as loud as thunder for the impact it makes. All eyes are on him.

"I am going to the sand people at the end of lambing season to exchange goods as I do every year. I will show him the way."

"Ofcourse... " My godmother looks convinced, and I am sure I hear more than mere agreement in her voice.

"I am still not convinced. An apprentice, and if we are to believe, a prophet of Apphat going on a perilous journey with a shepherd boy!" Giafar shakes his head.

I look at Halim who sits quietly undisturbed by Giafar's remarks. I look deep into his eyes, where the flames of the hearth are playing. A hint of blue now and then flashes across the darkness of his pupils.

Like the crash of an avalanche, it comes upon me suddenly in that deep resonance that cannot be denied for what it is. "Prince Ijlal and honoured Giafar, be on your way. The danger at hand is great, and the darkness has begun. Elwah Tahir, the Fair One, has been stolen, ripped from his people's crown."

The moment passes, salt hangs upon my senses like a

disappearing mist, and my skin still tingles. I look up to feel all eyes are now upon me.

"Damn! Every time I need proof, your nephew provides it, Aïschah. Very well, we will not tarry." Giafar is rubbing his arms in a manner that suggests he is suddenly cold.

"Godmother, what is Elwah Tahir?"

"I am not sure, Dear One, but my heart is full of foreboding. There is an old legend, which refers to one of the blue sapphires as the Fair One. It is a legend that comes from a strange and rarely heard of tribe in the far east of our country, near the cave of Gibrar. It is very serious if the Sacred Stone has been stolen, though no one in a hundred years has laid eyes upon the Sacred Stones.I sense the hand of the Sorceress behind this."

The following day, our guests depart. The parting is simple, but the feelings run deep.

Ijlal makes his farewells to Aïschah, thanking her for her hospitality. He then steps to Halim, holding his hands for a long time and finally embraces him. Halim, awed by the prince, accepts the gesture with all the innocence of a child. Ijlal then stands before me, a mixture of emotions race across his face.

"Azizi, my brother, in my heart I take the blue star flower of your forest. Like it, my heart awaits the spring of your return. May the Great Guardian Spirit bring you safely to my land."

∼‿‿

A WEEK LATER, HALIM and I make our preparations to leave, following the road that Prince Ijlal and his uncle have taken. My heart is full of mixed emotions.

My godmother has initiated me into the first Order of Lore and Magic. A different mark is made, this time on my chest, just below my heart. It is a circle that has been divided into seven sections. One has been filled with a symbol, marking me as an initiate of the first Order of Magicians. The other segments will be filled at each completion of further initiation. There are seven levels of Mastership to be achieved. I now hold the sacred vows of the Sacred Lore, handed down from generation to generation, and as well as the sign as a Healer of Apphat, I now bear the sacred sign of the first Order.

Late in the afternoon, I decide to go and see my father.

Opening the door to his house, I am filled with a sense of nostalgia. The familiar fragrance of leather-bound books and the smoke from his pipe, linger in the warm air leading to his study.

He is sitting at his desk, pouring over some parchments.

"Hello, Father."

He lifts his head, a serious look quickly replaced with a warm smile. "Aldrick, I mean, Azizi. I saw your god mother last week. She is very proud of you and your achievements."

"Thank you, father." A little awkwardly I make my way to his desk and sit opposite him.

"You have grown taller, than the last time I saw you." He smiles kindly at me.

"Father, I have come to say goodbye." The serious look on his face returns, "I have a task to fulfill and must leave for the Great Desert of Keyab."

My father is silent, looking at me quietly. "Your godmother has explained this to me." He fidgets for a moment, opens a drawer of his desk, and takes out a small pouch made of leather. He stands up and comes over to me, handing me the pouch.

"I am very proud of you, Azizi. This a small gift, at least to see you through on your journey. Use your skills well and come back to us safely."

I hold the pouch; it is heavy with coins. He holds me at arm's length, and then on impulse, he draws me into a warm hug. The sweet comforting smell of his tobacco pipe envelops us both.

"Take care my son and be well."

I leave his house with mixed emotions. I cannot say that we were ever very close, but at least I take his father's love, his pride, and good wishes with me. A little sadness is replaced with the knowledge that I will return to him one day.

<center>~~~</center>

STANDING IN THE HERBARIUM, looking once more at the neat rows of jars and herbs I helped collect and classify, I think of the five years that have passed. I stand there, excitement making me want to rush out onto the road, and yet with a knot in my stomach at the thought of leaving my beloved forest and mountains, as well as the gentle wise advice of my godmother. Aïschah prepared me for the journey and had also spoken long about my mission, telling me in the end to trust in the Great Spirit and trust myself.

Her last words to me in these matters make a lasting impression. She looks at me long and with much love. Tears roll down my cheeks freely and unashamedly.

Softly and with much simplicity she says, "Be still, be empty, be nothing. If you are filled with your worldly desires, you may not be filled with the will of the Spirit. Be a bell that is not a bell until it is rung, for then it is filled with the voice of Power of the Spirit. Do not desire to be filled with Power, for Power will only fill you when you have no desires. Therefore, empty yourself and be still. You will know and rejoice when you are, for you will be filled with the knowledge of the Universal Spirit."

The initial apprehension of the unknown, my nagging doubts at my abilities, the weight of responsibility to find what no one has seen for a hundred years, soon give way to a sense of exhilaration at this new adventure. I am like a bird stretching its wings for the first time. The pleasure of being on my own, with my own power, free to go as I will, or so it seems, is intoxicating.

Halim packed the mules the night before and had brought them to Aïschah's house today, laden with the goods he will trade. He added the essentials we would need on our journey. Some food items, some coats made of sheepskins for the still cool spring nights. I packed firestones to warm us and cook by. I also bring my satchel of medicinal herbs and implements.

Halim stands at the roadside patiently while I say my goodbyes. With my godmother's words full of wisdom still echoing in my heart, I turn to check the lashings of the precious cargo. Aïschah then steps forward to Halim.

I look over my shoulder. Aïschah speaks softly to Halim and gives him something. It must be a gift of great value to Halim for he looks awed. He attempts to kiss her hands but in a quick and simple gesture, Aïschah takes his hands into hers and embraces him.

As we come to the first bend in the road, I look back. My godmother stands watching us, and now she turns. She does not go into the house as I expect; instead, she heads up the little path that leads into the forest.

The mountain paths take on a singular beauty as if I am seeing them for the first time. I take in big gulps of air, greedy for the heady smell of ferns and wild herbs, warming in the early morning sun.

The forest is unusually quiet this morning, as if observing my departure. The methodical soft thud of the two pack mules is subdued on the still thawing ground.

~~~

THE DAYS WEAR ON quickly, and my excitement although still palpable becomes subdued. My mind is filled with thoughts of what is to come. I begin to focus more on the journey. Where I almost spoke incessantly to begin with, now, like Halim, I fall into longer periods of silence.

The trees that have witnessed my childhood grow sparser, the air is heavier and warmer, and the calls of the birds change to types I have not heard before.

The shadow of the mountain, cool and dark, takes longer to release us into the sunlight. The water streams that we follow are less tempestuous and meander amongst overhanging branches and polished stones. Its colour has changed from its cold, hard slate mountain grey to a shade of warmer yellow, sometimes green.

Small and unseen creatures make dry noises along the edges of the path we follow, and suddenly quieten at our approach, as if in an effort not to be detected, only to take up their chatter after
~~~

our passing.

I begin to feel like a stranger in an unfamiliar land. Still, the feeling of adventure has not deserted me; I am curious about all things and often ask Halim questions, about our surroundings and the strange animals we see. His knowledge, built from having been along these paths before, is deep and acute and shows his quiet powers of observation.

He still addresses me in his customary manner calling me 'Master'.

Gently I remind him, "Halim, we are travelling secretly in the guise of simple shepherds, and as such I am your equal. You must not call me Master."

There is a pause filled with the conflict of comprehension and confusion as to what he should call me.

"Call me Azizi."

"Oh... " is his only reply, and he blushes coyly, avoiding my eyes.

Often now, as he points out this or that landmark, he stands very close to me, occasionally resting a hand on my shoulder. The first time, I was filled with a shiver that made me forget everything he had just told me. Now, I look for those moments with quiet anticipation, but aware that I do not want to appear too eager. I don't want to force them.

On the sixth day of our travel, Halim who has been quiet, becomes very impatient, pressing the mules forward and telling me to ready myself for a surprise. No degree of warning could have prepared me.

We come around a bend in the mountain path, and there, framed by two slabs of the rocky walls that stand on either side of the path, is a view so spectacular it momentarily takes my breath away. The mountain opens before me and the land falls away suddenly. At the foot of the mountain lies a flat, yellow vastness, stretching as far as the eye can see. In the far distance, it meets the pale blue sky in one straight and uninterrupted line. I turn to see Halim grinning at my surprise.

"Oh Halim, it is beautiful."

Stepping closer, he wraps one arm around my shoulders to better direct my gaze, and he points to a slightly darker patch amidst the expanse of yellow.

"This is where we are heading. It is one day's journey from the well of Shahreza. There we will trade our goods."

I marvel at his eyesight, able to discern such a seemingly insignificant spot in such a vast expanse of yellow. It will take us another four to five days to reach this spot. We still have a distance to go to leave the mountain. There are some smaller foothills before we reach the great desert.

We leave the bend in the path and sadly, the great view disappears as we once more enter the last of the mountains. Halim advises an early rest as the last of the downward path is much harder to negotiate, and we, and the animals, will need all our strength.

We stop by a small pool in the shelter of some rocks and a single tree. The water looks cool and although clear, has a tinge of brown to it as if some of my forest herbs have macerated there for a while.

Halim has a fire going. Often, when we stop for the night and the fire is burning, I look into the flames and seek my godmother. She re-assures me of our safety; the woods have been watched and no trace of the Shadows or the Scarlet Robes have been detected.

Aïschah also gives me news of our home, and on occasion passes on some message for Halim. At first Halim is overawed at this and will hardly comment. As the days wear on, I begin to detect a degree of anticipation in him that makes me smile inwardly.

"Azizi… "

Still, now, Halim finds it difficult to call me by the name my godmother has given me. He looks down and speaks my given name at his feet.

"What is it, Halim?" I sigh. I have not been able to make contact tonight. My mind seems pre-occupied.

"Do you have troubling news?"

"No. I am troubled it is true, but other thoughts intrude upon my mind."

"Do you see her in the flames?"

"Huh?"

"The Mistress… " he looks furtively around. "Do you see her in the flames?"

"Oh. No, it is more like a dream but one in which I am awake. The flames help me focus inwardly."

The look of awe and desire on Halim's face makes me shudder.

"Halim, I do not always see pleasant things in my dreams."

His face clouds.

I do not add that the last few nights, late and as the embers died in the fire, I have followed in my mind Ijlal's return to his land. My heart is heavy with the knowledge that already he is far from me.

I witnessed one night as they stopped and made camp by a stream like the one we are following. Their mood was light, and Ijlal laughed easily at things his uncle was telling him.

It was one of those visions in which the words had no clear meaning. I could only hear sounds as if through water and understand only their intent.

Always I had watched for the Shadows and none did I see, but my heart was full of foreboding. Ijlal was toying with the fire while Giafar was preparing food for cooking. Ijlal's eyes were glowing, being drawn by the dancing flames. So clearly was his mind focussed on the face of his lover, that in my vision the flames drew me also. But strength suddenly seeped out of me like water through wet cloth as a black heart manifested itself at the centre of the fire. I called out a warning; Ijlal looked up as if surprised and at once the flames exploded and leapt at Ijlal's arm.

Ijlal yelled in terror and jumped back, finding himself sitting on the ground and looking around. The flames quickly receded and sputtered out as if water had been poured upon them. In my mind, I turned to the nearby bushes and hearing a malicious laugh, saw a dark Shadow lurk among the trees. With all my might, I made a dead branch fall from a tree into the nearby bushes.

A scimitar was drawn.

The Shadow melted into the depth of the dark forest.

"We will not cook our food by this fire. There is something unholy about it." Giafar had spoken sheathing his scimitar and looking around uncomfortably.

My dream faded, as the words were becoming clearer.

It seems the Scarlet Robes have not given up the pursuit of their quarry so easily.

"Azizi... Azizi"

I hear the wind whisper in dry leaves.

"Azizi…"

Dreamily I answer, and with a jolt I realise where I am. Halim's concerned face comes into focus close to mine; his hand gently shaking my shoulder.

"Are you well? Do you see evil things in the flames?"

"It is all right, Halim. I was just thinking."

His hand lingers on my shoulder for a moment and then brushes my arm as he goes to the fire to serve the meal that he has cooked. It is a simple meal, as all of them have been. It comprises of a stew of wild vegetables that grow along the way, which we collect during the day. To give the meal substance, we also eat flat, dried bread, which keeps well for long periods, and a small portion of strong cheese made from the milk of ewes, some months ago in the Asfaine Mountains. The strong, piquant flavour reminds me of my home.

Days go by with no further incidents. I search the fire for an assurance that Ijlal is safely home. As the flames dissolve, I see them clearly in daylight. They have just reached the outskirts of his father's kingdom at the place nearest the capital of Schiraz. Ijlal's impatience makes me smile; his uncle who is keeping up with the hectic pace, is muttering under his breath at the impetuosity of youth. There is, though, a hint in Giafar's countenance that suggests he is just as glad to be home.

The sand partly gives way to awkward, rocky paths and savage cliffs, sculptured by the raging and jealous winds. Ijlal drives his horse along paths only he can see; clearly this is familiar territory.

Ijlal, who leads, suddenly comes to a complete standstill. His head tilts slightly as if he is picking up a scent upon the wind. I have not detected any danger; the cliffs look deserted. All at once he gives a war like cry and drives his beast forward. Giafar, who at first lays his hand upon the pommel of his sword, now resumes a normal pace shaking his head slightly.

From the rocks they spring. With war like cries, men run forward to the prince and in moments have him surrounded. My heart sinks: I cannot understand the danger and Giafar's lack of concern. Ijlal leaps off his mount and steps forward. The would-be assailants come to a stand still in a group. Ijlal walks toward them, stands there for a moment and stepping forward, embraces the first of them.

Recognition fills my mind. These are his Companions, the pride of the desert. Their fame and renown for appearing swiftly seemingly from nowhere has become legendary. I look upon them now that their hoods have fallen; most of them are his age, some younger.

Pride and devotion bordering on fanaticism for their prince, burns in their eyes. These men will follow him into the jaws of death without question. Laughter erupts and all begin to talk at once.

Giafar approaches calmly and dismounts. One of the youths breaks away and steps forward to Giafar. They stand there a moment, eye to eye; no word is spoken, yet a world of words tumbles from each to the other. Then in complete unison, they take each other's right arm at the elbow and move into a warm embrace. This must be Giafar's own son, Faruq. He returns with his father to the group of youths who are standing at a respectful and silent distance.

They all greet him as the Sultan's general, as is their custom, with one hand on their heart, the other on their sword, and a short bow of the head. He in turn acknowledges them by name.

More subdued laughter and talk returns. Ijlal's eyes now dart around. Consciously, I too, look among them for the one whose name is already a legend of beauty and grace. Ijlal's beloved is not among them.

Faruq, Ijlal's cousin, steps forward with a smile of understanding and softly speaks to him. Shahulm is preparing to meet him at the oasis a short distance away. Disappointment quickly gives way to eager anticipation.

Smoke blows across the fire, and my vision melts away.

I am glad that he is safe among his people. In his brief stay with me, he had begun to teach me his language. He had been amazed at my aptitude for it and me at its simplicity and logical yet beautiful structure.

The smoke clears and once more the fire melts into a vision.

An hour or so has passed; they have reached the oasis.

The people have prepared a feast to celebrate his return. Still his beloved has not appeared, and Ijlal's disquiet begins to show. His cousin makes jest of it and teases him, saying this is a test of his enduring love.

Washed, refreshed, and dressed in finery, Ijlal looking every bit the royal heir to the throne, is led by his Companions in ceremony to a large tent prepared for a banquet.

He has just settled at the head of his clan, when all at once drums explode into an insane rhythm.

Like a burst of firelight when a log explodes, a human shape manifests itself in the centre of the tent. Truly, I behold him who dances like the fire.

In one fluid motion and yet appearing to move in all directions, a youth clad in a simple tunic, his skin oiled so that it shines at every turn, dances before his prince.

The beauty and grace of his looks transfixes the on-lookers, and even in my vision I cannot take my eyes off him.

The dance comes to an end with a crescendo of drums and pipes. Shahulm, bent low before his prince, looks up slowly. His eyes are embers, full of warmth and love for Ijlal. His jet-black hair falls in gentle waves around his face. He has the sculptured body of an athlete, the suppleness of a boy of twelve, and the fire of a soldier. Shahulm then smiles at his prince and in that moment, a thousand hearts melt. There is a long hush followed by cheers that rend the air.

Ijlal stands up and crosses the floor. They stand face to face holding each other's hands, tears race down Ijlal's face, and he takes his beloved and kisses him full on the lips. Wild cheers once more erupt.

Shahulm is content that his wait is ended; Ijlal his prince is pleased. The feast begins in full earnest.

I do not seek to see their private moments after the feast, for some things should be left concealed from prying eyes. I do know that the next time I see them his beloved is wearing the sacred talisman.

On other occasions I see them, their beauty together always takes my breath away.

Truly, they are a match, and all bless their happiness together.

Tonight though, the fire has burnt to ashes leaving me only my memories, an emptiness pervading my being. I shiver, despite the mild evening. I help Halim pack our things and go to lie down and sleep.

I lie there for a long time thinking of all the things that have led to this moment. Eventually, in fits and starts I fall asleep on the cold side of the mountain.

CHAPTER FIFTEEN

I hear a scream. Looking around it is still dark. Halim is not in sight, and strangely unconcerned for his whereabouts, I walk away from the campsite in the direction of the sound. The air around me is odd. I struggle to comprehend where I am.

There is a cave I had not noticed before, the mouth opening near a tree overhanging the pool of water. The water looks strange. In the grey light, it wavers and takes on a dark silky appearance. Circling the pool, I enter the cave.

Though there is no visible light source, I can see clearly. The floor of the cave is strangely smooth, though the walls are rough. The roof of the cave disappears into darkness. Here and there small ledges jott out of the walls, some have small openings; I venture further. I come to a turn in the tunnel, which opens onto a large chamber. On one side, a slightly raised rock formation is strewn with straw. Above this, distinctly etched into the rocky walls, long parallel marks stretch this way and that. I am fixated by these lines, which do not appear natural. A gust of air circles the chamber. A long moan echoes faintly, mixed with the distant clash of metal and faint human cries.

With a sudden shudder I realise that I must be standing in the legendary cave of Gibrar. My mind reels. How can this be since we are still on our journey and have not yet left my home mountain? Perhaps the legend is wrong. Perhaps the Princess of Moeurs had come to rescue her prince, here at the foot of the Asfaine Mountains, in this cave and not on the plains of Gibrar.

As I engage in this internal dialogue, the walls bearing the marks of the fire beast shiver and dissolve.

First, I hear her voice struggling to form words, then I see my godmother's face straining with effort and fatigue looking desperate as if trying to pierce a fog with her sight.

Her words become incoherent, but the urgency of her tone is unmistakable. She raises her hands in a plea. Black arrows shoot out of nowhere and pierce her hands. I cry out to her.

Her face twisting in pain, she mutters a few words, the arrows dissolve, and she resumes her struggle to make herself heard. The fog around her thickens, and I lose sight of her.

A soft, cynical laugh echoes in the chamber. I begin to shake uncontrollably, my insides suddenly cold. This laugh is filled with brutality and indifference.

The light in the cave wavers and changes. It takes on the hue of the thick sticky, reddish dirt found around some springs. The walls of the cave looke like the inside of a giant carcass. I feel nauseous. Again, I hear the murmur of the evil laughter. It is a woman's laugh, scornful and filled with the desire to cause pain.

Images of small children thoughtlessly tearing the wings off helpless insects fill my mind.

Shadows appear from the recesses in the walls and relentlessly surround me. I look upon them, struggling not to scream in terror. I remember the shadow world of Halim's mind in the days of his sickness.

The Shadows come closer. I call upon all my godmother's teaching, a little voice deep inside me telling me to be still... be still... be still.

All at once, I see their eyes, these Shadows, shells of humans. They are not vacant as I had thought them to be, but full of cold, impassive hatred, lusting for blood.

My body is shaking: a lamb at the mercy of hungry wolves, caught in a sticky trap of death.

I hear another laugh, this time triumphant.

"So, this is the one they have sent against me?! A mere child, unable to control his fear!"

I feel a cold dampness ooze down my legs. With great shame I realise the contents of my bladder has been released.

All the shadows at once erupt in snorts of mocking laughter. I feel naked, vulnerable, and ashamed.

"Halim!" I cry out.

"He calls for his shepherd boy. The lamb is afraid!" Once more they laugh and jeer.

The far wall once more shivers and dissolve into a blue mist. The Shadows recede and the laughter becomes distant.

My godmother is here. In one strong blast of her will I hear part of her message, "The Fair One is not a sapphire... The tribes are at war... Seek Elwah, for Sorrow is captured... "

A short spit of disdain and the fog seems to crystallize into ice; my godmother's face disappears.

Silence fills the cave. A palpable darkness surrounds me.

Like the hiss of a serpent, the woman's whispers penetrate my mind. "Do not meddle with me, little one. You are not worthy of being crushed!"

A dark hand appears in the air before me, gloved in blackness.

"Behold, I have the Stone of Sorrow. Long will the pain be for those who oppose my will."

The hand opens, and there a large, dark blue sapphire rests. Like clouds, dark grey spectres float upon its surface, rending it lustreless.

My heart is still. Despair rises into my being.

She utters a little laugh of triumph. I wonder about the other stone.

"I have the Fair One. I will have his stone also."

Out of the rocky walls a figure appears, faint and weak, still as a statue of stone. I can only see his eyes clearly. Slowly his eyelids open and he stares at me. Slow recognition fills us both. These are the eyes of blue I once witnessed in the fire.

A pleading look fills his eyes. I hear a faint, deep voice say, "Let your love keep me... "

Before he finishes his sentence, the gloved hand of black waves, his eyes turn to ice, and bitter coldness enters my heart.

"He is mine," the malicious whisper echoes.

I am overwhelmed by a sudden, ferocious blast of cold air, and I fall backward into a deep chasm, screaming now in full voice. I hit the icy water of a lake and I struggle to the surface gasping for air against the cold.

"Halim!" I scream, "I am cold. Halim! Halim!"

I awake suddenly, gasping for air and shaking.

Halim's strong and gentle arms are holding me, reassuring me. He is here, his body pressed against mine, comforting me. I must have had a bad dream.

Feeling the comfort of his body, I turn and embrace him. Sobbing with both relief and pain I tell him my dream.

He holds me and listens with grave attention.

As we set out on our journey once more, the light of dawn is grey and cold; a heavy fog lies over the land, and all sounds are muted. The soft thud of the mules' hooves sounds far away and dull. Boulders and trees occasionally appear as scant ghostly shadows and just as quickly are swallowed up by the mist. The cold air seems to penetrate to the very core of my body. I look away from the eerie scene. Closing my eyes, trying to shut out the cold, I stumble. I open my eyes again and look at my fingers clasping the blanket. The hard edges of my knuckles are white against the brown blanket. I shiver uncontrollably.

I stumble again. Halim stops the mules and turns to look at me. I see concern in his eyes.

"Master, we must stop and light a fire."

I do not have the strength to correct his address. I simply nod.

Halim takes the mules to the side of the road where there is a natural recess. Quickly he builds a fire and piles it high so that soon it is roaring. He helps me to the fire and covers me with another sheepskin.

I sit shaking for a long time. I cannot get the cold of the dream out of my mind. Halim sits next to me and places an arm around me. Softly he hums a low tune I had once heard him chant to his newborn lambs. It rolls like the gentle waves of a spring breeze over me, slowly swaying like soft, new grass in early summer. Golden rays of sunlight emerge in the depths of his song, warming me, comforting me, and slowly releasing me from the grip of the dark winter of my soul.

The fire becomes warmer, his hold softer, like snow melting at the sun's spring kiss, and my body yields. The fog melts and expands, and before me stands my godmother at the side of the hearth in the herbarium.

A look of concern on her face greets me.

"Dear One, are you well?"

With a heave of my heart, I tell her of my fearful dream. She listens gravely.

"I have been trying to get in touch with you but the scene you describe is not something I remember. I was not with you in the cave of Gibrar."

"Then who or what did I see?"

She pauses for a moment. With some hesitation she begins, "I am not sure. I did perceive a psychic attack during my contact with you. I am concerned. If your vision is true and the Sorceress holds one of the Sacred Stones, then we are all in grave danger."

A small crease furrows her brow.

"The Fair One I spoke of, is the Prince Regent and spiritual leader of the Naasséenes. He has been taken, as was foretold through you."

I remember the voice that spoke through me the day before Ijlal, and his uncle had left my godmother's house.

My Godmother adds, "The people of Naassée are fierce warriors and the taking of their prince has plunged them into anger and confusion. They are ready to march to war, only held back by the advice of their great council of priests."

I knew little of the Naasséenes other than the town gossip. I knew that they practiced the Mores of Apphat, which I had discovered reading on the Lore of the snakes.

My godmother explains, "They are an isolated people living in the Far East of our land. Their soldiers are revered as the fiercest warriors. According to legend, following the Great Cataclysm that befell the world, the Land of Apphat disappeared. It is said that a hundred years later a strange people emerged from the caves of Gibrar. They wore the same talismans and attire that Apphasians had been known to wear. They settled in the rocky hills facing the Great Ocean of Elwah.

"Their spiritual leader is said to be the incarnation of Apphat. The priests look for each new incarnation. His fair skin and blue eyes identify him in a land of dark-featured people. He is given the title 'Elwah Tahir,' the Fair One, and he holds the responsibility of spiritual leadership and guardianship of his people. Legends abound of his magical powers. His people are guided in every action by his every words. The taking of this person has enormous political repercussions. The words spoken through you this last winter in my house have come to pass. 'Elwah Tahir the Fair One has been stolen, ripped from his people's crown'."

"Then, Godmother, it is hopeless—my dream interpretation to the prince is misleading. It is not Prince Ijlal the sorceress is after but this Fair One. My quest is in vain. I am sent to protect the wrong one."

"The warning you heard me give you is true—the Fair One is not a sapphire." Aïscha pauses, her brow creasing once more,

"There is something that bothers me. No one knows where the sacred sapphires have been kept all these years. It is unknown if the people of Naassée were once the Sacred Guardians of one of the stones. Regardless of his status as a spiritual leader, the question remains, why abduct Elwah Tahir? Elwah, the second Tear of Apphat, has not been found. You must find it before the powers of the Shadows find it."

I sit unconvinced for a long time, exhausted from my recent ordeal.

"Azizi, your quest will not be in vain. The secrets of The Great Spirit are for Him to know. This much I know at least: He would not have sent you on a wild chase without a purpose. Trust in His judgement for even the Great Spirit can prove to be deceptive to His enemies."

She stands smiling warmly. The fire in her hearth blazes suddenly to an impossible intensity.

"Indeed, Dear One, the heart you have saved this winter is true to you. It shines like a summer sun upon your soul. Cherish him for he is sent to warm you by his light."

Her voice becomes soft and distant, the light around me becomes intense and I open my eyes, dazzled by the light on a shiny object. My eyes slowly focus. A silver object in the shape of half a sun and half a moon hangs from a cord around Halim's neck. This is the gift my godmother gave Halim—a talisman of life and protection. I look up to see Halim's concerned face close to mine, a butterfly hovering just behind him.

"Azizi, Azizi, are you well?"

My heart is indeed lighter, the fog around me has cleared and rays of brilliant light pierce the damp air. The brilliant blue butterfly still hovers behind him. I recognise it as a sacred symbol of the goddess.

I hug him tightly.

"Halim, I am well, thanks to you."

We spent the rest of the day quietly leaving the foot of the mountain and by the end of the day we finally reach the edge of the Great Desert.

CHAPTER SIXTEEN

Halim stands, a little amused, watching me when we first reach the Great Desert, studying my amazement. The first steps I take, the ground gives slightly underfoot, and I am slipping sideways and making a soft noise, like a whisper. With a shock, I remember my first dream of Ijlal in the desert and the strange way my feet had felt on what I thought was snow. I kneel upon the sand and touch it with my hands, scooping it up and letting it trickle through my fingers. It is warm, fine, and dry. I will soon learn to curse its fine grain, that seems to find its way into everything. Memories flood my mind. My first waking dream; the maps my godmother had shown me, her voice still echoing assuring me that I would one day see the great desert.

The sun sets in a blaze of glory, lighting the dunes as far as the eye can see in a glow of deepest red that gradually softens to a shade of pink.

The shadows of the mules stretch out to impossible length towards the East. Hours pass and the dunes now stand etched like frozen waves, glowing pale against a midnight sky.

The crescent moon has risen and now stands midway in the heavens. I sit mesmerized by this land. Halim patiently unloads the mules in preparation for our night's stop over.

That first night we sleep the sleep of the blessed under a canopy of stars. The next day we rise as the sky turns a pale shade of blue. Halim wraps padding around the animals' hooves, explaining that this is to protect them from the heat of the sand. I did not immediately understand, but by the middle of the morning, the air shimmers eerily with the heat of the sun, the glaring light stabbing at my eyes. The air is dry, and I imagine I am standing in front of the blacksmith's furnace on a hot summer's day. No sound other than the squeak of my steps on the sand and my hard breathing can be heard.

I begin to shed my clothing, which has taken a strangle hold on my body. Halim immediately rushes up with a strong admonishment. We stop long enough for us to change into clothing more appropriate for this climate. Halim pulls out a robe similar to the one I saw Ijlal wear on those early days of their visit to my mountain home. Halim explains how to wear this and the turban, calling it a Shemagh, which once wrapped over my head affords a little shade over my eyes. The remaining length, he explains, is to veil my face to protect it from the direct light and the dust. He shows me how to breathe to conserve my energy and what little moisture is left in my mouth. He advises me to breathe through my nose as much as possible and rubs some ointment on my lips, saying this will prevent them from drying and cracking. Handing me a full water skin, made from sheep skin, he tells me to only sip when absolutely necessary. Now at last I understand the ancient saying, "Do not cast your water upon the sand."

Halim also wraps a loose cloth over the beasts' muzzles.

What I had imagined would be such an adventure, at reaching the Great Desert, soon turns into a feat of endurance. Each step becomes harder as each foot slips in the sand, requiring just that little extra effort at each step. I observe Halim, wondering at his ease. I notice that he has a rhythm and movement different to a mountain walk. His steps flow with his body, adapting to the fluidity of the sand. I attempt to imitate this rhythm and at once fall face down.

I pick myself up, cursing the extra quantity of sand that has found its way into my clothing. Halim looks back and once he ascertains that I am unhurt, looks again to the front without pausing in his step. The sand, which at first had been warm, gradually becomes intolerably hot.

I begin to think that I cannot go on like this when Halim calls a stop. He explains that this is the Cârem, the hottest part of the day, when travellers stop and sleep, waiting for the sun to sink and the temperature to cool. From now on, we will be travelling mostly at night. Quickly using two sticks, he sets up a large, sloping shelter with a light gauze material. This provides enough shade for the animals, Halim, and me. He then spreads a slightly coarser material on the ground and instructs me to lie down and go to sleep.

Halim is soon asleep, his soft breathing settling into a regular pattern.

I watch him, marvelling at all that knowledge buried deeply into that soft gentle face. My heart is pounding in my chest, and the sensation of bees buzzing manifests in my stomach. On impulse, I lean over and very softly kiss his face. Then I settle back, my thoughts wandering the byways of my mind like an excited child looking everywhere at once.

I awake with a gentle shaking from Halim. The sky is already turning dark blue, strands of pink stretching across the sky. The shadows are again long over the dunes. Halim has packed most of the gear. I help him put away the rest.

He attaches a pouch to each of the animals and carefully pours some water in each. Not a drop is spilled as each beast drinks and eats thus. My lips and throat are parched.

The promised oasis is two more days of travel away. There, we will meet up with a desert tribe known to Halim. He will negotiate with them to take me farther, to the rendezvous place where I am to meet up with Ijlal.

We speak little about my mission. I do not know what I would have told him had he pressed me for details. I am not sure myself that I am on the right quest. It seems to me that the prince I was to protect has already been taken. All I can say to Halim is that this matter is now in the hands of the Great Spirit. I do not know what I will do once I meet up with Ijlal. Curiosity to meet his beloved, the one I have seen in the dancing flames drives me on in part.

This is a land where distance is not a physical concept measured in strides, but by the time it takes to get from one place to another. The second day, in the early morning about two hours following the dawn, the animals begin to show nervousness for no explainable reason and begin to look around from side to side. Halim looks up into the sky with a worried look on his face.

Everything to me seems absolutely the same as it has been for the last two days: an immensity of sand that stretches on forever, a relentless heat that saps my energy deep into the ground, and a sky of impossible blue with never a cloud in it. Halim's composure and the animals' restlessness combine to make me apprehensive. I think perhaps that we are lost and that the animals have at once sensed this. The land being so devoid of landmarks, I find it easier to trust an animal's instincts than any human knowledge of the way. Halim stops and the animals, still fretting are standing beside him. Halim first looks ahead, seemingly peering into the distance, then behind us, and then as if looking for something, now mimicks the animals by looking from side to side. Had I been in a better mood, the whole thing would have struck me as highly comical. Now, I just want to find out what it is that is so wrong. Surely the oasis cannot be too far away.

I am about to speak when Halim holds up his hand for quiet. I cannot hear anything. Just at that moment, a quick short gust of wind catches my turban and blows it across my face. That is all.

Halim at once whips around to the horizon ahead of us and peers into the distance. He quickly orders me to follow. As fast as dragging the animals behind him will allow, he scampers down the neighbouring slope of sand to a flat area. There he turns the beasts facing the way we have come. He orders me to sit behind the animals and to wrap my turban around my face.

I ask him what is wrong.

"It is the Cassim," he replies and points to the horizon. I look carefully. The horizon is still there, admittedly it seems a little blurry, but then in the heat of the day, I cannot trust my eyesight.

"I do not understand."

He looks at me, looks over his shoulder, and then again says, "The Cassim comes. Look again."

Once more I look. In the time that it had taken for that short exchange, the horizon is now a mountain rolling menacingly towards us. Terror seizes my heart. I cannot comprehend a storm cloud so low to the ground, and all the colour of sand moving at the speed of the wind, without a single sound.

"It is a sandstorm blowing from the Huda, the great mouth of the desert. It is the Cassim. We will wait here until it passes."

Mad! I think he is completely mad. We are to just wait until this inferno descends upon us and devours us? But then, where could we possibly hide in this featureless land? Hiding behind the animals seemed at least a solution, if not cowardly.

With the viciousness of a spring-fed torrent, the wind tears at us and then the sand blasts all around us relentlessly. Soon, I cannot see Halim who is sitting next to me. I hold out my hand, his meets mine and I hold onto him, my only link to the living in this land of death.

Disembodied screams whistle past my head, and ghostly fingers angrily grab at my clothes. No matter how tight I hold on to my garment, some piece of material becomes loose and flaps uselessly in the raging wind. The sand seeps into every loose flap; I can feel my skin being grazed wherever I have only a single layer of clothing.

The intensity of the storm grows and with it the pressure of the wind. My ears are hurting. Utterly confused and disoriented, I feel the sand slowly building up around me, immobilizing me into a sandy grave. I want to scream. I think I might die and briefly imagine my bones picked dry by the sand and sun, lying scattered in the vastness of the Great Desert.

I did scream Halim's name, the word snatched by the furious and jealous wind from my mouth, the moment it was uttered. With one final blast, the wind crashes like a wave upon my back and moves on.

Almost as quickly as it had come, the storm abates and disperses. Once more the sky is blue, and the deafening silence of the desert fills my ears. The animals behind us stir, half buried; they have taken on the shape of anonymous sand dunes. We rise slowly, and Halim shows me how to loosen the sand that has penetrated every fold of our clothing. I laugh, exhausted but relieved to have survived this ordeal.

The sun sets amidst an ocean of sandy waves frozen to a dusty pink. The sky once more ablaze in its final glory deepens quickly to dark blue.

On the horizon, now distinctly etched out in black silhouettes, stands a group of trees looking like tousled hair atop long, slender necks.

My heart races. This is the place where we will find the desert tribe. Halim will negotiate with them to take me to where I will meet Ijlal.

We agree that they should not know who I am. If asked, I have come from his village in search of my maternal grandfather who went abroad some years before. My family's affairs require him to return. I am to meet someone from Schiraz who saw him last.

We walk on, my thoughts racing. A little while later, a series of prickles run up the back of my neck and I turn around. But I resume my walk as there is nothing behind us that I can see. It must be nerves. I take long, deep breaths, mentally practicing a teaching of my godmother to still the mind.

As my mind grows quieter and we near the oasis, my perception confirms what my instincts have already picked up—someone is behind us, following stealthily some distance away. I do not alert Halim as my mind has now reached out to this presence and I do not detect any danger.

We reach the oasis; I am astounded to see so many green things flourish in the middle of this sandy landscape. A group of tribesmen some women and children have gathered to watch our arrival. They look upon us with open curiosity and I feel under scrutiny. Halim greets the people in their native tongue, in a strange exchange of formal greetings. He gives them first his greetings in the name of the Spirit, whose shed tears have given life to the world, and then asks them how their families are, and then how their animals are. Each question is answered formally with praise to Apphat and the Great Spirit; they respond with questions about how his family and beasts are doing.

Halim then asks them for the hospitality of the oasis. A long uncomfortable pause follows. At this point I turn and face the person who has been following us.

A little distance away, walking quietly towards us, is a single tall figure. I can make out that this man is carrying a sword at his side.

Halim turns in surprise and looks at me, with a questioning look. I keep my eyes on the soldier. As he walks past us and joins the assembled tribe, there is a palpable release of tension amongst the tribes people, as if by a secret means his movement has ordained that we are not a threat.

Only then does the leader of the tribe extend his welcome to us. He invites us in the name of the joyful Spirit to join them in the peace and life-giving sustenance of the oasis. I can feel the eyes of the soldier on the back of my neck.

I follow Halim and the tribesmen to the centre of the oasis, there to be amazed and mesmerized. First, I hear the distinct gurgle of a stream and beyond belief in this arid land, I see a stream. Clear and cool, it runs through the desert sand, and along its banks, fig trees and other plants flourish. My heart momentarily yearns for my forest and the cool rivers that run through it.

The people are warm and welcoming but very direct in their manner. I can tell that apart from the strange formalities of greeting, no time is ever wasted here in getting to the heart of things. I guess that for a people who live one moment to the next, never knowing when death will open its arms, little regard is given to matters of no consequence.

Sitting in the chieftain's tent, I admire the rich colours of the cushions and the tapestries that hang on the walls. I understand that they provide shelter from the elements, keeping out the desert wind and the cold of night. They also serve as a defined area for people to sit and meet, as well as creating a sense of status. Every object is a work of art but also has a function. Colourful objects, which I had at first thought to be purely decorative, also serve as implements for food or drink. Outside the tent, some of the tribesmen begin to sing to the dry beat of a drum. In the latter part of the song, I recognise descriptions of Halim, the two mules and myself. Already we form part of the oral history transmitted in song form.

While Halim speaks to the chieftain, I become aware of the intense gaze of the soldier. Something in his countenance both interests me and puts me on my guard.

The chief explains the political situation that requires the protection of the tribe by a soldier. Since recent attacks on other tribes by the Sorceress's Scarlet Robes, every tribe is now on its guard and at pains to protect itself. This soldier has offered his services and the tribe is glad of it. The chieftain explains that this is not an ordinary soldier, but a highly trained fighting machine, who can stealthily assess a situation before it gets out of hand. The chief relates an incident, where a pack of bandits was eliminated one at a time by this soldier, before the tribe had even known it was in any danger. There existed a covert sign between the soldier and the tribe. If the soldier approaches with his sword sheathed, all is well, if his hand rests on the pommel of the sword, there is suspicion and if the sword is drawn, whoever the stranger is, he or she will fall dead before a word is uttered.

I did not hear where this soldier is from as at that moment, my attention is drawn by his hand reaching out for his cup revealing a dark mark on his forearm.

The representation of a simple double axe, briefly sighted, scatters my thoughts as they flutter in my mind, attempting to remember where I have seen this symbol before. The double-headed axe with a line across it is the symbol for a Healer of Apphat. The plain double axe is of a different significance. Like butterflies caught in a capricious breeze, my thoughts find no definite place to land.

A scream rings out suddenly, accompanied by heavy, heart-rending sobs, and soon a cacophony of confused interjections and calls of concerns break the peace of the camp.

The chief gets up and walks out. The soldier is already at the entrance to the tent.

A man is holding a small boy of perhaps twelve years in his arms. Next to him and holding the boy's hand is his distraught mother. The boy appears limp and pale. He is conscious but terror fills his eyes. There is a large red swelling on his foot, and I quickly understand that the boy has been stung by one of the deadliest creatures that lives in the desert, a small animal that in self-defence if threatened, strikes much like one of the snakes in my mountains.

I make out from the dialogue that, though distraught, the parents are resigned to the inevitable death of their child. They come to the chief, as is their custom, to release him into his hands. As chief, it will be his duty to utter the ritual of prayers for the dead and dispose of the body.

The sobs receed from my consciousness. The night sky looks down upon me.

The rustle of a light breeze murmurs in the palm grove, the smell of wood fires drifts across the air like drying linen in the sun, and the moon shines like a polished scimitar amidst a dark blue sky of a thousand stars.

My mind reels at the recognition of my first waking dream. The sight of the sorrow in the mother's eyes, the defeat of the father as he holds his child, the gaze of the soldier upon my neck; I seek my inner being and ask in a silent prayer for permission. In the briefest moment, I know what has to be done.

Calling out to Halim, I instruct him to get my package of herbs.

There is a moment of hesitation as Halim speaks in his mind of the dangers of revealing my identity. I respond to his mind that I can be a healer regardless of where I come from. Halim goes to fetch the herbs.

I turn to the man and speak in a calm voice and with the authority that my godmother has taught me, one that will not countenance argument. "Place this child on the ground before me."

Halim, who has often seen me tending to his people and his sheep, brings a bowl of steaming water.

I hold the boy's hand and gently impress on his mind that all will be well and that there is no need for fear. Using the customary healing sign preamble of the Naasséenes, healers following the Mores of Apphat, I move my hand to align the boy's energies; my sleeve falls back too late to conceal the mark of my first initiation. I hear a sharp intake of breath and am aware that the soldier has moved and now stands before me and openly stares at me.

The poison is natural, and the method I will use is effective; a man-made poison would be a different story. The herbs slow the progress of the poison and draws it back to its point of entry. Then using my own mind power, a particular technique only recently acquired in my last months of apprenticeship, I begin to neutralise the poison and re-balance the boy's own system, encouraging it to fight this poison and awaken within itself the power to recognise its nature and oppose it.

The boy is young and open to the healing. It takes only moments before his colour comes back and his breathing eases. The stares and silence of the crowd upon my back are palpable, a burden I still find difficult to endure.

I turn to the parents and instruct them. "Make sure that the boy drinks all of the tea prepared from the remainder of the herbs. The poultice on his foot should remain until morning. He should rest for at least a day."

The parents stare at me in disbelief. The silence weighs heavily as the tribes people look upon the scene with ill-disguised doubt. I hear someone muttering that the child will die soon, that the poison will surely kill as it has always done.

"He is a healer of Apphat; he bears the mark of an initiate. Your child will be well."

The deep and firm sound of the soldier's voice could have been thunder for the impact it makes. The soldier challenges with his eyes anyone to disagree with him.

Halim looks at me.

I shrug my shoulders and go to wash my hands and splash water upon my face.

I come back to a hushed tent. The chief rises to welcome me to a seat of honour nearer him and a drink is offered to me. No questions are asked. It seems that the tribe has agreed without reserve that they will take me to the point of my rendezvous, and further if I require it.

The next morning, both father and mother, with the boy between them, have come to thank me. The little boy lunges forward and embraces me throwing his little arms around my neck and squeezing me hard and kisses me on the cheek. The gesture reminds me so much of the mind connection with Halim. My heart melts at this simple gesture. I hold him in return, thankful—bowing in my mind to the Power of the Great Spirit within—that this child has not died. Some of the people have gathered and cheer loudly, the sceptics if any now convinced of the healing.

The woman steps forward and introduces herself. "I am Fariqa, and this is our only child, Saeed. My husband and I owe you a life debt."

"Fariqa, I am glad your son is well. His smile and your happiness are enough for me. You owe me no debt."

Husband and wife look at each other. Halim who has been watching from a distance with a look of total devotion, catches my eye and makes a small gesture with his head. I understand that to refuse their offer will be considered an insult.

Realising that no amount of assurance that the life I helped save is sufficient reward, I agree, asking them to make themselves available if ever I require their assistance. In their eyes, this is but a small price to pay for such a large debt and so, reluctantly, they agree.

There is no longer suspicion in the soldier's eyes when I see him looking at me. Now though, I see a question and the answer makes me uncomfortable. In those moments I catch myself mentally classifying my herbs.

CHAPTER SEVENTEEN

The tribe packs its camp the next day and moves for a day's journey to a small town north of Schiraz. Once there, they will trade their stock of salt and other goods, before setting out again on their never-ending nomadic journey to re-stock. On the way to Schiraz, they will deliver me to my meeting place. We arrive in the late afternoon outside the walls that surround the town and set up camp there until the morning. Knowing that this will probably be the last of any rest I will experience, I take advantage to explore the town and further educate myself in the language and customs of these people.

I reach the marketplace in the centre of the old town. This is set up very much in the manner of all marketplaces, a fountain surrounded by low buildings. The building themselves look age worn and their walls made from mud and whitewashed, have over the years mellowed to a creamy yellow. I look around at the now empty square and turning into the setting light of the afternoon, a tall figure silhouetted against the failing light approaches me. It is the soldier who asks with deference if he can accompany me.

I nod in agreement, butterflies taking flight in my stomach. We walk, and he takes the time to point out things of interest commenting on the culture and customs of these people and comparing them with other tribes he has encountered on his travels. He laughs easily and often places an arm around my shoulders to better conspire in a joke. These are moments of sheer delight, savoured and looked for.

His name is Hasan, which in his father's tongue means 'Handsome and Good.' His dark brown eyes intrigue me. He comes from a tribe who live deep in the desert of Gibrar. I had overheard the tribesmen talk, and what snippets I could gather from the conversations around the campfire, indicated that his people are a fierce warrior tribe and very proud.

He stands a little taller than me, and his body, as far as I can tell from the flowing white garment he wears, is slim and sinewy. He rubs patchouli oil in his hair to stop it from drying, and this smell is most beguiling. He moves with ease, the muscles in his forearms fluid like a mountain stream emphasising the tattoos that I can now plainly see. His eyes capture my imagination. They are like deep caverns in which I can see flashes of warm fires that invite me to know this man better.

We wander aimlessly through the emptying stalls and then make our way through the meandering streets. I notice the respect from the people in the marketplace as they move aside when they see him. Several times now I catch him looking at me steadfastly. This unnerves me, and it reminds me too much of the serious way my godmother looked at me. At once I ask him why he is looking at me in this manner.

He looks around at the people and then in a slightly conspiratorial manner says, "Come, you and I must talk. I think it would make you feel better if we were out of earshot."

More butterflies take flight in the pit of my stomach. I push my feelings down and try to look for a rational reason why I am so happy to follow this man down a deserted alley.

We reach the outskirts of the market at a low city wall that overlooks the desert. Here, there is a large, paved terrace. He sits down and bids me sit near him.

Deeply, he looks at me. He stretches out his hand and caresses my arm smiling. "Relax, we are just here to talk. I know so little of your country, and I want to ask you some questions."

I nod, feeling a little disappointed.

He laughs lightly and then adds, "I think it would be better for us both if I come to the point."

He looks steadily and seriously into my eyes and says, "You are a lover of men."

I gasp, staring at him as my mind races for a reply, any reply. I am formulating a denial in my mind but catch his eyes requiring nothing but the truth. I remember my first apprentice's oath, to always tell the truth. I swallow and reply, "Yes."

"And you find shame in this?"

"Some."

"In my region, such men are honoured. They are the healers, the herbalists, the teachers, and Seers of our people, and more than a few of them become soldiers."

I look at him openly. He is a soldier. Here is a man like me who finds other men attractive and is so open and sure of this.

He continues, "These, as you have heard, are some of the fiercest warriors of the desert. Do you understand why they are considered so?"

"No."

"A man defending his lover will fight more fiercely by his side, than if he were defending a stranger."

"Is that the tattoo mark you bear on your forearm? Does it indicate you are one of these soldiers?"

He brushes his sleeve up and smiles. "Yes and no. Yes, this mark is the mark of a soldier who follows the Mores of Apphat. It also holds important details that mark my rank among my people."

I contemplate an army of such soldiers, standing resolute and proud in the face of adversity. Understanding dawns on me. The readings of the books in my godmother's house come to mind and their mysteries slowly fall into place. Even if one of these soldiers were to be killed or wounded, with what resolve he would be avenged by his lover.

Hasan continues, "Azizi, I do not understand the customs of your people who would deny such love."

I think long and hard, remembering past hurts in my hometown; the villagers' disapproving looks, the hurtful words and teasing of other children. I remember the anger of a man whose son I had embraced, not understanding why he was so angry. I could not even now understand what I had done that was considered so wrong. Then I remember the legends and stories, that had reached our village of the customs of the Naasséenes, lovers of men. How those stories were told in hushed and disgusted tones, and the words of loathing used to describe these people. Yet no one was ever willing to state the reasons. And so, I grew up with these impressions, avoiding village life and never speaking of them with my godmother, for fear of incurring the same disapproval.

I explain this to Hasan.

Love and comprehension in his eyes, he holds my hand. "Azizi, will you hear the true customs of the Naasséenes from one who has lived among them?"

I nod, thinking we would visit someone in the town.

Hasan begins, "It is customary for men amongst the Naasséenes to initiate a young man who has come of age into the knowledge and pleasures of love. It is a greater honour for the boy's family if the man is a soldier who follows the Mores of Apphat. This initiation is called Damna. Between both men a bond of great friendship is thus formed, which is honourable. The Naasséenes do not differentiate between the love of two mature individuals, regardless of their sex. Love is revered."

I swallow hard. "Your customs are beautiful and sacred."

"I will tell you of a sacred custom amongst these people. From time to time, a man and a woman who have coupled are unable to bring forth a child. Sometimes it is not the woman who is barren but the man. If this happens, the man will go to him who bestowed Damna, and they will agree that his seed be taken to the woman, that a child may be borne. He or she, who bestows life thus, becomes a guardian for the child. Many children are brought forth in this way. They are loved and cherished as other children are. All children are taught to have respect for their parents. Some children know that in addition to their mother and father they also have a secret guardian. In this village, the guardian could be any one of the men or women, and so each child learns to respect all and value all members of his community. The bond of love among my people is very strong."

He looks at me once more with those dark eyes. My whole being warms in the setting sun, and I shiver under his gaze.

Once more he strokes my arm and adds, "So, do you understand why you honour me, when I see the love in your eyes?"

I do not answer him. The dry desert wind is just beginning to blow from the East, stinging my eyes. A clap of wind echoes around one of the dunes. I bow my head in silence.

He takes my hand saying, "Come Azizi, I will not torture you with my taunts. Let us go back to the camp."

He helps me up, and together we walk quietly in the setting sun. The cooling wind brings upon it a myriad of smells from the markets. I step lightly, a weight seemingly gone from my shoulders. The sky is the colour of my heart.

I think hard and long about what he said. I suspect now so much of what my godmother has been trying to tell me. She knew my heart. I am restless for the evening, my whole being yearns for something, and now I think I know what.

I venture outside my tent that night for the evening meal. The camp has gathered around the fire. I sit as much alone as I can and quietly eat my meal. Halim has joined some of the younger men and seems at ease with them.

The flames are dancing across the circle, and the gaze of his eyes is upon me.

I look up. The sky is clear as water and adorned like the dark blue veil of the Tassili women, with a thousand shimmering jewels. The cool evening breeze blows from the East, from the

Ocean of Boundless Joy, whispering in the palm leaves. Children are laughing.

Embers in the fire are glowing. I see dunes in the distance scattered like white satin cushions in the moonlight. The sounds of voices and soft laughter breaking like small ocean waves, lull me into a sweet stillness. A waft of oranges and cinnamon caress my face and leaves me yearning.

I see him rise slowly and gracefully. He moves across the circle, his desert clothes flowing like white sea grass in the tide. My stomach knots as I realise that he is walking in my direction. The heady smell of patchouli oil announces his presence.

I look up and meet his dark eyes. He asks me to walk with him.

The world stops. My mouth is dry. I hear no other sound other than his words and my pounding heart.

I rise and turn to follow him. He is at my side and sounds of the camp return. I hear laughter and fear that someone is laughing at me.

We walk on, beyond the firelight, into the coolness of the moonlight.

We slow down, walking aimlessly. No words are exchanged. Suddenly I feel his hand take mine. I almost draw back in surprise, and gently he holds on to me. His hand is large, powerful, yet his skin is soft, his grasp firm. We walk further until we reach the outer edge of the oasis and begin to walk into the surrounding dunes.

There he stops. He turns slowly to me, looking deeply into my eyes. His hand that held mine now moves along my arm. Now both his hands are on my shoulders. He caresses one of my cheeks and taking hold of my head in his hands. Gently, slowly, he leans towards me. The touch of his soft lips on mine, I smell the patchouli oil of his hair.

I feel a fire in my groin. I surrender myself to him.

We melt upon the sand.

~

I AWAKE THE NEXT morning, a smile throughout my being, and sense of deep satisfaction at having fulfilled a longing. I experience a sense of pride at having come of age and no longer feel like a child.

As soon as I rise though, an irrational fear enters my mind and finds its way to my stomach, settling as a knot.

How will I face him, to whom I have revealed the most secret and tender part of myself? I will feel forever naked before his eyes. How can I look upon his face, when my eyes the night before, had voraciously gazed upon his whole naked form? How can I without blushing speak to him of my deep desire to lay with him again?

I consider the options: running away, staying in my tent, or just languishing to my death.

In the end, I consider running or hiding cowardly and a lie to myself. Since dying is not a practical option, I decide to muster my courage and face the day.

I reach the oasis to carry out my daily ablutions. Together with two of the other tribesmen, I wash in the clear, refreshing water. We exchange the customary greetings in the name of the God of Water, invoking blessings upon each other's families and beasts of burden. I notice that the men address me with unusual respect. I do not think that this is still a remnant of the healing and so I am puzzled.

I dress and turn.

There he is standing, obviously already washed.

I feel trapped. His broad, warm smile eases my embarrassment and slowly I move towards him, a little knot of excitement building within me. My worries melt slowly as I near him.

"The morning's greetings to you, Illustrious One."

I am taken aback by the greeting. He hands me a small parcel of yellow silk.

Puzzled, I unwrap it. Contained therein lies a short ceremonial scimitar. The blade catching the early morning light, shines out a flash of silver edged with a hint of rose. As I look up with wonder in my eyes, he smiles that warm smile of his and before I can utter a word, he places a small necklace around my neck. The necklace for the most part is made of small wooden beads, with one single triangular talisman in the centre of it. This is made of metal and bears a strange symbol. The triangle forms an arrowhead. The engraved stem extends all the way to the base, dividing the remaining shape into two. The left half contains a spiral, that unwinds downwards and runs across the base, to form another spiral rising on the right side. I turn the talisman over and on the other side, there is a replica of the simple double headed axe tattooed on his arm, freshly engraved.

"These are my gifts, Illustrious One, for the honour you have bestowed upon me by choosing me for the Damna."

I must look completely confused.

He laughs and then explains, "In my country, this is a tradition. As the one to have initiated you into your first love experience, it is my duty to bestow upon you gifts in honour of your coming of age. In my village, there would be feasting for three days, honouring you. No longer will others refer to you as a boy. You are bestowed the title of 'Illustrious One' and accorded the rights and privileges of manhood. You are permitted to sit on the Council of Elders.

"Since we are not in my village, the necklace that I give you bears both the symbol of your manhood, and my mark. This mark will be recognized by all those who know my tribe and me. It not only identifies you as a man, but that you are under my protection. Woe to any who would harm you, for they would answer to my wrath and that of my tribe."

"But I have nothing for you."

He laughs again, and caressing me most tenderly, he looks into my eyes saying, "Your gift is the honour of your youth, and the first of your love."

He looks long and lovingly into my eyes and with a note of sadness adds, "Although we have shared the rituals of Damna, and there will always be a bond between us, we must not enter into the union of Lovers. I sense that I am not the sacred one for you. Another awaits your love. I often glimpse him in the depth of your eyes and in those moments, I sense the wildness of the ocean in your soul."

This is the last day before the tribe will take me to the rendezvous. Halim has made all the trades he can and is packed. I give him some beautiful cloth and other practical items as gifts for my godmother and for my father. These are wrapped away, and Halim is preparing to make the long, lonely journey back to my beloved mountains.

As much as I long for my forests, something in me is changed. I feel older and the need for my maternal country is now subdued before the dawn of my manhood. A part of me feels right at last. My heart has opened and through it I can feel a strange and exhilarating joy flowing.

My godmother once said that I would not come fully into my power until my heart had found the flame of love, and my mind had found the way to sit by its hearth and contemplate its pure power.

I had not understood then. Now a fire rages at the centre of my being, struggling to find the air to combust it into an eternal glow.

I turn. Halim stands before me. He smiles warmly at me. I am lost for words; I have not spoken to him since losing my boyhood. I feel a sense of guilt that in some way I have betrayed his love for me. Memories of the time spent on the mountainside with Halim tending his sheep flood my mind. I remember those eyes of his, so deep and enticing, so full of promised warmth and love.

"Azizi…" Even now he hesitates to call me by my given name.

His eyes fall upon the talisman that hangs around my neck.

My breath catches in my throat, and I know my cheeks are blushing.

He smiles; tentatively he reaches and touches the talisman. A shudder runs up my spine.

I want to hold him; I want to tell him that he was my first love and always will be.

"Azizi… that is a beautiful talisman you wear." Tears are in his eyes.

"Halim…" Words from my heart are caught in my throat.

He looks at me with a serious look. "Azizi, I came to say farewell. I must return to the mountains."

"Halim," I struggle to find the words amidst the swell of emotions. "Halim, my love goes with you. I wish you safe journey. I will watch over you."

For a moment he looks upon me with awe, then resolutely and gently he takes me in his arms and embraces me, kissing me on both cheeks.

My heart feels like bursting. I hold him tight.

Releasing me gently he looks into my eyes. "Azizi, wherever and whenever you have need of me, send for me and I shall be there."

With one last embrace he turns, taking the mules' bridle and, without looking back, walks off into the vastness of the great desert. I stand there watching, until he becomes a speck on the horizon. A sudden breeze blows towards his disappearing form, and finally his small silhouette eclipses from my sight.

The sky has turned a deep purple with strands of dark red slashing across the night sky.

The gentle fragrance of warm hay lingers on my shoulders. I realise tears are running down my cheeks. I turn and walk to my tent.

C H A P T E R   E I G H T E E N

The following morning, the tribe packs and sets off to Schiraz. The tribes people have shown me great kindness and hospitality, and as a parting gift, they give me a small horse and a tent decorated in the traditional colours of their culture. This is a small affair cleverly designed to pack down to a minimum size and yet once fully erected, with the aid of concealed flexible bamboo rods, will accommodate four grown men.

Halfway through the day, they stop briefly to point out the road I should take to reach my rendezvous. It lies due west on the sandy edges of the Great Ocean of Malkizar. A shudder runs through me at the name of the Ocean of Great Despair.

The tribe heads southwest towards the great city of Schiraz. They are due to meet with the Sultan Rashãd, overlord of all the desert regions, and father to Ijlal.

My meeting with Ijlal is to remain secret, away from the prying eyes of a large city.

Hasan holds my hands and looks at me deeply for a long time. Finally, he says, "Azizi, beloved healer of Apphat, and more if my instincts are true. If I thought you needed me, I would be with you."

I can see him torn. He is a soldier hired to protect this tribe until they reach their destination, and he has also vowed sacred guardianship of me through Damna.

"My duty to this tribe will end once we reach Schiraz. If you have need of me, you only need to show the talisman you wear to any soldier. My mark will be known. If I receive such a message, I will be at your side with all speed. Farewell, Azizi, may the Guardian Spirit be with you."

He holds me briefly to him, the sweet scent of patchouli oil enveloping me like a cloud of protection. He then turns and with one last wave of his hand, runs off in his tireless soldier's stride to catch up with the tribe, which by now is some way off.

I remain looking out in the late afternoon, experiencing once more that total aloneness I have not felt since my childhood.

The silence of the Great Desert weighs all around me. A gust of wind blowing from the west stirs me from my reverie.

The tribe is but a dot on the horizon, and now and then a long moving shadow appears to float slightly above the ground. This is a phenomenon common to these parts. The air as it heats during the day warps and briefly acts as a looking glass. Objects a long way away suddenly appear like phantoms shimmering above the horizon.

The shadows suddenly wink off as the air shifts and cools. I walk on, alone with my thoughts, towards the shifting breeze that carry the unmistakable scent of salt.

The sun sinks in a fiery blaze, caressing the surrounding sand dunes and setting them like frozen waves in a shade of softest pink. The westerly breeze fresh from the ocean blows directly at me, setting tears coursing down my face.

I reach the meeting point late in the evening. Although the sun has set, the sky will remain light for many hours yet. This is a crossroads of desert routes, frequented by the sultan's couriers and traders, travelling between Schiraz and the Northern Kingdom of Glesskerel and its powerful ruler.

I have made good time, though this is the day prescribed for our meeting, I set up camp and wait for his arrival. I recall the maps of my godmother, when on long winter nights she would pore over the landmarks of our country explaining this and that. At each region, she would explain the landscape and instruct me on the culture of the people who lived there.

Although I can see the vast grey expanse of water that is the Ocean of Malkizar, I am not close enough to perceive the detail. A constant drone reaches my ears, now louder and then softer, a strange mixture resembling the loud wind in the mountain trees and the crashing of the streams down my beloved mountains. I shiver. The sight and thought of such an expanse of water challenges my rational mind.

To the north stands the renowned and treacherous Huda Pass. This is a narrow channel that snakes through a range of tall sandstone cliffs, home of the Huda people. These people have carved their homes out of the rock. They are a shy yet fierce tribe. Anyone who enters the pass is always secretly watched, and their presence known the entire way. If the Huda people take a dislike to a traveller, for whatever reason, he is never seen again. Many traders travel the pass accompanied by paid armed guards. Even this is not always a guarantee of safe passage. The Sultan of Schiraz has made a truce for the safeguard of his soldiers and tradesmen. They identify themselves by wearing the Badge of Schiraz. One of the Huda people will then guide them through the labyrinth of the pass.

Directly to the south, on a two-day journey, lies the great city of Schiraz. The region is renowned for its sacred Schiraz tree that flowers once every seven years and bears a precious stone.

The city itself is built on a rocky outcrop in the Great Desert of Keyab. Within the centre of the city is its famous well which, according to history, has never dried up in two thousand years. The city is defended on all sides by tall, solid walls carved out of the rock itself. It is said it could withstand an endless siege.

Lost as I am in my thoughts, waiting for the tell-tale sand flurries that would announce a horseman from the South, I do not see, and only too late sense, a presence nearby. I look up sharply and there is Ijlal but a dune away, looking at me and smiling. I smile back, acknowledging that I have been caught out. His Companions appear stealthily one by one and without sound. His followers stand a little aside.

They are the pride of the desert—sworn together as a band of youths to follow their leader in defence of their ideals. Passion glows in his followers' eyes—that they idolise him is obvious.

Ijlal approaches with his arms outstretched, his warm smile seemingly lighting up his whole being.

"Azizi, my brother, welcome!"

He embraces me and once again I experience an odd mixture

of emotions arise in me. Equipped with my recent experience of Damna, initial embarrassment gives way to knowledge of what it is to be held by one I love. He has not changed. If anything, he is more assured in his own territory. His skin still smells vaguely of cinnamon, and warmth fills my heart. I return his embrace, knowing for certain in my heart the nature of our deep friendship.

Upon a signal from him, his followers approach to be introduced.

It is with some curiosity that they look upon me, my fair skin and blue eyes contrasting with their darker features. The tallest among them steps forward. I recognise him immediately by his serious face and intense gaze that does not falter.

"Azizi, this is my cousin Faruq, eldest son to my uncle Giafar who accompanied me to your godmother's house last winter. Cousin, this is Azizi, my brother, beloved and favoured of the Guardian Spirit of Apphat."

That introduction did little for modesty. The Companions look upon me with awe.

Faruq stands a moment, appraising me. He then lays his hands on my shoulders and kisses me on both cheeks, as is their custom. He looks directly at me,"Welcome Azizi." Faruq steps back.

Curiosity possesses me to see in the flesh Ijlal's beloved, of whom stories of his great beauty have already sprung far and wide. I know, however, that in their culture the most important guest will be introduced last.

In turn they step forward and greet me in the same way, their warmth and sincerity unmistakable.

First comes Husam, whose name means 'sword edge'. Unlike his companions, he has thrown his outer robe over his shoulders, revealing the well-defined body of an athlete. A sword hangs by his side, his left hand lightly resting on the pommel; but I think his name refers more to his countenance, a look in his eyes that would not suffer fools and the ability to express an opinion with absolute honesty.

Then Fatin, whose parents have named him for his obvious intelligence. He is a about my height and looking directly into my eyes, with a gentle voice, welcomes me with the words, "Azizi. Beloved." He separates the two words with obvious intent, the second with a slight bow of his head. On the one hand acknowledging me by my name and stating that he not only understands the meaning of my name, but also defers to me as the beloved of the Great Guardian Spirit. He smiles knowingly and embraces me. It is as if I am embracing the softest pillow.

Next the twin brothers, Isamadeen and Rauf. At first, I think it will be difficult to tell them apart. Typical of their kind, their skin is the lightest honey brown. They are of similar build and looks. Both have beautiful, almost over-sized eyes. Isamadeen is a little taller and has a serious air about him. He stands with pride, relaxed and at ease, yet there is a tension about him that makes me think he will spring into action at any moment. The name Isamadeen does him justice; it means 'to guard.' His twin brother, Rauf, on the other hand seems playful, gentle, and soft. His doe like eyes remind me of Halim, gentleness, and mischief in equal amounts. His name means 'merciful and kind.' He smiles with such a sincere expression that it would melt the heart of an avowed enemy.

Cautiously, Rauf touches the skin of my forearm, sending shivers down my spine. He looks up and laughs like a child. Turning to the others, he proclaims, "It is still dough; his flesh has not yet been baked by the sun."

Laughing without malice, the others join him, the initial tension breaking once and for all. His twin Isamadeen, gently admonishes him, punching him lightly on the shoulder.

Jamal, whose name also means 'kind,' and close friend of Rauf, comes forward to greet me. Jamal and Rauf keep each other company and I imagine they would be a handful if they teamed up for mischief. Jamal is thinner than Rauf and shares his look of playfulness. The younger ones have turned fifteen only recently, yet they all move like soldiers.

A tall youth dressed in the traditional desert robes, his face covered except for his eyes, steps forward last.

His eyes meet mine and hold my gaze. My heart leaps as I recognise the flame in those eyes.

Deliberately, Shahulm takes off his head cover. My dream visions of him did hold witness to his beauty. Waves of light brown hair frame a perfectly proportioned face as if sculpted from the purest and lightest wood. His skin is lighter than the others, almost reflecting the fading light. Unlike the other Companions, his dark golden eyes contrast with his pale face, turning up slightly at the ends. He has a deep, expressive look, almost unfathomable, but light sparkles with every move. His top lip is full and shaped like a pair of wings that hover over his bottom lip, fashioned as a delicate petal of a rare flower.

I find myself staring at such impossible perfection. My knees are suddenly weak and may give at any moment. My inner being is trembling, and a vast hollow has opened in my stomach. Unsure of the feelings I am allowing to surface, I swallow, desperately trying to affirm my composure. My mind races with conflicting thoughts of desire and the need to recognise him as Ijlal's lover.

"Azizi, this is my beloved, Shahulm. Shahulm, Azizi, my brother whose wisdom allowed him to see into the stars and create the talisman that you bear, and which unites us."

Standing before me, his smile reaches up to his eyes, lighting his entire being. Shahulm bows placing one palm on his heart. Looking up, he steps close and kisses me on both cheeks.

"Welcome, brother." He speaks with a deep gentle voice that holds a strong foreign accent. The word 'brother' repeated, painfully closes the hollow in the pit of my being and clears my thoughts. A subtle fragrance of spices floats in the air around him. I smile back and bow my head in deference to him whom Ijlal has chosen as his beloved.

The introductions complete, Ijlal takes me by the arm and draws me towards the west, in the direction of the great ocean to speak in private. As we turn, I see the moon of Camlac rising above the horizon. Full and the colour of sand, it rises. A shudder runs through me at the sight, a vague memory taunting my senses. Unable to place the cause of this I turn and listen to Ijlal.

"Azizi, it is good to see you. Have you had a safe trip?"

Leaving out the vision I experienced at the watering pool at the foot of the mountain, I briefly tell him of our trip to the Great Desert. He laughs easily at my first encounter with the Cassim.

"We, on the other hand, had an easy trip of it. Except perhaps..." There he trails off as he reflects on the only incident by the cooking fire early that spring.

"You were psychically attacked one night while you were staring into the flames of your cooking fire. It was one of the Shadows. I was able to scare it away."

A moment of understanding at the recollection of his experience, and that of a branch seemingly falling by itself, is quickly followed by a look of awe. "I heard your voice calling out to me… " He trails off. "You were safeguarding us all the way?"

Within his question is also the uncertainty of how much I can see.

"Only in those moments where I sense danger." I add, "I cannot follow you in your private moments."

He laughs the comment off, but there is a sense of relief in his laughter.

We speak of the political situation. The tribes are all but ready to declare war against the Over Lord. Then we raise the question of the kidnapped religious prince, Elwah. Likewise, Ijlal thinks that perhaps I have been sent on the wrong errand and that danger to him has passed. I relay my godmother's opinion on this matter.

I shift to better face him in the fading light. I notice that his companions are speaking together a little distance away and that Shahulm is standing near the horses, which seem to be fretting. Far in the distance towards the south and the town of Schiraz, a telltale light cloud of sand blowing with the westerly wind announces a horseman. This is probably a courier on urgent business.

I ask Ijlal about the Naasséenes and their spiritual leader, Elwah.

Ijlal begins to give me the same informaton Aïschah has already conveyed to me. The beliefs concerning the reincarnation of the leader of these people, although the same, seem to have a particular significance for his people.

My gaze idly follows the courier travelling towards us,

wondering whether perhaps it is news from Ijlal's father. I can now see that there are two horsemen galloping together. They will be here within a few minutes.

Ijlal is telling me that his uncle is returning this night from the southeastern borders, where there have been rumours of skirmishes. He will be better equipped to give me information on the Naasséenes.

By a trick of the sunset, the moon of Camlac, which had been a pale yellow, slowly turns a blood red. Suddenly the horsemen are upon our group. Hardly anyone gives them attention. This is a well-travelled route for messengers.

Seemingly to avoid collision with the other horses, one of the horsemen goes around the Companions' horses, cutting them off from the rest of the group. Shahulm hesitates and finds himself between the two galloping men. The next few moments are a blur of dust, horse whinnies and confusion. The Companions attempt to cut across to help Shahulm with the horses, which are about to bolt. The second horseman, appearing to control his mount, which is rearing and stirring dust, prevents them from reaching Shahulm. The Companions' mounts stir creating more confusion, and keeping them at bay. Shahulm is in direct danger of being trampled.

In one sweeping gesture, one of the horsemen pulls Shahulm off his feet and throws him across the neck of his horse, knocking him unconscious. The horses of the Companions scatter in the fray.

We all stand there a moment, bewildered and unbelieving. Too late, my instincts are now screaming at the accumulation of warnings.

The horsemen gallop away. The robes of one, floating in the wind, comes loose and falls, revealing one of the desert dogs clad in the hated aquamarine: merciless mercenaries who will take on any task if the price is right.

Ijlal's scream of rage and anguish tears the air apart, as he starts to run after the horsemen.

I will never forget those screams. I feel a pain beyond pain, a heart torn from a chest, a cry that is beyond tears... and suddenly the air echoes with such cries. Before our unbelieving eyes, as Ijlal runs, his body melts away to the ground and a great kestrel takes off into the air, circling and crying for its lost companion. The great legendary magic of inseparable love manifests before us. In the echoes of his cries, that ring among the dunes is a sworn vengeance that he will not rest until the mercenary desert dog is dead by his hand.

The great bird swoops several times over the racing horsemen. Each time, the horsemen cower down on their mounts. I can sense their fear; no amount of reward will be enough for the death that awaits them at the hands of a vengeful lover, especially one whose love is linked to ancient magic. In desperation, they gallop on and disappear in the darkness of the mouth of a great cave at the entrance to Huda Pass, the piercing screams of the kestrel echoing like daggers at their back. For a moment, I pity their fate.

The Companions stand shocked, silent, and numb from the events that have just unfolded. Some of the older ones gather one or two of the horses but it is too late to give chase. We set out to search for the great kestrel, each in silent and remorseful contemplation at their inability to protect their prince and his lover. We find Ijlal in the sands in the late evening, naked, the passion of madness in his eyes. A grief beyond all grief has taken hold. The loss of his beloved will drive him until he no longer has a body.

I love him dearly, and yet not even I can reach him now. He is lost in that mysterious abyss of grief. A path that all know in their own heart yet cannot follow for another.

We retire to my camp. His Companions at first refuse to enter, but seeing the welcome extended to them and the concern I have for their leader, they soon feel an obligation to be by him. They are as lost as I am. The greatest puzzle to us all is the apparent lack of motive for such a heinous act. Although Ijlal is the son of the second most powerful ruler, the taking of Shahulm will not provoke Ijlal's father to war.

I am ashamed that I have failed Ijlal in the simplest of tasks. I do not tell the Companions of my mission. Still confused, I reflect on the events that have occurred. I remember the dream Ijlal had brought to my godmother for interpretation. The one to be taken would be a male of royal blood, beloved of another. To my knowledge, the only prince here is Ijlal. Shahulm is not of royal blood. The abduction of Shahulm does not make sense. I struggle to remember the details as I go about trying to calm Ijlal's convulsing body. It will be important to see that he is fed and looked after, as in his state he will not do so of his own will.

Prince Elwah has already been taken. This will be enough to provoke the Naasséenes to a holy war. I had thought that he had to be the male of royal blood referred to in the dream. If Ijlal is the intended victim, is this a case of mistaken identity? It was Ijlal who was attacked in the mountains.

Magic is not a new concept amongst my people. I have inherited my fair share of it. It may have been because of this that now Ijlal's Companions turn to me in desperate need. Yet even I had only heard of the great magic of love transformation. I look in vain in my crystals and amidst the flames for signs of where they have taken Shahulm.

A powerful magician must be working for them as well, for not a trace of him can I find. Some other means will have to be found. I fear moving Ijlal because of his weakness, and in the present politics of the realm, the fewer who know the situation the better.

I need to be certain of some facts before taking action. To alert too many about the recent events will only cause undue panic. I do not want the world to remember me for fuelling a war.

Nevertheless, I send one of the Companions back to Schiraz to fetch Giafar, Ijlal's uncle, and to deliver my talisman to one of the palace soldiers, hoping against all odds that Hasan is now free and will come with all due haste. I entrust Hasan's talisman to Faruq, Ijlal's cousin. He looks at the mark of the talisman, looks up at me in surprise, suddenly thrusts his closed right fist to his heart, bows deeply before taking his leave. Running with purpose, he mounts one of the horses in a single movement and takes off at a gallop.

The second afternoon at the same time that Shahulm was taken, Ijlal becomes feverish. No potions for sleep stop the convulsions. Suddenly, the great kestrel takes to the air again, filling the sand dunes with his cries. I stay until nightfall when the bird once again becomes human, though no human fire of life springs in his eyes.

The third afternoon, I again wait amongst the dunes for the return of my friend when, exhausted from his transformation, he comes plummeting down from the skies and lies not far from where I stand. I have begun to lose hope of ever finding a clue to where they have taken Shahulm.

My attention is suddenly caught, and shivers run up my spine. I look around intensely but only desert stares back at me, bare sand dunes on all sides. And then I realise that all I can hear is silence. It is not time for the bird to transform back to human shape. I look again fearing the worst. In the distance, towards the setting sun, I see a crouching figure. The air quivers still from the heat and it is difficult to make out what it is. I decide to approach it cautiously.

As I come closer to it, I realise that it is the bird, still in its shape. He looks at me with a cold hard stare, and I could swear that there are tears in his eyes. In his beak it holds a chain, on which hangs a golden pendant. This is the token of love that Ijlal gave to Shahulm as a declaration of his love.

The sun is just over the horizon, and the heat of the day, intense as it has been, is just beginning to shift. The token glimmers in the setting sun, appearing now and then to kindle itself in a fire of its own accord.

Gently, I take the token from the beak of the kestrel and turn to the sun to better look at it. A stab of sunlight shines at my eyes and I reel from the pain of it. I fall to my knees, momentarily blinded, feeling sweat pearl over my face. I can taste the salt of my tears. Blackness invades my senses.

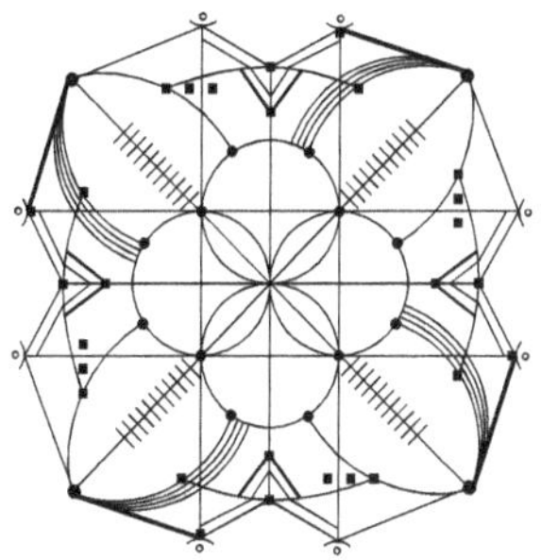

CHAPTER NINETEEN

I open my eyes and I think I have lost my sight. Everything is dark. My eyes begin to adjust, and I can see wavering, flashing lights and think of the talisman. Slowly I realise that I am in a tent and that it is lit with lamps and candles. The Companions stand around me looking very worried. I turn and feel another dull pain behind my eyes.

One of the Companions approaches me with a cup and holds it to my lips, and helps me drink. The drink is bitter but soothing, and I recognise with some surprise the bitter herbs of seership, given to those after a strong vision.

"Where am I?"

They look at each other, then Isamadeen speaks, "We found you near Ijlal. You were unconscious. You were holding this in your hand, and we had to prise it out, for you held onto it with all your might. Only then did you open your eyes."

Rauf shows me the talisman covered with a white silk cloth. He holds it with great reverence, almost bordering on fear. I recognise it immediately. Slowly I remember the stab of light, followed by the swell of grief in my heart and the invariable fall through the light. Something or someone was calling me urgently.

I sit up urgently and regret the sudden move. Holding my head, I exclaim, "Shahulm! I saw Shahulm."

The Companions fall silent and watchful.

I explain, "It is the sacred talisman that binds Ijlal's and Shahulm's love. I saw him; he is laid upon a bed of black stone, semi-conscious. He is calling with all the power of his mind to his lover or anyone else that might hear him. The talisman is the link—where before all has been hidden by magic, the love token broke through the veil and brought me there. And there was the vile horseman who abducted him, now bowing on one knee before his mistress."

I pause for breath, the Companions attentive to my every word.

"Try as I might, as in a nightmare, I was unable to raise my gaze to look upon that magician's face. But what I did see was unmistakable: the flash of the three intersecting black blades emblazoned on a red robe. I know where to begin to look."

There is a murmur amongst the young men. Some are pleased at the news; others look in awe at me and I can read a hint of fear in their eyes. I know though, that each one of them would follow me to the ends of the land, for the sake and love of their leader and his beloved.

They had retrieved him from my side in the sands and now he lies quiet and asleep for the first time since his ordeal.

"You have done well to wrap the token in white silk; you need also now to wrap it again in strong leather. The silk out of respect for the magic of their love and the leather to prevent its detection until needed."

Rauf offers it to me, but I shake my head.

"I am not strong enough yet to handle such a talisman of power."

Gentle Rauf trembles visibly at my words. I assure him that he is in no danger. Now that I am the talisman's link, it will only work through me. I must find a way of not loosing consciousness every time I touch it, however, and to this end I will need to consult my godmother, Aïschah.

I speak to all of them. "I need to think best on how to proceed. I will contact my godmother and seek her advice."

"What can we do, Azizi?" It is Isamadeen who asks, but eagerness to do something is plainly written on all their faces.

"Isamadeen, we must be certain of what we are to do. Let us wait until Faruq returns. We know at least where we can look for Shahulm."

"What about Ijlal? Will he be better?"

I look over to Ijlal who lies on a cot in my tent. He seems at last to be resting peacefully.

"I think Ijlal will be well. I think he knows what I have seen." Then I add, "The transformations, though will continue until he is reunited with Shahulm."

On instinct I also add something else, I am not sure what the words imply but I honour the feeling that makes me say them. "Know that I can face the witch, but I will need your strength to conquer the ones that guard her. I need my rest now; my head still hurts."

They leave the tent in silence. A ray of hope has penetrated the darkness of our despair, and it is with anticipation and a degree of restlessness that the Companions fall asleep, knowing at last that they can be of use.

Where we are heading, I will need strong fearless guards of the more conventional type—there are some things that not even magic can touch. My heart is glad that Hasan will be on his way. With a feeling of comparative safety, I fall in a deep sleep.

It is early morning; the air is cool. The drone of the Great Ocean of Malkizar can still be heard in the distance. My head has finally stopped hurting. I check in on Ijlal who seems to be resting peacefully. I am getting ready to gather some breakfast when a rustle at the front of my tent reveals one of the Companions. I recognise Husam.

One hand on the pommel of his short sword, he bows to me and gives me the greeting, which I had understood was reserved for the Companions of Ijlal's desert tribe, a bow and a closed fist to his heart.

He does me great honour to greet me thus and I am slightly puzzled by this.

"Master Azizi, Giafar has just returned from the northern borders, where they thought war might break out. Upon hearing of Ijlal's plight, the general requests your presence in his tent."

"Is he then in Schiraz?"

"No, Master, he is still some way north of Schiraz. Having received the news from his trusted couriers, he decided to hold audience with you at some distance from the city, so as not to arouse concern. His tent is nearby. I can take you there."

"Thank you, Husam. And please honour me and call me Azizi."

He looks up, surprised, and bows. It seems the honour is all his.

We cross a small oasis that is within easy reach. This is a much smaller affair than the one Halim and I had first stopped at. A well has stood in this place for decades and a few palm trees edge it on all sides, providing some shelter. We walk over the next sand dune.

Husam was right. Giafar has not wasted time. A large tent and several other small ones for his personal guards and entourage are pitched nearby. Small fires have been lit and lazy plumes of smoke rise in the early morning air, fragranced with the robust smell of roasted berries that will be crushed to make a strong drink. Soldiers stand in small groups around the fires speaking in low voices. They stare at me as I pass, some bowing their heads slightly.

It seems I am expected, and even the guards at the front allow me immediate passage. When I enter his tent, I am astounded at the richly appointed interior. His is not only the tent of a general but one that speaks of the Sultan's brother-in-law.

He reclines on a sumptuous divan covered with materials of exquisite designs and colours. A servant has brought him refreshments, which are laid on a silver tray atop a finely carved table of dark wood, encrusted with a pure white metal that filigreed around the legs of the table, and ending in an explosion of flowers on its borders.

Papers are strewn around on another table in front of him.

It is with a degree of anxiety that I face Giafar. Another event, which I feel in his eyes, will be another proof of my inexperience in handling the grave task of protecting the prince.

He looks up and much to my surprise comes to me immediately, holding out a hand in greeting.

Unexpected as his reception is, I offer my hand in return, which he shakes warmly, holding my right shoulder. He does me honour by this greeting.

"Azizi... may I call you by the name Aïschah gave you?"

I nodd my consent unsure and unsettled by his manner.

"Azizi, I thank you for your guard of Ijlal these last few days. His Companions are bewildered at the events that have taken place. They have spoken highly of your love and care of him."

"It is my duty," I answer.

He nodds, releasing my hand. He begins to pace up and down.

Always wanting to be direct and to deal with matters uppermost on my mind, I say, "I fear I have failed you and Ijlal's family in not foreseeing Shahulm's taking. For that, I grieve."

He stops and looks at me gravely. With unusual concern, he says, "Azizi, I am a soldier. All my life I have dealt with facts that may affect life and death outcomes. Magic is not my strength. I do not pretend to understand the powers that are at play here. I have always thought the love transformations to be fairy tales... that is until I heard of it for myself."

He shudders, lost in the thought of Ijlal transforming into a great kestrel and taking to the air, crying for his lost companion. "I have accepted long ago your role in this mission as Aïschah's hand-picked apprentice. Any magician trained and recommended by Aïschah is recommendation enough for me. Besides," he adds, with a wry smile, "I cannot so easily forget the words and voice of the Guardian when He spoke through you."

Once more he looks as if a chill wind has blown through the tent. Shaking the memory away, he continues, "I would welcome your interpretation of the events that have occurred. For my part, I am beginning to see a greater plot developing."

Cautiously I begin, "I admit to not seeing the whole picture yet. My first reaction at the news of Elwah's abduction was that the danger to Ijlal was now over. Yet, I cannot ignore the attack that were made on you and Ijlal during your sojourn to my home, and the one attack made during your return voyage."

He looks askance at me but allows me to continue.

"The taking of Shahulm at the meeting point speaks of two facts. Our enemies knew of our rendezvous and had planned this act well. The taking of Shahulm, however, seems to serve no other purpose than to anger Ijlal and provoke him to revenge. My first thought is that this is a case of mistaken identity, that the one to be taken has to have been Ijlal. Remembering Ijlal's dream, and the interpretation given, the one to be taken was to be one of royal blood. Only two to my knowledge fit this description—Elwah, who has already been taken, provoking his people to declaring a holy war, and Ijlal. It is doubtful that the Sultan no matter how grieved for his son, would be provoked to war over the taking of Ijlal's beloved... and yet war seems to be the prime motive."

There is a pause, filled with Giafar's pacing. He stops and looks at me.

"You summarise the facts well. I admit my thoughts coincide with yours. However," he went on, "there are other issues that have come to light recently, that alter the situation and the matter is now grave. You have done well to have remained here and kept this matter as secret as possible."

I wait for him to continue.

He seems to come to a decision but suddenly changes the subject, "You are held in high regard by the Naasséenes!"

I am puzzled.

"I'm sorry, I do not know... I have never been to Naassée, I do not know what you speak of."

He looks a little surprised. Then, remembering, he reaches for something on his table and hands it to me. It is a talisman hung on a string of wooden beads. My heart leaps into my throat in recognition.

"I am to offer you congratulations on your Damna, Illustrious One. You have found favour with one of the most feared and renowned Naasséene soldiers."

I can feel my ears burning and my cheeks begin to flush. With sudden realisation, I begin to understand his tone of respect towards me.

"You do puzzle me though, Azizi. Very few of your people accept the customs of Apphat, let alone the rites of the Naasséenes. Truly though, now I begin to understand the significance of your prophecy, when the Guardian Spirit spoke of an initiate of Apphat as the one for this mission. I do not pretend to understand it all, but it begins to make sense."

"But I thought Hasan was from Gibrar?"

Too late I realise that I have inadvertently spoken the name of the man who has initiated me into Damna. My cheeks grow hotter still.

Giafar replies almost casually, "No. No, Hasan is the Captain of the Royal Guards, duty bound as personal guard to serve Elwah of Naassée. He is the finest of them all. He was away abroad on a matter for his prince, when Elwah was taken. Great is his grief and greater is his purpose in finding his regent. He has followed a trail for many weeks now, but it has gone cold. But what is of greater importance at hand is this situation."

Giafar sits back on his sofa and invites me to sit opposite him.

"What I am about to tell you, must remain a secret. A little information in the wrong hands at this point can be a dangerous thing."

I nod my agreement.

"As you know I have been abroad. I had it put about that I was consolidating our borders. My mission was to find the family of Shahulm and ascertain their rank in the kingdom. Ijlal is an initiate of Apphat, and before the Sultan can approve Shahulm's title as Royal Consort to Ijlal, we had to determine his family's standing. The union would not have been disapproved of, only his title to rule besides Ijlal. How the two of them met is a matter of much mystery. Little was known of Shahulm, and he just appeared in the company of Ijlal. Only his ability to dance like wildfire is common knowledge." Giafar allows himself a wry smile.

I interrupt, "What of the blood line of succession?"

Giafar looks astonished. "Surely you are well acquainted with the customs of the Naasséenes. A suitable and willing concubine will be invited to bear his child. She would be accorded the honours and rights of royal concubine but would not be allowed to rule by Ijlal's side. That would be the place of his beloved. Shahulm would also be appointed special guardian to the children born under this arrangement." Giafar takes a deep breath and goes on, "What follows, is a matter of grave importance. I have found Shahulm's family." Giafar pauses a moment, as if trying to decide to go on or not.

"He is the eldest son of the most powerful king of the Northern Regions. The alliance between our two kingdoms resulting from such a union would make the Over Lord shudder in fear."

I draw in a breath at this news.

Giafar holds up a hand. "That is not all. Though the people of the Northern Regions accept that men who are lovers of men exist, and their love is natural, the rites of the Naasséenes are not so readily accepted. It appears that Shahulm had gone on his own secret 'pilgrimage' to discover the Naasséenes, seeking initiation, when he met Ijlal."

Giafar pauses momentarily.

My whole being is weighed down by the news of Shahulm's royalty. How could I have been so blind to the facts stated in Ijlal's dream: the joining of two golden snakes—two males of royal blood! With greater dread, I realise that Shahulm is obviously a virgin; he had not reached Naassée before meeting Ijlal, and therefore had not been initiated. Having found his soul mate, they would have agreed to wait for his formal union with Ijlal who would, as an initiate, take on the responsibility of Damna.

Giafar resumes. "This sudden disappearance of Shahulm, can be interpreted many ways by his family, none of which can result in peace. Whoever the family of Glesskerel allies itself to, will result in a force to be reckoned with. It is of course, to my brother, the Sultan's advantage to woo the king of the Northern Region, but the motives may be misinterpreted. This union of Ijlal and Shahulm is not entirely welcomed by Shahulm's family."

By way of explanation Giafar continues, "If Shahulm becomes the betrothed of Ijlal, Glesskerel loses an heir, and it forces the kingdom of Glesskerel to become annexed to the kingdom of Schiraz. I would rather see the two kingdoms form an alliance, but I do not think that Glesskerel sees it that way. They only see the loss."

There, Giafar pauses again and sighs. "I was told of your vision and the symbol of the three blades. From a strategist's point of view, if the taking of Shahulm is indeed the work of the Sorceress, it is a stroke of genius on behalf of the Over Lord. This act has a doubled edge: it will set the nations one against the other, and it serves as a powerful bargaining tool for the Over Lord if all else fails. What other motives the Sorceress may have I cannot foresee."

I shudder, and shadows pass over the tent, as I recollect Ijlal's dream, and the interpretation given by my godmother and me.

Giafar is openly looking at me. "What is it Azizi? What do you see?"

"Not so much see as perceive, Giafar. I have been blind. Shahulm's royal blood was stated in Ijlal's dreams. I do not think that political power is all that the Sorceress is after."

"Explain what you mean."

A stone seems to rest in the pit of my stomach. I can hear my heart pounding in my ears, as the seriousness of the situation dawns upon me. With trepidation I explain, "The sorceress is only after increasing her own magical powers; if in the process it benefits her king, then all the better for her. I remember the dream that Ijlal brought to my godmother for interpretation. There is a part of it which now fills me with dread."

Giafar's look urges me on.

"I will have to consult with my godmother. I want to make

sure that I understand her interpretation correctly. In my limited understanding, I refer to an ancient tradition amongst the early witches, the practice of sorcery in the group of islands of Brouille. At the full moon, as part of the final initiation rite, a new witch sacrificed a young male virgin by bleeding him from his sexual organs. I am not sure of the exact ritual, but it was supposed to give the witch greater power and acceptance amongst her sisters, more so if the male was of royal blood."

Giafar pales visibly. "I thought those savages had been eradicated three hundred years ago."

"Most of the witches may have been destroyed and the rites banned. But not necessarily abolished. They still live on in folklore and history. Nevertheless, Giafar, I will need to verify this with Aïschah."

Giafar gets up and begins to pace up and down. More speaking to himself than to me he begins to deliberate. "This is bad indeed. We cannot send an overt party to recover Shahulm without declaring war on the Over Lord. We cannot declare war on the Over Lord without an alliance with a powerful nation. The most powerful is the Northern Region of Glesskerel. Their king will not ally because he suspects foul play on our part. If we do not rescue Shahulm, we lose the beloved of the crown prince, and we potentially throw the nations into total warfare with each other! That son of a donkey's cronk... "

Giafar continues with a string of expletives, each worse than the previous, all alluding to various supposed aspects of the Over Lord's lineage and parentage. Some expressions I have not heard of before, and they are so explicit, that I do not know whether to be offended or just laugh.

Eventually Giafar subsides and comes to rest back on the sofa with a look of worried defeat.

"General, you mentioned a mission earlier on. Were you speaking of rescuing the prince Shahulm, or another matter?"

Giafar realising that he has abandoned himself to his emotions and language in front of me, looks abashed. "I was speaking of the Great Guardian Spirit's choice in this matter, Azizi. Though how far a rescue mission involving you personally is concerned, I am uncertain. We are no longer speaking of watching and protecting, but somehow gaining the upper hand against the Over Lord and that whore of an adviser!"

I can see what he is hinting at and my desire to serve Ijlal and rescue his beloved drives me to encourage him in this way. "Obviously, this mission would have to be covert and who better to send than a magician to throw a guise of concealment over the attack?"

Giafar sits up; a part of him is hoping against all odds. "Azizi, we are speaking of entering one of the most guarded citadels in the kingdom. Whether you personally can handle the witchcraft of the Sorceress, I am not able to judge. Beyond the outer defences though, we are speaking of highly trained guards whose sole purpose is to defend their king—to the death!"

Ijlal's dream is beginning to make sense. "Giafar, the remaining six Companions' reputation as skilled scouts and soldiers is the talk of your country. I have seen them in action more than once and know of their stealth, their skill as soldiers despite their age, their bravery, and most of all their sheer dedication to their prince. For all of that, I suspect some credit is due to you."

In spite of himself, Giafar cannot hide his pride in the

Companions. His own eldest son Faruq is one of them. Nevertheless, he dismisses the idea by stating, "They are boys."

"Then let me take with us one of the most feared and respected soldiers of Naassée, one who has vowed to protect and assist me whenever my need arises. No greater need is there than this one."

"Ah… " Giafar has no come back.

In the back of my own mind, I wonder whether Hasan will so easily abandon the quest for his prince to come with me on a reckless voyage, which could see the death of us all.

"Besides," I continue, "time is running out. We are at the wax of the season of Malkizar and only a month from the full moon."

"How is that important?" Giafar ventures to ask.

"According to the dream that Ijlal brought to my godmother, and if my interpretation is correct, the Sorceress is to sacrifice prince Shahulm on the first full moon of the season of Malkizar."

Giafar pales and thumping his fist down on the thankfully soft sofa beside him, he barks out an order for his attendant to call his generals together.

I leave Giafar's tent with a heavy heart. Giafar and his generals will come up with the best strategy for approaching the citadel of the Over Lord. The rest will be up to us. Once inside, nothing but our own wits, skill, and courage will protect us. My powers are limited. Out of necessity they will have to be saved for my confrontation with the Sorceress. Besides, it is forbidden me to intervene in hand-to-hand combat using a force far superior to that of ordinary men. The fighting, and there will be a lot of that, will have to be left to the soldiers.

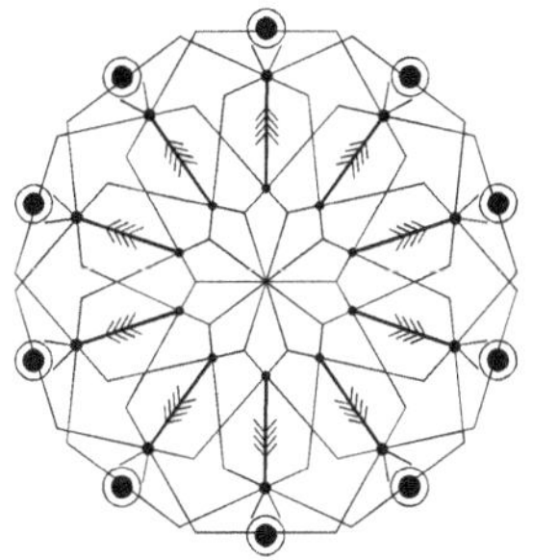

C H A P T E R   T W E N T Y

"Aïschah. Aïschah."

I sit in my tent, attempting to make a sending to my godmother.

I realise after a while, that my desperation overrides my sending and that my mind as a result, will not focus.

I abandon my efforts, resolving to calm my mind first and resume later.

I go to the tent where Ijlal has been moved, away from prying eyes, wondering how long the effects of transformation will continue.

Two of the Companions, Isamadeen and his younger brother, Rauf, are at the tent. They are both by Ijlal's side. Rauf is gently wiping Ijlal's brow, cooling him with a small hand-held fan. Isamadeen, the more serious of the two, is standing, watching with a mixture of devotion and tension.

I understand that the names given at birth in this land, as much as in my country, often, reflect the true nature of the person, although they are not always accurate. 'Rauf,' in his native tongue means merciful and kind, where his twin, Isamadeen's name, means 'to guard.'

Isamadeen first detects my presence, his hand ready on the pommel of his short sword despite the two guards that stand outside the tent. His fist touches his heart, and he bows to me upon recognition.

I stand on the other side of the bed; Rauf smiles meekly at me. Hardly out of boyhood, his dark eyes sparkle, like black pebbles at the bottom of a stream, glinting and inviting.

"How is he?" I whisper so as not to disturb the sleeper.

Rauf sighs, "He is restless. He calls to Shahulm in his sleep. He begs for him to be found, calling out 'he is so beautiful, my beloved, please, help him'."

The very words stab at the memory in my heart. With an effort I find myself suddenly holding back my tears. It was Ijlal himself who had called out in my dream, using those very words. So long ago it seems. I am determined more than ever to find a way to rescue Shahulm. I just don't know how at this point.

"Will we help him, Mahjir?" Rauf uses a term of great respect. The title Mahjir is given to one who has mastered the arts of magic and seership.

With the weight of responsibility in my heart at the answer I give, I reply, "We will help him. It is written that we will help him."

A silence falls upon the tent. Even Ijlal seems more at peace.

I become aware that tears are flowing down my face, and momentarily I panic, knowing what the taste of salt presages.

I wipe the tears quickly, and a little more bravely, I add, "Rauf, Isamadeen, thank you for your care of him. Now go and gather the others. We will meet in my tent at the rise of the moon tonight. I will tell you all how this is written that you may all understand what may be required of you."

They both bow to me and retire quietly. Again, there is this distance that my role places between my fellow men and me. *Will it always be like this,* I wonder?

I sit by Ijlal's side, lost in thought, my mind travelling to my beloved hills and the carefree times I spent by the mountain side, under the kind and wise tutelage of my godmother. The shepherd boy who befriended me, and who for the love of me, threw himself between this prince and one of the Shadows at a time of great danger. Halim was stabbed by the poisoned tip of the blade of that cursed dog, servant to the Scarlet Robes and the Sorceress.

At the prompting of Ijlal, I had used a mind meld to enter the young shepherd's heart and had rescued him from death. In the process, I witnessed the heart of the boy within and came to truly understand Halim, probably better than he knew himself.

I sigh. I am thinking of Halim, who so devotedly guided me down the mountain, who comforted me after my first confrontation with the Sorceress, and who gently led me through the desert. I also remember my dream of Ijlal when he first appeared to me. How naively I had wanted to believe that this was to be the love of my life. How gently and kindly Ijlal had taken me to his heart as a brother.

"Azizi?"

I can still hear the softness of his voice, in that melodious lilt that his native tongue plays upon my mind when I first heard it.

"Azizi."

I open my eyes. Ijlal is staring at me.

"Ijlal!" I take his hand and wipe his brow.

"Azizi, you are weeping."

"Ijlal. You are awake. I am glad to see you well again."

He looks at me with those wondrous eyes and that serious look on his face. He is weak, but there is a flame there that I recognise as my friend and prince. The transformations will surely abate now.

Ijlal's gaze becomes unfocused, as if trying to remember something. And then suddenly with a panic and despair gilding his voice, he utters a name that holds a world, "Shahulm?"

I hold his hand tightly.

"Truly I tell you, Ijlal, we will find him."

I do not dare think of the condition that we will find him in.

He relaxes a little and very soon, he is back asleep, his breathing steady.

I leave Ijlal to rest and signal to the guards to secure the tent. We are taking no chances. Guards are posted all around, and the shifts change at irregular intervals, often enough to allow the men to be alert.

I retire to my tent, my mind calmer. I settle back into my thought projection and again attempt to contact my godmother, Aïschah.

I slip into a comfortable state, almost like slipping into a warm bath. The result is immediate. Aïschah is there clear as daylight, sitting in the herbarium near the fireplace. Late spring nights are still cool. She is looking at me directly with searching eyes.

My heart feels like exploding. I want so much to be held in her arms as she often did when I was a child. "Godmother!"

A worried expression floats across her face and is quickly replaced by a stern but gentle look. "Dear One, you cause me concern. I thought you had learnt much greater self-control. I heard your call earlier, but it was muffled and distorted with all your other concerns."

I am safe in her presence. I want to cry; there is so much on my mind and in my heart. I murmur, "It has been harder than I thought."

She smiles warmly at me. "You look older Azizi. Yet it can't be more than two months since you left our mountains."

I am beginning to understand the burdens of adulthood. "Godmother, I need to speak with you on an urgent matter."

She holds up her hand, replying, "I know. What is the weather like?"

"Warm." I reply, a question of surprise in my voice at the sudden change of topic.

"Is there an oasis near by?"

"Yes... "

"Picture it in your head now."

Quite easily, I picture the tall palm trees in the moonlight, the deep well made of rocks. The picture slowly forms as a faint veil between us.

She is studying my mental picture and then suddenly waves her hand and it is as if a candle in my head has been extinguished, the picture disappearing at once. She looks at me with serious intent yet almost casually says, "Be there tonight, by the well."

Her presence vanishes immediately. The link broken so suddenly, leaves me momentarily stunned. I know my godmother's powers are great and often hidden. I can understand her ability to sever our link, but I cannot understand her reasons for departing so abruptly and seemingly dismissing me. Nevertheless, I have learned to trust her ways for her reasons are not always made clear immediately.

It is late afternoon; I decide to rest before my meeting to be clear-headed.

Several hours later, I wake up and make my way through the still warm sands, reflecting silver under the starlit sky. The first moon, Camlac is midway in the heavens, a silver crescent strand of light on its way out before the new moon. The second moon Ayshah, has not yet risen above the horizon.

In the distance, I perceive the outline of the palm trees, swaying gently in the early evening breeze. Turning slowly, I look beyond the camp and see low-lying tents made of white canvas, shining amongst beloved sand dunes. I hear the rustle of a light breeze in the palm grove, and the smell of wood fires drift across the air like drying linen in the sun. The moonlight shines like my polished scimitar amidst a dark blue sky of a thousand stars.

A soft, almost imperceptible voice is whispering to me, "This is your destiny; the moment has come."

Startled, I realise that I am looking and experiencing the first waking dream that I had when I was twelve. This is the vision I spoke of to my godmother. This is the vision that has placed me on this path, starting with my education with Aïschah.

I reach the oasis and wait with anticipation in my heart.

The place where I stand is elevated above the rest of the camp. I look beyond the sand dunes in the direction where I know my beloved mountains are. There, a sight catches my eye.

A flashing light, like a lantern carried by a traveller, is moving across the land. Riveted, I watch the movement of this light. It speeds like a golden night fly across the sand. I wonder at it, thinking that this must surely be such a creature. It is moving very fast across the desert.

A few moments go by, and I stand there focussed entirely on this approaching sight. Now it appears to be a large ball, soft and round and lit with an unearthly light that both glows and shifts in intensity as it moves.

Before I can gather my wits, the ball of light, which has now grown to the size of a man, has approached the oasis, and is slowing down to just a few paces from where I stand.

It comes to a stop; the sphere of light shifts in intensity and slowly pales before turning an iridescent blue. I know at once.

The light vanishes and there stands Aïschah, my beloved godmother.

I must be a sight; my mouth gaping wide open.

Aïschah steps up to me looking at me with that bemused smile, knowing that yet again she has caught me out. "Will I not be graced with an embrace?"

I throw myself at her, wrapping my arms around her. She feels so solid, so real. I can smell the aroma of the herbs on her still.

"Godmother... how did you... ?"

"Ummm. Gently, Azizi, I am still made of flesh and bones."

I release my embrace on her slightly, not wanting to let go.

"How? That is a skill of the seventh Mastership, which you will learn in due course. It is faster and safer for me to come to you."

"Safer?"

Aïschah looks around taking in the sight of the oasis. "Yes. I could not be sure that our mind link was not being spied upon."

I remember then the time I had a dream in the mountain cave, where the Sorceress had overpowered my conversation with Aïschah.

"Godmother, why did you not ever come to me in this fashion before?"

"Because it was not needed. This is a time of great urgency and need. And now, let us speak of the things that have been on your mind."

"Godmother, I hardly know where to begin."

She listens intently as I tell her of the Magic transformation. She questions me at length on this matter. She states that she has never witnessed the great Love Magic. She wants to know every detail. I tell her of the finding of the talisman and the effect it has on me, asking her in a way to tell me why this effect is so potent.

She asks many questions about my meeting with Giafar and she looks concerned. I come to the part of my interpretation of the reading of Ijlal's dream. She nods in grave thought, finally agreeing with the statements I made to Giafar.

We then speak of the other blue sapphire, and I express my anxiety at my lack of direction in this matter.

"Azizi, you have asked me many questions. Some I am able to answer, but others I cannot."

I realise that she is looking at the talisman that is now once more around my neck. The more I attempt to treat the object as just another trinket, the more conscious I become of it, and the more I am aware of her gaze.

My eyes start to wander. I cannot meet her gaze.

Aïschah speaks gently and softly and with great compassion.

"Dear One, I have always known."

"What? I... "

"I just did not know who and when."

"What do you mean?"

I am so embarrassed. I want to hide and at the same time, I want to know that everything will be right between us.

"My Dearest, it was always foretold in the ancient Lore, that an initiate of Apphat would one day come out of the Mountains of Asfaine and lead the people to a great rejoicing. I knew at once when you came to me with your dream, that you were that one."

A silence falls like the sigh of a falling star.

A little chokingly I ask, "Does this not bother you?"

She smiles warmly at me. "Dear One. How could your love bother me? Whether your love is for a man, a woman, or simply love of Life, it is still Love. You are a child of the light, created from the Tears of Creation."

I can feel tears running down my cheeks, my whole being sighing at the relief of an enormous burden that has suddenly been lifted from my heart.

"Azizi, would you honour me with the name of the one who so lovingly brought you to the flower of your manhood?"

And with that, I burst into tears, and she comes to hold me in her arms.

Haltingly I tell her, "His name is Hasan. He is a soldier."

Aïschah caresses my hair, her gentle strokes soothing away the pain of having carried this secret for too long.

I ask her what my father will think of me. She laughs light-heartedly, "Your father, Azizi, will love you as he always has. You are his son, no less for who you love."

"But why me? Why was I chosen?"

She pauses. "I do not know the answers to all questions, Azizi. There must be a way of the heart that only an initiate of Apphat can understand. In the ancient lore of the Naasséenes, it is said that those who follow the rites of Apphat, are blessed with a deep understanding of the opposing energies of the Universe. Remember that it was your love for Halim that allowed you to enter his heart and rescue him from the poison that was killing him. Only one whose heart was like his own, could achieve this."

I wipe my tears, and looking at her I ask her a little reproachfully, "If you have always known, why have you never spoken of this before?"

"My Dearest, I have. You were not ready to speak of it yourself, and so I waited."

I remember then the many times she looked at me, and how her gaze had made me feel uncomfortable. I remember a time in the herbarium after I had had my first vision, when I had spoken of the prince as 'so beautiful,' Aïschah had known then, in her inimitable way teasing me a little.

"Now, we come to the reason this talisman you had made affects you so much."

She pauses, looking at me with that little knowing smile of hers. She knew even that! She knew that it was I who had commissioned the making of the talisman.

"Do you remember my warning you once that unless you open your heart to your true destiny, in its attempt to flow through the power of love will always overcome you?"

I briefly remember words to that effect once, but at the time not really comprehending the meaning.

"Not until recently have you accepted a part of that destiny. You will find now that the talisman will not overpower you so much. You are an initiate of Apphat, according to the sacred customs of the Naasséenes. Be proud of this, rare and beautiful a creation you are."

My godmother has always been direct in the gentlest possible way. The burden has been lifted; there is no longer a need for shame or a desire to hide. I embrace her, thanking her.

She continues, "Now let us speak of the other matters at hand."

We speak at length about the blue sapphires, revisiting the legends. After the prophet had died, as none of his disciples were able to agree for which stone the warnings were made, the two stones had been separated and each kept in the guardianship of a spiritual leader. Long ago the stones had disappeared and were now only legend. No one knew for sure whether the sapphires actually existed. If Prince Elwah is indeed one of the chosen custodians, as his name and title implies, then his taking seems a demand for one of the Tears of Apphat as ransom.

We knew from my vision in the cave that the Sorceress claims to have one of the stones, the Tear of Malkizar. This, however, could have been a mental image created to fool us. Legend has it that an army that marches with both stones at its head, would be invincible. Giafar had once explained, that magic aside, if the enemy thought that its opponent had the two Tears of Apphat, then that would be sufficient to make it invincible. No soldier would stand against that kind of magical power.

I tell my godmother that the soldiers of Naassée are, according to Giafar, ready to declare a holy war against the kidnappers. The Naasséene soldiers have not swung into action yet, having been cautioned and held at bay by the will of their Great Council.

What puzzles both Aïschah and me is the fact that if the stone is kept secretly in Naassée, then why did the Over Lord not ransack Naassée and search for the stone? There is something amiss in all of this: the people of Naassée seem to cower, helpless at the capture of their leader and yet want vengeance. Could the Prince Elwah really be held to ransom for the Tear of Apphat? Would Naassée surrender the stone for their Holy Leader? It appears that the Over Lord's army has no intention of attacking Naassée. It is obvious that Prince Elwah will need to be found and rescued, as a matter of priority, and that will need to be done at the same time as the rescue of Prince Shahulm.

We cannot count on the soldiers of Naassée at this point. An army without a leader would have no direction.

The conclusion that the Companions and I will have to rescue both princes is undoubted. How, is the difficult question and more importantly, where is the location of the other sapphire—the Tear of Elwah? I will need that stone if I am to challenge the Sorceress.

Aïschah falls into a long and thoughtful silence. Finally, she addresses me with resolution, "Azizi, I will call a council of the Master Elders. It will be our task to attempt the discovery of the second stone. In the meantime, you will meet with Hasan and lay the plan for your mission. That is the dream that Ijlal brought to us."

I think for a moment.

"Godmother, in Ijlal's dream there were to be seven Companions to accompany the prince and me on this journey, the Companions only number six."

She looks at me.

I know the answer before I have finished my sentence. Hasan is the seventh.

She nods as if reading my thoughts and says she will take leave immediately.

"Godmother, will you not come to the meeting with the Companions?"

"Azizi, this is your mission, your quest. It is your time and destiny. I cannot interfere. This also was in Ijlal's dream. Besides," she adds, "I am not the initiate of Apphat."

I look at her, and pride is written all over her face. I embrace her once more.

Aïschah's departure is as spectacular as her arrival. A golden globe of light ascending from her feet envelops her whole being and she vanishes. Her voice echoes softly with a reminder that she will contact me soon.

The desert is cool and dark: the palm leaves rustle in the evening breeze, the melancholic call of a night bird echoes amongst the dunes, and the sound of soft air beneath its wings rises and falls as it hunts the sands for a prey. I stand tall, a weight has fallen off my shoulders. I feel a deep knowing that I am protected, and strength seeps into my very being.

With determination I go to Hasan and the Companions, my spirit once more buoyant.

As I look towards the horizon, the moon Ayshah is rising over the sea of Malkizar. It will be late; I run down the dunes, back to the camp. The Companions will be waiting for me.

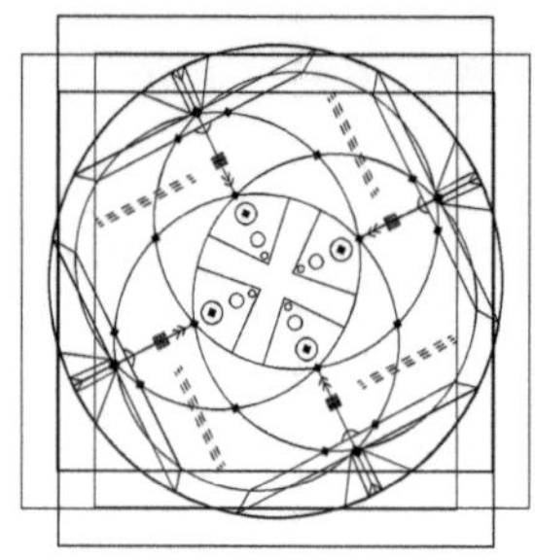

CHAPTER TWENTY-ONE

My tent is outlined in the moonlight against the desert sands. As I approach, I can detect light inside. The Companions must already be waiting for me. Erring on the side of caution, I approach slowly and carefully. I can discern a figure standing outside the entrance. With relief I recognise Isamadeen who is standing guard.

He acknowledges me and greets me in their fashion, with a bow of the head and his right fist clasped over his heart.

As I enter the tent, Isamadeen follows me on my right. A hush descends. Faruq is standing near the back of the tent and his presence dominates the small circle of young men. I know Faruq as the young soldier who took the talisman to Hasan. He is the tallest of them, built like a soldier, with a serious but not unkind face. In his native tongue, his name stands for 'one who distinguishes truth from falsehood.' Although he does not have the piercing eyes that his father, Giafar, has, nevertheless one could not easily lie to his open face.

As I enter, on my left stands a slim young man with an angular face. He takes up his position immediately behind me and to my left. I already know him as Husam, meaning 'sword edge'. He and Isamadeen share the same serious look and alert disposition.

Seated or kneeling, the other Companions are waiting in either pairs or alone. I identify gentle Rauf, who is engaged in quiet conversation with Jamal. Both boys are of the same kind temperament and seem to get on well.

Bright and alert as his name implies, Fatin sits on a cushion by himself.

All the Companions are wearing their traditional blue garments with short fighting swords at their sides. Four of them carry their emblem as initiates of Apphat—two golden snakes entwined around a sword, sewn into the garment near the left shoulder. A small red gem sewn at the top, represents their allegiance to the Sultan of Schiraz. Isamadeen, Rauf, and Jamal, as the three youngest have not been initiated. They are, however, accomplished in the arts of fighting.

All eyes are on me. There is no turning back now. I weigh up what I will say to them, how will I start. I decide on simplicity and straightforwardness as the language that they will appreciate.

I begin, "Many months ago, as you know, the Grand Vizier Giafar and his nephew, Prince Ijlal, came to my godmother, Aïschah, with a dream to interpret. The dream was in two parts and the first foretold of the taking of a prince who was also a follower of Apphat. No one could say for sure who that was, though we felt certain that Ijlal needed to be protected. Until recently we still thought that the taking of Shahulm was a mistake, that Ijlal is the one who was supposed to have been taken. It has since been discovered that Shahulm is of royal blood, and the eldest son of the kingdom of Glesskerel."

Here I pause. The lack of reaction proves to be revealing. Either the news is old news and a well-guarded secret amongst them, or the title of prince does not impress the sons of these nobles.

"Tell us of the second part, Mahjir."

Rauf had spoken softly bringing me out of my contemplation.

I smile at him and then at the entire group.

"You would honour me greatly if you were to call me by my given name. Please call me Azizi."

The Companions look at each other. It seems that the honour is theirs. They all whisper "Azizi" as if trying out the word.

"Now I come to the second part of Ijlal's dream. It was foretold that though an evil Sorceress would take the Crown's beloved, a seer of Apphat would seek him out. In this quest he would be guided by the Spirit of Hadid, Guardian of the Air, and assisted by seven companions. Together they will rescue the prince and reunite the lovers, and by the power of the Tear of Elwah they will destroy the evil one."

Now, at the mention of one of the Tears of Apphat, the Companions stir, and each makes a sign of respect that symbolises the unity of the universe and an acknowledgement of the force of creation.

"Azizi, we are but six," Fatin remarks.

Right on cue, the material at the front of the tent moves as if blown by the breeze. With great stealth that catches even Isamadeen by surprise, Hasan walks into the light and stands at the entrance of the tent.

I turn to face Hasan, my heart missing a beat looking upon his face and into the depths of his eyes. The companions are tense, an explanation is due. I walk to Hasan and stand beside him.

"Companions of Ijlal, honoured protectors of the weak in the land of Schiraz, I present to you Hasan, Captain of the Royal Guards to Prince Elwah of the Naasséenes."

Following tradition, Hasan rolls up his sleeve to reveal the tattoo of the double axe on his forearm. Simultaneously, Hasan gives me a perplexed look.

The Companions in unison, at once bow, right fists to their hearts. Though the reputation of Naasséene soldiers as the fiercest of fighters is well known amongst these young men, to come face to face with the Captain of the Royal Guard, is something few would have expected to have experienced in a lifetime. They each stand before him according to custom to look at the tattoo and salute him. I am secretly pleased at the awe and respect shown, even by Faruq.

"Hasan will be the seventh Companion on our journey."

Hasan gives me another puzzled look. I look deep into his eyes, with what I hope is a signal that I will speak to him in private. He seems to understand and retreats to crouch by the entrance and listen. With some amusement, I notice that Isamadeen and Husam both position themselves closer to him.

I go on to explain that we believe that Shahulm is imprisoned somewhere in the citadel of the Over Lord. Giafar and his generals will come up with a plan to approach and enter the citadel. Once inside, it will be up to us to find and secure the release of Prince Shahulm. I make it clear that this mission will be dangerous.

Although we will take every possible care, we cannot expect to come away without casualties. To their credit, the Companions listen gravely, and not one backs away from serving their Prince.

We will meet again in the morning with Giafar to go over the details of the mission.

The Companions leave quietly. Hasan listened without question, every now and again staring at me with piercing eyes. There is so much explanation I need to give him.

"Azizi, how did you know who I serve?"

"Giafar told me."

Hasan looks at me deeply. There seems to be something on his mind. "You indeed are not what you seem Azizi. My rank is a closely guarded secret abroad."

"I know."

Again, he looks at me with questions in his eyes. "What is this mission you speak of to these young ones?"

"To go to the citadel of the Over Lord and take back Shahulm, beloved of Ijlal."

Before I can go on, Hasan interrupts. "Azizi, I have promised to aid you if and when I can, but this you must know. I am on a sacred mission."

"I know."

Hasan looks up at me again, this time a little furrow creases his forehead. He laughs lightly then says, "You had better tell me all you know."

"Hasan, I know that your Regent Prince Elwah has been taken." Now, I have his attention. "I knew of the taking some months ago. I did not know until recently that you were looking for him."

Hasan's face becomes impassive. "Azizi how did you know of

this so long ago, it is only now becoming common knowledge in spite of the efforts of the Great Council to keep it quiet."

In matters of the soul, one cannot allow ego to interfere, so as plainly as possible I tell Hasan of the night in my beloved mountains, when the Great Spirit Guardian chose to speak through me and urged us to find Elwah.

There is a long silence. The intensity of his eyes is almost uncomfortable.

"Ah," he finally says. "Healer of Apphat, this I knew in the desert. Other things I suspected by the way you move and speak." He looks warmly into my eyes then, "And by the sign you bear over your heart, that of the first initiation of Seership. But a chosen voice of the Spirit? That, I did not know!"

He falls before me onto one knee, head bent. I am overwhelmed by shock and quickly kneel to better face him eye to eye. His mental guard falls then, and many thoughts race like clouds through his mind.

"Hasan, I may be the Guardian's chosen voice, but I am still a boy."

He looks up sharply, and in a firm but kind voice he reminds me, "A man, Illustrious One!"

I nod. "A man. I am still a man."

Hesitatingly, as if asking for a great boon, Hasan holds my hands and asks, "Azizi, you say you knew of the taking. I have long lost the trail. I do not know where Prince Elwah has been taken. I must find him, for his people are ready to wage a war to the death, a war which they will not win."

"He has been taken by the evil one, Sorceress to the Over Lord. He is where we will find Shahulm."

He looks at me incredulously. I tell him of the dream vision I had in the cave when the Sorceress confirmed she had taken him. Though I leave out many details including the references to the Tears of Apphat.

Hasan straightens and begins pacing. This is serious news to him. Why he had not suspected vexes his soldier's instincts and pride. He stops and turns, speaking with vehemence. "Azizi, of course I will come with you."

There he pauses thinking, as if unsure of what to say next. "The return of my prince to his people is important, Azizi, but there are other reasons why I must find him and safeguard his life. These reasons, I cannot speak of. I am sworn to secrecy on these matters, and I would not easily betray this. Please understand and forgive me."

I am puzzled. "Hasan, I understand, and I will not press you for details."

"When do we leave?"

I explain that we will wait until Giafar and his generals come up with a plan to distract the attention of the Over Lord's army, allowing us enough time to enter the citadel unchallenged. Once inside, we will seek out both princes and safeguard them out again.

He nods in a fashion that suggests that this will be easy work.

So, I add, "Hasan it is likely that the princes Elwah and Shahulm will be guarded by the Scarlet Robes."

The mere look of disgust that crosses his face tells me exactly what he thinks of these creatures. Resting his hand on his scimitar, he makes a motion to spit and says, "Not one that crosses my path shall remain alive to tell the tale."

"Be aware, Hasan, that they have powers and may not be overcome so easily."

"Azizi, do you know how they acquire their robes of initiation?"

I shake my head.

"Have you ever heard one of the serving Shadows utter a word?"

I say I haven't.

Hasan then proceeds to tell me a story of sheer horror. The Shadows who serve the Scarlet Robes are first initiated into the ranks by the cutting of their tongue. This serves two purposes: on the one hand, the Shadows will not betray their mistress or her secrets by spoken word, and on the other hand to 'encourage' the development of non-speech powers of mind meld.

The blood from the cut is used to colour a robe. Considering that when the robe is made it is yellow, many murders, usually small children, are used to colour the remains of the robe until such time it is deemed to be the correct shade of red. At this point, if the apprentice Shadow is considered worthy enough, they may complete their initiation and wear the blood that they have spilled by becoming a Scarlet Robe.

I feel sick to my stomach, at the thought of so many innocent beings had to die to enable one of these creatures to wear a vestment of their initiation. Now I remember the hatred that poured from the one in the forest the night Prince Ijlal had arrived at my godmother's house.

Hasan looks at me and goes to take his leave. He bows deeply in the fashion of Schiraz soldiers. Then straightening, he was about to turn and leave.

At once overwhelmed by the formality and realizing that this is the distance created by the aloneness of Power, I call him back.

"Hasan. Not you! Especially not you."

I go to him and embrace him.

He hesitates a moment and then he wraps me in his strong soldier's arms, holding me to his heart. Finally, he looks at me with tears in his eyes, "Azizi, how you honour me!"

I answer with an ancient proverb of the desert, "It is the honour of your love received a thousand-fold that I now give to you."

He leaves the tent and me to my thoughts. There is nothing to be done until the morning when we will meet with Giafar and so I go to my bed.

It is late, and when drifting off to sleep, I hear the Adhãn. *Much too late,* I think, and then I feel a pang of guilt for thinking that I am much too tired to get up and do my duty. I drift off again unable to get up.

I fall into Samå, the sacred state of meditation, that allows one's consciousness to fall away and enables the individual to experience Divine Joy. Faintly, I hear the melodious voice, singing the sacred words of prayer and yet my mind rebels. There is something different; this is not the prayer I know. This is different, beautiful, at once familiar and foreign. The words appear in front of me in the ancient calligraphy of the Masters:

'Ant Shajarat Jayira
Ahmi habi
La-ilaha illa-llah

Beautiful and haunting is this song. I can, in my sleep, feel tears welling up in my eyes. Over and over this song is repeated, in a soft plaintive male voice that modulates up and down the scale of unknown music, that my heart knows and yearns for.

Like a soft veil of silk, my tent is rent open, and a vastness of blue sky unleashes itself onto my senses. Without warning, my whole being is invaded by the taste of salt.

Like the star flowers of my childhood mountains, that burst forth at the first call of spring, a pair of eyes of the fairest blue looks upon me.

"My love sustains you. Look at my tears. My Love, will you come to me?"

I hear myself cry out, "I am here!"

I awake with a start, emotions choking at my throat, and my heart pounding so hard I find it hard to catch my breath. An old ache has returned.

This dream vision is so real, and this is the third time I have seen these eyes. Each time it has left me yearning for Eternity.

Dawn is breaking, and I walk out into the sand dunes for solitude. Even the blue sky above me is no consolation for the blue of his eyes that has confronted me, enticed, and enthralled me.

I recite my morning prayer and seek tranquillity in the exercises that I practice every day for mastership of the mind. Feeling a little more in control and with a flame not quite put out in my heart, I make my way back to camp.

On the morning breeze, I hear a faint familiar phrase and tune, repeated over and over again. Each time it rises a little higher until it reaches a pinnacle and then falls back to a low tone. I can now distinguish the sonorous tones of Hasan's voice. I come upon him unawares as he is finishing his morning prayer. I am transfixed. I suddenly recognise the phrase he was singing, "La-ilaha illa-llah", repeated.

Finally, he stands and turns. Seeing me there he looks momentarily abashed as if caught in the act of a personal and sacred moment.

"Greetings Azizi, the morning finds you well?"

"Hasan, what is that that you were singing?"

"It was my morning prayer. Surely you have a morning prayer?"

"Yes, but not like that. What is the meaning of the words you were singing?"

"Uh... you mean La-ilaha illa-llah?"

"Yes, those words, what do they mean?" A shudder runs down my spine as I once more hear the words from my previous night's vision.

"That means 'There is no god but God.'"

"Hasan, were you singing those words last night after you left me?"

Hasan looks at me strangely as if I have lost my senses. "No Azizi, this prayer is said at dawn, noon and dusk, not before nor after."

"Ah" was all I could manage to say.

"What is the matter, Azizi? You look troubled. What does my prayer have to do with anything?"

"I heard those words and others in a vision last night."

It is the first time that I see Hasan pale, and he looks positively shaken.

"What other words did you hear Azizi?"

"I do not remember; they were both familiar yet strange. I can only remember the phrase you sang in your prayer."

"Azizi, is it permitted to ask what you saw in your vision?"

I look at him, and the memory of the dream overwhelms me, tears well up in my eyes. Hasan comes over and holds me tight.

"Azizi, are we doomed on this mission? Is this what you saw?"

I shake my head. "No, I think it is the Sacred Eyes of Creation that I saw."

I can sense Hasan going through a dilemma. He does not know whether to fall on his knees at the mention of this sacred vision or to hold me. Since I am still sobbing, his resolve to comfort me is welcomed.

After a while he asks, "But why are you so sad? I would think that such a vision would fill you with joy and wonder."

"The day of my birth falls in the season of Malkizar. It is with the salt of sorrow that I see, Hasan, and it is the yearning for Eternity that I cry for."

Hasan holds me tighter; this he understands, he who deals with death in his profession.

We walk back to the camp together. At my tent, Hasan looks at me with concern.

"I will be well." I answer to his concern.

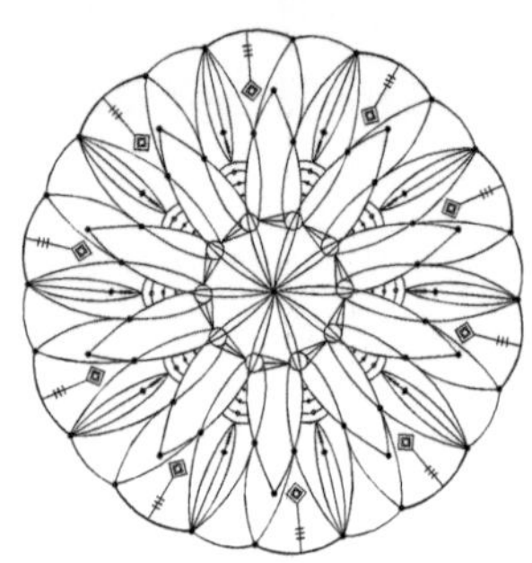

CHAPTER TWENTY-TWO

"The Huda Pass!"

Giafar is explaining the means by which we are to reach the northern regions and gain the Great Citadel, capital and home to the Over Lord.

There is a moment of disbelief followed by a resigned silence.

Apparently, everyone but I knows that this will be an almost impossible task. Faruq speaks up, "Father, I understand the need for speed. We have no leave from their tribesmen to go by the Huda Pass, and we all know that they are very reluctant to let anyone through. Negotiations with them will take more time than if we were to go back through the Asfaine foothills."

My ears prick up at the mention of my beloved mountains. Quietly, Hasan is explaining to me the dangers of the Huda Pass. The tribesmen are very fierce. The pass itself is at the base of cliffs so high that the sun never penetrates to the floor. The pass is so narrow in parts that a caravan may only progress in single file. This makes it extremely easy to defend.

The Huda people are very proud and protective of their homes. Caravans that have not had their leave to go through have been known to perish without trace. Furthermore, in this season, the winds can blow through the narrow passages with such force, that they can kill man or beast caught unawares. The Huda Pass is the conduit by which means the Cassim or great desert storms are made.

I am sure that I recall the horsemen who took Shahulm disappeared into a cave at the mouth of the Huda Pass.

Turning to Hasan, I ask him quietly, "If memory serves me right, is there not a cave at the foot of the Huda Pass?"

"Yes."

"The horsemen that took Shahulm disappeared into that cave. There must be a secret passage through it. Could we not follow the same route?"

"You are probably right, but for us to discover the secret way through that cave could take a year. We do not have the time, Azizi."

I sigh, resigned to let the soldiers who know the land choose the right route. I notice to my great surprise that Ijlal has quietly slipped into the tent and is listening. He is dressed for the road. He looks much better than he has done in a long time. His eyes shine with determination.

Giafar continues, "Time is short. You will have to take your chances with the Huda tribesmen. We have had dealings with them, and they are more accommodating to the Lord of Schiraz then any other lord. Royal couriers of Schiraz are usually allowed through in the low season. Besides, you have with you a soldier of Naassée. They are well respected by the Huda people. This may buy you passage through."

The Companions turn to Hasan.

At this point, Giafar notices Ijlal, "Ijlal! Ah, it is good to see you are well again. What are you doing here, nephew?"

The Companions surround Ijlal and their affection for him is touching to see.

"Uncle, thank you. I am well. I am ready to travel with you."

There is a moment of disbelief, followed by a hush that is almost deafening.

Giafar looks as though he is about to explode but regains control and in his most commanding voice replies, "Nephew, we will do everything in our power to return with Shahulm. I do not think that you are well enough to travel. Time is of the essence, and you may slow us down."

Ijlal looks directly at me and replies, "Was it not said in my dream, that there would be seven Companions together with the prince of the land and the seer of Apphat who would rescue the Beloved of the crown?"

I want to support Ijlal's claim to come with us and yet I can see Giafar's point. But Ijlal looks well enough to travel. And as far as I am concerned, yes, my interpretation stands: there will be seven Companions accompanying us.

Giafar scoffs. We have reached a stalemate.

"Pfhhh! Dreams! If every soothsayer has his way, the land would be filled with dreamers. No disrespect meant to you, or your godmother, Azizi." Giafar quickly adds.

There is an awkward moment. None of the Companions want

to disappoint their leader, yet all know the realities of travel through harsh country. Ijlal looks at me pleadingly, begging with his eyes for me to find a way.

I will not speak with the voice of the Guardian Spirit this time, but I think that at least I can speak with the voice of reason.

"With great respect Giafar, is it not ordained that an initiated soldier of Apphat, should stand in battle side by side with his beloved? And if he cannot, should he not fight with his Companions until he joins his beloved?"

Hasan looks at me with a broad smile. "Giafar, indeed Azizi speaks truly, that is the ordination of the initiated soldier."

Giafar mumbles something to the effect that he should have known better than to contradict the voice instrument of the Spirit.

Ijlal looks at me with words of thanks in his eyes.

"Azizi, if you think that he is fit enough to travel, I will allow it. But see to him, for you will be responsible for his well-being along the way."

I bow my consent to Giafar, giving him the deference that a wise general is owed.

Giafar continues to lay out the plan for our approach to the Great Citadel of the Over Lord. The place is built on a great hill that stands in the centre of a wide plain, between the Ocean of Malkizar and the Isthmus of Mina. The only approach to the great city is along a well-maintained road that runs directly across the plain and on which travellers can be seen approaching for many days. The aim will be to distract the forces of the citadel long enough to allow passage even of a small caravan, unchallenged.

"I have sent an envoy to the Great Council of Naassée, requesting that the armies be gathered and begin a march toward the Great

Citadel. The armies are to travel through the Asfaine foothills and make landfall on the coast nearest the Isthmus of Mina. The army from Schiraz will split at the Glesskerel foothills, and one contingent will move towards the Giant's Footsteps two days after your caravan has crossed the isthmus."

"My Lord Giafar, if they think they are under siege, will not the guards of the Citadel close the doors to the city well before our caravan reaches it?"

Giafar looks at Fatin with the eye of a general that recognises quick wit and intelligence. "Yes, Fatin. Though our plan is intended to confuse and give the impression that we are standing against Gleskerell, there is a possibility that the Over Lord's generals will see through that ruse. That is why the caravan will not enter through the main gates of the city but make its way to the west of the Great Citadel."

Isamadeen interrupts at this point. "The Great Citadel is built on a cliff face in the west." Looking briefly at Ijlal he adds, "there is no hope that we can scale that cliff to gain entry into the city."

Giafar although appreciative of the Companions' quick grasp of matters of importance, is nevertheless losing his patience at the interruptions. "Yes, Isamadeen. That is why you will not scale the walls of the cliffs."

"Then how... ?" Jamal is quickly silenced with one look from Giafar.

"A spy from the Royal Guard has informed us that there is a secret passage. It is situated at the base of the citadel at the bottom of the cliffs. However, this pass can only be accessed at the low tide of Malkizar. You will receive the instructions on how to gain this pass once you have reached your destination. We cannot risk this information falling into the wrong hands. You will agree that timing will be of the essence. We will require you to be in constant communication with us." Looking at me he continues, "Azizi, with your permission this is where I would request your assistance. Our court Magician and Seer Haroun-al-Rashid will act as the link between us and your caravan through you."

"Giafar, I had expected this and of course I will be happy to play my role in this."

The Companions looked on in awe. Ijlal smiles to see their wonderment at something he experienced firsthand with me when we were a little younger.

Giafar continues, "Hasan, I have not heard back from the Great Council of Naassée. It is possible that with all the events that are occurring, the Great Council may think it a ruse and a trap of the Over Lord. I know how important it is for you to be with the Companions. However, your physical presence at the Council, would do much to convince them to order the armies to march. I would ask your favour knowing your speed as a Royal Guard, to reach Naassée within the next week. You will still have time to rejoin the Companions in the Huda Pass and assist with the negotiations."

Knowing Hasan as I do, I can detect that under that cool, emotionless surface he is put out.

"Giafar, since time is of the essence, would not the token from Hasan have the same effect?" I am holding up the talisman offered to me by Hasan for my Damna.

"Azizi, yes it would, but it would take longer for one of my couriers to reach Naassée than for Hasan to do so."

"It can be there tonight Giafar."

If the Companions were awed before, now they positively paled. "Explain this Azizi."

"I will contact my godmother tonight, and she will personally deliver the talisman to the Great Council."

Giafar thought for a while. "I will not ask how this is to be done, Azizi, but yes, Aïschah there with Hasan's talisman would have twice the impact. So shall it be, then."

Hasan nods, gratitude written on his face. His place is with soldiers not politicians.

"Very well, if there are no questions, then your departure is tonight. All your travelling needs have been made ready."

Giafar looks fondly at Faruq and then at all the other Companions. "I have no need to tell you that in the next month, you will need to use your greatest skills, your greatest cunning, and all of your courage. I wish you the speed and blessings of the Guardian Spirit and will pray for your safe and speedy return. All praise to the Spirit!"

In one voice the Companions shout, "Sri Akall!"

A shudder runs through my spine at the sound of these sacred words.

Before retiring to my tent, I check in on Ijlal. His spirits have lifted remarkably. He greets me with a warm embrace and a kiss on both cheeks. "Azizi my brother, thank you for your support."

I smile at him. It is both my duty and my pleasure.

"Ijlal, you look well enough to travel. However, I must ask you to tell me if you feel unwell in any way."

"Brother, nothing can stop me now. We are on our way to seek my beloved Shahulm."

I hold his hands and look at him deeply. There is a question that is burning on my lips. He must have sensed this.

"What is it Azizi? What is on your mind?"

"I do not wish to pry, Ijlal, but I wondered what it was like when… " I hesitate to go on. He looks puzzled for a moment and then laughs light-heartedly. "I remember prying myself on such matters, when the Guardian spoke through you."

I remember the moment. It seems so long ago, that winter day in my godmother's house.

His face clouds a moment thinking about how to put his experience into words.

"Azizi, it is when I am overcome with grief. It is first as if I am falling into a deep well. My whole body aches, but there is a will in my mind that forms, wanting… no, demanding justice. Then a picture appears in my head, I know not from where—a picture of ancient times—and I see a great bird flying directly towards me. It calls to me, and I recognise its cry. Then it swoops down, and before I can avoid it, I can feel its presence filling my mind and my body. At once I see what the bird sees and feel what it feels, and I realise that I too am now as one with the bird as it is one with me."

It is as my godmother, and I had discussed and concluded, that the magic of Love Transformation is rooted deeply into the magic of the Ancients. Everyone in his or her fundamental essence, belongs to an animal group spirit. In Ijlal's case it is Hadid, the spirit of the air, and it is this spirit that assumes authority in the face of grave danger, where love is concerned. Why it is so rare and affects some and not others, is another mystery.

"Azizi, what is it to witness this transformation?"

"Ijlal, it is the great Love Transformation. It is both sacred and awesome to witness."

"Do people think I have gone insane?"

"No. They are deeply respectful of the sacred love you bear for your beloved. Once you asked me if Shahulm was your star soul. Truly Ijlal, the Love Transformation would not be made manifest if he was not."

"Azizi, my brother, beloved of All, how fortunate I am to have you by my side."

He comes over again and once more embraces me, in that warm sensuous manner of his that makes me forget all my worries and my woes.

"Ijlal, one more question if I may."

He smiles most graciously and straightens himself in the manner of a child when required to answer a serious question by his teacher.

"Ijlal, do you think you could call the great bird and make manifest the Love Transformation at will?"

Ijlal is deep in thought for a momen. "I do not know Azizi."

I make a mental note to begin training Ijlal in the powers of his mind and see if he indeed can call the Transformation at will.

It is still high noon as I leave his tent. I instruct him to rest before we set off tonight.

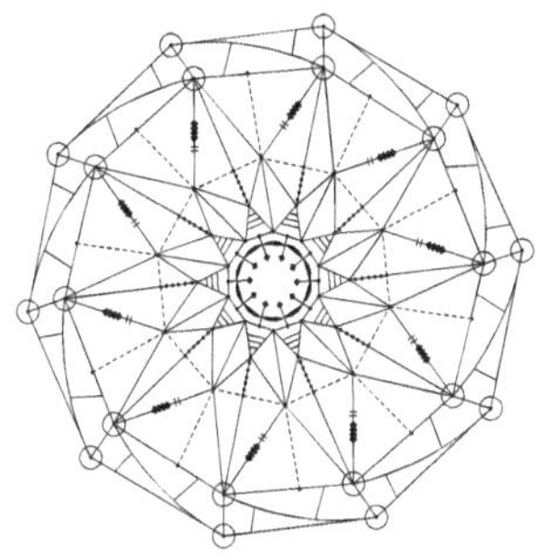

CHAPTER TWENTY-THREE

The moon of Camlac disappears in its final ebb. Now begins the season of Malkizar, as slowly Camlac will renew itself until full. We need to reach Shahulm before it reaches its fullness. Ironically, I remember that it will soon be my nineteenth naming day.

As our caravan makes its way north to the Huda Pass, I look over my shoulder and see the moon Ayshah rise slowly in the east, it takes the shape of a thin silver crescent, its empty receptacle facing heaven. A shooting star runs across the heavens above the moon, heading north.

Each member of our caravan is mounted on a horse, and each has packed lightly in the manner of desert travellers. I am still unused to my mount that the tribesmen have given me, having only experienced the sure-footed mules that Halim and I had brought down from the mountains earlier this spring. The first day is uncomfortable and I find my body aching in places I did not think could ache. Rauf shows me how to best move with the horse and adopt a rhythm that eventually eases my discomfort.

This is another new beginning. I feel a sense of relief to be on the move and left alone to my own thoughts. We depart under the cover of night to leave as little trace of our movements as possible. By the morning, the desert wind will have erased all traces of our passing. In the manner of desert travellers, as Halim had taught me, we journey at night until mid-morning and then take a rest during the Cârem, the hottest part of the day. It will be a two-day journey to the base of the Huda Pass.

Earlier that evening I contacted Aïschah with Giafar's request. She understood the urgency and at once disappeared with the talisman.

Out of curiosity, I looked in on the Great Council meeting.

Aïschah did not wait upon ceremony to be invited in. She had manifested in the middle of the room, much to the astonishment of the gathered elders, some of whom knew of Aïschah by reputation although only two had met her. With very little embellishment she delivered Giafar's request and underlined her speech by presenting Hasan's talisman. The effect of Elwah's personal guard's symbol was immediate; the Council called for its generals and issued the orders to march.

I told Giafar and Hasan of the decision of the Great Council.

Giafar was relieved and immediately ordered his own troops to march towards Naassée, where they will join the Naasséene soldiers. The Over Lord's spies will report the march north towards Glesskerel and hopefully this will confuse him. The intention will not be clear and this will buy us time.

During the next meal break, I take the opportunity to check in on

Ijlal and see how he is faring. I need not have worried; his energy is at a peak. He's glad to be on the road and doing something.

I teach him a simple exercise of mental imagery to allow him to focus his mind power on a desired outcome. This comprises of a technique of breath control combined with simple physical manipulation of certain fingers, known as 'mudras' in ancient cultures. I ask Ijlal to keep this ritual a secret, as it forms part of the sacred Lore of Seership. Suffice to say that it enables Ijlal to still his mind quite effectively within a short period of time. He seems naturally adept to the work and pleased that I am teaching him something that he considers sacred.

The nights of travel are uneventful, though I am always overwhelmed by the great, uninterrupted vastness of the sky and its countless stars.

The times when we make camp and take our rest become more and more difficult. My sleep is restless and always haunted by an urgent call, which is never clear. All I can remember is the sensation of floating in a vastness of blue sky, a sky that caresses me and urges me on.

On the second night, before we set off for the base of the Huda Pass, I focus on establishing contact with Haroun-al-Rashid the court magician. This is a mere formality, to establish the link that will from now on be our constant source of information. Giafar will know of our progress and our group that of the armies of Giafar.

There is also a necessity to ensure that in some way our communication will be protected from intrusion. This is a more difficult task, as it requires constant vigilance and a split focus of the mind, to monitor the field of protection around the communication. Haroun-al-Rashid will be the main source of power for that aspect, as I have not yet been trained in this technique. Out of necessity, we also keep our communications brief.

The communication is successful and clear. Through his magician, Giafar sends his greetings to the troupe. When I relay this to the Companions, there is a hushed welcome and amazement in their eyes, like Halim's look when he first received news of his family through me.

We arrive at the base of the Huda Pass at the break of dawn and make camp. Hasan has gone ahead to organise a meeting with the chieftains. Faruq goes with him as a capable soldier, whose skills have commanded even Hasan's respect. He will also bear the appropriate gift of greeting on behalf of his prince. Once the appointed time has been set up, Hasan will send Faruq back to bring the rest of the caravan to the meeting. We hope that, in addition to Hasan, the presence of Ijlal as the crown prince in the caravan will add weight to the request for a safe passage.

At one point, Rauf asks me if I cannot in some way influence the minds of the chieftains at the meeting, to allow us to go through.

I smile at his innocence and reply that it is forbidden for me to use my powers to influence my fellow human beings, unless it is in defence of loved ones who are in some danger. Then, and only after careful consideration will I allow myself to impel the mind of the offender with more positive thoughts.

He asks me to tell him a story of such an event, and I relate the story of their prince Ijlal. I speak of the occasion when he and I took a walk into my beloved forest and unbeknown to him, he had just been lured and almost trapped by a Scarlet Robe. I explain that as a last resort, having sensed the danger too late to do anything else, I was obliged to take control of his mind and bid him walk to me and away from danger.

When I look up, all the Companions are either sitting or standing close to me, listening in rapture. They clamour for more stories, and so I tell them the legend of the first great Love Transformation, that they might understand their prince a little more. Constant friend to Rauf, Jamal, who is sitting near Ijlal ends up with his arm around his prince, hugging him in obvious affection and admiration. Their lack of inhibition in demonstrating their true feeling for each other, will never cease to amaze and inspire me.

It will soon be noon, and Hasan and Faruq will not return until late afternoon. We settle for the mid-day rest and wait for their return. Our camp is very close to the ocean of Malkizar. The incessant sound soon lulls me to sleep, though it is with some reluctance that I allow myself to slip into slumber. The odour of salt on the afternoon breeze brings too many visions with it.

I find myself standing on a dune. I am staring at the entrance to the cave of the Huda Pass, and in the distance, I can see a lone figure walking towards me. His desert clothes of the brightest white are floating and moving around him like sea grass in the afternoon breeze.

It will be Faruq returning to us. I should call out to the Companions and tell them to prepare. I find myself paralysed on the spot, unable to take my eyes off the young man walking towards me.

Soon I make out his slender figure. The noon haze of the desert heat that surrounds him, at first begins to change and waver with his every move. It now seems to surround him in an impregnable silvery light. He is very close and still his face is covered in the manner of the desert traveller. This is not Faruq nor is it Hasan; this figure is much too slender.

The figure now stands in front of me and still I cannot move. Slowly and quite deliberately he removes his face covering.

My heart and mind explode in a myriad ways, in both recognition and shock. His eyes are of the brightest and deepest blue—these are the eyes that have haunted my dreams. His is the fairest face I have ever beheld; my breath is taken away. I struggle to stem the flow of tears of both joy and longing I feel. His skin is the pure white of snow and his hair is the colour of the desert sand. He looks at me.

He has such longing in his eyes, and then as I think my heart cannot bear more, he softly speaks my name, "Azizi, at last."

I want to throw myself at his feet. He holds out his hands and takes mine pressing them gently in his.

"Dear One, we do not have much time. A question burns in my heart."

Bewildered, I hear myself answering, "Ask what you will. The answer is yes."

He looks so deeply into my eyes that all the sky enters my being. He smiles then and again speaks, "Azizi, I would ask for your love for all Eternity."

I speak from the depth of my being, "With all of my heart I give you all of my Love, now and for all Eternity."

Something both strange and wonderful happens then. He sheds a tear and catching it on the tip of his finger, he places it delicately and deliberately in his mouth. Then softly like a summer breeze he leans forward, and he kisses me.

A sweetness the like of which I have never experienced fills my entire being. All taste of salt is banished, sunlight engulfes my mouth, and a wondrous warmth descends to the very pit of my being.

"Immortal Beloved, receive my gift."

A whistling wind begins to blow, harsh and intrusive. The silvery haze around us begins to shimmer and waver. He smiles sadly and his form starts to fade from my eyes.

I call out to him, but he hushes me saying we will meet again. The wind starts to tear at the fabric of his garment.

As his being disappears in a white haze of light, I can still hear his voice singing to me, urging me to learn and repeat this song everyday. Our love and the safety of the world are at stake. Softly I hear that magic song:

Alsafinat Almuqadasat
Astaqbal Hubiy
Qum bi'iiuua Habi

Just as his last words fade, I hear a woman's terrible scream filled with hatred and rage.

I open my eyes and find myself sitting bolt up right on my sleeping mat. The bare and bleached desert light is tearing at my eyes.

Isamadeen is next to me with concern in his eyes.

Tears are flowing down my face. I shield my eyes with my hand.

"Azizi, you were having a dream. Are you well?"

Feeling a little disoriented, I answer, "Yes... I think so. Thank you, Isamadeen."

I look up to him grateful for his concern. I have never seen Isamadeen frightened; he looks at me and backs away with several stumbling steps paling visibly.

He mumbles 'Mahjir' several times.

Rauf stirs awake and comes to stand by his twin brother's side. With hoarse sleep in his voice, he asks, "What is it, Isamadeen? What is the matter?"

Isamadeen, who had turned to look at his brother, returns his gaze to me and there is another look of astonishment, bordering on disappointment. Perplexed and obviously confused, Isamadeen replies, "It is nothing Mahjir... Azizi... was having a dream."

I am now concerned. What was it that Isamadeen saw that has so disturbed him, which obviously now has disappeared?

Rauf gives both of us a blank look before walking away shrugging his shoulders.

I am still filled with the vision I have just experienced and want very much to be alone to reflect. So, under pretext to see if Faruq is on his way back, I say that I will go and look out for his return.

I stand on a nearby dune, looking out out over the surrounding desert and search for the mouth of the cave at the base of the Huda Pass. It is not far from here that Shahulm had been taken. I can make out the cave and its dark, gaping entrance. The sun has begun to sink low on the horizon, turning the dunes into a deeper shade of gold.

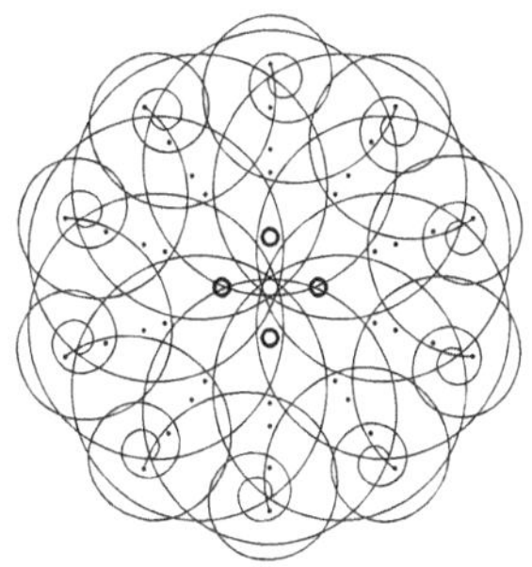

CHAPTER TWENTY-FOUR

With a pang of longing, I recall the vision I have just had. Softly, I hear the words of the song he has urged me to learn. Using the art of memory that my godmother taught me, I remember all the words and the tune he used to sing it. With a small shock, I remember the dream in which I first heard this sacred song.

Softly, I sing this song to myself. Very gently and at first without much awareness, I begin to feel a glow of warmth in the pit of my being, and I remember his kiss. Such a longing wells up in my heart, and yet strangely gone is the sadness that I have experienced so often in my life.

I finish the song and looking up towards the north, I see dust blowing in the wind and a figure on a horse. Faruq is on his way.

I walk back to the camp to tell the Companions to make ready. I see that Isamadeen and his brother Rauf are deep in conversation, which stops when I reach the camp. Isamadeen seems to be less controlled than usual, and his brother, on the other hand, seems to be reasoning with him.

I tell them all that Faruq is on his way and to make ready for departure.

We are packed and ready when Faruq arrives. He looks exhausted and tense. Despite this, he insists on leaving immediately.

As we ride towards the cliffs of the Huda Pass, Faruq draws rein and sidles his horse next to Ijlal's and mine.

"Hasan has negotiated for an audience with their chief for the evening of tomorrow."

An insightful ruler in the making, Ijlal remarks, "The request was not granted easily Faruq?"

Faruq looks in the distance for a moment and then answers. "No, cousin. There is something that bothers me. I thought the chieftain was not speaking as freely as she wished."

"Who else was present when you made the request?" I ask.

"Advisers and other tribesmen. All decisions of the Huda are shared amongst those who wish to take part."

"Faruq, was there anyone present who either stood apart or who seemed to want to force their will?"

The young soldier reflects for a while. Ijlal looks at me inquisitively.

"Yes, Azizi. There was one who spoke loudly and whom the others seemed to resent when he spoke."

"Describe this person to us, Faruq."

His perfect soldier's mind, trained to remember the smallest detail, enables him to recreate the meeting and all who were there. "His hair is the colour of the cliffs of Naassée at sunset, and he wears a beard of the same colour. His eyes are dark. He is about the height of Jamal though stockier. When he walks his steps are uneven, as if he is nursing an injury to his left foot. He bears no marks on his skin that I can tell. His voice is harsh, and he often speaks of the rights of his people. Judging by the reactions of the other tribesmen present, he spoke of this too vehemently and too often."

Faruq pauses a moment, seemingly remembering a detail.

"He made a reference to the sovereignty of the Huda people, insisting that they did not wish to become involved in the petty wrangling of the Sultan of Schiraz."

Ijlal straightens a little in his seat and states, "It seems that this person knows more of our mission than we would wish."

"That is what I thought," replies Faruq.

Ijlal turns to me. "Azizi what are your thoughts?"

"I agree with you. There is something here that is disturbing. I will wait until the meeting before I can say for sure what it is."

Faruq nods and spurs his horse forward to the head of the caravan.

We ride silently, Ijlal understanding that until I see this person, there is little I can surmise.

We approach the base cliffs of the Huda Pass. On our right, the mouth of the cave gapes dark and forbidding, set in a silent groan.

I sense Ijlal's sadness at the memory of seeing his beloved abducted into the depth of this cave. Much to his credit, Ijlal takes control of his emotions, and his grief does not provoke the transformation it has in the past. I am pleased to see the progress he has made with the mind exercises.

The cliffs of Huda are aglow with the setting sun, burning a deep orange. Travelling up a short, winding path that seems to lead to the base of the cliff face, we suddenly come up to a dark narrow fissure in the rock. This is the entrance to the Huda Pass.

No description of it can have prepared me for this sight and the feeling of brooding power. We are forced to enter one rider at a time. The air is suddenly cool, and the cliffs rise on either side, smooth and to great heights, leaving a ribbon of dark blue sky mimicking our path. The trail is sandy, resulting in an eerie silence, which is occasionally broken by the sound of a falling pebble echoing down the passage, leaving us tense and alert.

There are other passageways that open on either side from time to time. This is a veritable labyrinth. I am glad that Faruq's memory leads us in the right direction.

We travel on, hushed by the strange majesty of the place. The path takes a turn and opens abruptly onto a large sandy clearing. The tops of the cliffs are still aglow with the sunset.

I am awestruck with the sight of the rocky cliff now facing us. The façade of a temple full of ancient majesty, stands carved out of the rock. An elaborate entrance flanked by mighty columns opens directly before us. This entire construct has been shaped out of the solid rock face. As we approach, the details of sculpture showing clearly and seemingly untouched by the ravages of time, astonish me with their beauty and precision. Ancient stone creatures stand guard at the base of each column. Geometrically centred, the imposing entrance made of solid stone slabs, heavily decorated in ancient scrolls, leads straight into the cool, dark heart of the cliff. I feel dwarfed by this mighty building and awed at the prospect of meeting the descendants of the ancient artisans who devised and carved this monument.

Here we dismount taking our personal belongings. Four small men appear silently, seemingly from nowhere, and take our horses leading them away through another passage.

Faruq signals us to follow him.

He leads us through darkened passages that are occasionally lit by deep clefts in the rock rising to the height of the cliffs. These allow light to filter through from the surface. Whether these are natural or man-made, I cannot tell. The darker passages are lit with torches, and the rocky surfaces of others seem to glow of their own accord, giving off a pale light sufficient to see the way.

We come finally to a large room that opens from the passage we travelled through and find Hasan waiting for us. His manner is subdued and giving the Companions a signal, he indicates that it is not safe to talk here at this point. He leads us to rooms farther down that will serve us as sleeping quarters for the night ahead.

Two men resembling those who took our horses come in and quietly place wooden plates on low tables in the middle of the room.

The food consists of several dishes. Some with dried fruits and nuts. Other bowls contain different pastes that are tangy, and which go well with slabs of unleavened bread. Smaller containers hold varieties of oils, herbs, and spices in which the Companions dip their breads. Drinks are served, one of which is particularly strong tasting, quickly setting my head spinning.

After our meal, we are shown to a small cave in the centre of which is a depression forming a pool deep enough to wade to waist level.

This is the washing facility. Water forced under the great pressure of the sandstone rocks of the pass, springs up in a gentle waterfall at one end of the pool. Hasan shows me how to use some of the sand, combined with some dried herbs that lie in a wooden container by the pool, to wash and refresh myself.

This done, I put on fresh clothes and retire to the communal rooms we will share. A small opening carved out of the rock at the far end of the room, looks out onto one of the meandering passageways we followed earlier. Amazing that the openings are not visible from below. At least now I understand how these people know the movements of strangers below.

Hasan comes into the room smelling sweet from his bath and a fresh application of the patchouli oil that I find so beguiling.

He embraces me and sits next to me on a low mat woven of some kinds of reed, on top of which are several sheepskins. I wonder with a tinge of melancholy, whether any of these have made their trading journeys through Halim.

Hasan is looking at me.

"Hasan, tell me of your meeting with the chieftain. Faruq tells me that it did not go well."

Hasan nodds. "It did not. I have met these people once before. They are very proud and straightforward in their dealings." Hasan pauses. "This time, though it was different. They seemed tense, as if they were hiding something against their will."

"Faruq also told us of the man who spoke loudest against our passage."

Hasan looks thoughtful for a while. "There is something not right, yet I cannot put my sword's point to it."

As we speak, I continue to nibble at the foods on the table. "Hasan, what do you think is making them so nervous?"

"I do not know, Azizi. The tribes throughout the land are suspicious of each other. Alliances are not easily formed. Betrayal is always on their mind."

I take some bread and following Hasan's example, dip it into some savoury oil and then dip it into a greyish substance that for all resembles coarse sand.

My mouth is suddenly filled with the taste of salt.

I reach quickly for a drink. Hasan smiles a little at my discomfiture and refills my goblet. My head swims, I feel disoriented, and perspiration begins to bead on my face. I look at Hasan and can hear his voice still speaking of desert politics. Then concern appears in his eyes. I drop the goblet spilling its contents on the ground.

Everything suddenly goes still. My eyes become unfocused; the rocky wall opposite me shimmers then dissolves.

I see a room with a man kneeling on the ground. From Faruq's earlier description, this is the man who has previously so vehemently objected to our passage.

The walls around him darken and though I cannot sense smell, I am suddenly nauseous and repulsed with what would have been a rotting stench. Part of the wall before him seems to detach itself. A Shadow!

There are two of them in the room now. No words are exchanged, only mental images. The red headed man is being threatened. One of the Shadows draws a short knife and holding the man's forearm, slides the edge of the sword across his wrist three times. With shock, I realise that they have just marked him with the symbol of the Scarlet Robes—the three crossing blades. He is now their property. They will give him an antidote in small portions; enough to keep him alive but not enough to let him forget his mortal danger.

The man winces in pain but dares not withdraw his arm.

Malicious laughter echoes in my mind as the vision dissolves. The walls close in again. My eyes once more behold Hasan, who is sitting bolt upright his eyes full of concern.

I choke and catch my breath. My clothes are damp from perspiration. "Hasan! Shadows! There are Shadows here."

Hasan immediately draws his sword and stands up looking around.

"No!" I gasp. "With the red headed man—he is marked."

Then at once realising a greater danger, "Ijlal! Where is Ijlal?"

Hasan rushes to the doorway then hesitates.

"I will be safe. Protect Ijlal!"

I have recovered from my vision by the time Hasan returns with all the Companions and Ijlal. Scimitars drawn and with serious looks on their faces, they surround their prince.

They sit down, placing themselves between their Prince and the entrance. They seem to be waiting so I relate to them my vision.

I then explain, "We now have a bargaining position. This man is marked by the Shadows. He is now the property of the Scarlet Robes to do their bidding. If he is identified though, it will be his death warrant."

"Has he not been poisoned by the venom on their blades?" Hasan asked.

"They have administered an antidote in small doses, enough to keep him alive, with the promise of a full dose as his reward. He has been fooled, though, as once he has outgrown his usefulness, they will let him die."

We pass a tense night, the Companions taking turns in pairs to watch over the safety of Ijlal. The next day Ijlal is accompanied by at least two of the Companions wherever he goes. This leads to strange looks. The culture of the Huda dictates that the people are responsible for the safety of their guests. A guest who looks uncomfortable or feels unsafe, will be seen as a great personal shortcoming in the host and an insult to the guest. Nevertheless, we endeavour to defer to the royal status of Ijlal and make it look like part of our way of life.

The appointed time of evening arrives, and we make ready for the meeting with their Chieftain.

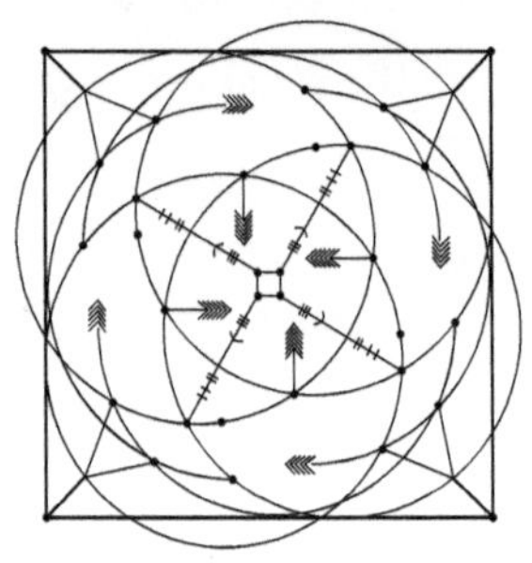

CHAPTER TWENTY-FIVE

Various torches mounted on the walls light the room we enter, and several smaller candles have been placed around. Cushions are arranged around the room in a circle, but the room is otherwise bare.

The chieftain is already seated at the far end of the room. She is an elderly woman several years older than my godmother. I had heard that the women fight as fiercely and as well as the men in these regions. She sits quite erect surrounded by several tribesmen and women. She is engaged in quiet conversation when we come in. She watches very carefully as our group enters and no detail escapes her sharp eyes as the Companions position themselves in the most defensive places around Ijlal. I decide to take on a less prominent role, so that I can survey the entire room, enabling me to sense the energies around the gathered people for any danger. It is agreed also that my role as Seer will not be divulged unless absolutely necessary.

The meeting opens with the formal greetings common to all desert tribes.

I look around to identify the red-headed man. He is seated slightly behind the chieftain and to her left. He wears a garment with a hood of a dark colour. Even under his hood I cannot mistake his eyes. They have already acquired the essence of crazed confusion. He moves on his cushion slightly, I notice that his left arm is bandaged at the wrist, and some blood has oozed into a tiny spot on the surface.

Prince Ijlal speaks first, "Gaisha, I thank you for this audience and present my compliments from my father, Sultan Rashãd."

"Prince, thank you for your gift which your kinsman presented to us before your arrival."

Ijlal bows slightly.

"Prince Ijlal, are you well and have you been well treated in our house?"

This is a double-edged sword. She looks at him kindly, but her sharp eyes wander ever so slightly, yet meaningfully, over the surrounding Companions in obvious guard position. The innuendo is not lost on Ijlal.

"Your people have been most kind and have taken care of all our physical needs."

She appears a little amused at the cleverness of the response. She understands that Ijlal is not going to commit himself to criticizing any perceived lack of safety. She decides not to pursue the matter.

"You have requested safe passage through the Huda Pass. You have chosen an ill time for your passage. At this season, the pass is often ravaged by the Ahl-Cassim, and it can shred a man or beast to death who is unprepared for it."

"It is a risk we are aware of, and a risk we are prepared to take if you will permit one of your guides to accompany us. Your people are well known for their ability to travel through the Huda Pass in any season."

The red-headed man leans forward and whispers something in her ear. She seems a little annoyed at this and raises her hand to silence him. He is angered by this and glares at Ijlal.

"Prince Ijlal, can I not persuade you to enjoy our hospitality, until the season of Malkizar is over?"

This will be difficult.

"Gaisha, I thank you for your offer but alas our affairs are urgent and require us to hasten north without delay."

"What is your urgency?"

The bluntness of her question takes me by surprise, but Ijlal seems almost prepared for it. He pauses a moment allowing the tension to peak and pass.

"We are on an urgent errand to the Kingdom of Glesskerel. My Beloved, Prince Shahulm, has been taken ill. We are to meet with his family and escort his mother back to my father's palace."

She looks at him directly in the eyes. I hold my breath. I am amazed at Ijlal's self-control. He has not lied; he even paused between the words 'taken' and 'ill.' Shahulm certainly has been taken and would be ill. How he is able to mention his beloved's name without falling prey to the grief that will herald the Love Transformation is in part, I believe, due to the mental exercises he has been practicing.

In a tone that borders on sarcasm she responds, "Your father boasts many speedy couriers that usually have leave to pass through. Surely one courier would be faster than an entire caravan? Even this Naasséene soldier," she points to Hasan, "would have no difficulty reaching Glesskerel in less than a lahae."

"You will agree with me, Gaisha, that sending a courier, even a Naasséene soldier on royal business, could be interpreted as an insult. Accompanying the Queen of Glesskerel with less than a royal escort, would be unforgivable. However, since you offer safe passage for my father's couriers, what difference would you draw to safe passage for a royal caravan?"

She looks at him for a long pause. Then she laughs openly. "Well answered young prince. You will make your father's tutors' proud."

The red-headed man again interjects in her ear. "However, Prince, the majority of my people have to agree on this, and there are those among us,"—here she pauses long enough for most of the tribe people to look at the red-headed man—"who oppose this passage. Also, one of my people will need to volunteer their services to safely guide you through the Pass. To date no one has offered."

The red-headed man looks spitefully pleased with himself. I catch a movement on one side of the room; a small figure exits quickly through a side door. I extend my mind to this presence, trying to follow it quickly before it is too far out of my reach. I cannot sense any immediate danger, and yet there is a familiarity I cannot identify, as if a shield of protection has been drawn. It sets my mind racing. The presence is too far now for me to further probe, leaving me with a sense of unease.

The red-headed man is making a vehement speech, about not getting involved in the petty affairs of Sultan Rashãd of Schiraz. In an oily tone, he asks what we have to say to the rumours of the armies moving north through to Naassée.

The chieftain looks directly again at Ijlal and re-phrases the question. "Would you care to speak to these rumours, Prince, of your father's armies moving north to Naassée?"

"Gaisha, if our intent had been hostile, we would now be accompanied by my father's army. Instead, I hear you say that you have rumours of my father's armies travelling north to Naassée. On these rumours I cannot comment. Our caravan has not seen, nor received a single courier since we left Schiraz two days ago."

Ijlal is a true diplomat. He has not lied once and yet he does not give anything away.

This response seems to enrage the red-headed man even more. He is alienating himself with his tribe, though. It appears that more and more the group is becoming ambivalent to his ranting.

After careful consideration and having consulted those of her tribe who are present, the chieftain speaks, "Prince, if the majority of my people agree, your caravan will be allowed to pass. However..." here she pauses, "you will only be allowed to pass if one of my people will agree to guide you through the Pass."

There is a long pause. All the tribe people look at us with a neutral stares. No one steps forward. The red-headed man looks pleased with himself, almost chuckling out loud.

With my mind I call his attention, and as soon as our eyes lock, I look down and openly stare at the bandage around his wrist. The spot of blood has grown a little more, and his sleeve, which he had allowed to fall back during his speech, now reveals almost the entire bandage. He looks at once at his wrist and as he lifts his eyes again, I once more lock eyes with him. Suddenly he seems nervous. He pulls his sleeve forward and makes to stand up. He is about to say something when a movement catches my eye at the side entrance.

A woman steps into the circle. Behind her a smaller figure follows and remains in the background. "Gaisha, I will guide this caravan through the Huda Pass."

Palpable relief, accompanied by a sense of disbelief passes through our group. The assembly looks to this woman. She has her back turned to us.

The chieftain looks at her and asks, "Fariqa, no one is forcing you to do this. Are you making this decision of your own free will?"

"Yes. It is a life-debt I owe one of theirs."

She turns then. I recognise her immediately. This is the desert woman Fariqa whose child I had saved from the bite of a poisonous desert creature. Looking to the back, I see and recognise her child now grown taller, looking well, and smiling at me. My heart leaps in gratitude at seeing them both.

Such is our relief that in the time it takes for the chieftain to agree to Fariqa's offer, both Hasan and I are the only ones to notice that the red-headed man has slipped out of the meeting room with a look of rage. My instincts tell me this will not be our last encounter and we will need to be on our guard.

Fariqa and I speak for some time. Her family often travels with the caravan Halim and I had first met. It is her husband's tribe. They first met as his caravan had travelled the Huda Pass. She and her son, Saeed, would stay with her tribesmen, the Huda people during the season of Malkizar.

Little Saeed stands hidden behind his mother and then as his shyness wears off, he begins to join in our talk, and tells me of the things he does here and the games he plays. With great pride, he tells me that his father has promised to bring him back his first short scimitar.

The Companions hear firsthand from Fariqa the story of how Saeed had been near death when the Guardian Spirit, in His great mercy, had sent his servant and healer to halt the poison and miraculously heal her only son. She leaves no details out, down to the doubts that her husband's kinsmen had openly voiced, until Hasan, the soldier protector of the tribe, had affirmed the healing powers manifest.

This story does nothing to diminish the awe that the Companions hold me in. I protest that my role was only as an instrument. In the end, I accept that this will always be a part of my life. I am glad that Saeed has been saved. And as long as my ego does not get in the way, I reflect that as an instrument of the Spirit, no matter how imperfect, I will always serve His greater purpose, where and when the need arises, with all my heart. I will continue to do so in the greatest humility for the honour He bestows upon me, by choosing this imperfect vessel to manifest his might.

The conversation turns to the coming trip and how we will handle the various dangers, especially the Ahl-Cassim.

"It is a simple task but one that requires experience," Fariqa explains. "Reading the weather is important. There are certain signs that will signal the Ahl-Cassim."

"Does Ahl-Casim, not mean 'the Breath of God?'" I remember with a shudder the great sandstorm, Halim and I encountered on our way into the desert. "What if we are caught? How do we escape?"

Fariqa smiles and then explains, "The passage is dotted with small side caves. These were dug long ago to allow caravans to take shelter if necessary. The caves are marked with secret signs that only the Huda people know."

"You should rest. We will leave early in the morning, and you will need your strength if we are to complete the journey in time and before the height of Malkizar."

We part and return to our sleeping quarters where we spend a vigilant night's rest.

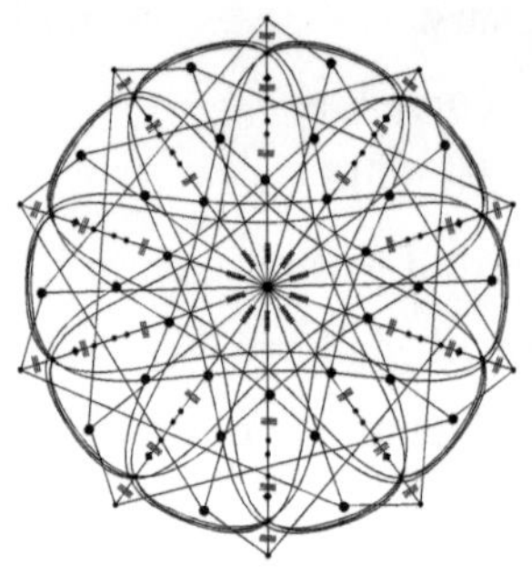

CHAPTER TWENTY-SIX

We do not see the Huda people again; the decision having been made to allow us through, they have withdrawn to their own activities. Only a message of well wishes from the chieftain is delivered to Ijlal through Fariqa, our guide. Her son, Saeed, will stay with his maternal grandparents over the next two or three duna. The Companions wear the same shepherds clothing that we set out with. Scimitars and short swords are kept under their clothing. Their blue robes are carefully packed away in satchels caried on the horses.

The horses have been well looked after, groomed, and fed and are waiting for us tied to several iron rings mounted into the rock. Fariqa looks anxiously at the sky through the narrow openings of the cliff tops. A pale blue sky is lacerated with thin strands of soft pink clouds, showing like fresh wounds. The air is still and cool.

Turning back to us, Fariqa remarks, "There is a good chance

that an Ahl-Cassim will strike during the day."

We set off in the silence of the dawn. The pass soon narrows, and we are forced to travel single file. I am glad of Fariqa's guidance as the Huda Pass proves to be a labyrinth of confusing passages that begin to criss-cross in absolute confusion. Whenever I think we should make a left turn, Fariqa leads the caravan to the right.

As the Huda Pass is protected completely from the harsh desert sun, it is safe for us to travel during the day. I was glad of it, as I do not know how comfortable it would be to endure the eerie atmosphere of the pass in complete darkness, when at every turn a Shadow could detach itself from the rocks. As we progress, Fariqa, at the head of the column, points out some of the safe recesses that can be used to shelter from the Ahl-Cassim. Faruq, in turn points them out to the companion following him and so on down the line of the caravan.

To the unaccustomed eye, these could just be another irregularity of the cliff face that at first glimpse, would not offer much shelter.

I notice that preceding the mouths of these caves, a curious symbol of a circle with three intersecting lines had been carved into the rock. This obviously signals to the initiated traveller that nearby is a shelter. The symbol fascinates me. In the ancient hieroglyphs of the northern regions, this symbol represents both danger and safety. It is strange to see how the ancients of the north have influenced the cultures so far to the south. Or maybe it was the other way around.

Eventually we come to another large clearing, similar in proportion to the one where the palace of the Huda people was carved. Here, though, are just plain cliff faces on all sides, save for three other passages that lead out from it. Hidden to the eye, behind a fold in the cliff is a steady trickle of water that surges from the rock and runs down its face. It gathers into a small pool, only a few hands wide. It then disappears into a crevice at the base of the cliff, softly gurgling out of sight.

We refresh ourselves and refill our water pouches, before watering the horses. We then settle to a modest lunch.

Following our meagre meal, we resume our trek through the pass. We decided earlier that an attack would be more likely to come from behind. Not wanting to take chances though, for the protection of Ijlal, since Fariqa leads, Faruq will follow immediately behind followed by Isamadeen. Although all the Companions are trained in the art of defence and offence, Faruq and Isamadeen are the most highly regarded for their fighting skills. Jamal and Rauf follow. Being smaller in stature, they will find it easier to manoeuvre in the narrow passage to protect their prince. Ijlal and I follow. The caravan's back is guarded first by Fatin, whose quick wit would be of use if any attacker made it past Faruq and Isamadeen. Finally, Husam, an accomplished fighter reinforces the rear together with Hasan.

Every now and again, the pass widens into small circular openings, before it narrows off and the caravan is forced once more to travel single file.

I am preoccupied with my own thoughts, the silence of the place engendering in me a peaceful state of reflection. We come to another of those clearings when I see Fariqa hold her hand up in a signal to stop. It is some time before the next meal break and so I am perplexed. As we gather behind her, I notice that the pass ahead is blocked by a fall of rocks.

The way is barred. Some rocks look to have been pushed from above and have fallen in an avalanche of debris, rising to the height of a man on horseback. This will take at least a lahae to clear. There is simply no time.

At this point my skin begins to crawl and I turn. Hasan follows my gaze. Only a few kershel away, movement manifests itself in the form of indistinguishable creatures. Dark against the eternal gloom of the pass, two Shadows creep out, not willing to come too close.

A hysterical laugh breaks the silence and ahead of us, jumping out of a side cave, is the red-headed man. He is quite beside himself swearing and jumping around, informing us that our way is barred.

The Shadows creep as far as they dare, lurking under the cover of the overhanging cliffs. The stench of their presence is detectable even at this distance.

The Companions gather around Ijlal, forming a protective circle.

Fariqa steps towards the obstacle of rocks examining it, ignoring the crazed man who steps back momentarily. Then she comes back to us and speaks directly to Hasan, "We cannot go this way. There is another way, however we will need to retrace our steps, and this will take another two dunae of journey; not to mention getting past these foul creatures."

Hasan looks at me, and I shake my head.

"We have no time to spare."

"And," Hasan adds, "there is no guarantee that we will not encounter the same fate further down."

There seems to be no answer. I look up at the narrow ribbon of light above us. Impossibly high above sheer cliffs, a pale sliver of the moon Ayshah hangs late in the day sky at one end. An imperceptible draft of cool air caresses my face and a sense of peace descends into my being, I detect a subtle aroma of wood fires, a gentle knowing that permission is granted.

A quick resolution is needed. "Hasan, can you and the Companions hold these creatures where they stand and not let them come near?"

Slowly he answers, with a question in his eyes, "Yes, Azizi, but what are you planning?"

I sigh, not knowing how to explain, nor knowing whether what I have in mind will work. "I shall deal with the crazed man and the rocks."

Hasan looks at me in a way that suggests he thinks that I may have lost my mind, and then, checking himself and remembering a healing in the desert he bows. "We will hold them, Azizi."

The Companions look at me wondering what, if anything, I would be able to do. Fariqa at first looks at me with incomprehension, then smiles and takes up her position beside Hasan.

I face the creature, which by now is almost unrecognisable as a man. He is screaming at me, hurling insults, and laughing in a hysterical fashion. Never have I asked for the power, but now feeling the acute need to help my companions, I surrender myself to the will of the Great Spirit Guardian.

In a loud, clear voice that comes from the heart, invoking the Spirit of War and Conquest, I shout with all my might, "Hjaldr Tyr! Hakka Päälle. Sri Akall!"

The sound reverberates for ages. It appears time itself stands still at the sound of the words. Even the mad man in front of me looks subdued and only after a long pause starts to snicker nervously.

With one voice and with one accord the Companions reply, "Sri Akall!"

Once more the sound echoes for what seems an eternity.

Unheralded, the power comes. A deep current rises from the base of my spine. Hotter and hotter it grows, until all else around me fades into hot molten light.

The current rises, reaching my heart. A burst of flames fills my head, my eyes water, tears stream down my face, and my hands rise slowly of their own accord. I taste the salt of my tears on my lips. Like an avalanche crashing, a booming sound echoes in my ears. With a surge of fire, I feel the power flow through me.

And suddenly it ends: a cool torrent of energy pours down upon me, and the fire abates, trickling down my spine. The power has flowed, and my eyes clear. I see what the power has done.

The mound of rocks has been utterly reduced to powder; not a trace of it remains. As for the red-headed man, he is gibbering at the side of the road, looking dishevelled and confused. Truly now I think he has lost his senses. I turn to the Companions. Awe and a hint of fear are in their eyes.

No matter how I explain it, saying that I am an instrument of the Great Guardian Spirit, they only see the power and me, so I let it be. I bow silently in my mind to the Flame in my heart and surrender my thoughts and feelings to Him who has chosen me as His instrument.

These are moments when I experience the loneliness of power. Though they love me and respect me as their friend and brother, they are in awe of me.

Only Hasan senses this; he comes to me and tentatively reaches out. Gently he enfolds me in his arms, whispering, "Sri Akall, my beloved Azizi."

The Shadows disappear at the first sign of power. They are cowardly creatures and will not so easily stand their ground if outnumbered.

We resume our travel a little more wary of who might be following us. Fariqa says nothing. Though she is obviously affected by what she has seen, she also knows the power having witnessed the saving of her own son. As far as she is concerned, even if a fire beast manifests in front of her, she will graciously make way for the Guardian Spirit's instrument and wait patiently until the obstruction in our path is removed. I dare say that on her return, she will earn a few coins in the telling of the story she has just witnessed. Not too many people could boast having witnessed the might of the Guardian Spirit's power firsthand.

Strangely, the power has not affected me in the way I thought it would. None of the weariness or heaviness that I had experienced in my early years follows. This is a welcome change. Though I do notice on more than one occasion, one of the Companions ahead of me, turning and openly staring at me. They seem to be looking directly into my face before bowing and saluting me. This is the same look Isamadeen gave me when I woke from the vision in the desert, while waiting for news of Faruq.

We travell for some time; I am lost in my own thoughts when again I experience that creep of the flesh in the back of my neck. As I turn, I meet Hasan's eyes. He nods acknowledging that he too is aware of the Shadows following just out of sight.

I immediately go to a level of inner focus that allows me to expand my consciousness, to find out if there is another ambush ahead of us. I cannot detect anything ahead of us and so check to sense what is behind us. I experience something peculiar. It is as if there is something missing. I turn to look just as the rest of the caravan is coming around a double bend. I must wait a few seconds, before I can see the remaining troupe. Fatin is behind me followed by Husam. Shortly after, Hasan's horse comes around and my heart leaps. Hasan is not on it. I am about to call out when I catch Husam's eyes as he gestures to keep silent.

This is a desert trick I have seen Hasan practice, when he was guarding the travelling caravan. He would quietly and furtively disappear and catch anyone following unaware.

My stomach tightens. These are Shadows, and I am not sure he is a match for them. Their fighting techniques are cowardly. Just a scratch from the tip of their blade will send him into an oblivion of pain, quickly followed by death. I have not brought with me the herb we used to heal Halim. This herb needs to be used fresh and drying it would have the singular effect of neutralising its potency.

I am suddenly afraid.

Fariqa comes to a halt shortly to stop for a quick break and allow us to water the horses. This clearing is much narrower and for the first time since we set off, I feel powerless, imprisoned, and uncomfortable.

As we sit down for the meal, Faruq inquires about Hasan and Husam tells him that he had dropped back a while ago because we were being followed.

Faruq immediately orders a watch at both ends of the passage.

Shortly, a figure approaches. I recognise Hasan, and I am

relieved to see him, apparently unharmed. As he approaches, he finishes the task of wiping his blade on a cloth, which he throws aside with disgust. The cloth is stained red.

Quietly, Hasan sits down and drinks some water. When asked, he explains that he had dispatched the two Shadows that had been tailing us since our last encounter. There is not a scratch on him. The Companions nod their approval, and a glint of admiration appears in Isamadeen's and Husam's eyes.

Fariqa has been busy with the horses, and I have been thinking about what I will say that won't unduly worry Giafar, when I contact them later this the evening.

I notice the air around me becoming heavy. The next moment blurs into a series of images and shouts. Fariqa's suddenly tilts her head up, the way forest creatures do at the first sign of danger. The air changes again, and it prickles along my arms and face.

Fariqua is yelling, "Quickly to the horses! Follow me!" She takes two of the horses by the leads and hurries down the passageway ahead of us, not waiting to see if anyone follows her.

We stand dumbfounded.

Fariqa yells again, "The Ahl-Cassim!"

Hasan reacts first, picking up his travel things and running to the nearest horse, when all at once we hear a long deep wailing sound growing louder by the moment.

We make it to the nearest shelter. Even the animals seem to know the urgency.

If I thought that my experience of the Cassim in the desert with Halim was bad, what follows is nothing short of terror. The air in the cave we take shelter in is suddenly sucked out and my ears hurt incredibly. Disoriented and unsteady on my feet, I decide that sitting down is not a cowardly thing to do. A scream of fury erupts outside the cave as the Ahl-Cassim rages, where we stood but a moment ago. A veritable barrage of sand speeds past the entrance of the cave obliterating all light. The mouth of the cave looks like an angry moving torrent of dark brown water that defies gravity.

The horses are terrified and seem ready to bolt. It is all that Fariqa and some of the Companions can do to keep them inside. One step outside would be certain death.

The Ahl-Cassim howls for an eternity and then as suddenly as it came, it passes. With an audible smack the air returns into the cave and my ears pop. I look around and see that the Companions are in much the same state of shock that I am. Rauf is terrified and tears of shock are streaming down his beautiful face. I go to him and placing my arm around his shoulder I reassure him as best I can. He leans his face into my chest and cries a little more, then looks up meekly and smiles, wiping his face. The rest of the Companions are visibly shaken, only Hasan and Fariqa appear impervious to the events that have taken place.

Fariqa advises us to stay put a while, not only to regain our bearings, but also to make sure that we are out of danger. From time-to-time, dangerous flurries of sand blow down the rock passage, tagging behind the Ahl-Cassim like wayward children. The sand eddies still capable of causing harm will whirl around for a while before disappearing.

Finally, we make it out and I am glad to see daylight again. The sky is once more a ribbon of blue above us, and the pass looks peaceful, as if nothing happened.

We resume our travels, when a little way farther down we come upon a sight that makes my stomach churn. A human skeleton caught in the wedge of two rocks has been picked clean by the storm. A small tuft of red hair still clinging to the head is all that remains of the man. I reflect that at least his death has been more expedient than it would have been at the hands of the Shadows.

Though we are on our guard, the remainder of our journey is uneventful, and we eventually reach a large opening where a few low shrubs grow. The height of the cliffs has gradually dropped over the last few hours of travel. The sun is setting and lights the topmost reaches of the cliffs. The rocks, which were bathed in the sunlight during the day, are still warm. We will rest here until dawn when we resume our march.

Fariqa tells us that despite the incidents we encountered we have made good time. By mid-morning tomorrow, she tells us we will come out of the Huda pass and into the great marsh. From there it will be another two days before we reach the lower lands of the Isthmus of Mina.

Hasan must have known my thoughts for he adds, "If the sky is clear, you will see the Asfaine Mountains in the far east."

A twinge of excitement makes my heart skip a beat at the name of my beloved homeland. Hasan smiles at me knowingly.

We eat and build a fire to keep us warm for the night. The Companions gather, and I announce that I will contact Haroun-al-Rashid. In my last session I spoke directly as an intermediary between Giafar's magician and the Companions.

I relax my mind and gaze into the heart of the fire. Like an irresistible scratch at the back of my neck, I sense Haroun-al-Rashid making contact. As agreed, I wait until I can feel the field of protection before opening my mind. A warm impression of safety that carries with it the scent of Schiraz is the seal that signals the security of our communication.

I can then see a tunnel of light opening before me. Though the sensation is that of falling forward into this tunnel, the reality is that the connecting energy field simply collapses the distance between us. Shortly I stand before Haroun-al-Rashid, a benevolent old man smiling at me.

Giafar asks after our welfare. I assure him we are all well. I then relate the events of the last two days. I speak both in my mind and aloud to enable the company to listen to the thread of the conversation.

Giafar listens silently as Haroun-al-Rashid relays my words. I have come to the account of our taking shelter from the Ahl-Cassim, trying to convey the terror of the storm, when Isamadeen in jest interjects with a comment that it was so scary that Rauf had cried.

The link must be clear, for quickly comes back the answer, "It was not so long ago that your nurse tended to your tears, Isamadeen." Giafar says this in good humour, laughing.

Isamadeen blushes heavily at the words relayed in a voice that had taken on the tone of the general.

The Companions smile but there is no malice between them. Each knows the others' weaknesses as much their strengths. More than blood allies them. In any case, Rauf's apparent weakness is also the strength they all rely on in moments when kindness and mercy are called for.

Giafar is curious to hear that the news of the march north of the two armies is already known. He is pleased, nevertheless, that it seems to have created confusion and approves of Ijlal's responses to Gaisha. He expresses concern that we have been followed by the Shadows and though he supports Hasan's actions, states rather sombrely that once those two fail to report, others will be sent to make inquiries. He warns us therefore, to be on our guard. Obliquely, Giafar inquires after Ijlal's health and is pleased to know that he is well.

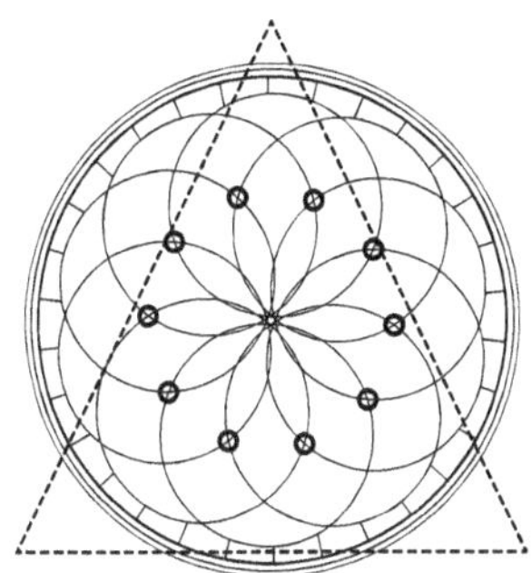

CHAPTER TWENTY-SEVEN

Communicating with Giafar's magician has become easy. Tonight, the Companions heard and saw the presence of their general through my eyes and voice. Because of this, his belief in the powers I hold, or because of what lies so heavily upon his heart, Ijlal waits until all have retired before asking me if I will attempt to see Shahulm.

My heart sinks. The desire to help him conflicts with the sadness that I might not be able to do so. I hesitate a moment, recalling the horror I have seen inflicted on Shahulm. It is not just the memory of his torture at the hands of his captors but also wondering if this will throw Ijlal into a greater despair.

The talisman is the only link to his mind, and that now scares me. For the love of him, though, and witnessing the desperate yearning in his eyes, just to know that Shahulm is still alive and because he has always held me as his brother, for the love of them both, I concede.

I seek out Rauf, whom I have appointed as the Haafiz or Sacred Keeper of the talisman.

With a mixture of curiosity and his natural wish to offer support for his prince, Rauf comes along as well. We take a small piece of lit kindling and some wood and move a little away from the camp, to set up a small fire for me to gaze at.

Rauf brings out the leather pouch that holds the talisman and holds out the sacred symbol.

I signal to Rauf that I will take it when I am ready and that he should hold on to it for now.

I take a breath, focussing my mental energies, and brace myself for the inevitable onslaught of power. I think of what my godmother has told me regarding love and think of the times my heart has spoken to me.

Looking deeply into the flames, I see the face of my first love. Deep brown eyes stare at me. The simple melody of a young shepherd boy's flute floats on the air. I see again the face of prince Ijlal when he first appeared in my dreams, and then, with the passion the sun has for the desert sands, I see Hasan's face. Just as his smile fades in the light of the embers, I see again a pair of eyes like two blue star flowers. My heart sings. I am ready and signal to Rauf.

With a slight shock the cold talisman falls into my hand; soon though, it glows of its own will, and warmth travels along my arm to my heart.

Myriad stars explode in my mind and the sound of the wind whistles in my ears and reminds me of my mountain trees. The mists clear and, like an eagle, I float above water and towards a group of islands.

With a leap in time, I am inside a rocky stronghold. It is night here too and the clammy walls are lit with smoky torches.

I move silently among the cold stones. A small fear enters my thoughts. What if I am not able to return? I double my efforts to focus on my search, calling to mind the flames of the fire, and the first image of Shahulm dancing for his prince.

Like a lodestone, I am drawn to the depths of the earth; down and further down I spiral until I enter a place that is filled with loathing and darkness.

I see a frail young body strapped to a godless slab of stone, lit by candles made of a dark wax. He lies there almost lifeless, all colours drained from his youthful form. There is enough there of him for me to recognise Shahulm. They have tortured him. Not so much by way of inflicting bodily pain, although there are marks upon his flesh that indicate he had suffered that as well. His torture is more of the mind. They are weakening his will to resist; they are draining his determination ever to see his beloved again. They are attacking the essence of his love and chastity for his prince in the hope to turn him into their puppet. They have touched him to the point of indecency but not to the point of seduction. This they are to leave to their mistress for the ceremonial sacrifice.

The room is filled with their dark thoughts and lusts. Rage wells up inside me, and fear also, for this is a room filled with hopelessness. Dark Shadows move on the peripheries. Closer to the stone slab where the prince lies, a circle of Scarlet Robes stand, their lust polluting the already filthy air.

One stands a little apart observing the proceedings. Waves of cold fear wash through me, and I begin to shiver involuntarily. With grave dread I realise that this is the she-monster, the Sorceress.

I must make contact with Shahulm and give him the hope that he so needs. I focus my mind banishing the fear that threatens to engulf me. With all my heart, I picture Ijlal and the talisman of their love. Using the powers of sending that my godmother taught me, I project this into his mind. Like a straight arrow of light my thought runs true to its target.

At that precise moment, with my right hand, I reach for Ijlal's chest and touch him just below his heart. The result is immediate. Now Ijlal sees what I see. The Scarlet Robes stagger backwards as Shahulm relaxes, and takes a strengthening breath, and briefly opens his eyes; hope enters his spirit once more. I release my connection with Ijlal.

A cold heartless laugh echoes in the cavern. She turns and I see her eyes. They first flash an ugly green, which then slowly change to the yellow of the eyes that had stared at me in the garden of Halim's heart.

For a moment, her gaze wanders here and there searching the air. With deadly accuracy they come to focus where I stand and again, she begins to laugh.

Looking at me directly, addressing all my fears and all my deepest secrets, she pronounces, "So often have I been your goddess. Now you have come to worship me."

As much in fear of what I know she touches upon, as well as a refusal to bow to her, I scream a denial as the sight vanishes from my eyes, with her evil laugh still echoing in my mind.

I am back in the desert staring at the embers of a dying fire, the scream of 'no' still echoing in the cold night air. There is enough grief on Ijlal's face for me to know that he has seen what I have seen, such is the power of the Talisman.

Quietly he stands up, "Azizi, it comes over me. I must be alone with my grief."

At this he turns, walking away, and slowly and quite deliberately his body transforms into the great brown kestrel, the lonely call to his mate reaching out to the stars.

Rauf stands there a moment not knowing what to do, then as he wraps the talisman back in its coverings and walks back to camp.

I wake up the next morning with Ijlal's cold and naked body shivering against mine. I hold him as long as he needs to be held. I remember in my mind the cold night I spent on the mountainside once, but I also remember the soft song of a shepherd boy whose music evokes the warm sun of spring. I sing softly to Ijlal, cradling him in my arms.

At last, his convulsions ease and stop. He relaxes and breathes more easily. He turns to me and says, "It came to me Azizi. I called the great bird spirit, and it came to me."

A mixture of exhilaration and shock shines in Ijlal's eyes at the realisation that he can now master his transformation at will.

In some ways that realisation gives me mixed feelings. On the one hand, I am glad to have someone who can, in a small way, understand the burdens of magic, but on the other hand, this is a power linked to Love in its purest form, something that, for all my gifts, I am still a stranger to.

"Azizi, will we reach him in time?"

I look deeply into those wondrous eyes, "We have until the full moon of Camlac, Ijlal. We will be there for him. It has been written."

He waits a moment, uncertain, and then asks, "Was it not also written that the Evil One would do everything in its power to stop us?"

"When the rules of war between Good and Evil are drawn, no guarantees are given, for Man is given free will to fight for either side. It is the good in us all that we must believe in Ijlal. It is our will to triumph. For though evil has strength and many allies, it cannot stand in the way of Love, for that is the weapon it cannot defend itself against."

Ijlal looks at me and asks, "What then must I do, Azizi, to conquer the evil that attacks my beloved?"

"Send him your Love to fight the despair he faces. If he cannot remember it of his own free will, you must bear the burden of remembering for him, and send him your love, with all your heart."

He lies there a moment then looking at me, his eyes shining once more with hope. Then he embraces me and murmuring thanks, he gets up and leaves.

I speak the words again in my own head to remember the wisdom that has flowed through me. The message has been spoken for both of us.

I get up and walk not far from camp to give my morning prayer.

I reach a small patch of sand and rocks atop the smaller of the cliffs and turn to face the rising sun. As I stand there a movement catches my eye. Hasan is already there as if waiting for me.

"Greetings of the morning to you Hasan."

"And to you also Azizi."

I can sense that something is on his mind and so wait.

"Azizi, I have a favour to ask of you."

"What is it Hasan? What can I give you?"

He looks at me lost in thought for a while, then in his usual fashion comes straight to the point. "For the last three nights, and more intensely than ever last night, my dreams have been haunted by my prince who keeps urging me to protect the Haafiz. I keep pleading with him that I am here to protect him and do his bidding, but he keeps saying, and this I cannot understand, 'Hasan protect the Haafiz; he should not be here alone.' I keep calling to him saying, Master you are not alone, I am here.' He just smiles at me and repeats what he has just said."

Here he pauses, clearly confused and much distraught by the dream that he has experienced. His prince is commanding him to protect the only being Hasan has been taught to protect—Elwah himself, his prince.

"Azizi, is my lord rebuking me? What am I to make of his command?"

For no reason that is clear to me at the time, I look up and away from him and over his head and say, "Come Hasan, it is time for the Morning Prayer."

Without thinking he stands with me and facing the rising sun bows deeply. He begins to intone the Morning Prayer I have heard him sing. The first rays of the sun explode over the horizon. I hear my own voice intone after him the words I have memorised.

Alsafinat Almuqadasat
Astaqbal Hubiy
Qum bi'iiwa Habi

Almost unconsciously, lost in the sacredness of the words and the melody, a small part of me notices that Hasan's voice has faltered and stopped.

I finish singing the Morning Prayer and open my eyes to the blue sky of a new day.

I am perplexed to see Hasan on his knee before me, a look of total amazement on his face. As soon as I look at him, he lowers his face in an act of humble submission.

"Hasan, what is it? Why have you not finished singing your prayer?"

"Mahjir, I cannot. I must not look into your eyes. It is not fitting. I do not understand, but it is you. May my prince forgive me, I did not know who he was asking me to protect."

Tears are rolling down his face. It is breaking my heart to see Hasan in this state and so I go to him and place a hand on his shoulder. I am just as confused as he is. I do not understand what Hasan is saying.

As soon as I touch him, Hasan shudder and breaks into sobs, holding my hand on his shoulder.

Tenderness washes through me and I hear myself speak, though not in the voice of the Spirit Guardian. This voice is soft and grave and though I speak the words, I do not understand what they mean, "Hasan, my faithful one, you now have the answer to your dream. Do not speak of this to anyone."

We return to camp and for a while Hasan appears to be subdued. If he faithfully attended to me before, now he veritably shadows me.

CHAPTER TWENTY-EIGHT

By mid-morning we reach the outer ranges of the Huda pass. Before us lies a vast flat plain that stretches as far as the eye can see. The surface is a patchwork of sand, water, and spindly looking grass, occasionally dotted with small dry-looking shrubs.

Fariqa pulls out a small parchment, on which a map is drawn showing the safe passage to follow. "These lands are treacherous," she warns, pointing to various parts of the map. "The sands here make up most of the marshlands. These are known as quick sands, that will swallow an animal the size of a horse in moments."

She waits a moment for her words to sink in, but she did not need to. The Companions are only too aware of the dangers, as quicksand is common in the Great Desert of Keyab.

"You will need to refill all of your water skins at the spring nearby. You are not to drink the marsh water, as it is certain death. If stung by one of the many insects that populate this land, crush and rub the leaves of this shrub on the affected area to ease the pain and swelling." She points to one of the small dry looking shrubs.

She then begins her good-byes to the Companions.

Finally, she stands silently before me.

"Fariqa, thank you. The life debt you spoke of is more than repaid."

She smiles and takes my hands in hers. Her skin is callused, yet her touch is warm and gentle. "Favoured of the Great Guardian Spirit, it has been an honour and a privilege. I have many tales the telling of which will fill my moments to the end of my days. My son also will tell the tales and perhaps to his children and his children's children."

With light in her eyes, she adds, "And if he does not wish to marry and have children, then his path will be to seek you out and tread the steps of sacred Lore you would show him."

I embrace her then. "Blessings on you and all your family, Fariqa."

We part and I catch up with the Companions who are waiting at a distance.

We set off upon the path that lies according to Fariqa's map, ahead of us with the sun on our right.

Already the air is thick with heat and moisture. I struggle to adapt to the new conditions. I notice how my body has become hard and slim following the rigours of my journey.

The passage through the marshlands is uneventful but we have recourse to use Fariqa's medicinal advice many times.

With his newly discovered power, and to the wonderment of the Companions, Ijlal more than once transforms into the great bird and at divisions in the trail, flies the length of the path to lead us in the correct direction.

As we draw closer to the kingdom of the Over Lord, Ijlal's fever begins to return, though it does not affect him as it did. His eyes glow with the hunger to see his beloved safely in his embrace again.

The Companions grow accustomed to his transformations and regard them as their sacred and secret bond. Their love and respect for their leader deepens and, if possible, draws their band closer together than before.

On the second day of our journey, we reach the other side of the marshland and as night falls, we begin our march to the Isthmus of Mina.

That night, as arranged, I once more contact Giafar. I tell him that we are about to reach the isthmus, making sure that his troops are positioned to take away the attention further north. I also contact my godmother to learn the Lore of concealment and seek news of the search for the second Tear of Apphat.

Camlac, the moon of chaos, its heavy crescent hanging low to one side in the evening sky, looks yellow and pale, almost sickly. The season of Malkizar is reaching its peak. It will not be long now before the moon is full.

The Companions gather around the fire with me for the ritual of the contact. It takes no time at all before I sense the familiar sensation of the link, accompanied by the safety of the scent of Schiraz.

Haroun-al-Rashid and Giafar stand before me. Giafar is pleased that we have made good progress. Within the next day as we cross the Isthmus of Mina, the troops of Schiraz will be assembled on the north shore of the great inlet of Gleskerrel. The Sultan's armies are poised and to confuse the Over Lord's spies, the armies are facing north looking upon the great forests of Glesskerell.

An envoy has been sent to the regent of Glesskerell with greetings and good wishes and an invitation to join them in a 'friendly' military exercise. Glesskerell for its part had secretly extended a welcome to the Southern armies and had invited them to encamp on its southern borders.

Openly, the armies of Glesskerell are slowly amassing north of its forests, apparently readying to defend itself from the invading armies of the South. The troops of Naassée have camped just northeast of the tongue of land that leads to the Over Lord's stronghold, ready to cut off the Over Lord's only means of escape by land. From an onlooker's point of view, it is also possible to assume that the armies of Naassée are lying in wait to lend a hand to the victor.

Giafar's spies have reported that the city of the Over Lord is in a state of nervous apprehension, and though no open moves of defence have been made, some of the Over Lord's armies have been secretly dispatched to the north side of the Isthmus. The regent's ships are waiting ready, to the west of the citadel out of sight. Any envoy that the Over Lord had sent with requests for an explanation, has been imprisoned, and no response have been made.

Greater numbers of Shadows have been seen along the shores of Glesskerel and all soldiers have been warned to always move around in groups of ten or more. In spite of this, the bodies of careless individuals have been found tortured and disfigured.

The Over Lord, it seems, is keen on obtaining news in whichever form it takes. The soldiers have not been told of the strategy, so there is no danger that the secret would be revealed by ordinary means.

It looks like Giafar's plan is working. The enemy is confused and unaware of the unassuming caravan of wandering shepherds that is about to cross the Isthmus.

Giafar, nevertheless, cautions us to be on our guard; a cornered animal will behave dangerously and unpredictably. The fortress has been built to withstand a long siege, and its greatest weakness is that its only means of escape is by way of the isthmus or by the slower, more dangerous ocean, Malkizar.

If threatened sufficiently, it is always possible that the Over Lord will attempt to charge his troops down the isthmus, and we will be in the thick of it.

We break our communication, and the Companions fall into deep discussion amongst themselves on the politics and the adventure to come.

I move away at a distance, not wanting to attract attention and to be alone for my meeting with Aïschah. I signal as much in a gesture to Hasan.

He understands and though he will leave me alone, he will follow at a distance and keep me within his sight.

Not wanting to use the previous technique and lead unwanted, curious travellers to our location, Aïschah uses a different method of arrival, although no less spectacular for the onlooker.

While I sit on the ground, not far from me, a patch of sand begins to glow and slowly, beginning with her face, Aïschah materialises before me in a continuous glow of golden light. The light vanishes and she steps forward to embrace me. She looks at me bemused, measuring me with her eyes. I have grown another good hand span and now stand almost eye-to-eye with her.

She comes directly to the point of our meeting. "The Great Council of Magicians has met. We discussed the possible location of the second stone, for no one has been able to scry for it. As a sacred talisman it is protected by strong magic, which is preventing its finding. It is also said that one does not find the stone, but rather it finds you. We re-examined the ancient Lore and predictably old arguments flared up between the two factions, on the interpretation of the danger alluded to by the Great Seer."

Aïschah sighs in memory of the turmoil.

"As one of the Elders, I called the meeting to silence. I urged the Council to put aside their differences. I reminded them that finding the stone was of greater importance than to come to some conclusion of the Seer's cryptic death note. We could not allow the second stone to fall into the Sorceress's hands. We found many references to Elwah, the Stone of Joy, in both sacred texts and historical accounts but neither gave any clue as to where the stone has been kept."

Aïscha goes on, "The difficulty with the Lore, is that no one is completely sure of its vocabulary and many symbols. Words in the ancient tongue are interchangeable in meaning. It is thought that the ancients not only relied on the written word but its inflections in the spoken language for the correct meaning. Unfortunately, the key to inflection has been lost and the inflections of the spoken words were rarely written down, relying instead on the age-old tradition of passing the knowledge orally from magician to apprentice, particularly in relation to sacred and secret Lore.

"Often the people of Naassée are referred to in text. It tells of a prince of Naassée who won a battle to secure and return the Stone of Elwah. As a reward, the Great Council of Magicians declared the people of Naassée the Sacred Guardians or Keepers of Elwah. Here the words again are interchangeable. They could mean either guardian in the sense of one who protects, or keeper in the sense of one who actually holds and protects. It makes sense then, that their spiritual leader, the Prince of Naassée, would take on the honorary title of Elwah the protector.

"In some way, Naassée is directly connected with Elwah. When questioned, the high priests were silent and would not speak of their Lore or of the possible location of the sapphire. They insisted that only their Prince could speak of this and therefore it was imperative to have him returned safely. One amongst them stressed that this must be done before the full moon of Malkizar waxed, or grave consequences would follow. The Lore itself referred to this and so did Ijlal's dream. This was not anything we did not already know. If wielded by the Sorceress, the powers of the Stone of Malkizar would rule the emotions of the people and the world would be plunged into despair and chaos."

Aïschah looks concerned that she has not been able to locate the stone. She continues, "Alone and unaided, I delved further into ancient texts at the Ancient Library of Keesha. For I believe that the answer to the riddle is not to be found in the past. The Lore also foretells future events."

I wait for her to go on as she frowns slightly.

"There is a parvus which reads:

Nautiz dar tetra kah (*Na-ootëez dahr tetra ka*)
Othilda 'ra Elwah (*Otilda rã–El wah*)
Elwah isa mar (*El wah eesa mar*)
Haafiz 'ra sowelu (*Hâfiz rã so-way-loo*)
Aziz thurisaz ku (*Azïze thooreesãz koo*)

Literally translated and making liberal use of ancient mythology, the text means:

Constraint in the dark hour,
Separated will be Elwah.
Elwah stands still, 'or,' joy in a moment of stillness
The Sacred Keeper makes whole,
The Beloved is the gateway.

"The best translation I can give it, taking into account the various possible inflexions and the context of the words, the text could read:

'Threatened in its darkest hour,
Elwah will be separated.
In a moment of stillness and joy,
The Sacred Keeper will make whole,
The Beloved becomes the Gateway.'

"As you can see, there are some words the meaning of which are open to interpretation." She pauses a while and almost apologetically continues, "At least we have some assurance that the stone will be safe though... "

Aïschah looks up and is now staring at me with the grave attention I remembered so well from childhood.

The silence and her stare become uncomfortable.

"What is it, Godmother?"

I look around in case she is looking at something over my shoulder, and when I look back at her, her face has lost her previous astonishment.

"Ah. It is nothing. For a moment there... but it is nothing."

I speak more sternly than I have ever dared to speak to Aïschah, "Godmother, what was it?"

More to herself she mutters, "Is it possible...no, it can't be." She momentarily shakes her head as if to clear her thoughts, "No. It is the blood of your ancestors, Dear One. It happens to almost all of your line that inherit the sight. As you grow into your adulthood, your eyes take on a stronger colour of blue." She nevertheless continues to look at me with an odd expression.

I have heard this before though I'd forgotten it. This explains the reactions I have had from some of the Companions. The change comes and goes, often accentuated by the emotions; much like the changes in the voice of a boy as he grows into manhood. Something in my godmother's countenance still makes me feel uncomfortable, though.

As in the past, I change the subject. "I will need to learn the Lore of Concealment, Godmother, to take this group safely across the isthmus tomorrow."

A shooting star traces a silent silver arc in the dark blue sky. A soft freshening breeze plays with my hair, as over the horizon the moon of Ayshah rises slowly, gilding the edges of the dunes with her silver light. My godmother looks over her shoulder and sighs. This is perhaps the best omen we will see.

"The Lore of Concealment is simple but requires great concentration and attention to detail. You will do well to prepare for it tonight. It is simply a way of bending the light around those that you wish to conceal. To the outside eye, you will appear to be invisible. I must emphasise that this is not a 'trick.' If someone were to walk directly at you, both would experience the same physical impact. Also, you cannot conceal sound, so the Companions will have to be warned to be very quiet, especially if others are nearby. Light, like any other substance, is malleable, so long as one has the proper tools." She waits a while to make sure that I have understood.

She explains then the state of mind that I will have to enter to see the light beams that affect us. It is then a matter of projecting with my mind, a field of energy that will act like a mirror. The light will flow around us and re-form behind us, much in the same way as wind blows around a ship's sails. To those ahead and behind us, the light seen will only be the beams touching objects around us, and we therefore will become invisible.

Like the meticulous teacher she is, she makes me practice there and then. I succeed in concealing myself from her on the first try, much to her satisfaction.

"Azizi, this is a technique of the third initiation. There are Varye, sacred moral duties and codes, that bind the Magician to using certain powers and techniques only under specific circumstances. These apply to this technique, which I do not have the time to teach you. You must therefore promise me that you will only use this for the purpose you have stipulated."

I duly promise. Aïschah once more looks at me in silence before entering into the state that will dematerialise her. She turns and off-handedly asks, "Have you summoned Halim?"

The thought of the young sixteen-year-old shepherd who accompanied me out of my mountains into the safe hands of Hasan makes me smile. Aïschah gave him a talisman that would allow him to be a kind of protector against evil energies around me.

"No, I have not." I add with a melancholic smile, "We have all the soldiers we need. Is he well?"

"He was well the last time I saw him. He has not been seen recently. It is possible that he took his sheep further up the mountain, for he knows of pastures even few of his people know. I thought perhaps you had summoned him; I know how devoted he is to you."

The moon of Camlac rises then, its cycle reaching midway to a climax. It bloats yellow over the opposite horizon to the moon of Ayshah. The signs are beginning to align. The weight of responsibility falls on my shoulders like a heavy coat. I shudder at the thought of the tasks ahead.

Aïschah smiles at me once more and bids me farewell before the light engulfs her. A short time later, there is nothing, but sand, rocks, and a dark sky dotted with a million stars, and two moons opposing each other.

C H A P T E R T W E N T Y - N I N E

I rise with the sun and having fulfilled my duties of prayer. Then I turn and, with Hasan on my right walk back to the camp.

The others are ready and waiting, the horses packed. A mist covers the spit of land, which we are heading for. I have practised the mind state most of the night and now a little apprehension fills me at taking this last step towards our goal.

I ask the Companions to listen carefully as I explain what I will be doing to conceal our caravan. They are to look to me for signals that I make to impart instructions, and Hasan will repeat the signals at the rear of the group. No one is to stray beyond a certain distance, past which the concealment will not work. If need be, we are to gather as close as possible in a small group, ensuring that even the horses should be silenced by covering their heads with a soft cloth.

I must look tense for Rauf then comes over and embraces me

in a reassuring way. My tension melts and I smile at him and the rest of the Companions.

"Hjaldr Tyr! For Shahulm!"

The Companions echo my cry and prepare to depart. The Companions are still dressed as shepherds, their short swords and scimitars concealed under their garments. Their dark blue robes still carefully packed in the cases that the horses carry.

I raise the shield of concealment, and we make our way forward to the small strip of land that leads to the citadel of the Over Lord. The fortress is still hidden by short hills and mist. We have just about reached the isthmus when my heart leaps. A shapeless movement detaches itself from the mist ahead of us. I can now distinguish a Shadow on horseback heading straight for us. I signal to the Companions to stop and hold still. I hear behind me the soft whisper of a scimitar being drawn.

The Shadow suddenly pulls his mount to a standstill and sniffs the air.

I look at Hasan who seems ready to lunge forward and dispatch the creature. I signal for him to keep still. He looks annoyed but stands his ground.

The Shadow's horse pricks its ears in our direction. All will be lost if I do not think of something fast. Remembering the encounter of the Shadows in our mountains long ago, and while still focussed on the concealment, I send thoughts of green grass to the horse's mind.

It works almost instantly; the horse lowers its head and looks for the illusive grass amongst the rocks. Frustrated, the Shadow pulls hard on the reins and kicks his mount forward. He trots past us, obviously searching, scanning the landscape ahead.

When the danger is past, Hasan comes up and whispers, "Why did you not let me finish him off?"

"A Shadow dead along a path that no one has seen travelled, will raise many questions. Enough doubt could be raised that even the Sorceress might suspect more than just zealous soldiers. I do not want to alert anyone to our only advantage so soon."

Hasan shrugs his shoulders, signifying, 'a dead Shadow is always a good thing,' and resumes his place at the rear of the caravan.

I allow the concealment to dissipate slightly as I find it drains my energies. The effect, if we were to encounter anyone, would be as if they were looking at a distant and distorted image, common in the great desert at the height of noon.

Taking advantage of the cover of mist, we make good time and reach the Isthmus of Mina by the middle of the day. I turn often to see if the whole group is still with me, and to check if Hasan has anything to communicate with me. Occasionally, and with little hope, because of the mist, I look into the distance to see if I can at least glimpse the Asfaine Mountains.

By the time we reach the end of the isthmus, the sun has warmed sufficiently that the mist begins to clear, revealing in the distance the top towers of the Great Citadel.

In ancient times, a powerful and kind ruler who had united all the lands under a common law had built the fortress. The Great Citadel had been as much a fortification against attack, as a gracious city of great culture for his betrothed. It was said that all the great teachers and artists made their way to the city at least once in their lifetime.

In recent times though, disturbing reports were received that the streets were deserted by night, people feared for their safety, and very little culture ever made its way in or out of the city. Strange creatures roamed about, and it was rumoured that even ordinary people practiced the dark arts.

The roofs of the towers glimmered in the sunlight. I begin to wonder how I will be able to sustain the mental capacity to hold the shield of concealment for the rest of the day and the next. We reach a small hillock behind which we take shelter and I signal to the Companions to stay within earshot, as I am about to let the shield go.

We cannot light a fire, and though we have no need of it in the warming sun, the feeling of oppression as we near the citadel is palpable; a fire would have been of considerable cheer.

I speak softly to the Companions, "I am unsure if I will be able to hold the shield of concealment throughout the whole of tomorrow. It requires a great deal of concentration, and I am new at this. From what Giafar told me, there are very few features from here to the citadel. The land was mostly flattened long ago to better detect approaching armies."

Unsure of what I am asking them, I pause to gather my thoughts. "Do you all feel safe in enough in our present disguise for me to occasionally drop the shield?"

"Azizi, would it not be worse for us to be seen appearing and disappearing by anyone who could be watching our approach?"

It was Fatin who had spoken. My ears burn at the simple logic in his statement.

"Certainly, that is true. However, a concealing shield will be of no use at all if I am not able to use it, or if I cannot hold it at a crucial time."

"How long a period would you be able to hold the shield?"

I turn to Hasan and answer, "Probably for no more than half a day, as I have done so far."

"As you say, Azizi, the land was cleared to see approaching armies. A group of poorly dressed shepherds with a few mounts would not attract a great deal of attention at this distance. By my reckoning, it will take us at least two days to reach the ramparts of the citadel."

This time Isamadeen interrupts, "We can then easily walk unshielded for the remainder of this day and part of the next. What do we do if we encounter another Shadow as we did earlier on?"

There is a pause.

"Other than kill it." Husam spoke with a wry smile intended for Hasan.

The Companions laugh light-heartedly. These are soldiers; they can laugh at death.

"Who has travelled this road before?"

"I once came here with my uncle a long time ago, when I was still a child." All look at Ijlal. "It is true, Hasan. The land is mostly flat for a great distance around the citadel. However, as one approaches the city, the ramparts that have been built to protect it, are embedded into the flanks of a great hill. The only access to the city itself, is along a road that snakes its way up the hill. There are many turns in this road that will shield the traveller from the gates of the city."

"The alternative," Fatin adds, "is the secret way Giafar has spoken of, and which will only be revealed once we have made our way to the west of the city. However, we are not sure how long it will take to reach the other side of the city."

Like the true general he is destined to become, Faruq listens, weighing each argument and each person until he is ready to suggest the best option.

"I think that we should continue on our way unshielded, leaving Azizi his strength for when it is most needed. The Shadow that we passed earlier was obviously looking for something or someone. We have no way of knowing whether that was us or not. We cannot take any further risks of being discovered. So, if we encounter another Shadow, and we can see it before it sees us, then Azizi you will shield us. Otherwise, we will kill it. We cannot afford to let it return with news of our approach. Once we are nearer the citadel, then Azizi, it will be most useful to be shielded until we reach the western side of the citadel."

All the Companions nod in accord. Hasan appraises Faruq and nods his agreement. I think for one moment before adding this caution, "The Shadows are creatures that act often of one mind, and that is because they are linked in their thoughts by a governing Scarlet Robe. If we encounter one, we had better be prepared for it and not allow it to see us as a group. It could raise the alarm with its thoughts in an instant."

The Companions look at me for an answer and I cannot give them one. To attempt to disrupt the thought transmission of a Shadow, would be as good as to broadcast our exact whereabouts.

Hasan gestures, taking in the companions, "These men have been trained in the desert skills of stalking and scouting. We will need to change the organisation of our group slightly. Faruq has good sight and would do well as the lead protector of the group. Isamadeen is a strong and cunning soldier who could take my place at the rear of the caravan. I will take Fatin and Husam and travel at a distance ahead of you to clear the way of any wandering Shadows. We will travel on foot without beasts. That will leave Ijlal, Jamal, and Rauf to protect you personally, Azizi." The last he says pointedly to ensure that the two youngest understand he is not giving up this role lightly.

"Azizi?" Ijlal speaks up hesitantly. I turn and wait.

"Would it help if I were to take the shape of the great bird and spy out the land for you?"

Even so close to his goal, Ijlal is thinking of the safety of his Companions. Hasan nods his agreement. The Companions look at me waiting for my decision. Though the strategic advantages are obvious to soldiers, this is a matter of magic.

My greatest concern, apart from the emotional pull that Shahulm's proximity might have on Ijlal, is the possibility that such a transformation might act as a pebble in a pool of water. It could send shock waves throughout the realms of the world for anyone who is sensitive enough to magic to detect the transformation. This could act as a calling card to the wrong person and destroy the advantage of surprise we have built.

Looking at it from a strategic point of view, I decide that given Ijlal will not venture too close to the citadel, knowing what awaits us on the road, will be an advantage.

"I agree that this will give us great advantage. However, so close to Shahulm I am concerned that someone sensitive to magic could detect your transformation." Conscious that they think I might advise against it, I add cautiously, "I think we should limit your transformation to just one at this point. I will give you special instructions later to make sure that you do not exert your powers too much."

We resolve that we will move as planned, with Hasan, Fatin, and Husam some distance ahead of us. Faruq a little behind them, will lead our small company, and Isamadeen, positioned a little farther behind, will protect us from a surprise attack from the rear. This leaves Rauf and Jamal who proudly position themselves on either side of me, hands resting at the ready on their concealed scimitars.

Ijlal transforms into the great bird. The love for Shahulm and his nearness make the transformation almost instantaneous. The large kestrel at first circles above us, before flying west.

We journey without incident until the Cârem when we stop to take refreshments. Hasan, Fatin and Husam will be pausing also for this part of the day wherever ahead of us they are.

I attempt to link with Ijlal's mind, but the power of the great bird is beyond my comprehension. I catch a glimpse of blurred sand dunes, as if drawn on a map that my godmother kept in the herbarium. The dunes are moving very fast beneath my gaze, and dust is blowing in the distance. The image does not last long enough, nor is it clear enough to tell whether I have contacted his mind.

We have just settled for a rest when upon the afternoon breeze I hear a cry; a cry that to this day haunts me, the cry I first heard when Shahulm was taken.

The Companions are already up, scanning the horizon.

A great brown bird is flying low in our direction. As he nears the ground, the bird begins to lose its shape and takes on the human form of Ijlal. He tumbles upon the sand and lies there. We rush to him. Faruq reaching him first holds his head gently in his hands, and eases some drops of water from his water skin between Ijlal's parched lips.

Ijlal is panting and is obviously trying to get some words out, but has little strength left. Finally, he allows the Companions to minister to his needs.

Rauf gently wraps a light garment around his naked prince, more to protect him from the harsh rays of the sun than out of modesty, for these young men have no consciousness of shame for their bodies.

In the time it takes Ijlal to recover, Hasan, followed by his two companions, arrives at a run. Quickly they tell us that the Great Kestrel had swooped over them and flew on to us, signalling his intent for them to follow. Hasan quickly asks what the matter is.

All eyes are now on Ijlal whose breath still comes in shallow gasps.

His words rush out and tumble over each other so much, that we had to ask him to repeat them twice before we understood. "An army. A vast army is heading towards us now. They come from the citadel. The Over Lord is marching."

Most of the Companions including myself instinctively look to Hasan. "How far are they Ijlal? When will they reach us?"

"No more than an hour or two!"

Hasan and Faruq both stand and find a mound of sand that provides a slightly better vantage point. They stare into the distance narrowing their field of search towards the citadel. Then they come quickly back to us and kneel beside Ijlal who is now sitting up.

"It is true, they are in the distance now. Ijlal, how many men would you say there are?"

Ijlal, who has been trained in the arts of war and reckoning, thinks for a moment before replying, "I would estimate close to six thousand men."

The effect is sobering. This is enough to pose a serious challenge to the army of the South.

The Over Lord's army during times of war could be as much as five times that number. The Over Lord is making a decisive offensive move, but the bulk of his force is still to the north of the city walls. Is this a ruse meant to distract or is this a force meant to be punitive, and bring the army of the South to its knees?

If caught unawares, Giafar's armies could be overtaken and the men of Glesskerel and Naassée would not have enough time to respond.

"We must inform Giafar immediately. This army must be met and defeated," Faruq states vehemently, expressing what most are thinking.

Hasan speaks up quietly, "Faruq, Giafar's men will not make it in time. They are too far to the north. It is the men of Naassée that must cut this army off."

There is another question burning in my mind, one that is further removed from the practicalities of soldiers, nevertheless one that is intrinsic to the outcome of any conflict. "Ijlal, were you close enough to see who was marching at the head of the army?"

Hasan looks at me, comprehension slowly dawning on his face.

"No brother, though the standard of the Over Lord is clearly raised."

Isamadeen breaks in, "It is unlikely that the Over Lord himself would be at the head of the army. The man is a well-known coward."

Muttering and nods of agreement quickly race around

the Companions.

Ijlal is now worried at my question and asks, "Azizi, what does it matter if it is the Over Lord or one of his generals?"

"It was said that the Over Lord's armies would not march until the Sorceress had both of the Tears of Apphat, for then his army would be invincible. Mad for power as she is, she would never allow the sapphires to leave her hands. If she heads the army, she may be bluffing, but that bluff may cost us many men. If it is not her, then her power upon the will of the Over Lord may be slipping, or he has panicked, or this is a ruse to unnerve us. Which ever way we look at it, many others will ask the same question without a clear answer."

The Companions fall into silence.

"I must attempt to contact Haroun-al-Rashid and my godmother. She will contact the armies of Naassée."

"What will we do when the army reaches us?" Though Jamal is not frightened and looks ready to take on a good portion of the six thousand men, there is some concern about the practicality of the situation.

"I will raise the shield of concealment and we will wait for their passing."

"It is as good a plan as any. Are we all in agreement?" All the Companions nod their agreement to Hasan and, all in one movement, part their robes and unsheathe their scimitars.

Contacting Haroun-al-Rashid was easier than I thought, although he is initially surprised to hear from me as we were not due to contact each other for another day.

He understands the urgency, and at once has one of his servants call Giafar. Upon hearing our news, Giafar immediately sends aides to signal his troops to prepare to march. Unwilling to disclose his plans in a mind meld, he tells me he will contact the troops of Naassée. He asks me to safeguard the Companions as best as I can and to make haste for the city and enter it in whatever way is most expedient.

Hasan and the Companions discuss the possible direction that the approaching army will be taking, and the best spot to conceal us in this near featureless land.

Ijlal says that there is a small outcrop of rocks about a half hour's distance away. The army will be passing by this outcrop, though in his estimate, not close enough to be of any concern.

We prepare to travel and I tell the Companions to keep our disguises on in case the shield fails. In a land of myth and magic, a troupe of simple shepherds appearing out of thin air will still be a better omen than a group of soldiers.

We reach the outcrop that Ijlal spoke of. It hardly stands more than a man's height above ground. It consists mostly of a few large, flat rocks that seem to grow out of the infertile soil, and a few small blades of grass clinging to the crevices.

Spreading some loose pieces of clothing we settle on the rocks, which are still hot from the mid-day sun. Not long after, a cloud of dust stirs on the horizon, signalling the approach of the army. They have obviously timed their march to allow the night to conceal their crossing of the isthmus.

The Companions wrap their brown desert robes to protect themselves from the still harsh sun. I look upon our group, which is settling into uncanny stillness. This is their skill of stealth I am witnessing firsthand. Their breathing deepens, as their bodies relax yet remain vigilant.

To maximise my power over the concealment, I am to wait for Hasan who will signal to me to raise the shield. We will wait until the last moment. The passing of six thousand men will still take an hour or two, even at desert speed. We have tethered the horses on the side furthest from the way the army will come and shielded their eyes and muzzles with a piece of cloth. With all the skill on animal handling skill my godmother taught me, I calm their minds into a state of near slumber. This requires a great deal of effort, as even animals have a clear sense of night and day as well as danger.

Time passes. It seems interminable. The sun creeps nearer the horizon; the dust from the road to the west turns the early afternoon light into an orange haze.

The Companions could have been asleep for all the movement that comes from them. I admire their ability for perfect stillness. I breathe as Aïschah has taught me and settle as best as I can.

Finally, the dust that had heralded the approaching army turns into a clear outline of men on horseback. My heart leaps into my throat and my stomach churns at the sight of such an army. I look at Hasan who sensing my unease, smiles reassuringly before returning his calculating stare to the oncoming forces.

I am to throw the shield over the entire outcrop to include the horses. It will have to be timed at a point when, from a distance Hasan had calculated, the outcrop will just come into their sight. Even if one of their leaders' notices that a dark spot on the horizon suddenly winks out of existence, it will be discarded as 'sarab,' an ordinary phenomenon that occurs at this time of the day, as the heat from the land plays with images that are a long way away.

Hasan raises his hand slowly. I swallow and enter into the state of mind that allows me to see the light that bounces from the rocks.

The air in front of me swirls and is filled with many colours. Each colour separates itself into minute beams and flecks of gold dust. I can sense with my mind the subtle strength of those beams of light as they hit my garment, transmuting themselves into the colours and outline of my clothes and body, then bouncing back in all directions.

Hasan's hand comes down.

I project an energy ball that emanates from the centre of my forehead and grows outwards. At first, this is a soft sphere that allows some of the light beams to penetrate, then as my will becomes focussed, the sphere hardens into a perfect reflecting surface. The beams of light will gently shift and follow the outline of the sphere, assuming the shades and contours, of whatever lies around us before bouncing back. The atmosphere within this bubble becomes like a strange midnight devoid of light. Strangely, we can discern each other, and see outward objects losing some of their detail in a more subdued daylight.

This process, though elaborate, will look as though if it happens instantaneously.

The head of the army becomes visible. I struggle to hold onto my concentration as next to the general leading his troops, riding a horse as black as night, sits a creature dressed in a red robe.

Straining to remain in control of my emotions, I focus on the face of the Scarlet Robe who rides with a look of utter disdain for the men who accompany him. With a small shock that threatens to unsettle my attention, I recognise the look of hatred in those black eyes. This is the Scarlet Robe who had organised the attack on Ijlal and his uncle on their way to my godmother's house.

Whether he senses anything or not, the Scarlet Robe begins to move away from the column of men. His mount is now heading directly for the hidden outcrop of rocks.

Hasan looks up at me, drawing his scimitar. I shake my head and hope he interprets it to mean that he is not to move yet.

As the shield hardens around the outcrop of rocks, my consciousness also takes in the living creatures that take refuge in its shade. I become aware of the grass blades defiantly clinging to the rock. As my awareness expands, I also become aware of one small deadly desert serpent, the colour of the surrounding sands. This particular species makes a dry rasping sound if disturbed. With considerable joy, I discover that this one is a female guarding its nest of two eggs.

Immediately, I reach out with a part of me that can busy itself with the mind of the serpent. I send out a signal of danger with the vibration of every approaching hoof. The danger takes the form of a beast that could in one instant crush and destroy its nest.

Within a moment, the serpent slithers from under the rock and appears upon the sand near the hidden outcrop.

As the Scarlet Robe approaches, the serpent begins its rasping sound, soft and intermittently at first. The black horse is almost upon us when the serpent raises its head and makes a threatening sound. The horse rears and refuses to go further. The Scarlet Robe cruelly brings his mount under control, thrashing the flanks of the beast. With a hard yank on the bridle, he returns to the column of soldiers.

I release my hold on the serpent's mind as it slithers back

towards the rocks. One moment the serpent is upon the sand, the next it has winked out of existence, just as the Scarlet Robe turns his head to look at the creature that caused his mount to rear.

Hatred pours out of those black eyes as they search the surrounding sands.

The eyes continue searching as malice gives way now to malevolent curiosity. Slowly the Scarlet Robe edges his horse back towards our hiding place. He pauses, sensing the air around. I begin to feel his evil thoughts as he searches. This is not a mind of intellect and reasoning, just sheer hatred, and blood lust.

My concentration begins to waver under the weight of such darkness.

At the last possible moment, the general at the head of the army shouts some orders, which distracts the Scarlet Robe's attention. With a look of malevolent regret at not being able to inflict pain, he rides off to the head of the column.

A flood of relief washes through me. Hasan, though, keeps his scimitar unsheathed.

The army passes on uneventfully, the men looking dejected at being conscripted to fight a war they have no conviction for.

The sun begins to set in an eerie yellow glow, in the aftermath of dust and dung that marked the passing of the army.

I release the shield and ease the tension in my mind and body, shifting and stretching my muscles, until I can feel sensation returning to my limbs. Like rocks becoming fluid, the Companions stand up and prepare to remount their horses.

We set off at a faster pace than before, a sense of urgency spurring us on. The sun has just set, and the sky is turning a darker hue, the shadows of the horses stretching far behind us.

Suddenly, Hasan pulls his mount to a stand still and motions to the others. It is difficult to see in the early evening with the light of the fading sunset in our faces. The Companions at once dismount and gather around Hasan.

"What is it?" I ask, "Why have we stopped so suddenly?"

"There are three horsemen coming in the wake of the marching army," Hasan replies.

We move slightly off the tracks, Rauf and Jamal making sure that our trail is brushed to leave no marks. I raise the shield of concealment once more and we wait.

It is not long before the stench that comes on the evening sea breeze, announces the presence of Shadows. The three riders ride slowly not taking any particular care where or how they ride. They occasionally scan the horizon and the trail left by the army. Now we know why there are so few deserters in the Over Lord's armies. These creatures follow the march and simply catch, torture, and kill any who attempt to escape from the marching orders.

As the riders approach, I realise that not all three are Shadows. One of them is a desert dog mercenary dressed in a robe of aquamarine. These men are without scruples and take on any task if the price is right.

A scream rips through the air.

The great kestrel manifests itself in a surge of power and blinks into existence from the shield.

I am still reeling from the burst of energy of the transformation. I realise too late, that the face of the desert dog is that of Shahulm's abductor. In the instant that it takes me to realise his identity, the bird attacks the man, literally tearing him off his horse and rending his flesh to pieces.

The desert dog screams belatedly, recognising the creature that is attacking him, the nightmare that has haunted him since the taking of Shahulm suddenly and unexpectedly made manifest.

Though also taken by surprise, the Shadows are now enjoying the terror of the man being torn to pieces. They unsheathe their poisonous swords intent on killing the bird once they have enjoyed the feast of its kill.

Hasan's scimitar flashes first in the late evening light, closely followed by Faruq's. In the instant that it takes for a candle to be blown out, the Shadows are lying dead on the sand. The desert dog's body is strewn in pieces as his blood seeps into the thirsty land.

I allow the shield to collapse. The great bird, looking distressed but avenged is slowly losing its shape.

"Please forgive me, Azizi, I could not let him pass by. It was he who took my beloved."

The Companions are standing protectively around their prince.

I go to him and taking him into my arms, I embrace him.

"We will find him, Ijlal, and he will be well."

He releases himself to his tears then and cries bitterly for the lover who was taken from him.

The Companions quickly bury the bodies in a makeshift pit and scatter fresh sand over the blood. As quick as the killing of the Shadows was, I cannot be completely sure that they did not raise an alarm, nor for that matter that the controlling Scarlet Robe has not perceived the images that they had witnessed.

We hasten with greater speed towards the citadel intent on reaching its walls under the cover of night.

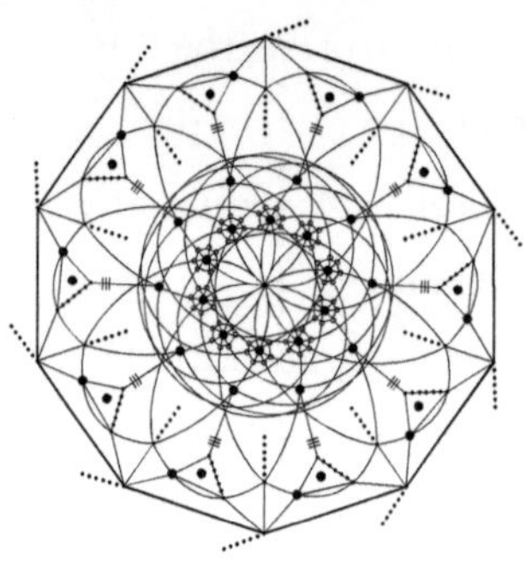

CHAPTER THIRTY

Hasan calls a brief stop to discuss how we will enter the citadel. Referring to Giafar's calls for urgency, we decide to investigate entry through the main gates of the city.

It is late at night when we reach the citadel, its walls rising from the surrounding plain like mountains. Tall towers stand like dark sentinels outlined against the starlit sky.

We make our way up the steep, winding road Ijlal had spoken of. Even by the light of the stars I can see that it is well built and broad enough to take ten men on horseback.

The faint light of pre-dawn is beginning to light the horizon as we reach the city gates. I turn to look at the way we have come and see the vast expanse of the plain below. My heart misses a beat; in the distance I see an outline of the Asfaine Mountains etched on the horizon, a hint of white glinting in the early morning.

The city gates, though shut, appear to be unguarded. The

height of three men, they are made of heavy wood reinforced here and there with large bands of dark blue metal.

I turn to Hasan, "Hasan, this does not seem right. Why are there no guards on duty?"

With a worried look, Hasan considers my question. Ijlal and Faruq listen with grave attention.

Keeping his voice low Hasan answers, "I have also noticed that there are very few soldiers patrolling the ramparts. There are only two possible options I can think of: either the Over Lord is too confident and has committed all his soldiers to the defensive force we saw earlier, and he has kept a small contingent for his personal protection. Or he has split his force into two, directing the remaining force to the west side. Perhaps he fears an attack from the Ocean."

Faruq nods his agreement. Ijlal looks at me, "Azizi, I can take the shape of the bird and fly over the city to check."

My immediate instinct is against it. "Ijlal, if there are archers behind this gate, one desperate arrow shot out of fear could mean your death." I consider the options, only one presents itself and that will involve my ability. "I will use my skill to sense what is behind this gate."

Leaning against the gate, with both my palms on the wood, I focus my energy to the other side. Closing my eyes, I relax as best as I can. I do not have the skill my godmother has to be able project herself on the other side of a solid object, but at least I can project my energy and sense what I feel. The gate feels solid. Gradually I can sense my energy on the other side. Taking a few deep breaths, all I sense is a strange emptiness.

Taking my hands off the gate, I turn to the Companions who

look upon me with concern. "There is no one behind the gate."

'How will we get in then, if no one is able to open it from the inside?"

I answer, "We can try the smaller gate." Pointing to the left of the main gate, stands a small door, presumably to allow a single courier or messenger, to pass through quickly without them having to unlock the main gates.

The smaller door is made as solidly as the main gates. I reach beyond the door with my consciousness and can detect no presence. To unlock and open the door will be a simple matter. My godmother taught me the power of moving objects in my early training.

With the palm of my hand flat against the door, I send a pulse of energy to act upon the mechanism. With an audible sound, the lock snaps open. We are through in moments, being careful to lock the door behind us.

As we step into the citadel, my heart is beating so loud that I think it will give us away. The first thing that strikes us is the eerie silence and the lack of soldiers patrolling the ramparts or the streets. A dark and oppressive energy fills the air. I look at Ijlal. His eyes burn, and his whole body is alert. The soldier in him is not going to allow his heart to rule.

We find an empty stable, built for visiting merchants, where we tie our horses and quickly eat some of our remaining rations. In low voices, we speak to determine what our best plan of movement will be over the next few hours. We agree that since we have made our way into the city, we will attract very little attention, as long as we watch the way we act. The fluidity of movement of an Apphatian soldier can be identified by almost anyone. It will be important for all the Companions to mask their identities, as much by their outward disguise of simple shepherds' clothing, as by adopting a walk and attitude that will suit that disguise.

I, on the other hand, can easily pass for a scholar, who has come on pilgrimage and who has early in his travel joined a caravan of shepherds for his safety.

Ijlal tells us where the palace is situated. We are to make our way to the top of the city on foot as our horses will attract too much attention. Ijlal proposes then to find the entrance by which servants and suppliers enter the palace.

By the early afternoon, we reach the upper level of the city. We split into smaller groups or pairs, and by carefully observing the comings and goings; we soon discover the servants' entrance to the palace.

Two soldiers closely guard the way. They check the individuals who come through the door, and any items being brought into the palace.

The guards are young and more attentive to their duties than most. It will be difficult to get past them. We sit in some quiet corner speaking in hushed tones and deciding on how best to get past the guards. Using the seal of concealment would be difficult, as it would have to be done in pairs. That would mean going back and forth eight times, the chance of discovery increasing each time.

Suddenly a roar arises from the lower reaches of the city. The sound of people screaming and rushing about is getting louder and louder. The guards look at each other and leaning over the nearest wall overlooking the city, decide to rush off to see what's happening.

No sooner have they turned the corner than we move inside without the use of concealment.

In a low whisper, Faruq exclaims, "My father and his troops have made good speed!"

In one movement the Companions draw their scimitars. The look of boyish innocence in Rauf and Jamal's eyes is quickly replaced by one of cold determination.

Very slowly, we make our way from one level to the next, but the palace appears oddly quiet and deserted. Occasionally we hear distant footsteps hurrying down an adjacent corridor.

Finally turning a corner, we find ourselves at the end of a long corridor, broad and richly decorated. Hasan raises his hand to signal a stop and we retreat to the shadows of a nearby alcove. He does not need to point. At the other end of the corridor, a group of soldiers has just arrived, forming a double protective rank in front of a richly carved door, painted in deep reds and gold.

As we look on, a messenger dressed in the royal colours, rushes to the captain of the guards and whispers to him. He is immediately let into the chamber. The captain looks from side to side in nervous apprehension.

I have never witnessed the Companions in a fight. With common accord, Hasan and the Companions step out into the light and walk almost casually towards the standing guards.

Taken by surprise by the sheer affront, the soldiers stand there a moment. It is all the time the Companions need. They almost reach the guards before the captain shouts an order and the soldiers draw their swords.

In true Apphatian combat formation, the Companions move

in such a way that at any moment, they form a pair with each protecting another's back. Apphatian soldiers will fight thus to the death in protecting their beloved. This is what makes them the most renowned and feared of all fighters.

The Companions' scimitars wave in mesmerising, graceful movements, each stroke a calculating blow meant to distract the opponent or reach to make a kill. Every time a scimitar moves, and I expect it to flow in one direction, it comes from the other. The superior technique of these young desert fighters overwhelms the guards. As the soldiers fall one by one, others drop their weapons and run before the fury and righteous vengeance of the Companions, nevertheless still falling in their tracks from a blade thrown at them. Hardly a cry is uttered and in a little while, all is quiet.

I stand before the door and push it open.

The young messenger is standing in the centre of the room looking unsure, and when he sees us, he slowly recedes against a far wall. A small squat man crouching in a far corner of the room is rocking and muttering to himself. Judging by his attire, I realise that this is the Over Lord.

I look at the young, frightened messenger, and I realise that it will be difficult to obtain any information, not because of his fear but possibly from a sense of loyalty he may still have for his master.

I signal to Rauf and softly speak to him, "Rauf, see if you can befriend the messenger and bring him to me."

Rauf shields his scimitar, turns to the young lad, and beaming his most boyish and disarming smile, gently walks over, speaks softly to him, inviting him to come and join me.

The messenger taken by Rauf's kindness, hesitantly follows him.

Wasting no time and having assured myself that the lad will not recoil and run, I place my hand on his shoulder, then gently slip my hand to the back of his head. Applying a gentle pressure just to the side of the base of his neck, I trigger a point that will make him compliant.

"You will not be harmed. Now tell me what message you have for your master, the Over Lord."

As in a trance, the young messenger relays the message, which he had but moments before delivered to the Over Lord.

"The armies of Schiraz assisted by soldiers of Naassée, have defeated the army on the Isthmus of Mina. They have now overrun the city. Their leader is demanding unconditional surrender."

It appears that Giafar, on receiving our news, has wasted no time. He somehow conveyed a message to the army of Naassée. The army then crossed the isthmus before dark, and in true desert fashion concealed themselves in the sands. Once the Over Lord's armies had reached the isthmus, the Naasséene soldiers leapt out of hiding, taking them by surprise and making short shrift of the battle. In the meantime, Giafar took a small contingent of soldiers on horseback, and at desert speed, rushed to the Isthmus of Mina reaching it before dawn.

The army of the Over Lord was caught in a well-laid trap between the two armies and was quickly defeated. The remaining soldiers from the North had then joined forces and they had simply attacked the citadel.

The few guards on the ramparts, seeing the Over Lord's pennants flying at the head of the approaching army, had thought that the previous day's contingent was returning, and had not bothered to raise the alarm. The city was invaded quickly and was now in possession of General Giafar and the Naasséene soldiers.

Little wonder the Over Lord is looking a little bewildered. Judging by his mumbling, he has lost most of his senses. It will not be hard to convince the remaining nobles to surrender to the invading armies.

I release the mind of the messenger. He rubs the back of his neck and smiles at Rauf.

"I promised that you would not be harmed. Now go to your home and take shelter. The Over Lord is no longer your master."

If anything, the lad looks relieved, and without further prompting, leaves the palace rooms.

I turn to the Companions. "The city is in the hands of Giafar. This man can wait here for his fate. We must find Shahulm quickly."

Ijlal is at my side at the mention of his beloved. "Azizi, where do we go?"

"When I sought Shahulm for you that night, he was deep in the bowels of this palace, so we need to find a way down."

The Companions look around hoping against all odds that a way down will manifest itself. I close my eyes and look inwardly, re-living the night that I had sought Shahulm. I hunt through my memories for the feeling that drew me to him.

Something on the edge of my inner consciousness rings softly, like a glimmer of sunlight caught in the ripple of water, or the moon behind a cloud seen at the corner of my eye, bright one moment and gone the next.

I open my eyes and look around the room. A little to one side of the throne of the Over Lord, is a large tapestry depicting an ancient war. Men are frozen in silent screams of either attack or death, charging on horseback, thundering through fields of blood-stained grass. In the background of all that noise and pain stands a clear sky with a small sun painted high above the plains in one corner, and a moon in the other. It seems that it is both night and day.

I point at the tapestry and declare, "We go through there."

Faruq, the distinguisher of truth, is the first to reach the tapestry and in one movement, draws it aside to reveal a small open archway that leads to steep stairs.

Still with their scimitars drawn, the Companions rush after Ijlal down the stairs that descend into darkness. I feel a sudden pang in my heart and in that instant, I can smell salt. In my mind I hear a faint echo of a song gilded with sunlight, that caresses my inner being like a summer breeze. Thinking that the realisation of our goal so close at hand is the cause, I put it aside and resolve to calm my mind for the final confrontation with the Sorceress.

We descend for an eternity. Finally, we reach a large dark room, barely lit by torches that line the damp walls. A smell of mould and rotting permeates the air.

I ask Hasan to stop a moment to let our eyes adjust to the new light.

The Companions gather and looking at them, softly I whisper, "Shield your eyes and prepare your weapons."

I gather a small ball of energy in my mind and direct it to the palms of my hands. With a small explosion, I release the energy as it fires across the chamber releasing an intense light.

Multitudes of high-pitched screams are heard, as Shadow after Shadow melts from the walls and staggers in the searing light of the chamber. Blinded, the Shadows are no match for the Companions and succumb easily without a fight.

We move down the corridor, cautious of what might lie in our path.

Finally, we reach a door I recognise, and I know we are outside the chamber where I have seen Shahulm. We make ready for what lies behind the door.

In one swift movement, Hasan and two of the Companions throw open the doors. We rush in, prepared to fight to the death, and come to a sudden stop. The chamber is empty, the altar of stone bare of its previous sacrifice.

Ijlal's eyes burn with a fever, and I can see that the transformation is simmering beneath his self-control.

"They have taken him away. Azizi, where have they taken him?"

I stand there a moment wanting to obliterate this chamber and all the pain it has ever held. A vague taste of salt again floats on the air.

"They must have taken him to the ships. Did Giafar not tell us the ships are being made ready on the west side of the island?"

There is another door that leads from the chamber. Relying on instinct rather than a plan, we take to the door immediately. This leads down a slightly wider passage, which curves at one end and looks as though it opens into another chamber.

The Companions stop ahead of me. Thinking there is some confusion on which way to take, I rush up.

A Scarlet Robe stands in our way. He is holding a small body in front of him dressed in brown rags.

CHAPTER THIRTY-ONE

The ground wavers beneath me. I freeze as I see Halim held in the murderous hands of this hateful creature. Like a distant dream, I remember my godmother asking me if I had summoned Halim. The echoing strands of a spring song fade into darkness.

Silence fills the world, the silence that holds its breath before the roar of thunder. *Halim,* I think,*'Halim, stand still. Do not be afraid you cannot be harmed'.*

I call out to him, "Halim..." a rasp in my voice betraying my emotions.

With a grin of spite and evil pleasure, the Scarlet Robe slowly raises his short sword to Halim's throat. Deep brown eyes look at me, look and smile.

A hateful laugh gurgles, as in one movement the Scarlet Robe slides his knife across Halim's throat. A small red necklace appears on Halim's neck, as incomprehension and then pain fills his eyes.

I scream his name and run forward, not caring any more for the deadly point of the knife's blade. Several silver flashes whistle by my side as the short blades of Hasan and the Companion's pin the Scarlet Robe to the wall behind him.

"Halim!" I scream his name, cradling his head to my chest, warm red blood wetting my hands. I struggle to stem the flow; I want to put it all back into him. I lean close to his face and whisper his name, calling him, begging him not to go. His face blurs in my tears. Angrily, I wipe them away. A sickness envelops me.

The light in his eyes flickers and he lies limp in my arms.

I can no longer move; my body has turned to stone. I want to scream at the world. Darkness engulfs my sight. I hear myself calling his name, over and over. Someone is lifting me. Halim is being carried away from me. I cannot tell where I am, everything blurs, my senses leave me, and I do not care where I am going or why. Darkness falls.

⌒⌒

My godmother is sitting beside me.

I cannot catch my breath. I try many times to say that he has died, that they have killed my shepherd boy, that Halim is dead. The words catch in my throat; unable to breathe, I cannot bring myself to say the words. If I am to pronounce them, my world will explode into a million pieces never to be put back again. I try to breathe, but the words still do not make their way past my heart.

Halim's murder does not make sense. Why him? He was no

danger to them. He is a simple shepherd boy. There is no power in him but his simple love for me.

Aïschah waits. She sees my pain; she is powerless to master it.

In her compassion, she does the only thing a mother can do. Gently she holds me. My tears flow so hard that I find it difficult to breathe. She holds me in her arms until the flood of tears ebbs.

"Why him? I do not understand."

She looks at me tenderly. "His death is the only thing that could send you into despair. Killing him makes no sense to you, only to them. They are hoping to destroy your hope, your courage and your will to fight them."

My godmother's words to me, contain wisdom but not the comfort I yearn for, only the reason to fight. Halim's death will not throw me off my goal and destiny. Still, no matter how many times I tell myself that I have only witnessed the passing of his outer shell, that his spirit still lives on, the grief at his loss weighs heavily upon my heart.

It is the determination not to allow the Sorceress a victory over the life of an innocent that now drives me. Sorrow and despair cannot be allowed to rule.

I learn later that the Companions had asked Haroun-al-Rashid to contact my godmother. It was she who had advised them to continue the quest and take me with them. They had seized upon and were sailing a small ship that had been prepared for the Over Lord, the master of the vessel only too willing to serve a great general now that the despised Over Lord had been dethroned.

I sleep for several hours and awake disoriented, unable to comprehend where I am. I join the Companions on deck. They come to me, their love and concern is clearly etched in their faces.

Ijlal holds me, having witnessed my love for Halim. In grief, we are closer than we were before. No words are spoken. The Companions' love for me does much to ease the burden I am carrying.

My godmother has returned to our village and has taken Halim's young body with her. It will be hard to confront his mother and cousins with the news of his death.

Trying to distract myself, I step to the front of the boat, this strange sensation of fluidity beneath my feet a new experience for me. We are sailing to the island of Brouille where it is said the Sorceress has taken refuge. According to folklore, the island is the retreat for an ancient and vile sect of witchcraft, which saw many young male virgins sacrificed as part of the final rite of initiation of witches. The rites have long been banned, the witches exiled and, in some cases, executed.

Mist envelops the ship like the grief around my heart. There is no need to conceal the vessel and a light easterly wind is blowing, pushing waves of mist before it, rolling like clouds upon the water. We are making good headway.

The smell of patchouli announces Hasan's presence. He looks at me with a mixture of sorrow, remorse, and concern. I understand his remorse at not having been able to save Halim. I go to him and take refuge in his warm embrace.

We reach the island of Brouille by the end of the day. Despite the wind and the late afternoon sun, the island and the surrounding seas are still enveloped in thick mist.

Here and there, large dark outcrops of rocks on the edges of the island stand out.

The boat is tied to the end of a long wooden quay that stretches out from the island into the sea. Four soldiers have been assigned with us at Giafar's command. They now stand, guarding the ship waiting for our return.

We walk some way onto the island carrying torches to light our way, before we come upon the dreaded sight of a small fortress that grows out of the surrounding rocks. The island is devoid of vegetation, the rocky landscape adding to the depressing atmosphere. Pockets of thick white mist still hang like long strands of torn, bleached flesh.

We stop awhile, scanning the outer defences of the fortress. The structure is old and in parts are crumbling. The walls are made of ancient black stone that glistens in the late afternoon light. The function of the stones is not to protect: I can sense that there are enough spells that ward off unwelcome and unwary travellers.

The air feels weighed down with a darkness that confuses the senses and gnaws at one's resolve. Rocks appear to waver, their outline dissolving and shifting with the mist, only to re-appear somewhere else.

We make our way towards the fortress, its dark walls looming above us. The Companions walk with their scimitars drawn.

I am wary of the unnatural silence, then a chatter of malevolent whispers arises. I hear many voices on the mist, but I cannot make out any words.

Every now and again a malicious laugh hangs in the air. Then I hear a name, which freezes me in my steps.

"Halim," the laughing voice whispers with venomous sweet-ness.

Laughter erupts.

Fleetingly, I see Halim's face and the horror in his eyes as the

Scarlet Robe's knife sliced across his throat.

I moan and find myself doubled over. Hasan is kneeling next to me his arm around my shoulders.

He says nothing. His presence lends me the courage to stand.

I perceive the link between the Sorceress's image of Halim dying and my mind. Using the knife Hasan gave me, in a ritual gesture I ruthlessly sever the link. The chattering voices disappear.

The path we take leads resolutely to a solid wall. This must be a charm of some kind. I search my mind for the teachings of my godmother and find nothing. As I face the black stonewall, I hear again in my mind that cold laugh and my gut fills with icy apprehension.

The wall in front of us shimmers and dissolves. A dark passage lies open before us.

"This has too much of the appearance of a well-laid trap." Hasan speaks quietly but confirms the thoughts of all in our party.

We stop, considering what options lie before us. The icy knot in my gut still twists. Hasan's hand comes to rest on my shoulder. I shudder and taking in a deep breath, a warm glow forms in my stomach and expands to slowly melt the icy uncertainty.

"What should we do, Azizi?"

"Rauf, bring out the talisman. Ijlal, do you feel strong enough to wear it?"

It takes a short moment before Ijlal nods, willpower shining in his eyes. He places the sacred Talisman around his neck and immediately, the coiled snakes take on an unearthly glow.

"Ijlal, follow the song of the talisman, and go where it leads you. We will follow."

The Companions once more form a guard around Ijlal. Wary

of sudden attack, we enter the fortress. A dull, oppressive stench reaches our senses. The air is both heavy and cold.

An array of corridors leading into all possible directions confronts us. Without hesitation, Ijlal turns to his left and leads us without pause, until we reach a large circular room, which again splits into several corridors.

I notice that the further we go, the harder it is to focus. Walking becomes difficult, as if we are dragging ourselves ankle deep in sand and water. I am fighting to keep awake.

We pause; even Ijlal seems tired and unsure.

Hasan, who is bringing up the rear, comes to stand beside me. "We are being followed."

I too had sensed some time ago the slithering, murky presence of Shadows. "It was inevitable that we would be."

Hasan nods. We need a plan if we are not to become trapped like rats. The Companions gather around.

Hasan speaks in a whisper, "We are being followed. We cannot allow Azizi or Ijlal to become trapped. And trying to outwit these Shadows would be a waste of time. We should split the party and draw off the Shadows that follow. This will leave Azizi and Ijlal to find Shahulm quickly.

Hasan looks at me. I know who else we need to find, if indeed he is being held here.

"What if Ijlal's party comes under attack?" Fatin's question is reasonable.

"I propose that Rauf and Jamal go with them, and Isamadeen to guard. This will leave Faruq, Husam and you Fatin to come with me."

All nod their agreement.

"How will you find us again in this maze of corridors?" I ask.

Hasan's hand clasps Faruq's shoulder. "As his name suggests, he who distinguishes truth from falsehood will show us the way! Besides," Hasan adds with a smile, "I will smell the talisman you wear, Azizi, it is my seal of protection."

That was that, then.

"What shall we do once we encounter the Sorceress if you have not re-joined us?" Isamadeen looks worried.

Hasan's face is grave. "Neither your sword nor mine will be of any use, Isamadeen. This is magic—it will be up to Azizi to deal with her. Your task is to protect him and Ijlal against all else."

My body shivers at the weight of responsibility. Will my training be enough? I am only an initiate of the first order, still an apprentice. She on the other hand, is an adept, albeit of the dark arts. Her powers will far surpass mine.

My godmother's wise words come to mind then. "Do not trust 'your' powers, Dear One; they are not yours. Rather trust the power of the Great Spirit for He is all."

The plan is for me, Ijlal, and the others to take refuge in a side corridor and for me to project a shield of concealment around us while Hasan and his Companions move away with the Shadows in tow.

We move a little farther down a passageway and seeing a small recess along the wall, we quickly take shelter in it, while Hasan moves down with Faruq, Husam and Fatin, making a little more noise than they normally would.

Quickly, I create a shield at the entrance of the recess as the rest of my party quietly draws their scimitars.

My heart sinks as I watch Hasan and the others move down

the dark corridor, which soon engulfes them.

We don't have to wait too long before the putrid stench of Shadows announces their approach.

Like slime, they silently move after Hasan's party. There are no more than twenty of them. The fighting odds of five to one gnaws at my conscience for agreeing to this plan.

As soon as the Shadows and their lingering stench have moved beyond our senses, I release the shield and Ijlal leads us back to the previous division of passages. We resume our frantic search using Ijlal's talisman as our lodestone.

I notice that the feeling of confusion and weariness has gone. We emerge out of the passageway to enter a corridor twice the width of the one we have just left. Small slits open into the walls, and I catch glimpses of the water surrounding the island. The sun has set, and the mist lifted to reveal a pale dusk.

The roof of the corridor is lost in darkness. At the far end I can perceive a large door flanked by two smoky torches. The door is crossed and studded with metal.

I pause, unsure. Everything is too quiet. The end of the passageway seems to invite us.

The Companions gather around. I link briefly with Hasan, wanting to know where they are and how they fare. My mind is overwhelmed with a dark passage filled with confusion. The noise of battle fills my consciousness. I see the faces of the Companions strained and worried. They are under attack.

The image is suddenly snatched from my mind, and I am left with a cold feeling of ruthless invasion. We cannot help them. A glint of yellow light catches my eye—in one of the openings in the rocks, I behold the rising full moon of Camlac. We are running out of time. I signal that we will make for the door.

Cautiously, we move down the passageway. We reach the door when a rustling noise behind us makes us turn. Ten Scarlet Robes with drawn short swords, blades glistening with poison, stand barring our only exit.

Isamadeen at once takes a protective position between his prince and the creatures.

No matter how skilled the Companions are, this will be a futile battle. A mere scratch from any one of these blades will mean certain death. Hatred pours from their hooded faces. They stand silently and motionless. I can sense their minds attempting to destroy the resolve of the Companions.

We hear an audible click and as I turn, I see that the large wooden door has swung open.

A dark chamber lies beyond, lit by torchlight. The Scarlet Robes as one take a step forward, forcing us to retreat through the doorway.

I enter the chamber followed by the Companions. The chamber is made of the same black stones as the outer walls. The surface is uneven and glistening with dampness. Many black candles light the space. Openings are cut into the rock, and I can see the surrounding island and the waters of the inlet.

At the far end of the chamber, the floor rises by several steps. On the uppermost step, four more Scarlet Robes stand facing us. Each holds a ceremonial knife and bowl. I shudder to think for whom these are intended. The door to the chamber slams shut behind us and the following Scarlet Robes form a guard in fron of it.

The Companions look helpless. For a moment as I turn once

more to face the dais, I think I see a face in pain, frozen into the rock. An evil cackle echoes around the chamber. A movement emerges from behind the four Scarlet Robes and she, my mortal enemy, appears. She is dressed in a red gown overlaid with her ceremonial black robe, three red intersecting swords stitched on her lapel.

A smile of utter disdain floats across a cruel mouth. She savours the moment.

I am surprised to see how small she is, standing perhaps a head shorter than I am. The colour of her eyes shifts from green to fluorescent yellow.

"Ah, here is the little lamb who has lost his shepherd. Now he has boy soldiers! How amusing!"

I sense anger and frustration building in the Companions.

Looking them over, and as her eyes rest upon Rauf and Jamal she laughs. "At least you have brought me two young virgins, how kind!" She shakes her head, throwing back her long black hair over her shoulders.

"You seem surprised, little one!" She speaks directly at me. Her tone becomes acid and full of disdain. "I drew you here. Every move you made was fore planned and manipulated."

She laughs again. "Men!" She spits the word. "Men are such pitiful creatures! Give them a scent to follow and they will walk in their own delusion to their own deaths! And you!" She looks at Isamadeen. "Soldiers of Apphat you call yourselves! Even weaker, for you follow those who would follow me! Why do you think only men serve me? Futile creatures! You and your kind will pay dearly for the destruction of my sisters. The rites of initiation were sacred—men served their purpose, and we sacrificed them.

At least their blood was of use."

She looks to one of the Scarlet Robes at the back of the chamber and pointing to Rauf she commands, "Bring me that one!"

The Scarlet Robe takes several steps toward Rauf, when in one swift movement of cold rage, Isamadeen steps forward and cuts the Scarlet Robe down where he stands. Even in death the creature did not relinquish either hatred or silence.

She laughs again.

"Never mind, there will be time later. You will pay for his killing."

I turn to her, determined to deny her perversion of the truth.

"The beliefs of Apphat and his philosophy were not about man or woman. It was about both, as a balance and a union of creative force. Those who follow Apphat understand that within oneself lies the duality of creation. Your kind has perverted that truth. That is why the dark arts are reviled."

She stares blankly. The concept is beyond her warped and limited understanding.

She changes her demeanour then. I reel back, feeling the full impact of her mental attack. "Did you bring me the other stone?"

A long pause follows as I sense her mind probing my thoughts. Strangely, a power wells from within me and I can sense that where she would have searched my heart, she cannot pass this gate of power.

My heart is filled with a wondrous feeling. Fleetingly I remember a kiss in sunlight.

"I know you met him in the desert, yet I am sure that he did not give you the second stone." She looks at me again with a mixture of disdain and curiosity.

Again, she points to some Scarlet Robes at the rear and orders, "Strip him and search his clothing. And this time do not be so careless as to allow yourselves to be killed."

Isamadeen and the others moved in a semi circle behind me.

I wave my hand, "I cannot bear the touch of your creatures. Leave them. I am able to undress myself."

Slowly and deliberately, I remove my garments. Naked and defenceless, I stand before my enemy. Her avaricious stare probes my vulnerability. Strangely, I almost feel pity for her. The love in my heart has no shame of my nakedness.

She turns then, almost nervously. "It is as I thought. You do not have the stone!"

She turns back having slipped her hand into one of her sleeves. "I, on the other hand, possess this one." She brandishes a large blue stone the colour of the sea in a storm.

The Stone of Malkizar, the Stone of Sorrow, one of the Tears of Apphat lies there in her corrupt hand. A quick intake of breath comes from the Companions—this is legend they are witnessing.

Fury and rage overtakes them. Like a master's angry dogs, they fret to be let loose. Rauf fetches my robe and helps me back into it. He then draws his scimitar at the ready.

"Where is Shahulm?" Ijlal demands. His patience has run out.

Covetously, she caresses the stone. "You are right." She muses, "The time has come."

She moves to the side and motions to the four Scarlet Robes. They part revealing a large black stone altar.

Naked, pale, and semi-conscious, Shahulm lies upon the ungodly slab of stone. His head lolls to one side. His eyes are lustreless, blankly staring at us. He has lost so much weight that his ribs show through his pale parchment like skin.

Once more she smiles to see the horror in our eyes.

The cry of rage echoes throughout the chamber and a shadow flies across the lamplight, followed by the agonizing guttural wordless screams of one of the Scarlet Robes.

At the sight of his tortured lover, the prince transforms himself in one last act of fury and desperation and is tearing the creature's eyes out.

With an almost tired and careless gesture, the Sorceress throws powder at the attacking bird. The kestrel is flung to the ground where it lies panting in exhausted fury, slowly losing its bird shape.

Rage fills the Companions to see their leader and his lover so contemptuously dealt with. Yet they are frustrated at their inability to do anything, for this is unnatural power that cannot be vanquished with swords and knives.

I feel their look of despair upon me. For some time now a ball of fire has been forming at the base of my spine. I stand with quiet certainty, confronting my worst enemy and the enemy of all that our Order of Magic stands for. This is the time of reckoning.

I stand empty, a bell waiting to toll.

The moon Camlac rises full and shines a sickly yellow over the island. This is the night at the height of the season of Malkizar. Behind her, through one of the openings in the wall that face east, lies the vast stretch of water beyond the isthmus of Mina, and beyond still is the Great Desert of Keyab, just south of my homeland.

Slowly in the east, the crescent moon of Ayshah rises, its silver light spreading along the ripples of the water. For a moment it sits poised on the horizon and its reflection so perfectly mirrors in the water, it looks like the sacred double axe of the Naasséenes, followers of Apphat.

I hear her gluttonous laugh echo once more.

"Enough! Let us proceed with the sacrifice."

A part of me is fighting not to lose consciousness: light is tearing at my brain, my eyes water, and my senses are invaded by the taste and smell of salt.

Like a blast of hot air everything around me explodes into fury, and the elements of air, fire, and water manifest without warning. Wind suddenly rages in gusts, dark clouds gather on the outer edges of the cave, and within these, dark forms take shape in the shadows. Beasts of prey materialise and stare with their hungry yellow eyes. Growls echoe throughout the chamber and grow into thunderclaps. All around is storm and fury. Lightning bolts strike outwards from my body, highlighting streaks of water trickling down the walls of the cave.

Awed, the Companions involuntarily step back. The Shadows cower.

I take a breath. I will not lose control of my emotions. Deep within myself I seek the teachings of the Way. I seek the centre of my being. At once, I am as calm as the eye of the storm and this eye watches the Sorceress. She smiles contemptuously.

"Impressive! But you do not think that I drew you here to lose this battle now, little one? Wait but a moment and I will show you how to destroy."

She brandishes the blue sapphire, ready to begin her ritual. Malkizar has paled and softly it calls to its mate for release. Staring at the Stone, compassion overcomes me.

Elwah calls to be released. The time for Joy to be born again has come. The time for balance is here. Like a sky opening itself to the sunrise I understand.

I understand the kiss in the desert. The stone of Elwah was truly within him. He merely passed it to me for safekeeping in a kiss of bliss and joy:

> *"...And in its darkest hour*
> *Elwah will be safeguarded, for*
> *In a moment of bliss and Joy, the Sacred Keeper*
> *Will make his beloved whole,*
> *And his beloved will become the Gateway."*

In my mind I surrender myself and I sing the sacred song of the stone, a song of Divine Love. Slowly, like a warm fire that feeds my heart, the Tear of Apphat named Elwah rises from my inner being, striking me like a bell, filling me with its most wondrous song.

I put my hands to my mouth and receive the magical gift. It glows the pure blue of the clearest sky. It warms in my hand. A knowing from deep within me calls softly and with authority.

"It is time to restore balance."

With a look of incredulity and rage the Sorceress steps forward. "Give me the Stone!"

The world holds its breath.

I proclaim, "Water and Salt that maketh

The Tears of Joy and Sorrow

Cannot be One without the other.

Pain and sweetness go hand in hand

I release you.

Let the lesson begin!"

Without hesitation, I throw the stone at her. A look of disbelief crosses her face, then avaricious triumph overcomes her composure, as the stone flies straight into her outstretched hand.

She catches it and takes a breath, looks at me directly, and begins to mouth the word "fool," when suddenly her composure changes, a look of incomprehension, then horror.

She screams out "No… " Her hands are paralysed, and she can no longer let go. Both stones glow, one with the blue of a summer sky, the other with the blue of the deepest ocean, dark and foreboding. All the horror of her vile deeds attacks her, her own conscience and her own terror eat at her.

She once more lets out a blood-curdling scream of utter despair. The test has come before the lesson. The storm at once rages around me, utterly unleashed, and the shadows within the wind attack her, devouring her. Before my very eyes, the Sorceress slowly shrivels, dries, and collapses into a mound of salt.

The Scarlet Robes collapse senseless on the ground. The storm abates, and wisps of air pick up strands of dust and whirl them around the cavern. Balance is restored, at least in this chamber. I sense the Companions' emotions, a mixture of awe and satisfied justice. Soldiers are used to the sight of blood, but the utter destruction of an enemy, who knows as she dies that this is the end—there is completeness in this. They begin to move to their leader and his lover.

At that moment, Hasan and the others burst into the chamber making short work of the semi-conscious Robes.

The sapphires lie still glowing on the ground where they

have rolled.

I advance to pick them up and hear a deep voice gentle as the morning sun, "No, Dear One, do not touch them, it is not yet your time."

At this a sphere of light engulfs both stones and they disappear.

I can taste salt; tears are rolling down my cheeks. With some sadness I think I will not see such blue light for a long time.

The same voice speaks again, gently, and deeply, "Then Dear One, until then, content yourself with my gift and look upon my light that shines forth from the blue of his eyes."

I turn.

The rock walls of the chamber still trickle with water. The rock takes shape and slowly, like a frozen statue melting, I see the form of a young man emerging out of it.

He is released as the witch's powers have been destroyed. Faltering a little, he steps from the rock. He opens his eyes and looks directly at me.

Blue eyes stare at me with all the love and tenderness of his heart. The lover of my dreams is here. The one I have so often dreamt of is here in the flesh. Gently, he steps forward and takes me in the warm and strong embrace of his arms.

Softly he whispers, "I am Elwah Tahir, Haafiz of the Sacred Stone for the people of Naassée. Dear One, you have promised me your heart; now, accept mine."

THE END

Book 1

The Tears of Apphat. Immortal Beloved

Book 2

Silence of the Stars

Chronicles of Azizi, Seer of Apphat. Immortal Beloved

Chapter One

The Return of the Prince

My heart, heavy as a storm cloud with the memory of Halim's death, nevertheless found a rainbow of hope at Prince Shahulm's rescue into the arms of his beloved Ijlal...

DICTIONARY OF
WORDS AND PHRASES

Aldrik Azizi's child's name. Made up of two parts: ALD/ADAL Norse for 'noble' or 'kind'; and RIK, Old Germanic for 'mighty'. Born on the second hour of the second day of the second month of Winter—A Child of Stardust. Pale, slight of build. Ice blue eyes. Holder of magic. Often misconstrued as 'distant', 'aloof...'

Adhån Call to prayer. The faithful do their duty of prayer at least three times a day when they hear the call from the High Priest. 'My Heart is trembling. Look at my Tears. There is no God but God' (page 260 – song).

Ahl-Cassim (pronounced *ahl-caseem*) The Breath of God, the precursor to the great desert sandstorms the Cassim.

Apphat (pronounced *ap-fat*). Apphat the Wise. Ancient king of Naassee who founded a philosophy based on androgyny. His philosophy was that the duality of creation existed in both men and women. The Apphatians were known for its fierce, honoured, respected and feared soldiers. The Royal guards in particular who were all homosexual, had vowed total allegiance to their King. These soldiers were not allowed into battle unless they had taken a lover. They would fight side by side and could only be defeated in death.
The Apphatian soldiers began the practice of 'Damna': a sacred initiation of boys that have come of age (around 17 years), into

the secrets of love making. It was considered an honour to have one's boy thus initiated.

The kingdom of Apphat was destroyed in the great cataclysm and its people disappeared. Many hundreds of years later, a strange people emerged from the Caves of Gibrar wearing arm bands and amulets that the Apphatians had been known to wear. This people settled in the east of the land and became known as the Naasseenes. They practiced the rites of Apphat. (Refer to 'Apphat The Wise').

Aïschah (pronounced *a-ee-sha*) In the Ancient tongue means 'Silver Moon' (see also Ayshah). Godmother of Dear One. Seeress Magician, Teacher and Healer. Mahjira or female master of the seventh rite. She lives in the Asfaine mountains and honoured friend and guardian of the Hills People.

Ayshah (pronounced *a-ee-shü-ha*) The second moon of this world is smaller and has a silvery appearance. According to legend, this moon can overpower the ill omen of Camlac especially if it eclipses the latter during the season of Malkizar.

Azizi Name of power given to Aldrik ('Dear One'), by his godmother. It means 'beloved'.

Brouille Group of islands in the northern seas. Said to be haunted, constantly enveloped in mist. Tradition has it that for many years it was the secret meeting place of the early Black Witches.

Camlac Name of the first moon of this world. It usually appears first in the cycle of moons and is usually a pale yellow in appearance. Depending on the season, it usually is taken as a bad omen. It was named after the demi-god its name meaning 'chaos'.

Damna Apphatian for 'Sacred Initiation'.

Duna Equivalent to one day, or the time that it takes for the wind to re-sculpt a sand dune in the great desert.

Duwae Equivalent to a year.

Elwah The season of Joy, associated with re-birth and reincarnation. Also the name of the Prince Guardian of the Sacred saphire by the same name. In our culture Spring.

Fariqa Meaning 'woman companion'.

Faruq (pronounced *farook*) Meaning 'One who distinguishes truth from falsehood'. Eldest son of Giafar.

Fatin One of the Companions, his name means 'clever', 'bright.'

Glesskerel Kingdom of the Northern Region and country of origin of Shahulm. The nation is situated far north of the Asfaine Mountains and is separated from the Asfaines on its southern most border by a large glacial wilderness.

Gaisha (pronounced *ga-eesha*) Title of respect meaning 'Great Mother'/ 'Great Father' depending on gender.

Gibrar Foreboding and desolate cave legendary place thought to be the last stand of Princess Baltazar and her lover. Renowned for the strange beasts that inhabit the surrounding lands. Used as test of bravery by early Apphat soldiers, also thought to be the place of origin of the Naasseenes.

Hala Aura or energy field. Visible to those with the Sight.

Halim Meaning 'gentle'. Shepherd boy of the Hills People. Destined to befriend Dear One.

Hakkaa Päälle Literally 'Cut Them Down!"

Hasan Meaning 'handsome'. Naasseene soldier, Captain of the Royal Guard and personal protector of Elwah, regent prince of the Naasseenes.

Haafiz Sacred Keeper

Hadid One of the twelve ancient guardian spirits. Hadid was the guardian of the air taking the form of a great bird; he was also the messenger of the sun god.

Haakon Aldrik's father. His name in old Norse means 'high son' or 'descendant'.

Hjaldr Tyr Invoking the name of the God of War.

Haroun-al-Rashid (pronounced *ha-roon-al rasheed*) Seer and magician at the Court of the Great Sutlan Maltiza, ruler of Shiraz.

Hreinn / Hreindyri Old Norse for reindeer.

Huda Literally meaning 'conduct'/'guide', interpreted as Great Mouth. This pass acts as a channel for fierce winds, known as the Ahl-Cassim.

Hummel (pronounced *who-mēl*) A stag having no horns, or unable to grow horns. English slang for homosexual.

Husam Meaning 'sword edge'. One of the companions.

Ihram Restriction / forbidding to engage in any mundane activity, including arguing, sexual activity etc. This is a time of spiritual cleansing.

Ijlal Heir and prince to the Kingdom of Shiraz. The leader of the Band of desert youths, trusted for his courage and fierce fighting skills.

Isamadeen Meaning 'to guard'. One of the companions, older brother to Rauf.

Isthmus The Giant's Footsteps: a group of islands so called as they appear to be steps across the inlet from the Great Citadel to the coastline south of Glesskerel.

Jamal Meaning 'kind'. One of the companions.

Jörmungandr In Norse mythology, Jörmungandr—also known as the Midgard Serpent or World Serpent—is an unfathomably large sea serpent who dwells in the world sea, encircling the Earth and biting his own tail, an example of an ouroboros. As a result of it surrounding Midgard it is referred to as the World Serpent

Kershel Measure of distance approximately equivalent to a metre and a half.

Knut Aldrik's bully and nemesis in the village. The name means knot.

Lahé Equivalent to a week.

Mahjir (pronounced *ma-here*) for a man; **Mahjira** (pronounced *ma-heera*) for a woman. Term of great respect, literally means 'Master' and is given to one who has mastered the arts of magic and seership.

Majlis Audience with the King.

Malkizar The coldest and most turbulent season of the Country. The season of Malkizar sees the Asfaine region covered in snow and cut off from the rest of the country for about 3 to 4 months. In our culture it would be known as the winter of the long night.

Mina The 3 stone pillars. The isthmus of Mina that leads to the stronghold of the Over lord—the great citadel.

Naassée A strange and enigmatic country built on the cliffs overlooking the Great Ocean of Elwah, its people known as both the Naasseenes as well as the old Apphasians. According to legend the people of Naassee emerged from a deep cave following the great cataclysm that destroyed the kingdom of Apphat. They wore the same clothes and talismans as the traditional Apphasians. They are ruled by priests of immense magical power and their leader is one known as Prince Elwah. It is said that he is a reincarnation of unbroken lineage of such individual and is identified by the priests as one of fair skin and blue eyes. Naassee is also known for its fearsome army of unconquered ruthless soldiers, who also follow the ancient rites and lore of Apphat.

For it is the Tears of Creation that are
the waters of the oceans. Tears that are made of
the waters of Joy and the salt of Sorrow.

Parvus Sacred rhyming verse written in groups of five lines, mostly used for epic poems and sacred text.

Rauf Meaning 'merciful and kind'. One of the companions.

Saeed Meaning 'Happy', 'Lucky'. Son of Fariqa.

Samå Listening, sacred form of meditation that allows the person to transcend consciousness and having removed all illusions feels the shudder of Love and stands in the Presence of God.

Sarab Mirage: a common phenomenon that occurred at certain times of the day as the heat from the land played with images of caravans of water that were a long way away and made appear to be close.

Shahulm (pronounced *sha-hoolm*) Named after the Guardian of the Night, meaning Lord of Dreams/Hope.

Sri Akall! Great is the Great Spirit.

Steggi / Steggr Old Norse for Stag.

Suffrah Mahjir Mahjir Suffrah is one of the revered Elders and Magician, the master who initiates Azizi into the First Order of Apphat the Healer.

Taqe Arabic for 'energy'. This is the type of energy that Azizi is trained to see; that is the energy field surrounding all living things.

Tekbiek (pronounced *tekbyek*) Predatory bird rarely seen. Dark in plumage it is adept at camouflage. Amongst the simple folk it is associated with the dark spirits that are said to roam the forest at night.

Varye (pronounced *va-ri-yay*) Sacred moral duties/codes that bind the magician to using certain powers or techniques only under specific circumstances.

War Cries see chapter 28 at the Huda Pass. These are of Sikh origin and combine Vikings cries of war:

> ***Hjaldr Tyr*** (pronounced *halder tear*) Invoking the name of the God of War
>
> ***Hakkaa Päälle*** (pronounced *haka pahl*) Literally 'Cut Them Down!"
>
> ***Sri Akall!*** Great is the Great Spirit.

THE COMPANIONS

Ijlal (pronounced *eej-lal*)
Prince of Shiraz. Same age as Azizi— 17.

Faruq (pronounced *fa-rook*)
Meaning 'one who distinguishes truth from falsehood'. Cousin to Ijlal, son of Giafar. A year older than Ijlal, aged 18.

Husam (pronounced *hoo-sa-m*)
Meaning 'sword edge'. Will not suffer fools and can express opinion with brutal honesty. Aged 17.

Fatin (pronounced *fa-teen*)
Intelligent and perceptive. Aged 17.

Isamadeen (pronounced *isa-ma-deen*)
Twin brother to Rauf. His name means 'to guard'. Always at attention, ready to pounce. Aged 15. He is the eldest of the twins, only by minutes, but he never lets Rauf forget this.

Rauf (pronounced *ra-oof*)
Gentle and kind, twin brother to Isamadeen, born a few minutes later. Aged 15.

Jamal (pronounced *ja-māl*)
Means 'kind'. Similar personality to Rauf and just as mischievous. Just turned 15.

SACRED VERSES

Alkhalid Alhabib
Immortal Beloved

Page 260
'Ant Shajarat Tayira
You are a Plane Tree
Ahmi-habi
My Beloved
La-ilaha iilla-llah
There is no God but God

Page 279 & 317
Alsafinat Almuqadasat
Sacred Vesel
Astaqbal Hubiy
Receive my Love
Qum bi'iiwa Habi
Shelter my Love

www.ingramcontent.com/pod-product-compliance
Lightning Source LLC
Chambersburg PA
CBHW061053100726
47911CB00012B/208